DISHONOUR

Jacqui Rose is a novelist who now lives in London, although she hails from South Yorkshire. She has always written for pleasure but the inspiration for her novels comes from her own experience. Her previous novels *Taken* and *Trapped* were Kindle bestsellers.

For more information about Jacqui please visit www.jacquirose.com or follow her on Twitter @JacPereirauk

Also by Jacqui Rose

Taken
Trapped

JACQUI ROSE

Dishonour

AVON

AVON
A division of HarperCollins*Publishers*
77–85 Fulham Palace Road,
London W6 8JB

www.harpercollins.co.uk

A Paperback Original 2013
1

A catalogue record for this book is
available from the British Library

ISBN-13: 978-0-00-750359-9

Set in Minion by Palimpsest Book Production Limited,
Falkirk, Stirlingshire

Printed and bound in Great Britain by
Clays Ltd, St Ives plc

MIX
Paper from
responsible sources
FSC **FSC C007454**
www.fsc.org

Acknowledgements

I loved writing this book but none of it would be really possible if it wasn't for an array of wonderful people behind the scenes. I'd especially like to thank Caroline Hogg, my editor who now has sadly left, Caroline Ridding who steers the helm of the wonderful ship which is Avon/HarperCollins and my new editor Lydia Newhouse and of course the fab art team behind the fantastic covers of my books. I'd like to thank my agent, Judith Murdoch who is constantly in the background, supporting and giving me invaluable advice.

On a personal note I'd like to thank my best friend of twenty five years, Timothy Daniels, who sat and listened whilst I read endless chapters to him then was brave enough to give me his honest opinion. Big love and thanks to 'Denzel' and his wonderful boys who light up my life and bring me so much joy. And of course I'd like to thank all my friends, family and my beautiful children who continue giving me love and support on this rollercoaster ride of life. Thanks to Sanja and Sheeja from Solace women's aid for their continual, unwavering support and lastly thanks to you, the readers who make this wonderful fairy tale possible.

Dedication

For my mum, Patricia 'O' Neill,
because I know it'll make her smile.

'Everyone has the right to life, liberty and security of the person.'

Universal Declaration of Human Rights, Article 3

'IZZAT'
URDU FOR HONOUR

1

BRADFORD

Laila Khan opened her mouth to scream but the sound of the sharp slap across her face shocked her into silence. A tiny red mark appeared on her cheek, turning quickly into an angry raised welt as her uncle leaned into her face, spitting with rage. 'You will do what I say, child. The time has come.' Wide-eyed with fear, Laila stared at her uncle.

The aromatic smells from the palak chicken and rice on the plate in front of her began to overwhelm her senses. Her body jerked as a wave of nausea hit her. Hurriedly she jumped up from her chair, but her path was blocked by the imposing figure of her angry relative. Unable to stop herself, Laila deposited the contents of her stomach all over her uncle's brand-new shoes.

Horrified, Mahmood Khan looked down at his feet before throwing Laila back down on the chair. Gripping hold of her hair, he snarled, hatred shining from his eyes. 'I have been patient with you. Treated you like my own daughter. I allowed you to go to the funeral of your Aunt today, but now my patience has come to an end.'

Trembling, Laila felt a scratch on the palm of her hand and realised she was still clutching onto the reason for her nausea. It was a photograph. Loosening her grip, Laila allowed herself to look at it once more. It was a picture of a man. A man she'd never seen before yet her uncle had just informed her that in less than a week, she was to become his wife.

Tariq Khan sat across from his sister at the dinner table, noticing how her eyes were red, blotchy and swollen. Reminding him of a bullfrog he'd seen last year in Pakistan.

He'd come in later than the others from the funeral and had been greeted by screaming. When he'd gone to investigate, he'd seen Laila kneeling on the floor at their uncle's feet, begging and pleading with him not to force her to marry.

Tariq had watched as their uncle had called his sister names. A whore. A slut. Accusing her of being nothing short of a disgrace. Spitting at her in disgust, putrid yellow phlegm sliding down Laila's face. She'd then turned to him. Pulling at his trouser leg and looking up with her big almond-shaped eyes. Begging him to do something to help. But what could he do? How could he have helped her? He'd been powerless. So, unable to see the pain in Laila's eyes, he'd turned his face away from her, leaving her begging on the floor.

She knew what their uncle was like. Didn't she understand everything would be easier for her if she didn't put up such a fight? Couldn't she see she was making it harder for herself? She knew she had a duty. A duty to their uncle. A duty to their family.

What did she think her uncle was going to let her do? Had she really thought her uncle would let her run around like the other girls in her class? She was sixteen, almost seventeen. Old enough their uncle had told her, too old nearly.

Gravely, his uncle had told him word had got back that Laila had been cosying up with some English boy at school. 'Flaunting herself, making a fool out of our family name.'

He'd tried to persuade his uncle that no dramatic course of action was needed but his uncle had just stared at him with hostility. 'She has brought this on herself. You cannot feel sorry for her Tariq, you cannot show weakness. This sort of behaviour has to be stopped. To be punished. We have our family name to think of. *Your* family name.'

And then their uncle had straight away put what was needed to be done into action.

As Tariq continued to look at Laila, still sobbing, he knew she didn't know how thankful she should be to be getting married. Her life wasn't over; though it would've been, if his uncle and the family had had their way.

Their uncle was from a certain mindset. A small, but dangerous one. A dark sinister part to the otherwise warm, friendly Pakistani community they'd always lived in. His uncle believed in punishment, not forgiveness; revenge instead of mercy. And according to their uncle – just like the father who'd recently been found guilty of killing his daughter after finding text messages from her boyfriend – bringing dishonour to the family had to be avenged.

Tariq had found himself having to beg with his uncle and other relatives, pleading for leniency on Laila's behalf. Trying to make them see the punishment didn't fit the crime. Eventually they'd backed down, but on one condition; that Laila get married.

'Is everything in order?'

Tariq's thoughts were broken as his uncle spoke to him in a gruff tone. Putting his head down, Tariq muttered in reply, wishing that what was about to happen didn't have to. 'Yes, everything's sorted; just like you asked.'

Mahmood Khan looked at his nephew. There was a lot to do before tomorrow. He was feeling tired but he prayed he would be given strength to deal with the next few hours.

He glanced quickly at Laila as he reached for another helping of rice. Girls were a curse. Especially beautiful ones. The more beautiful, the more of a curse.

Quite frankly, he wasn't sure what wrongs he'd done to deserve to be blighted with three nieces. But then, Mahmood knew he

5

shouldn't question what he'd been given – only make the best of it, which if he were to be honest, was very hard to do.

Laila had always been spirited. Her two sisters, who were older than her and already married, had been different. They'd been quiet and willing to please. Understanding what it was to be a woman. Neither of them had the brains nor the dazzling beauty of Laila; they'd been blessed with simplicity and plainness.

From the moment Laila was born, Mahmood knew his youngest niece was trouble. As a baby she'd had the cry of a lion, roaring with discontent. When she was little she'd suffered with stomach problems, no doubt caused by the fire of the warrior in her belly fighting to get out. She absorbed knowledge like the jacaranda tree absorbed water. Her defiance whirling and gliding like a Middle Eastern Sufi dancer.

It was all too much. She was nothing like her mother who'd been a good wife to his brother, although admittedly he'd sometimes needed to show her his word was final. Nevertheless, his sister-in-law was silent and attentive. Two traits a woman should possess, but two traits his niece didn't come close to holding. Thankfully though, by this time next week, Laila would be someone else's problem.

It felt to Mahmood that all he'd done for the past few years was battle with his niece to keep her in her place. With each passing year it became more of a struggle as he fought against her unwelcome curiosity of the world. When his brother, their father, had died, the responsibility of looking after them had fallen on his shoulders. Neither Laila or her brother had liked the changes at first but it'd been necessary. His brother had been soft; far too soft for a man who carried the Khan name. Often Mahmood had disapproved at the freedom his brother offered his wife and children, giving them leave to argue, question and educate. He'd often chastised his brother but the admonishment had been wasted, falling onto deaf ears. But then his brother had passed away and everything had changed.

6

Under Mahmood's guidance, everyone, including Laila and Tariq's mother, had been shown the error of their ways. And though the changes had come up against long faces and the occasional question, they'd all eventually accepted the way it was going to be under his rule. All except for Laila.

Mahmood looked at his watch. 'We better go Tariq, time is short.'

Mahmood pushed his chair away and looked once more at Laila. Her face was marked not only from her tears but also from the fresh bruise now forming on her cheek. Tomorrow when they went out, he'd make her wear her burka, to hide it. By next week the bruise would be gone, and then maybe, for the first time in his life he could be proud of her. Proud to give her away.

Laila's eyes widened as she watched her older brother and uncle. She was terrified, but she had a rising suspicion something worse was about to happen. Her uncle rarely ventured out at this time of night, preferring instead to have his friends come to him.

Mustering up some courage, Laila directed her question at her brother. 'Is everything all right, Tariq?'

Before Tariq had a chance to say anything, Mahmood snarled at her, his strong accent punctuating the words.

'You bring dishonour on this family, then you ask if everything's alright?'

Laila sat up in her chair, her face reflecting the puzzlement in her tone. 'Dishonour? Tariq, what's he talking about? I don't know what he's talking about.'

Mahmood banged his fist on the table. 'Laila, don't pretend to be the innocent, it's too late for that . . . I've heard the talk. The whole of the community has. You've brought shame on us. On me. Well, it stops right here.'

Laila's face was drawn and her fear was apparent. It made Tariq feel uneasy and he turned away, not wanting to see the terror in his sister's eyes.

'Tariq, please . . .'

Mahmood's arm shot out, sweeping the supper dishes off the table, sending Laila's untouched plate of food to stain the beige carpet rug.

'Don't make a fool of me. Do not make me your enemy Laila . . . I know all about you and the English boy.'

'English boy?'

Mahmood clenched his fist. His niece was a liar. He'd always known it. He'd seen the slyness in her large almond eyes the moment she'd been delivered into this world. It put him in mind of what his grandmother had always told him when he was a boy; *'the larger the eyes of a woman, the easier for the devil to dance into them.'* And looking at Laila now, Mahmood knew the wise woman who'd lived in a tiny house on the outskirts of Turbat in Pakistan had been right. Mahmood leant forward, leaning his arms on the table; ignoring the fact he'd just put his hand in a pile of cold rice. 'Raymond Thompson. Ring any bells Laila?'

Laila Khan swallowed hard. She knew the name. She knew the boy. But not in the way her uncle was trying to imply.

He sat next to her in class. Yes, she'd talked to him. He made her laugh. They were friends; special friends. She'd even given him a CD of her favourite songs, covering the case with pink smiley stickers. But it'd all been innocent.

He hadn't been at the school long, moving up north from London to come to live with his mother on the south side of Bradford. He was popular and handsome, his cockney twang adding to his appeal, though it wasn't just the girls who flitted around him and swooned over his six foot frame. The boys wanted to be his friend too. They seemed to respect him, understood he could handle himself. That he wasn't going to be messed with. Even Mrs Rigby, the sixth form maths teacher, blushed when he went to talk to her.

So she'd been surprised when Raymond had moved his desk

next to hers, though quietly pleased. At first she'd ignored him, but slowly she'd started to smile when she'd heard his jokes. Then the smiles had turned into laughter and they'd become friends. Good friends.

Laila didn't know why he'd chosen to be her friend but she'd cautiously welcomed it. She loved it when he teased her as his blue eyes twinkled back at her. A smile. A laugh. A tease. That's all it *could* be. Even if she'd wanted to take it further, she couldn't. She knew that more than anybody. But what they had was still special to them and no-one could take their special away.

There hadn't really been any physical contact, apart from that one time. That once. The day she'd decided to forget she was Laila Khan; respectful and dutiful daughter of the late Zarin Kahn and niece of the ever-present Mahmood Khan. That day last summer she'd chosen to walk to the bus stop with him instead of with her friends and they'd held each other's hands.

'Laila, your uncle will kill you if he sees you.'

'He won't though will he?'

She could hear the conversation now between her and her best friend and she'd been right; her uncle *hadn't* seen them. Nobody had. But she hadn't needed to be seen had she? All it had taken were words and as Laila sat at the table, trying to ignore her uncle's cutting stare, she knew her friend had talked. Not intentionally, but talked all the same. Probably to her sister who in turn had no doubt talked to her mother or an elder before the words had found their way back to her uncle. And it was this talk which had her uncle staring at her with so much contempt. 'Uncle . . . it was nothing. Nothing happened . . . I was . . .'

The look on her uncle's face made Laila stop talking. The rage which was already there in his eyes had turned into something else. Hatred. But worse still, when she glanced at her brother and saw what looked like disappointment on Tariq's face, she couldn't bear it. She couldn't bear to have her brother, who she loved more than anyone in the world, look like she'd let him down.

9

She watched as her uncle nodded his head to her mother – who'd sat silently throughout – gesturing to her to leave the room. Laila could feel her legs trembling as Mahmood walked round the table towards her. He pulled her up as he grabbed her arm, painfully squeezing it as he did so. She saw Tariq step forward, then stop. Her uncle's face pressed onto hers as he spoke in a hiss. 'There is no place in this life for little whores. So understand this; if it wasn't for your brother pleading your case Laila, you might not have had a tomorrow.'

Laila pulled back, terrified by what her uncle was insinuating. Though it wasn't an insinuation was it? It was an outright threat. Clear for her to understand. She knew her family respected their cultural teachings, as she did. But this? She knew this wasn't part of it. Couldn't they see she hadn't done anything wrong? She'd tried so hard to be obedient for her uncle but the harder she tried, the angrier he seemed to get. The more she asked questions about things, the more infuriated he got. She'd heard time and time again about what happened to girls in the community who brought shame and dishonour on their family. But *she* hadn't brought shame. She'd walked less than the length of the high street with Raymond. Refusing his requests to go to McDonalds. Refusing his requests for him to walk her all the way home. It'd been innocent.

Mahmood dropped her arm and walked towards the door, deciding not to bother with a jacket. He turned to Laila as Tariq opened the dining room door.

'*You* might have been lucky, but your boyfriend's not going to have such an easy ride.'

Laila ran to her uncle, grabbing at his sleeve. 'What are you going to do? . . . Uncle, please. He's done nothing wrong.'

'For someone who's so innocent you seem to care an awful lot about what happens to him? You're a disgrace.'

'I don't care . . . I mean I do care but not like that, I care because he's done nothing . . . uncle, please, don't touch him.'

Mahmood grabbed Laila's hair, pulling her head back. 'Try stopping me.'

He let go of her hair and started for the front door, but Laila refused to let him walk away. She grasped hold of him, trying to pull him back. She was beside herself with anguish and the tears rolled down her face as she cried. Her uncle sneered. She was out of control and he was going to enjoy seeing Raymond Thompson squeal. '*Izzat*, Laila. Honour. Doesn't it mean anything?'

'It means everything to me uncle, you know it does. But not like this. It isn't about this.'

She let go of her uncle and ran to Tariq, pulling on him and hearing his shirt tearing as he tugged it away from her grip. 'Tariq . . . no, stop. You can't do this, leave him alone.'

The fear in Laila's heart was mirrored in the look on Tariq's face. He spoke in an urgent hush to his sister. 'What do you *want* me to do Laila? I've got no choice.'

'For me, please Tariq. Do what you want with me but leave him alone.'

Tariq couldn't listen any more. He didn't *want* to hear his sister like this. Couldn't she see what harm she was doing by acting like this? It was just making their uncle more determined. More angry. And it made Tariq afraid his uncle would go back on his word and instead of just marrying Laila off, something worse, something more permanent would happen to her. Pushing Laila to one side, Tariq walked out of the dining room.

'Tariq, no!' Laila shouted after her brother. She needed to stop them but she didn't know how. No one would help her. No one would get involved. This was family business; family *honour* and most people she knew would either think her uncle was doing the right thing or be too afraid to say anything.

She didn't even have Raymond's telephone number to warn him but she couldn't let them hurt him. Not because of her. Without thinking, she picked up the phone.

'Police, please.'

11

The phone went dead. Laila turned round. The first thing she saw was Mahmood come back into the hallway with the telephone wire he'd pulled out of the socket in his hand. The second thing she saw was his fist coming towards her. A moment later, Laila Khan blacked out.

2

Raymond Thompson or 'Ray-Ray' as his friends and family called him, looked in the mirror and smiled. He'd been blessed with good genes. His natural sun-kissed blonde hair tumbled onto his forehead, falling short of his dazzling blue eyes. And his big white smile gleamed out cheekily, charming both old and young.

He didn't have to search far to see where his looks came from. His parents were a handsome couple. In his youth, his father, Freddie, had made Robert Redford look plain. His mother, Tasha, had been a hostess in one of the Soho clubs, persuading the punters to part with their cash for expensive glasses of champagne, whilst keeping their straying hands away. But she'd turned her back on it when she'd fallen in love with his father. And even years later, he knew his parents still turned heads.

Thinking of them made Ray feel sad; taking the edge off his good mood. He sighed heavily. His missed his father. He missed his old life. He wasn't used to being up north. He was born and bred a Londoner, and had spent his whole life growing up in Soho. And then ten months ago, everything had changed. His father had been given a stretch and everyone, including the police, had been surprised when he'd *actually* been sent down.

His father was Freddie Thompson. The biggest face in London. One of the untouchables, or so he was supposed to have been, until the coppers had come knocking.

Almost three million in stolen jewellery had been found in one of the hundreds of lock-ups his father owned. Of course, everyone knew it was a set-up. A sting.

It hadn't mattered that the coppers on the case had been bent, or that the evidence had been tampered with and the jury members squeezed. The powers that be had just wanted to get him off the streets, and the end result was the same. They had Freddie Thompson. The most dangerous man in London. The biggest villain in the south. But to Ray-Ray Thompson, they had his dad.

The eight year sentence had been bad enough, though the barrister and his father's highly paid legal team had put in an appeal based on a technicality, getting his sentence reduced. So at worst they'd said his father would be walking free by Christmas.

That had been the plan and everyone had been happy. A couple more months inside had been doable. What wasn't good was what happened after his father's successful appeal. That was where the real problem lay. And that problem had added a life sentence to his prison term.

Ray-Ray shrugged his shoulders, trying to get rid of the sadness he felt. He didn't want to think any more. It was summertime, and he refused to let another month go by when all he did was mope around.

Only this morning his mother had told him the best news he'd heard in a long time. They were moving back to Soho. By the end of the summer they'd be back in London amongst their friends and family. They could finally try to start to get some of their life back.

Neither his mother or him had wanted to come up to Bradford, but his father had insisted, and no one argued with Freddie Thompson. Not even when he was sat behind a bulletproof screen in Belmarsh prison. They'd moved to the north for two reasons.

Firstly, his Dad hadn't known exactly who else besides the coppers were behind the set-up, so he'd wanted to get them out of London whilst his men sounded out the danger; if of course there was any. The second, and the reason they'd ended up specifically in Bradford, was that one of his father's friends had moved to the north a few years ago to get his daughter away from the drugs scene, and his Dad had asked his friend to keep an eye out for them.

Putting on his black Alexander McQueen shirt, Ray-Ray knew he should've been more excited about the move back down South than he was. Yes, it was good news, but each time he thought about it, within a few moments the shine had been taken off his excitement. And two small words told him why. Laila Khan.

It was stupid. She hardly even talked to him. It was him who did all the talking. Bunnying away ten to the dozen whilst she just sat and listened. Staring up at him with her beautiful eyes. Ray-Ray felt soft admitting it, but she was special. What they had was special even though he didn't quite know what they really had. Even when he'd walked with her to the bus stop together, all she'd really done was occasionally glance at him with her huge brown eyes and smile, holding his hand gently but fearfully. But that had been enough for him. Just being in her presence was enough.

She was shy. He liked that. But more than that, she was different from any of the girls he hung around with in Soho. Instead of legs and tits, blow jobs free and paid for, Laila covered up wearing long skirts and loose tops. She fascinated him. And as his father always said, he knew how to appreciate real beauty. She was stunning and the more she covered up, the more alluring to him she was.

She had long jet-black hair which touched the base of her spine. Big almond eyes pooled with warmth and kindness. To Raymond, Laila was perfect. And as his father used to say about his mother, 'she was a diamond ring in a muddy football pitch.'

The sound of a car alarm made Ray-Ray look at his platinum

Rolex watch; a seventeenth birthday present from his father. He needed to stop thinking about Laila and get a move on. He was supposed to be at the cinema on the other side of town by eight with some of his mates.

He turned to see his mother, Tasha, watching him. She gave him a big smile before gently rearranging his shirt collar.

'You look a sort, babe. Going anywhere nice?'

His mother's voice was soft and lulling but her cockney accent was clear to hear.

'No, just going to the cinema. You don't look too bad yourself.'

'I'm going to meet your Auntie Linda; she came up for the day.' Tasha smiled at her son, holding him a little tighter and a little longer than normal. Both of them knew what she'd just said wasn't true. Her stepsister Linda was no more likely to leave Soho than the Queen would leave the royal family, and Tasha was grateful to her son for playing along with her untruth. She knew he didn't feel comfortable with what she was doing; of course she hadn't said anything to him, but he wasn't stupid. She knew Ray-Ray would feel like he was betraying his father by not saying anything and therefore feel like he was somehow complicit in the whole situation.

But Tasha also knew Ray-Ray would be in no doubt what would happen to her if Freddie ever got even the slightest hint she was seeing someone else. And no one wanted that. Not her, not Ray-Ray and in a way, not even Freddie. So Ray-Ray played along, not wanting to know any more than he'd already guessed and not asking any questions. And as she said to herself in an attempt to make herself feel better; *what he didn't know, wouldn't hurt him.* The last thing Tasha Thompson wanted to do was hurt her precious son.

He was so like his father in many ways, but in the one way that mattered he wasn't. Ray-Ray was kind. He had a heart. Her husband was the opposite. It always amazed her how, despite this, Ray-Ray doted on his father, and his father on him. They idolised each other and turned a blind eye to the parts they didn't want to see.

Ray-Ray chose to ignore what his father did, much in the way he chose to ignore what Tasha was doing now. Freddie was notorious; putting the fear into the hardest face. That's what had attracted her to him all those years ago.

Tasha's father had been a bully and handy with his fists, and her mother had been nowhere to be seen for most of her childhood. The combination of an absent mother and a bully of a father had driven Tasha into Freddie's arms, seeing him as someone who could protect her from her father. And he had.

Tasha could still remember the day it had happened as if it was yesterday. Her father had been sitting on the outside toilet, reading the *Racing Post* with his kecks round his ankles and no doubt the usual sour look on his face.

After hearing the way her father treated her, Freddie had pulled up outside their house in his Rolls Royce, walked through the house, into the garden, and kicked down the door of the toilet. Her father's face had been a picture; surprise, then shock, then fear.

Everyone in the East End knew Freddie Thompson and her father hadn't been any different. The last thing anybody wanted was to be on the wrong side of Freddie, especially with their trousers round their ankles.

Freddie had dragged her father through the kitchen, before kicking him out onto the doorstep. Even now it made Tasha smile to remember her father pleading with Freddie not to hurt him, his trousers still down and his pasty, spotty white arse on show for all the neighbours to see.

That day Freddie had packed up her stuff and moved Tasha in with him. And she'd been with him ever since. Within a week she'd realised she was only swapping one controlling man for another, rather than the man of her dreams.

Even though Freddie was just as much of a bully as her father, at least in his own way Freddie loved her. Her father hadn't even come close to loving her. Freddie had looked out for her and wouldn't let anyone hurt her, and for that Tasha was grateful.

He'd never raised a hand to her, whereas her father constantly had. However, there was one big difference between the two men. If Tasha ever cheated or said she was leaving, even though he'd never laid a finger on her, she knew Freddie Thompson would kill her.

Tasha looked over her son's shoulder to check herself in the mirror. She looked good. Her blonde highlighted hair tumbled past her shoulders. Her constantly tanned skin glowed and her curvaceous figure hadn't changed much since she was twenty.

She knew she was taking a risk. A huge risk. But she couldn't help it. Last month she'd tried to stop it but after a week she'd found it impossible to curtail her feelings. Her sister had told her it was madness. 'Tash, Freddie ain't going to be happy with just giving you a hiding. He'll kill you and what's more, he'll probably bleeding kill me an' all.'

Tasha didn't need to be told; she knew. She'd never meant it to happen, but some things in life you just couldn't help. And love was one of them.

Tasha sighed, watching the frown forming on her forehead in the mirror as doubt started to show on her face and a sudden dread swept over her. She turned away, not wanting to see her own fear reflecting back at her. She didn't want to think about it anymore. Freddie was banged up, she was in Bradford. Perhaps it would be alright . . . it had to be.

Standing on her tiptoes to kiss Ray-Ray on his cheek, she purred as she spoke. 'Okay baby. I'm going.'

Ray-Ray watched his mother as she walked out of the room but before she got to the doorway he grabbed her hand.

'Mum . . . be careful . . . please.'

Tasha smiled; a deep warmth showing in her eyes, before turning to walk away without another word.

Ten minutes later, Ray-Ray rushed down the stairs. He was going to be late. As he got to the bottom of he heard a loud bang then

18

froze as the front door was kicked open and four men he'd never seen in his life forced their way into the hallway.

Instinctively, Ray-Ray ran towards the kitchen and towards the back door, hoping to grab hold of one of the kitchen knives in the wooden block on the side. Fear didn't rush through him, only survival.

He hadn't reached the door before he felt a hot pain at the back of his head, then the warmth of his blood trickling down his neck as he continued to run for the door. The kitchen knives were over in the far corner. He hesitated, only for a fraction of a second, trying to decide whether to grab one, but it was enough to cost him the chance.

Ray-Ray felt his arm being pulled, causing him to spin round and face his attackers.

'Motherfucking pig. You stay away from her,' Mahmood screamed at Ray-Ray, enjoying the rush of adrenaline. He would make him pay for the dishonour he brought on his family and was going to teach him a lesson he wouldn't forget.

Holding onto Ray-Ray, Mahmood could feel he wasn't as strong as him and if he wasn't careful he'd soon be overpowered. He quickly looked around for Tariq who was standing back doing nothing, with a look of shock on his face.

'Tariq, what are you doing? Get hold of him.'

After a moment's hesitation Tariq grabbed hold of one of Ray-Ray's flailing arms as his cousin, one of the four of the group his uncle had recruited, held onto the other. Mahmood drew back, clenching his fist before he began to pummel Ray-Ray's stomach. Over and over again he brought back his hand, until Ray-Ray began to noisily cough up blood, the sound of it drowned out by Mahmood continuing to shout, his eyes wild with rage, 'You will never see her again. Never.'

Tariq and his cousin let Ray-Ray fall onto the floor. Tariq stepped away towards the door, wanting to go. It'd gone far enough. This isn't what he'd thought was going to happen. Maybe he'd been naive, but he'd believed his uncle when they'd told him they were only going to shake him up; *scare him a little*.

He watched as his uncle drove his steel heel sideways into Ray-Ray's nose, crunching the cartilage down as he groaned in agony, splattering the area with blood.

'Pour it.' Mahmood gave the order, passing a small bottle to Tariq. 'I said, pour it Tariq.'

Tariq froze, staring at the bottle, then looked at his uncle in horror. 'No, uncle, I can't. Not this. Stop it, please.'

Mahmood's face creased into anger. 'Do not disobey me and bring shame on me boy.'

Tariq felt the bottle being snatched away from his hands by one of the men who'd come in with him. A man Tariq hadn't seen before. With a smirk he spoke to Tariq. 'Give it to me. I'm more than happy to do it.'

The agony and the smell of his own burning flesh was the last thing Ray-Ray Thompson remembered.

3

She was perfect. Just perfect. Stroking her head of soft curls streaked with warm browns and honeyed blonde, he smiled warmly at her. 'It's not good for you to go without food. Eat something.' He paused and looked down intently before adding, 'Please.'

It was no good. She'd no intention of eating the chicken soup he'd spent the past half-hour lovingly making. 'I suppose you're on a diet. Maybe I should've made you a salad instead. If it helps any, I think you're lovely just the way you are.'

She stared at him before she turned her head to one side. He wasn't going to push her. He didn't want to upset her. She'd eat when she was ready, like she'd talk when she felt able. These things took time; he knew that. Pushing back her curls, he kissed her gently on her forehead.

She coughed, making him look up at her, worried. He couldn't remember a July as warm as this one but for some reason she was still trembling. It was true the evening's were cooler, but it worried him the way she was shaking. It certainly wouldn't do for her to get cold. He turned up the heating before standing up from the small metal-framed bed.

'Try to get some sleep sweetheart. You've got a big day tomorrow.' Heading for the door, he stopped. 'Silly me, I almost forgot.' Turning back, he picked up the rope. 'It wouldn't do now if I forgot this, would it?' With a sweeping movement he grabbed both her arms behind her back, making her cry out from the pain. He bound them expertly, pulling the bonds tighter than necessary to secure her incarceration.

'One more day my beautiful; that's all it'll be. Just one more day.'

Putting her gag back on, he smiled. She was ready.

4

Freddie Thompson stood observing the prison's pool table. He was the wing's pool champion and nobody had ever come close or ever dared to beat him. This time however, he wasn't playing; he was watching.

Rubbing his chin and thinking he needed another shave, Freddie saw one of D-wing's lifers take one of the worst shots he'd ever seen, sending the white ball careering into the top right-hand pocket. Freddie sneered.

'Hey, are you fucking blind? I bet a ton on you to win. Don't try to turn me over Craig. You're taking liberties.'

Forgetting himself for a moment and fed up of being pushed around, Craig snarled at Freddie. 'Piss off.'

It didn't need the silence which fell on the prison's recreational room to tell Craig he'd said the wrong thing. The sick feeling he had in his stomach was real and felt by all the other prisoners as he stood facing Freddie Thompson.

Freddie smiled slowly. He laughed as he spoke to the now-visibly shaking Craig in front of him. 'I don't think I heard you right. I thought for a moment there you told me to piss off.'

Before Craig could utter a word, he found himself forced backwards against the pool table with the cue stick being rammed hard on his throat. He wheezed as he tried to catch his breath as Freddie pressed down.

'What am I going to do with you Craig? What's that? Can't quite hear what you're saying mate.'

As Freddie continued to press down on his throat, gurgling sounds competed with Craig's gasps as he struggled to gulp mouthfuls of air. The normally pallid Craig started to get some colour as his face and the whites of his eyes turned a crimson red.

Freddie grinned, bemused at the wet patch slowly appearing on the front of Craig's trousers as he pissed himself with fear.

'I don't like rude people and I don't expect people to be rude to me on my wing. I don't like your sort; thought what happened to your friend would've told you that. Do you know what I do to people like you?'

Craig tried to shake his head, but unable to move, he just closed his eyes, bracing himself for the inevitable.

'I'll take that as a no shall I? So let me show you.'

The other prisoners, although hardened by their own life of crime and violence, still winced and turned away at the sound of the cue stick gouging out Craig's right eye and his screams of fear and pain.

A few hours later, when all the prisoners of D-wing had been questioned by the screws, swearing on their loved one's lives that they hadn't seen, heard or even frequented the recreational room that day and had no clue how Craig had sustained his injuries, Freddie Thompson sat in his magnolia-painted cell.

He looked around, curling his nose up. The slop buckets were full to overflowing. The heavily stained sheets – which were supposed to be fresh each week – looked like they'd just been swapped from one dirty set to another. And the cold July evening's air whirled in through the barred prison window as if looking for some warm sanctuary.

24

Freddie wasn't sorry about putting Craig in hospital. Fuck it; he hardly had anything to lose now. And besides, Craig was a friend of Benjamin Bradley. He'd been there that day in the showers. The day Freddie had used up his get out of jail card. Closing his eyes, he remembered it like it was yesterday . . .

It'd been a day like any other when Freddie walked into the showers, hoping they wouldn't be filthy. He never understood why the men had to behave like animals and shit all over the cream tiled floor. The screws didn't care; it only sealed their belief the courts had been right to lock them up.

No one was willing to clean it up, so it stayed there, mixing with the soap suds along with the cheap shampoo before finally disintegrating down the shower plug holes.

The only time the showers were fit for human use was on a Wednesday morning, when the cleaners came with a look of disgust and made a half-hearted effort to clean them up.

Taking his frayed towel, given to him at her majesty's pleasure, Freddie made his way to the showers expecting them to be empty, having sacrificed his breakfast of an undercooked egg to get a shit-free shower. So it surprised and annoyed him in equal measure to hear voices.

Coming round the corner he saw the wiry form of Benjamin Bradley laughing like a hyena and jumping around on one foot in excitement as he huddled up in the far corner with a few other men.

Freddie glanced at them, pleased the men were fully clothed with no obvious intention to shower and took no more interest in them than he would a pesky gnat. Until a moment later that was, when Benjamin dropped something on the floor, making him frantically scramble to pick it up.

Curiosity took hold of Freddie as he walked across to the shifty-looking men.

'What's so interesting Bradley to make a grown man roll

on the floor like a fucking circus clown? What have you got there?'

Benjamin Bradley looked up and froze. Freddie knew most prisoners and come to think of it, most people were scared of him. His formidable reputation always preceeded him. It was clear to Freddie, from the sweat breaking out on Bradley's face, he was afraid as any other man.

Freddie watched as Bradley stayed frozen on all fours, with his mouth opening to reply but closing again seconds later.

'The cat got your tongue? Because if it hasn't, you better have a fucking good reason for not answering me. Otherwise I'll be the one having your tongue Bradley, and you really wouldn't want that.'

Freddie looked round at the other men, who quickly averted their eyes. This was going to be very interesting. Again, Freddie could see Bradley was trying to find an answer but it was clear he didn't have one. With the speed of a fox at the sound of a hound, Benjamin Bradley rammed the evidence into his mouth.

Freddie Thompson was dumbfounded. He'd expected the man just to tell him what it was; instead here he was shoving it into his mouth as if it was the last supper. It only took Freddie a moment to snap himself back into action. He reached quickly down with one hand, putting his fingers between Benjamin's teeth as the other men stood frozen He yanked open the squirming man's mouth with the other, making Benjamin shriek with pain and spit out the contents which he'd manically been trying to chew.

Freddie held Benjamin's gaze for a moment before picking it up and unfolding the soggy mess. It turned out to be a photograph. As the photo unfolded, Freddie's eyes widened. Lying in his hands, covered in Benjamin Bradley's warm saliva was a photo of a little boy, no older than two or three. A mask of torturous pain covered his face and his big green eyes were wide open in manic terror.

Bradley was in the photo as well, and there was no mistaking what he was doing to the boy.

Freddie had seen and done a lot. Hurt people for just looking at him. Nothing could touch him, but this image of the little boy made him want to drop to his knees and cry. Instead he used the ache he felt inside of him to clench his fist and bring it down in a haze of raging fury into Bradley's face.

Ten minutes later Freddie stood under the cold shower, not feeling the icy sting on his back. Not caring that a dead man lay at his feet with a fractured skull and a small rich trickle of blood coming out of his ear. The only feeling Freddie Thompson had at that moment was one for the nameless boy and the image he knew he'd never get out of his head.

When they'd found Benjamin Bradley's body, all the prison inmates denied knowing anything about the murder despite everyone knowing *exactly* who had done it, and how.

Freddie had decided with that with all the DNA tests, and the fact just a microscopic drop of blood could put you in the frame for something, it was best for him to admit he'd slapped Benjamin around a bit but deny all knowledge of the murder; adding that as Bradley was a known nonce, he was a sitting target.

Not having enough evidence to charge him for murder, due to having over twenty witnesses suddenly remember they saw Freddie Thompson slap Bradley about a bit before leaving him very much alive and well to go to play pool in the recreational room, the CPS had no alternative but to stop pursuing the case and let Freddie get on with appealing against his original sentence.

Freddie had thought it was all behind him, until one morning the police came to see him, informing him that one of the men who'd been there that day was willing to give evidence against Freddie.

The case had gone to trial a couple of months later and it'd only taken the jury two hours to come back with a guilty verdict. With no mitigation to speak of, Freddie had received a life sentence.

He'd honestly thought no one would've been brave enough to give evidence against him. But according to Freddie's sources, the man who'd grassed on him had got early release for grassing him up. Not that it'd done him any good. Freddie's men had found the geezer a week after the trial and three weeks after that his bloated decaying body had been found in the Thames.

Freddie sighed heavily bringing him back to the present. Killing the man hadn't done Freddie any good; he was still sitting on a life sentence. He tried not to think about that day. Not because of the nonce's brains all over the shower room floor, but because of the image of the little boy, which haunted him still.

On some days it made him squeeze his eyes tight shut so the tears wouldn't seep out, and on other days, it simply made him want to beat a man within an inch of his life.

If getting a life sentence meant the boy could be saved from a life of abuse, Freddie Thompson would've happily served his sentence without another thought. But he could no sooner find and rescue the boy than he could walk out of prison. And the way it was looking, he wouldn't be walking out anywhere until he was doing it with a walking frame.

Freddie put his head in his hands. He took a deep breath and tried not to think. But as he'd discovered in the last few months, not thinking was easier said than done.

He didn't want to think about his house in Soho or his villa in the Costa Del Sol. He didn't want to think about his beautiful wife, Tasha, because he missed her too much. He'd never told her that or even thought about telling her, but he did. He didn't want to think about his son Raymond, who he was so proud of, and he certainly didn't want to think about the next twenty-five years. The one thousand, three hundred weeks, or the nine thousand, one hundred and thirty-five days – give or take – he had to serve.

Whichever way he looked at the numbers it was a hell of a long time. Freddie Thompson found it was *all* he could think about and it was beginning to fuck him up.

How had he got himself into this situation? After all, he was Freddie Thompson. *The* Freddie Thompson. Since he'd been legally accountable, the longest he'd spent behind bars was eighteen months. He couldn't remember a time when he hadn't been able to get out of something, whether it be grief from his wife for boning some Tom from the clubs, some ruck with the South London boys or even the other charges of murder he'd been up for. He'd always been able to talk, to pay or threaten his way out of the situation; hell, he'd even had his original sentence reduced to a streak of piss, but as he sat in his cell, Freddie realised there was no getting out of this one.

He wanted to cry but he didn't know how to. Tears were as foreign to him as a heatwave was in the Arctic. He couldn't cry. He couldn't escape. He was fucked.

'Hey, Thompson. The governor wants to see you. There's been a phone call.'

Freddie looked up. Eyeballing the prison officer with as much contempt as he could muster, he snapped, 'Ain't you heard of knocking? Don't walk into my cell again without a tap. Anyway, what phone call?'

Without thinking the prison warder snapped. 'How do I know, Thompson? I'm not a mind reader.'

Freddie Thompson stood up. He stepped towards the officer, purposely standing within an inch of him, watching as the screw gulped and the colour drained away from his face.

'I may be in here, but that don't stop me getting to you out there. One nod from me and my men will come looking. And it won't take five minutes to find you. How do you fancy being

29

woken up in the morning with a fucking axe in your head, *Officer* Davies?'

'All . . . all I meant to say is, I don't exactly know what the call is about. But I think it might be about your son. I think there's been an accident.'

5

'You must think me awfully rude. I've spent all this time with you and I haven't even told you my proper name. It's Arnold, but my friends call me Arnie. It means powerful eagle you know, derived from a Germanic name.'

Arnold beamed, whilst thinking how much smaller than usual she looked as she lay naked, curled up shivering in a foetal position on the single bed, her hands tied.

He couldn't understand why she was still shivering. He'd turned the radiator up to full blast even though he knew it would cost him an absolute fortune. But still, he didn't want to be selfish.

A horrifying thought came to Arnold's mind as he gazed at her. A fleeting, disturbing thought passed through his mind. Perhaps she was unhappy; perhaps she wanted to go home, instead of being with him?

Dismayed, he caught a reflection of himself in the mirror which was placed above the small white bookcase. He saw the worry lines etched into his forehead and he saw the anxiety in his eyes. He had to stop this. He had to stop torturing himself thinking she didn't want to be with him. Why wouldn't she? He wasn't going to let himself start thinking negatively, especially not today of all days.

'Are you still cold Izzy?'

'My name's not Izzy.' She spoke and it shocked him. He wasn't sure if it was the Scottish accent which he didn't remember her having when they'd first met, or the obvious hostility in her voice. It made her sound coarse. But what shocked him the most was her denying her name was Izzy.

The other girl had said the same thing. Telling him over and over again her name wasn't Izzy and he'd got the wrong person. Though eventually he'd seen she'd been telling the truth. He'd got the wrong person. He'd made a mistake and he didn't mind admitting it. How he'd thought she was Izzy, he didn't know. He'd been wrong. So very wrong. She'd been nothing like her.

The girl spat her words. 'You're fucking sick, you know that? My name's Lucy, fucking Lucy, you sick fuck.'

Arnold scowled. Not wanting to listen to any more abuse, he placed her gag back on, watching as she squirmed and made grunting sounds until she'd exhausted herself. Touching her gently, Arnold stroked her head as he talked. 'That's my girl. Nice and calm now. You really shouldn't get so angry Izzy. It's really not good for you. My silly little Izzy; my Isabel. It means God's promise you know.' Arnold sat looking at her warmly, before feeling overwhelmed with emotion and having to brush away tears.

The knife he'd bought had cost a small fortune. It was over two hundred pounds, but looking at it, Arnold had to admit, the craftsmanship was beautiful. A Gerber Harsey silver trident made with a double-edge fixed blade, a thick rubber handle for a better grip and according to the man in the shop, made to US military standards.

He had everything ready. He placed the knife back down on the table, trying to remember the rhyme he used to sing. For the life of him he couldn't remember it, but hopefully it'd come to him later. 'Now then Izzy, it's time. Are you excited?'

Arnold stood in front of the bed completely still for a moment, then he seized hold of her legs in a swift movement, dragging her off the bed; making her face smash onto the floor, oozing blood all over the cream lino. 'Whoops-a-daisy, silly me. I'll have to clean that up later. Not to worry Izzy, not to worry.'

The knife did what it said on the box; it cut. Deeply and precisely. It was so much better than the other one he'd struggled with last time. He whistled, enjoying his work. She was still moving, still wanting to show him she was boss. He chuckled warmly; that was Izzy alright. Always wanting to be in charge. Always wanting to get her own way.

He walked round to her front, warmed by her show of defiance. He carefully took the blade and placed the sharp point at the top of her pubic bone. 'Fiddle sticks! Well I'll be blown; look at that, my hands are shaking Izzy. I didn't know I was so nervous. I better be careful.'

Arnold smiled as he took off her gag, wondering why a shrill piercing scream came out of her mouth.

It was way past his bedtime now and Arnold could feel his eyes burning. The rhyme which had escaped him before suddenly came flooding back into his memory. He started to sing as he sat in the corner of the room. 'Izzy shall have a new bonnet, and Izzy shall go to the fair, and Izzy shall have a new ribbon to tie up her bonny brown hair.'

He laughed out loud, pleased at how the words came flooding back to him. 'And why may I not love Izzy, and why may not Izzy love me?' He stopped and paused for a moment as he got to near the end; frowning, he spoke the last lines very quietly. 'Because she's got a kiss for Daddy; a kiss for Daddy, not me.' Bending down, Arnold smiled sadly before kissing the severed head.

6

It was late by the time Laila found the courage to knock on her mother's bedroom. Tentatively she tapped, hoping her uncle wouldn't return home now. He'd forbidden Laila to speak to her mother on her own, telling her she would find no comfort in her arms. So instead she'd lain in bed with her face sore and swollen, waiting to hear the familiar sound of her uncle's car coming down the drive, willing to hear the sound of the tyres on the gravel, but it hadn't come. The terror Laila felt inside her, knowing her uncle had gone to see Ray-Ray and hadn't returned, filled her with so much dread that it overrode the fear of making her uncle angrier by disobeying him.

The bedroom door was opened by her sleepy mother. 'Laila! What are you doing here, you know what your uncle said. Go back to bed.'

'I need to talk to you.'

Laila's mother looked up and down the corridor nervously. '*Please* Laila; just go back to bed, we can talk in the morning when uncle's here.'

Seeing her daughter trembling, Laila's mother's voice became softer as she took hold of her hand. 'If uncle catches you up at this time, you know there'll be trouble. Please, try not to be so headstrong Laila. You must learn to quell your spirit, child. No good will come of it. Women have no place to question men, no matter how great a test it may seem.'

Laila scanned her mother's face, not truly recognising the person in front of her. Before her father had died her mother had been open, warm and loving. Now she was closed, distant and worse still, afraid.

'Mum, please. I need you to help me.' Laila's eyes filled with tears as she watched her mother wrap her shawl tightly round her shoulders. Her mother's voice was hesitant when she spoke. 'Laila, what do you want me to do?'

'Speak to uncle. Explain I haven't done anything. He might listen to you. Tell him I don't want to get married.'

Laila's mother slowly shook her head, pain for her child in her eyes. 'Things have changed now. You don't have a choice and your insistence in having one has caused all the problems. Did you really think hanging around with the English boy would've been acceptable to your uncle? Didn't you know you'd cause trouble?'

'Trouble? There's that word again. We didn't *do* anything.'

'Laila, why do you always have to argue? Why can't you just accept this?'

In frustration Laila raised her voice at her mother, tears streaming down her face as she spoke. 'How can you say that to me Mum? You always taught me to think for myself; you told me I never had to accept anything I didn't want to. You know we talked about me going to university. You told me you wanted me to do the things you'd never done.'

'Shhh Laila, stop talking like that. You know all girls must get married eventually. It's either now or later, so what's the difference?'

Laila's face was full of bewilderment. 'There *is* a difference; you know there is a difference. Daddy would never have allowed this, he wouldn't have wanted you to allow it.'

Her mother put her head down as she talked, fidgeting with

the sash edge on her cream shawl. When she spoke, her voice was laced with warmth. 'Laila, I know it's been hard for you since your father passed away and today we buried one of your aunts. But doesn't that show you Laila that life changes? We take things for granted when we shouldn't do. Life moves in ways we sometimes don't want it to move in. No matter how in control we think we are, we have no real power and we have to accept our destiny. And yours is to get married. Laila, you have to do this, not only for yourself, but for all of us.'

Laila could hear the hysteria in her own voice as she threw herself at her mother, wrapping her arms round her as if she were a child. 'I can't. I can't. I can't do it. Please Mum, help me! I don't want to do this, I'm scared. I promise I'll behave in the way uncle wants me to. I won't complain again. Please tell him I'll behave . . . *tell* him.'

'The decision has already been made.'

'Mum . . .'

'Laila, if I could, I would help you, but there's nothing I can do.'

'But you're my mother. You must be able to help me.'

Laila's sobbing echoed around the upstairs landing and it became louder as she felt her mother stroke her hair in the darkness. 'Laila, my beautiful, beautiful child, I'm so sorry. So, so sorry.'

'Laila? Laila? . . . Wake up.' Mahmood Khan lent over his niece. He could see her face was swollen but chose to ignore it as he shook her awake. Bruises faded, swollen lips went down but defiance had to be tamed. It was as simple as that.

It was still dark outside, though the beginning of the crimson morning sky was just appearing over the chimney pots of the rows of terraced houses. Mahmood paused for a moment, deep in thought. They had a lot to do today and he hoped his niece would understand there was no room for hysterics.

Mahmood sniffed, realising the smell of last night was still lingering on his clothes. Last night had gone well; better than expected. He was proud of what he'd done. Taking control. Being fearless. Being driven by honour. Protecting their family from the shame Laila had brought or was about to bring onto them. And Tariq? He'd let him down; hesitated and had been unable to do what he was supposed to. But perhaps that was only to be expected from his brother's son.

Sighing, Mahmood turned to face his niece. He scowled as he saw her roll over. 'Laila. It's time you got up.'

Laila groaned. Her face was hurting and she'd spent most of the night spitting blood out of her mouth. She was exhausted, but most of all, her overriding sense was fear. A thought flashed through her mind. Ray-Ray. She span round, feeling the twinge in her ribs. She'd only discovered her bruised swollen side in the middle of the night after she'd spoken to her mother. Laila guessed that when she'd been knocked unconscious her uncle had kicked her.

'Ray-Ray? What happened to him . . . what did you do?'

The tears ran down her face, making the scowl on her uncle's face deepen.

'Please uncle; please tell me he's all right.'

'Have you no shame?'

'Please.'

Mahmood looked at Laila. The thought that she'd be someone else's problem soon made his heart soften slightly. 'You don't have to worry about him anymore. That life is over. You have a new one Laila. Today, we'll be taking a trip.'

'A trip?'

Mahmood bristled. He hated when she questioned him and challenged his authority. It was for this reason the whole marriage had to be arranged so quickly.

'Yes, Laila. A trip. A trip to Pakistan.'

The scream which left Laila's lips was heard all the way up the street.

* * *

Leeds Bradford International Airport heaved with the rush of excited laughing outbound holidaymakers and inbound sullen tired ones. Businessmen and women distanced themselves from the crowd, sitting with laptops precariously near their over-frothed cappuccinos. Honeymooning couples, families and security guards filed past, wrapped up in their own world, blind to Laila and her agony as she sat in her full burka, her face covered, with only her almond eyes showing.

The airport was overly hot as signs dotted around the airport apologised for the breakdown of its air conditioning. Laila could feel the sweat running down her back, changing from hot to cold as the heat of the July day mingled with the chill of her fear.

Her head was pounding and she felt ill, though no one could tell. No one could see her light brown skin become pallid and ashen, nor could they see the strain and bruises which were both imprinted on her face. All they could see was a person head to toe in black.

Laila's eyes darted to the right, but her view was blocked. She looked the other way but that too was blocked. Both ways blocked by the sides of her burka, making her think of the horses she saw on match day wearing their blinkers, stopping them from seeing what was really going on around them.

A sense of panic started to creep over Laila; starting from her feet and slowly wrapping its way around her body, tightening her breathing and her chest. A cloying, nauseating feeling stuck at the back of her throat, causing her breath to rasp and making her feel as if she was being crushed by a heavy weight. She pulled at her burka but it was unrelenting; tight and unforgiving around her neck. The sense of claustrophobia was overwhelming.

It was the feeling of claustrophobia and panic which made Laila get up and run, scraping back the metal chairs and turning heads. She didn't know where she was going but she had to get out of there. She couldn't just sit there waiting for the hand of fate to happen. Maybe if she could get to a phone, perhaps then she'd be all right. But who would she ring? She knew it would be impossible to call her friends; they'd be as frightened as she was. Terrified the same fate would fall to them.

As the thoughts passed through her mind, Laila kept on running, hearing the muffled voices of the disgruntled crowd as she pushed past them, frantic to get away. She looked up at the signs. Which way out? Her eyelashes caught her veil, making her flinch. She ran forward towards the throng of people, hoping it was the exit.

Laila hurried on, seeing the curious looks from the passersby. Couldn't they see she needed help? Help from what was about to happen. But how could they? They could no more help her than she could help herself.

Tears started to spring into her eyes, disrupting her vision even more.

'Hey! Hey lady, calm down. Anyone would think you were in a hurry.'

A large security guard blocked Laila's way. His arms outstretched with a large kind grin on his face.

'Excuse me; can you get out of my way?'

'Pardon?'

The material deflected the sound of her voice causing Laila to speak louder. 'Can you get out of my way?'

'It's fine, she's with me. She's a nervous flyer. She's never been one for planes, have you Laila?'

Laila turned to see her uncle, out of breath, standing behind her. His eyes were cold as he looked down. He took her tightly by her hand, pulling her away from the gaze of the guard.

'Going somewhere Laila?'

'No . . . no, I just needed to get some air.'

'I hope you weren't thinking of running to that boyfriend of yours? Not sure if he'll be fit to see you.'

Laila screamed. She started to sink to her knees, but was held up by Tariq who'd come up behind her as well. He pulled her gently back to the coffee shop. His words were a warning as well as his tone. 'If you want some advice, please do yourself a favour Laila and make this easy on yourself. Don't mess with uncle.'

A crash of luggage falling off a trolley distracted Tariq, causing him to loosen his grip on his sister's arm. Knowing it might be her last chance of freedom, Laila bolted. Running, ignoring the cry of her name, she lifted up her burka, revealing a pair of jeans underneath as she ran up the stairwell in front of her. If she could just find the exit, at least then there was more chance of getting away.

At the top of the stairs, Laila was breathing hard and was still no closer to finding the exit of the overcrowded airport. She hadn't noticed the way she'd come in. Even though she didn't know which way she was going, Laila continued to run, sensing an ever-nearing threat behind her. She was too afraid to turn around, knowing it could cost her vital seconds.

In the distance she saw two police officers. She hesitated. Perhaps they could help? But then, what would she say? She didn't want to get into trouble and she certainly didn't want her family to be in trouble. Besides, she wasn't entirely sure if she could trust them. She'd always been told the police weren't sympathetic and wanted to keep out of these matters; worried they were too culturally sensitive to get involved.

Pressing on, Laila continued along the upper level of the airport. 'Could Laila Khan please come to the check-in desk? Laila Khan to the check-in desk.'

The voice over the airport tannoy sounded loudly, making Laila feel exposed. She whirled around as if a thousand fingers were pointing at her, uncovering her whereabouts, but she only saw the milling crowd of travellers. As oblivious to who Laila was as they were to her fear.

Then through the crowds Laila saw what she hadn't wanted to see. Something which made her recoil into herself making her stoop in panic as she stood frozen to the spot. She saw the jet-black head of hair, distinctive by the way it bobbed and flopped. She saw the camel-coloured suede shoes paired with the green linen trousers. It was her brother, with his gaze transfixed on her.

Laila span round to run, but less than a meter away stood her uncle, disdainful and angry. Terror took over and she took an involuntary step towards the glass railing overlooking the drop to the busy ground floor thirty feet below, where people milled about in shops and drank coffee in the overheated airport.

She pressed her body against the barrier, clinging onto it and standing on tiptoes as she did so. Could she do it? If she jumped it'd all be over. She wouldn't have to go to Pakistan. Wouldn't have to marry a man she didn't know. All her fear would go away in one swift movement. Looking over the barrier, she urged herself to do it as she felt her legs trembling. Her uncle walked slowly towards her, speaking with quiet menace. 'Don't be silly Laila; just come here, no one wants to make a scene. Not here. Not now.'

'Please uncle, just let me go home.' Laila's voice sounded child-like as she struggled to hold back the tears.

'That's exactly what you are doing. Going home.'

She turned to Tariq, desperate for him to help her, but seeing her uncle take another step towards her made Laila turn away, her attention back on her uncle, hoping she could appeal to him. 'Just let me finish school, like Daddy wanted me to, and afterwards, I . . . I promise uncle, I'll do anything you say.'

'We've been over this Laila. The life you had is finished. Your new life will be with your husband. Duty. Honour. Now come away from the balcony Laila, you'll have people staring.'

Laila didn't move. From behind her uncle she saw two large security guards looking over, concerned puzzlement on their faces.

Tariq spoke to her now, his jaw clenched in tension, desperately wanting his sister to stop causing herself more trouble. 'Laila, there's nowhere for you to go. Please. The best thing you can do is to make it easy on yourself. In time you'll get use to it. One day you will come to love him. So please come here. *Please.*'

Mahmood interjected, pushing Tariq out of the way, irritated by his soft tone. 'We both know you're not going to jump Laila, so stop this nonsense and come here now. As your uncle, I'm ordering you to.'

He put out his hand for Laila to take, but she only looked at it, unable to take it, knowing if she did it would only harm her rather than help her. She turned her head and looked down at the drop below again, her heart racing.

'Is everything alright Miss?'

The security guard from earlier spoke as he walked towards Laila. From the expression on his face it was clear he didn't know what to make of the scene. Her in her burka clinging onto the railing as if it were her life raft with her brother and uncle on either side, their arms stretched open, looking as if they were herding up a stray sheep.

Tariq spoke to the guard, not taking his eyes off Laila. 'Everything's fine.'

'I was talking to the lady.'

'Well *I'm* talking to you, and I'm telling you *everything is fine.*'

Laila watched the security guard. His shirt, at least a size too small clung to him, and perspiration sat like angry storm clouds around his armpits and across his protruding stomach. As he spoke, he wiped the sweat away from his top lip. 'Are you all right love?'

Tariq quickly whipped round. 'She's not your love. She's my sister.'

The security guard, slightly thrown but not put off, spoke again. 'I need you to tell me everything's all right.'

Laila stared at him. It was now or never. This was the moment she could get away. Be taken somewhere to work things out. She could finish school and go onto university as she'd hoped to do. Then she could travel. See the world, before settling down to someone who loved her and who she loved. Now was the time to say what her family planned to do with her. This was the last

42

chance she'd have. But then wouldn't it also mean getting her family in trouble? And then what'd happen to her mother? Her brother? Could she really do that to them? Could she really live with the fact she'd never be able to see them again?

With her big almond eyes darting between the security guard and Tariq, Laila opened her mouth and spoke as confidently as she could manage. 'Yes, I'm fine. Everything's fine.' As the words came out of her mouth, Laila could almost feel something dying inside her.

7

Tasha sat and waited. She'd been waiting now for several hours, though it could've been days or even weeks, maybe even years. Each second she waited seemed like a lifetime. Waiting for the doctors to tell her if Ray-Ray, her son, her baby, was alive.

Had it really only been last night when she'd got the call from her next-door neighbour? Tasha had expected to hear there'd been a parcel delivered or the alarm of her house wouldn't stop. She wouldn't have even minded a call telling her the kids from the local school had been trying to scale her large gated walled house. But this? To hear her house was on fire with her son inside? That call she'd never wanted to get.

With her head in her hands, Tasha sat on the uncomfortable red plastic seat in the long corridor, staring down at the floor. Hearing, but not seeing the hospital staff and visitors walking by. The strong smell of disinfectant, though overpowering, was slightly comforting. Sterile and sanitary. Completely opposite to how she felt.

What had she been doing when Ray-Ray was screaming for help? When he was trapped by the fire and overwhelmed by the smoke? She closed her eyes, squeezing them shut but it didn't take away the images, it only stopped the tears pouring out onto the floor. Nothing could take away her guilt. Even if Ray-Ray pulled through, she would know what she had been doing. Simply put, she'd been in bed with another man.

'Tash!'

The sound of his voice made her look up. It was Freddie. She stood bolt up and stared hard at him. She hadn't seen him for over a month but he still looked the same. Actually, he hadn't changed much over the years. He wasn't typical of a man of his age. At fifty-two there was no sign of a middle-age spread creeping up. No receding hairline, no lined face, only a body which a twenty-year-old man would envy. Her husband had had it all. The looks, the money, the gift of the gab, and most of all, the fear factor, but now he was paying a high price for being Freddie Thompson.

Tasha could feel herself turning red. She knew Freddie couldn't read her thoughts, but it didn't stop her feeling like he could. It was as if it was written all over her; as if Freddie could see the guilt on her face.

When she'd got the call, she'd pulled on her clothes and been driven straight to the hospital. No time to check to see if her usually immaculate hair was in place. No time to check to make sure there were no creases in her clothes. And if Freddie looked closely, he would know. The telltale signs were all there.

'All right babe.' It was all she could manage to say. She didn't trust herself to say any more. She was trying to keep her voice steady. Hoping Freddie would think her nervousness and her appearance was all down to what had happened to Ray-Ray.

She'd missed the last prison visit and she knew Freddie had been pissed off. He'd sent one of his men round to see her, which she thought he might. Nothing had been said apart from, *'Freddie was worried you weren't well; wants to make sure that there isn't a problem.'*

But she knew it hadn't been a bedside visit, but a little warning to her. Letting her know no matter where she was, no matter what she did, he would be there, right behind her. She belonged to him.

Freddie held her stare and it was only then Tasha became aware of the two screws on either side of him, handcuffed to him. They stood uncomfortably on either side. Both tall and lanky and nondescript, they could almost be mistaken for brothers.

They looked hot in their ill-fitting jackets and matching nylon trousers, unsuitable for the July heat. But more than that, they looked nervous being locked on the arm of the notorious villain, Freddie Thompson.

Tasha didn't bother to acknowledge them. She hated screws nearly as much as she hated the police. She'd come across enough of them in her time when she'd visited friends and relatives in prison to know the majority of them were trumped up little bullies who would, if they had the guts, give Freddie a seeing to.

Freddie watched his wife. He hadn't seen her for a while after she'd cancelled the last prison visit. It was good to see her, especially after a sweltering two hundred mile ride in the prison van, stuck listening to the two muppets who called themselves prison officers brag about their latest bit of pussy.

All he wanted to know was how Ray-Ray was doing. Nobody had told him anything. The prison officers had only smirked at him when he'd fought back the tears on the journey, wanting an update and asking if his son was still alive. Tonight though it'd be him who was smirking, after he'd put in a call to one of his men to pay them a little visit. To show them just what happened when they tried to make a fool out of him.

Tasha's face was drawn and tired, but she still looked as beautiful as the young woman he'd fallen for all those years ago. Not that he'd tell her. He had a reputation to hold onto, even with his wife.

There was something else though, another look on her face he wasn't quite sure of. She looked nervous. Jumpy. Though he guessed it was to be expected under the circumstances, it somehow made him feel uncomfortable.

He needed her to be strong. To be the Tasha she'd always been. Resilient. Headstrong. Loving. A woman who didn't demand the emotional attention from him most women would. He didn't go in for all that crap, but even if he wanted to give it to her, he didn't know how.

He didn't like to see her like this. He could see her vulnerability but he didn't know what to do to make it better. So he did what he did best when he felt unsure. He got angry.

Instead of smiling at Tasha and comforting her like he wanted to do, he snarled, letting his anger show in every word he spoke. 'Tasha, what the fuck is going on? One minute I'm sitting in my cell feeling jack arse sorry for meself, then the next thing, I'm being told something's happened to Ray-Ray, but they don't quite know what, or rather, they won't tell me what. So now I'm asking *you*. What the fuck is going on?'

Tasha swallowed. She could see Freddie was frightened because that always made him angry, but then so was she.

'I don't know *exactly* what happened but I know there was a fire and Ray-Ray was in the house. That's all I know. They're operating. It doesn't look good. They don't know if he's going to pull through.'

Freddie's powerful muscular shoulders visibly slumped. His head couldn't get round it. How was this possible? He'd sent them up to Bradford to be safe. He had to find out if it was an accident. A faulty switch. A gas explosion. Something. Anything.

Nobody had known where they were or at least not many people, but the thought that he could be somehow responsible for his son lying on an operating table tightened Freddie's stomach. He didn't want to think about the possibility of a revenge attack because of something he'd done to someone. There was a lot Freddie Thompson could live with but that just wasn't one of them.

'Where were you Tash? Where the fuck were you when this was happening because clearly you weren't at home?'

Tasha paused. She knew Freddie was going to ask this question, but for some reason she hadn't prepared an answer. She could feel her mouth moving. Twitching to say something, but unable to find the words. Anything she did say would sound like a lie because it would be. And the truth? She just couldn't say, because her husband could never find out the truth.

Freddie stared at his wife. At forty-four years old she was stunning. Even with her messy hair and crumpled designer clothes, her beauty still shone through. Her skin was pale and lineless. Her face held the darkest, yet softest blue eyes and her lips were full and red.

When he looked at her, he found himself being overtaken by an uncontrollable jealousy. The thought of another man even looking at her made him rage violently inside.

When he'd first met her she was hostessing in a nightclub but he'd put an immediate stop to that. He couldn't bear the thought of anyone else lusting after her. His jealousy, however, hadn't done her any favours. It hadn't given her the romantic weekends and bunches of flowers, though of course she'd always had access to as much money as she'd wanted. That much was a given. What his jealousy *had* done was make him treat her harshly. Almost as if it was her fault it made him feel that way. Although he hadn't used his fists as most of his friends did with their other halves, he'd hurt her in other ways; with verbal punches and put downs which were as harsh and cruel as any physical blow.

He'd shot her down when he knew she hadn't deserved it. Humiliating her in front of friends and other well-known faces because of his seething jealousy. And the more he'd done it, the angrier he'd got with himself. And that anger had in turn made him do it more. He hadn't wanted to but he hadn't been able to stop himself either.

Tasha was smart and he hoped she was smart enough to know that even with all the verbal, he loved her. He'd lay down his life for her. In fact, he'd lay down *her* life too if she ever thought about cheating or leaving him. All in the name of love, of course.

He knew every part of her so well and as much as his main focus was on Ray-Ray, he continued to look and wait for an answer, because he knew she was up to something. Problem was, he didn't know quite what.

'Mrs Thompson?' The surgeon broke the atmosphere, and the relief even from the prison officers was palpable.

'I'm her husband, so you can speak to me. Anything you've got to say to her. Tell me mate.'

The surgeon looked at Freddie before letting his eyes wander down to the handcuffs, staring at them with clear disdain on his face. Freddie sneered as he leaned in towards the surgeon, causing the man to blush and take a step back.

'Never been chained up before doc? You don't know what you're missing.'

'Freddie!' Tasha shot her husband a stare as she tried to take hold of his hand, both for support and to try to calm him down, but she found it being pushed away by the slightly taller guard.

'You know the rule, Mrs Thompson. No physical contact.'

Ignoring and turning her back on the prison officer, Tasha spoke to the surgeon, afraid of what she might hear.

'Sorry darlin' but don't mind Freddie, as you can imagine it's very difficult for both of us. Is our son okay?'

Bristling, and unnerved now by Freddie's continuing hostile stare, the surgeon tried to create a professional environment once more. He cleared his throat and directed his entire conversation to Tasha. 'We've just finished the operation and we've taken him to intensive care now.'

'But he's going to be okay though Doc?' The tone in Freddie's question frightened Tasha into answering her husband before the surgeon managed to. She'd never heard him sound so vulnerable.

'Of course he is; why wouldn't he be?'

'He's got some extensive injuries. Look Mrs Thompson, shall we go somewhere and sit down, so I can explain properly what's happened to your son?'

Agitated now, Tasha snapped at the surgeon. 'I don't need to bleeding sit down, ain't nothing wrong with me. Just tell me what's going on.'

'Okay well, we removed his clothes under anaesthetic and he's sustained a number of burns, unfortunately including burns on his face, which will probably be quite disfiguring.'

'Oh my God.'

'But he's been lucky.'

Freddie growled at the surgeon. 'You call being turned into the fucking elephant man lucky?'

'I know there'll be a lot of adjusting but he *really* is lucky. It could've been much worse. He'll be in intensive care for the next few days and after that we'll reassess the situation. The other thing I . . .'

The black beeper attached to the surgeon's scrubs sounded loudly. Glancing at it, he quickly started to rush away down the corridor. 'I'm sorry I have to go. I'll come back later to explain anything else, but he's in good hands and the intensive care nurses will be able to answer any of your questions.'

Part of Tasha wanted to be angry and call after the doctor for leaving without telling her all the facts, but the frightened part of her was happy to let him go; relieved for just one more moment where she could pretend everything was going to be fine.

Standing in the side room with Freddie and the prison officers, Tasha wrapped her arms around her waist as if somehow it would stop the wailing sound that seemed to be resonating from every pore in her body. The only thing she could see through the tears was Ray-Ray, lying unconscious, almost unrecognisable in the mummifying bandages.

The smell of Ray-Ray's burnt skin held thick in the air. Sweet, coppery and nauseating. Tasha was unable to look at her son's face, not wanting to see the bandages, knowing the sweet, beautiful face she kissed only a few hours ago was no longer there. In its place was the face of a stranger.

She looked down his body and saw what looked like metal clamps sticking out of his leg.

'Why has he got them?'

The nurse smiled sympathetically and spoke in barely a whisper. 'His shin was splintered in three places. The surgeon needed to . . .'

She was cut off abruptly by Freddie. 'Splintered? What . . . what are you talking about? I thought he was caught up in a fire.'

'He was, but he also has damage to his leg.'

'Can a fire cause that?' As Tasha said it she knew it sounded ridiculous, but rather ridiculous than let the thought which was slowly coming into her head creep in.

Freddie turned to Tasha, his face red. 'Don't talk fucking bollocks Tash. There ain't no fire which breaks legs.'

The nurse looked at them kindly. 'Didn't the surgeon tell you? The fire didn't actually cause any damage.'

'But I don't understand; he's been burnt?'

'Not by the fire Mrs Thompson. He only suffered smoke inhalation from that. His burns have been caused by acid. They're chemical burns.'

It took Tasha only a moment. Only a slight pause, before she leapt at Freddie. She lashed out, throwing her arms everywhere and bringing them down into contact with Freddie's powerful chest. She reined the blows down as the prison officers tried to pull Freddie away, but he stood firmly rooted to the spot, watching as his wife's tears poured out and he allowed her to take her anger out on him. And although the punches didn't hurt on a man like him, the physical contact made him feel slightly better, although his expression stayed the same. Cold, hard and unmoving.

Tasha stopped, exhausted and her speech was laboured as she hissed at her husband. 'This is your fault Freddie. The reason my son is lying here is because of *you* and your stupid, stupid business. Because of you his life is ruined. I will never forgive you for this. You hear me. *Never!*' Tasha screamed out the last word then ran out of the private room, almost knocking into a group of student nurses.

In the corridor, she leant on the wall, breathing deeply, and welcoming the feel of the cool of the concrete seep through her shirt onto her skin.

'Tash!'

She turned her head and saw Freddie being walked down the corridor the other way, being taken back to the prison van. He shouted to her as he was led away. 'Tash, I'll sort it. I'll get whoever did this . . . I promise. Tash, don't ignore me. For fuck's sake, I didn't want this to happen did I? Tasha? . . . Tasha? . . . I'll call you, okay?'

Tasha Thompson didn't bother looking at her husband. It was the first time she'd ever turned her back on him, and both of them knew it. As she walked into the July sunshine she looked up, enviously watching a single plane cut through the crystal-blue sky. She'd no idea where it was going but that didn't matter; if she was given half the chance she'd be on it, because it was going somewhere. Somewhere other than here and somewhere would've been good enough for her.

Getting out her phone she sighed, knowing today was a turning point. Today, Tash's life had changed forever.

'Hello, it's me.'

'Hey, is everything all right?'

The voice on the other end was warm and kind, making the guilt Tasha had disappear. Despite what she'd thought earlier, she needed him now more than ever. His voice always had that effect on her. It always made her ask herself how could something this good be wrong?

'No, not really it's . . .'

Tasha trailed off, unable to explain and not wanting to break down into tears.

'Listen, don't try to tell me now. Shall I come and pick you up? Are you still at the hospital? We could have a coffee or something.'

Tasha paused then quickly said, 'Yes, okay, I'd like that. I'm at the entrance but I can't go far in case he wakes up. I want to be here when he comes round.'

'I'll jump in the car now. I'll only be ten minutes. And sweetheart, try not to worry.'

As Tasha put the phone down, Arnold smiled to himself as he got his car keys out. He liked her. She was perfect. *Just perfect.*

8

Laila could see the grounds of Bradford Royal Infirmary as she looked out of the plane window. Everything seemed so small and unreal from the air, like a picture postcard from the sky. A leisurely summer's day in Bradford, everyone getting along with their lives without a care.

She was invisible to all of them. High up in the sky, no one knowing where she was going. No one caring. But Laila cared, and she was terrified. There were so many questions she wanted to ask but there was no one to answer them. So the questions just went round and round in her head, terrifying her more with each recurrence of thought.

How long was she going for? When would she come back? *Would* she come back? That was the worst question of all and part of Laila was pleased her brother – who was sitting next to her, flicking through a motorcycle magazine – wouldn't answer.

Islamabad. She hadn't even been to Spain, let alone a country thousands of miles away. She didn't know anything much about the country, not *really* about it. Not the things you really needed to know. Of course she knew about the history, the culture, the food and where it was in relation to Afghanistan; she'd learnt it all in school. She even knew enough about the conflicts and the different religious divisions to get an A-star in her history home-work. She knew *all* that. What she didn't know was about the real things. The things that mattered to everyday life.

How could she possibly go somewhere when she didn't even know where to take a bus, where to buy chocolate or some under-wear, or even where the Ladies toilets were? It was those things that *mattered* and it was those things she didn't know.

Yet the biggest thing, the thing which scared her the most besides marrying a stranger, was how to live in a country when she didn't speak the language. Yes, she knew and understood the odd word of Urdu but not enough to live there. But that was the point wasn't it? She didn't want to live there and until yesterday she hadn't planned on even going. She didn't *want* to go, yet here she was sitting on a plane, unable to get off, unable to do anything apart from what her family told her to do.

With the thoughts came the tears and Laila sniffed loudly. A moment later, Mahmood's harsh voice was heard. Not for the first time that day, Laila Khan wished above all things her beloved father was still alive.

'I can tell you this now Laila; I'm not sitting here the whole way to Pakistan with you sniffing away.'

Tariq looked at his sister. The guilt he felt was indescribable and the last thing he felt he could cope with was a whole journey of his sister's tears whilst his uncle chastised her. Even though he'd been told both by his uncle and his mother it was part of his duty as her brother to take Laila to Pakistan and see her married off, truthfully, he could do without the whole trip.

Still, perhaps it'd be worth it in the end. Once she was married their uncle could stop being so angry with Laila. Tariq hated seeing him being so cruel to her. And as long as she didn't mess up, maybe Laila's torment would soon be over.

Exhausted, Tariq leaned back in his seat moving his head slightly to get a more comfortable position on the hard headrest. His uncle had refused to pay for first class and so for the next few hours he was going to be stuck squashed between his sister who didn't sound like she was going to stop crying and his uncle, who'd somehow managed to get through customs with a container of homemade stuffed paratha and was already tucking into it, stinking the stale air.

Tariq closed his eyes and thought about the events of last night. He shuddered. Partly from what had happened to Ray-Ray and partly through his own fear and shame of being involved with it all. He supposed lying low in Pakistan until everything had died down wasn't a bad idea. He didn't think anyone had seen them but Pakistan was a good place to hide. It had different rules. His uncle had told him over and over again how the country acknowledged the importance of men being men. Only a few months ago they'd had the conversation.

'How can men and women be equal Tariq? It's like saying a zebra is the same as a lion.'

'What about education uncle, don't you think women have a right to that? Maybe it'd be worth Laila finishing off her education. I know my father would've wanted that?'

His uncle had stared at him and shook his head as he stood in the kitchen at home, a look of disappointment and scorn on his face. *'Your father did a lot of damage. He made the mistake of letting you think we can choose our paths, when in fact our paths are chosen for us. Why fill Laila's head with things which will only lead to disobedience? We will guide her and then, when the time comes, her husband will guide her. That's the way it should be.'*

Tariq broke his thoughts, uncomfortable, as he moved his head again hoping for some slight relief on the headrest. He sighed. How could he think his uncle was right, because that would mean his father had been wrong? He didn't like to think like that. In fact, Tariq didn't like to think of his father at all; it was easier. For one thing, it meant he didn't have to question his uncle or for that matter, himself. But mainly he didn't like to think of his father because he missed him. Missed the life which used to be.

* * *

Laila watched her brother, who was asleep. Gently, she placed a blanket over him. It was getting dark outside and it was also getting cold. The air stewardess smiled at Laila but wasn't able to see the small smile in return. Her uncle hadn't allowed her to take off the burka and she didn't suppose she'd be able to until they arrived at wherever they were going.

Laila glanced at Tariq again, trying to keep her thoughts away from Ray-Ray and trying to stop herself imagining what her uncle might have done to him in his anger. Tariq had also been angry last night which she hated to see, but now as he slept he looked a different person, his face relaxed and free of any sternness. It was tragic, but it felt like it was only when he slept that she could be close to him, closing the void which had developed between them and recognising the brother she so dearly loved.

When their father had died a year ago, and their uncle who they only knew from short, strained yearly visits had come across from Pakistan to live with them, he'd taken over as head of the family, and Tariq had changed, although admittedly he had been forced to. He'd gone from a protective loving brother to a chastising angry one, who each morning scolded her over the breakfast table or when he came home from work at night. It was almost as if he was playing a role. A role their uncle had given him; one which didn't really fit. At times Tariq seemed cruel, harsh, but Laila knew that wasn't who he really was, but what their uncle expected of him.

The pressure to be a man when he was only a boy had taken its toll on Tariq. Like her, he'd been expected to take on a different role overnight. A role no one had warned them about when their father had still been alive.

When he'd been alive they'd talked, dreamt and loved one another. But their uncle had put a stop to that before their father had even been cold in the ground. Now she barely said a word to her mother or Tariq, and neither did they to her. And even though she knew hatred was against all her teachings, Laila struggled not to hate her uncle with a vengeance.

Tariq had been good at so many things when he'd been younger; he'd been especially good at football. Their father had often told Tariq he was certain he'd be the first Pakistani goalkeeper playing for England.

But only a month after the funeral, Tariq had come home from school, walked into the garden and set his football kit on fire. Their uncle had stood a few feet behind Tariq patting him on the back as the flames leapt into the air.

She'd looked at Tariq from the kitchen door, watching in puzzlement before her brother had turned to her angrily, answering a question she hadn't asked but only thought.

'There's no point in having it Laila. There's no time for playing; that's what boys do.'

'But Tariq . . .'

Mahmood had jumped in then. 'Enough Laila. When will you learn it's not our place and certainly not *your* place to question what we're called to do? Your brother's made up his mind.'

'You mean *you've* made up his mind for him? You haven't even bothered to see him play. Have you ever thought he could've been called to do that? A gift he was blessed with, uncle?' That day was the first time Laila's uncle had hit her.

Tariq stopped playing football. Stopped playing sport and even stopped making an effort at school, leaving with no qualifications but stepping straight into a job within their uncle's business. Laila tried to talk to her brother about it, but he refused to talk to her and shut her out of his life.

She was certain if their father was alive Tariq wouldn't have chosen the path he was now on. He seemed to be trying to convince not only his uncle but himself that his life was what he wanted it to be. And with it, the Tariq who'd once loved her, kindly teasing her as he pulled on her pigtails as they walked to school, had disappeared, along with his burning football kit.

9

Arnold drove steadily to the hospital. There was a sense of urgency to get there but a stronger sense of not wanting to break the thirty mile per hour limit speed. He didn't want to hurt anyone, or perish the thought, kill somebody by driving too fast. He'd never been one to break rules even as a boy. Especially as a boy. His father had made sure of that.

1973
Northumberland

'Arnold! Arnold, come here.' His father's voice echoed round the large hallway and Arnold shivered. Even though he'd just turned eleven he still never knew if his father was cross or happy when he called him. The tone was always the same; low, soft and devoid of any emotions which might give away his true feelings.

Coming down the stairs, Arnold made sure his shirt was without creases and his tie was straight; his father liked that, liked him looking smart, looking better than the other boys.

'Now son, I want you to take your sister out, it's not good for you to be cooped up in here all day. When I was a boy, the holidays meant adventure, not sitting in your room reading books. Go up to

the woods; have fun, but mind Arnold, you know the rules. Don't get dirty. You know what happens to dirty boys.'

Arnold glanced at his father; he actually didn't know what happened to dirty boys. From as far back as he could remember, his Father had always said the same thing, and although he'd never heard his Father raise his voice or seen him lose his temper, there was something in the way he spoke, something which warned Arnold and made him afraid to ever dare to come home covered in dirt. He didn't want to break the rules.

Arnold watched his sister stand on her tiptoes as their father bent down slightly to receive a goodbye kiss. He then turned to Arnold and reached out his hand for his son to shake it. 'Have a good time children. And remember what I said.'

'Fiddlesticks.'

'What is it Arnie?' His sister looked at him with soft big eyes and a mop of honey-blonde hair. He loved that she called him Arnie. She was the only one, and she only ever did it in secret when their father wasn't listening.

'I've forgotten our damn sandwiches, we'll have to go back and get them.'

'No Arnie, I'm too tired to go all the way back, you go.'

'Then if you're too tired to walk, you'll be too tired to eat, so I'll only bring mine.' His sister looked at him before her cheeks flushed red with anger, which always made Arnold laugh; she had such a quick temper.

'Arnold Wainwright, you'll get my sandwiches for me or I'll tell Pappy you said damn.'

'You'll do no such thing and if you do, I'll tell him you call me Arnie.'

His sister, who was three years younger than him and four inches smaller than him, swung her fist violently. Arnold ducked out of the way and laughed, making his sister angrier.

'Tell me you'll get my sandwiches for me Arnie, tell me.'

'Yes all right, I'll get them, I was only teasing. Wait here for me. I won't be long. Now, where's my goodbye kiss?' Arnold stretched his arms wide open and put out his cheek, expecting the loving kiss his sister always gave him; the only bit of affection he got.

'I shan't give you a kiss Arnold, I shan't.'

'Well I'll give you one then.' He bent forward but his sister darted away, still annoyed at her brother's teasing.

Sighing, Arnold started to walk back through the woods towards the house, stopping for a brief moment as his sister shouted out to him.

'Arnie?'

'Yes?'

'Do you still love me more than life itself?' Arnold smiled before he replied to his sister, whose face was lit up with eagerness.

'Yes. Yes Izzy, I do.'

Arnold ran as fast as he could back to the house to get the sandwiches he'd forgotten. The grass made him feel as if he was springing along as he bounded down the hill towards the isolated house. The River Coquet ran alongside and though it looked particularly turbulent today, hungrily sweeping along broken branches and leaves, many a summer had been spent paddling in the shallow part of the river, followed by a desperate attempt to dry out their clothes before returning back home.

As he ran he thought about Izzy. He hated it when she was angry with him. Hopefully when he got back she would cheer up and be his friend again. As long as he had Izzy he didn't need anyone else and hopefully neither did she.

Approaching the house, Arnold was cautious to check his clothing, making certain no stray piece of mud or grass had surreptitiously got onto his trousers.

The large wooden front door creaked open. Standing in the entrance hall, Arnold contemplated going straight into the kitchen to pick up the lunch he'd left on the side and hoped his father hadn't heard the door. But then it would mean breaking rules and he was loath to do that; even for Izzy.

The mahogany stairs leading up to his father's office were highly polished, as was the rest of the house; pristine, with nothing out of place. Pictures of unknown relatives stared out from their gilded frames and the gold ornate wallpaper gave a feeling of formality to the high-ceilinged hall.

The mock-crystal candelabra with the glass droplets was in the exact same place, turned the exact same way it always was and Arnold was careful not to go anywhere near it as he passed, recollecting what had happened last year.

It was a simple mistake. An unintentional one when he'd run past the decorative candelabra, trying to get to his room before his father had finished counting to ten, being warned but not knowing what would happen if he didn't make it to his bedroom by the end of the countdown.

He'd been aware of knocking it slightly, but he hadn't thought anything else about it, until his father had come into his room in the middle of the night. Waking him up, suppressed rage in his voice, sweat dripping down his forehead, wanting to know who'd smashed the light. His father had dragged him out of bed and along the corridor to look at the candelabra.

'Look at that Arnold, look at it. I didn't know I lived with vandals.' Arnold had looked, but hadn't seen anything different. The candelabra still stood in centre place on the carved red wood table and the glass droplets gleamed as much as they always did.

His father had leaned into his face, punctuating each of his words as he spoke. 'It's. Been. Moved. Arnold.' The fear Arnold had experienced only allowed him to mutter two words before he'd wet himself.

'Sorry Papa.'

'Well Arnold, you know what happens to boys who destroy people's things. They have their own things destroyed.'

His father had then spent the next two hours quietly breaking all of Arnold's treasured possessions which, in the absence of any toys, were made out of things Arnold had collected and found in the woods for him and Izzy to play with. The origami birds he'd made which Izzy loved. The pictures he'd painted at school and the stories he'd written for her to read up in the woods were cut up with a shiny pair of scissors, along with anything else Arnold held as valuable.

Clearing his thoughts of that night, Arnold stood outside his father's office, hoping his Father would open the door straight away and let him get the sandwiches to take back to Izzy. He was aware his hand was shaking as he knocked lightly on the panelled door. A voice came from inside.

'Yes?'

'Papa, it's Arnold.'

'I thought I told you to go to the woods son.' Pushing himself further against the thick door, Arnold spoke again, hoping his father wouldn't think he was shouting, but at the same time needing to be close enough to hear him, as his father never repeated anything twice.

'We did go to the woods but I forgot the sandwiches Papa.' The long silent pause was exaggerated by the solemn ticking of the grandfather clock in the hall below. Eventually the door was opened and Arnold jumped back, standing up straight with his hands firmly by his side.

It was only his head his father put round the door but curiously, Arnold could see his shirt was without a tie with the top two buttons undone. The normally immaculate black hair was ruffled and a slight red flush sat on his cheeks. A strong sweet smell hit Arnold's senses. His father glared and Arnold wanted to be sick.

'Forgotten your lunch? Then what does that make you Arnold?' Arnold put his head down and muttered inaudibly.

'I can't hear you Arnold.'

'I'm stupid Papa. I'm just a stupid ignorant boy.'

'And what else Arnold?'

Arnold stood in silence before his father promoted a reply. 'Say it. I want to hear it boy.'

'Izzy . . . Izzy doesn't love me. She only loves you and not me.'

'That's right, and don't you forget it. Run along now Arnold and get those sandwiches.' As Arnold turned to go, his father's words stopped him. 'Shouldn't you say something to me Arnold?'

'Yes Papa. I love you more than life itself.'

Arnold was singing now. Singing a number song he'd made up about Izzy. He didn't know why and he certainly wouldn't tell Izzy this, but numbers made him nearly as happy as she did. Wherever he looked he would count and see numbers. It was almost as if the world was made up of them; rushing into his mind as if they were trying to tell him something. If he looked at the trees within a matter of minutes he could count the leaves. If he looked in the sky he could see how many clouds there were. If he saw numbers written down he could add them up, take them away, his brain making constant patterns with them.

It was his secret comfort, and in the back of his mind he had a memory of a lady who'd sung a number song to him as he lay curled up in bed when he was small. Singing to him; making him feel safe. He'd often wondered if it'd been his mother, though he had no one to ask. His father had always warned him never to ask about her – 'You know what happens to boys that ask about her.' Arnie didn't, but all the same, he didn't ask.

The tree he'd left Izzy by was the tallest in the woods, flourishing with branches which intertwined with the surrounding trees. He'd carved Izzy's name on the base of the trunk two years ago and much to her delight, it was still clearly visible.

The vibrant green grass growing around it was like sitting on a mattress; soft and comfy. When they lay on the ground they'd watch the clouds go by, promising each other when they were older they'd always be together. It was their special place, but looking around now, he couldn't see Izzy.

'Izzy. Please come out. Izzy, I'm sorry I made you cross.' The trees in the warm wind blew gently, caressing the air with their scents. Arnold sighed and hoped the whole afternoon wouldn't be spent searching for Izzy as she watched him, laughing and looking on from a hiding place she'd found.

He started heading up towards the river; it was the only way she would've gone. He knew she wouldn't venture deeper into the woods, she was afraid of the chattering branches and whispering leaves.

'Izzy? Izzy?' His feet were beginning to throb in the tight brown lace-up shoes he was wearing. They weren't really suitable for walking or for the summer months but his father insisted on them being smart, even if it was only to go out and play.

Sitting down on the grass in the clearing, Arnold took off his shoes and rubbed his right foot; he could see a blister forming and if he put his shoes back on it'd only get worse.

The dancing sunbeams on top of the flowing river were mesmerising, making the water look like crystal glass waves, bubbling and breaking against the edges of the steep bank. As he watched the birds dive in and out of the water, Arnold noticed a large black bundle which looked like a bag on the side of the bank near the disused watermill. Getting up and shielding his eyes from the sun to see it more clearly, he realised that it wasn't a bag at all; it looked more like a heap of material.

Leaving his shoes and enjoying the sensation of the grass between his toes, Arnold walked round the arch of the river towards the heap. He stopped dead. His heart banged in his chest and his breathing became shallow, then his legs started to run as his mind screamed. It wasn't a piece of material. It was Izzy's jacket and he could see it moving. He could see something struggling. It was Izzy.

The river gushed over her face as she fought to keep her head above the water level, clinging onto the side of the broken submerged limestone wall of the mill. The river careering towards the weir a few feet along.

'Izzy!' Arnold threw himself down on the ground, leaning his body over and hoping to reach his sister.

'Help me Arnie. Help me; I fell.'

'Hang on Izzy, I can't reach you, I'll get a branch.' There were twigs, ivy and broken pieces of brushwood but nothing that would do. Arnold tried to pull on a hanging branch, hoping to break it off, whilst all the time calling encouraging words to Izzy, but the branch simply bowed, holding on solidly to the body of the tree.

Running back to the river empty handed, Arnold leaned over the side again, pushing himself further forward than last time.

'Izzy, you've got to try to reach up and hold my hand.'

'I can't Arnie, I can't let go.'

She was right. It was impossible for her to let go of the wall with one hand and stop herself from being swept along into the weir.

'I'm going to go and get help Izzy.'

'No, Arnie, no; don't leave me.'

Arnold looked into his sister's eyes, wanting to stay but knowing he needed to get help.

'Izzy I have to go. Promise me you'll hold on until I come back. Promise me Izzy even if you don't think you can any more; I need you to hold on. Don't leave me.'

'I promise I won't let go; I won't leave you. Come back Arnie, come straight back.'

'I will. I'll never leave you but you've got to be strong.'

Running faster than he ever thought he could, Arnold darted back through the woods towards the house, calling his father as he ran. 'Papa! Papa!' Arnold opened the door wide, running into the hallway and shouting to his father. 'Papa, please come quickly.'

The thunderous sound of his father running down the stairs and the wrath he saw on his face didn't stop Arnold from screaming. 'Papa, it's Izzy.' His father grabbed him, shaking him in frenzied anger. Arnold felt his head jolting back and forth as he swallowed the words he was trying to say.

'Where are your shoes Arnold? Why are you covered in dirt?'

'It's Izzy, Pappy; please there isn't much time, she's in trouble.'

'Answer me boy. Where are your shoes?'

Arnold looked at his father, then at his feet. Almost immediately, *a different kind of fear hit him; he'd forgotten to put his shoes back on. He didn't bother looking up, but was well aware of his father's rage towering above him as he continued to speak. 'Rules, Arnold. Rules are here to be adhered to and not to be broken. Haven't I told you not to shout? Haven't I told you never to get dirty? I've told you about the rules haven't I?'*

'Yes Papa.'

'Then why would you come running in here covered in dirt with no shoes on?'

Terrified, Arnold answered. 'I left them up by the river Papa.'

The clump of hair being pulled from his head made him yelp out as he was dragged silently by his father into the quiet of the front parlour.

His father threw him towards the dark oak chair which was already placed in the middle of the room.

'Sit down Arnold.'

He couldn't sit down. He needed to be brave for Izzy. She was relying on him. He had to get his father to understand Izzy was in danger. 'No, Papa.'

Arnold watched as his father gave a bemused smile and squinted his eyes, reminding Arnold of the monsters he'd read about in the storybooks at school.

His father's footsteps sounded on the wooden floor as he unhurriedly crossed the room. Arnold trembled and imagined that every pore of him was beating.

He continued to look straight ahead; his view out of the far window blocked by the looming figure of his father centimetres away from him. The view of his father's chest became the view of his father's face as he crouched down to Arnold's eye level.

'What did you say boy?' Arnold thought he was going to be sick; he could feel his knees tapping together and his body felt like his spine was no longer supporting him. His tears interfered with his speech as he clenched his fists desperately wanting to find strength. 'It's Izzy Papa, she needs our help.'

'Sit down Arnold and listen to me. I'm going to go back to my office now. I'm going to leave the door open and give you the choice of staying here as I told you to, or break my rules by leaving this house without permission. Think carefully Arnold; the choice is yours.'

His father swivelled on his heels, creating a squeaking sound on the highly polished floor as he went to leave. He stopped in the doorway, not bothering to turn to look at his son, only to give him a warning. 'As I say son, it's entirely down to you, but remember; bad things happen to boys who break the rules.'

The room seemed to be spinning round as Arnold sat on the chair. He tucked his hands under his seat as his legs spasmodically shook. He needed to get to Izzy, he'd promised her he'd come back with help. If his father wouldn't help, then he'd have to do it all on his own. He looked across at the open parlour door. It was only a few feet away, but for some reason Arnold couldn't move.

All he needed to do was to stand up and run; run out the door and go to help Izzy. But he couldn't. Something he couldn't see but could feel was holding him back. Fear was pinning him to the chair. Fear was stopping him going to save his sister.

Arnold went to get up but found instead he sank ever deeper into the chair. His head became filled with a high-pitched scream unheard by the rest of the world. 'Izzy, I'm sorry. Izzy please forgive me.'

Arnie stood next to his father; as still and as silent as Izzy who lay on the mortuary table. It'd taken a group of locals several days to recover the body – decapitated by the steel mechanisms of the weir – from the turbulent waters of the River Coquet. The rescue team had stopped the search for her head, hoping it'd eventually be washed up on the mud flats further down the river.

Nausea swept over Arnold and the overpowering smell made him think he was going to pass out. The remorse and the guilt; Arnold could almost taste it. As they stood alone in the room looking, his father spoke to him. 'Your sister broke the rules Arnold; you see what happens when you break rules.'

His father had told him not to, but he couldn't stop the tears running down his face. The loud voice made him jump.

'Stop those tears. Tears won't bring her back Arnold. You made your choice. I gave you the opportunity to go and help your sister, but you decided to sit in the parlour and do nothing. In my books at best you're a coward and at worst . . . at worst you killed your own sister. Now I want you to look at her Arnold. See for yourself what happens to people who break the rules.'

Arnold span round to his father, who stared at him with a mocking sneer.

'I can't Papa. I can't.'

'Do it.'

'Please Papa.'

'Do it.'

Trembling with fear, Arnold walked up to the sheet covered body whispering under his breath to himself. '6, 8, 10, 12 . . .'

'Stop muttering boy.'

Arnold's fingers reaching for the sheet were almost rigid with fear. He felt the bile rise up in his mouth as he took hold of the starched cotton sheet. Pulling it back, Arnold froze, as his eyes rested on the headless torso of his sister. He screamed, then turned to run out of the morgue with the image and the echoing of his father's laughter following him.

Outside the mortuary the local priest came up to give his commiserations to Arnold's father, turning to Arnie afterwards. 'As for you young man; all you have to remember is it's only the body of your sister that's been taken. Her spirit is still with us. The body you saw in the morgue is no longer Isobel's. She's left that one now. She no longer needs it. As long as a person's spirit lives on; so do they. Isobel is all around you. She's here, and you'll find once your grief eases, you'll see and feel her everywhere.'

'But where . . . where will she be?'

The priest smiled at the peculiar little boy in front of him. 'In all *that is beautiful Arnold, you'll find Izzy. In all that is perfect, she's there. You just have to look.'*

Arnold nodded his head but his mind was elsewhere. Izzy was still here. She was still alive. She hadn't left him after all. She loved him. And now all he had to do was find her.

The horn being blown startled Arnold, stopping the flood of memories. He drove into the hospital car park and could see her standing by the entrance of accident and emergency.

Opening the passenger seat door Arnold smiled, speaking warmly. 'I'm sorry I'm late, it seems to be a thirty mile per hour zone everywhere; I didn't want to get caught speeding.'

Tasha smiled, looking at his handsome face. 'It's all right babe. I'm just grateful you came.' She leaned over and gave Arnold a kiss on his cheek.

He'd been right, she was perfect. Just perfect. *His perfect little Izzy.*

10

'Fuck.' Freddie threw his unauthorised mobile phone at the door of his cell. He watched it break into pieces, making him angrier than he already was. Turning his rage on the leg of the metal bed, he kicked it until the viewing window of the cell door slid open.

'What's going on Thompson? You better not be wrecking your cell, otherwise it'll be a stint in solitary.'

Freddie stepped towards the open hatch and saw the bearded face of the deputy governor peering through. He sneered at him. 'I think we both know how that ain't going to happen. I ain't going nowhere. But if you *insist* on playing at being superman, go ahead, be my guest. It just could end up getting a bit messy though. All I want is to let off some steam in me cell without a bleeding screw sticking their frigging neck in.'

The deputy quickly looked around; hoping no one else had heard Thompson's threat. It wouldn't do to lose the authority and respect he'd worked so hard to establish within the prison. But it wouldn't do either to pass off the threat as idle. He knew Thompson's reputation. Knew it wouldn't take more than a nod for Freddie to get his men to pay him a visit at home. He had a wife and daughter to think of. He'd been in the service thirty-odd years now and it didn't get any easier. He'd spent more years behind the high grey prison walls than most lifers had. Retirement couldn't come soon enough.

Clearing his throat, he whispered through the hatch.

'Okay Thompson, what's up? What do you want? Just whatever it is, keep it down.'

'I need to use the phone.'

'You know the rules; no phone calls on lock down.'

'Yeah and you and I both know I don't give a shit about them.'

Even through the hatch, Freddie could see how nervous the deputy governor looked. He could see the sweat coming through the wiry whiskers of his greying beard. 'It's more than my job, Thompson.'

'Not my problem . . . *governor*.'

The cell hatch door closed and a few moments later, Freddie could hear the rattle of keys.

'Okay make it quick . . . and mind, I don't want any trouble.'

Freddie didn't bother answering. He smirked as he was led into the main section of the prison wing. Even though the wing was on lock down due to a fight in the recreational area earlier, it was as noisy as ever. Shouts and bangs were heard coming from discontented prisoners behind the rows of slate grey steel doors.

His reputation and influence made it possible for Freddie not to share a cell with anyone else. The other cells in the wing were overcrowded, four men to a two man cell; but he'd made sure the screws had been paid off nicely. Having the eight feet by ten feet cell was the only slight comfort he had in an otherwise relentlessly harsh regime. There was no way Freddie could serve time *and* share a cell with a stinking farting stranger.

Freddie picked up the phone and dialled the familiar number. He'd been calling all day and there'd been no answer. Even in normal circumstances not being able to get in contact would've driven him crazy but being inside, it was a whole new level entirely. The call connected then cut into voicemail. 'Shit . . . Tasha it's me. I don't know where you are or what the fuck you're playing at but you *need* to answer . . . I'll call back later and you better start picking up.'

Freddie slammed the phone down back in the cradle. Breathing quickly and deeply he bit down on his knuckle, noticing his wedding band as he did so. What he really wanted to do was put his fist through the wall.

'Missus playing away Thompson?'

The smirk and the narrowing of Freddie's eyes was enough to tell the deputy governor he'd said the wrong thing. The fist hitting his mouth confirmed it. Later the deputy governor would tell his wife it wasn't the blow which had surprised him, it was how much it'd hurt.

Supper time clanged out the usual sounds of metal trays and plastic plates. Mashed potatoes and meat stew slopped onto the blue dishes, with a lucky few coming away with apple pie and custard, the rest coming away with only overripe and undercooked fruit.

Freddie sat in the corner of the large canteen, waiting for his meal to be brought to him by one of the other lags. His fist throbbed and he rubbed it absent-mindedly. He'd spent the last couple of hours in his cell awaiting his punishment but as the whole of the wing had been on lock down anyway, it hadn't really been much of a hardship.

Freddie knew full well no real punishment could be dished out to him. The person who was supposed to reprimand him was the person he'd hit. And the person he'd hit had taken him out of his cell, letting him use the phone when he shouldn't. Stalemate.

'All right Freddie? A hooker for your thoughts?'

It was Eddie Davidson. An old acquaintance of Freddie's and

a fellow lifer; sent down for putting an axe in his long-term girl-friend's head. A couple of months ago he'd been moved from Parkhurst for trying to start a riot, transferring to the same prison as Freddie but to a different wing, making this the first time they'd had a chance to meet up. Freddie smiled.

'You know how it is Eddie. But good to see you mate.'

Eddie sat down, glaring at another prisoner who'd come to sit at the same table but catching Eddie's hostile stare, thought better of it. 'I wanted to thank you for getting me moved to your wing Freddie. Appreciate it mate.'

Freddie waved away the thanks. 'Turn it in Eddie. You and me go back a long way. The minute I heard you'd been bounced here I had to make sure you were looked after. I couldn't have you holed up with the nonces on E-wing. Anything you need, come to me.'

Eddie smiled, showing off a mouth of neglected teeth. 'I'm the one who owes you pal, so if there's anything I can do for you, let me know.'

'To tell you the truth Eddie, it's just good to see an old face. I could do with the company.'

Freddie stopped abruptly as his food was put in front of him and waited for the lag to walk away before he continued. Pushing his food round the plate and putting anything looking like onions to the side, he talked, trying to keep his voice free of the emotions which were gnawing away at him. 'I'm strug-gling here Eddie. Finding it a bit rough. You heard about Ray-Ray?'

Eddie nodded his head. 'Yeah, I'm sorry.'

'Cheers. He was given a good seeing to before they crisped him with acid. Odd thing is, nobody's come forward to say who did it yet. I don't know what to do mate, it's crippling me up. I'm stuck in here and I need to be out there finding whoever did this.'

'You've no idea who?'

'I'm racking me head and no one comes to mind; but in saying that, *everyone* comes to mind. You've got no fucking friends in this business. My son needs me. I want to get out and put me ear to the ground. Get it sorted and be there for him. And then the other thing doing me nut in is . . .'

Freddie paused and glanced at Eddie, deciding if he should confide in him. But there was no need, the look in his eyes seemed to give Eddie the clue he needed to guess. 'You worried about Tasha?'

Freddie shrugged his shoulders as he pictured the way Tasha had walked away from him in the hospital. 'A bit. I dunno, she seems different somehow. I know it's hard on her me being in here, but I've done bird before and she never behaved the way she is doing now. You know, stuff like not answering my calls, cancelling visits. I asked her where she was when Ray-Ray was attacked; she couldn't give me an answer. I'm at a loss mate and I don't want me brain imagining things which might not be true. But I know she's angry with me. Blames me for what happened. And a woman scorned and all that . . .' Freddie trailed off, slightly embarrassed.

Eddie gave a wry smile. 'Seriously? You're asking *me*? I'm not exactly the best person to get marriage counselling from.'

Freddie blinked then leaned back in his chair roaring with laughter, remembering the reason Eddie Davidson was doing life.

Starting to eat his apple crumble, Freddie listened as Eddie bent forward and spoke in a whisper.

'What you need to do is break out.'

Freddie looked at him in bemusement. 'This ain't the 1960s Ed, and it certainly ain't *Midnight Express.*'

'I'm being serious.'

Freddie stared at him. 'You and I both know people don't escape from prison; not any more anyway, and certainly not from a high-security one. Nice thought though.'

75

'Freddie, hold up. I'm not saying to break out from here; you wouldn't stand a fucking option mate. Pull me up if I'm wrong but I'm presuming you'll get compassionate visits to go and see Ray-Ray in hospital?'

Freddie raised his eyebrows, and for the first time since the conversation had started, he began to take some real interest in what Eddie was saying. 'Yeah, go on.'

'Well, I know it'd be no good either to try to do a runner from the hospital but *going* there or coming back. Different matter entirely. What you got to lose? You're serving minimum of what? . . . ten, fifteen years?'

'Twenty-five.'

Eddie whistled, shaking his head. 'Fuck me. Twenty-five long 'uns for killing a nonce. World's gone mad.'

'Eddie, remind me to come to you when I need cheering up won't you?'

Eddie grinned; thankful they could both hang onto their sense of humour. 'Okay, so you're burning a quarter. If you're lucky you'll be out in eighteen, maybe fifteen, but it's still a long time.'

'This still ain't helping.'

'Think about it; money's not going to be a problem to you when you're out, so the only two headaches you'll have are finding the muppets who thought they could get away with turning Ray-Ray over, and sorting out the missus. And once that's done, you get on a plane and live happily ever after, sipping sangrias in the sun.'

'Sounds easy when you put it like that, but ain't you forgetting the one small matter of how I'm actually going to get from being inside a reinforced prison van to lazy days in the sun?'

'You've got enough men to sort out being sprung.'

'The being sprung part ain't the big pain Ed, though it'd still take some doing. The authorities being clued-up is the pain. They don't take chances now. Each time they take me to see Ray-Ray, they'll use a different route. They could easily add another two hundred miles on, just so we don't go the same way.'

'That's where I come in.'

'I'm desperate to get out to be there for Ray-Ray, so much so I don't even know how I'm even going to get through the next few hours, but that don't make me stupid Ed.'

Pushing the bowl of cold apple pie to the side, Freddie sighed and started to get up from the table. He liked Eddie and trusted him, but he certainly didn't want to talk shit with him. Half the inmates in prison spent their time talking about escape plans; the other half spent their time feigning their innocence.

Freddie understood it was a way of the men coping, but personally, he wasn't interested in living in a fantasy world. His way, whether he liked it or not, was to face the time he had in front of him. He wasn't sure exactly how he was going to get his head round it, but bullshitting himself wasn't an option.

Eddie continued. 'I know a driver who works for the security firm who provides the transport for here. He sorts out the rosters so it won't be a problem for him to be the one who works the day you visit Ray-Ray. He'll also be able to tell us the day before which route he'll be taking.'

Freddie sat down. His mind was racing. What he was hearing sounded almost too good to be true. 'Is he trustworthy?'

'Yeah, trust isn't the issue. I've known him a while and sorted out a few things in the past for him.'

'So what's the issue then?' Freddie paused, squinting his eyes and letting Eddie have a flash of the hardened face everyone was scared of. 'What's in it for you Ed? I know you and me have a history, but I also know no one in life gives a bag of candy without wanting a blow job in return.'

Eddie licked his lips nervously. 'I want to come with you.'

Freddie laughed ruefully. 'Stop wasting my fucking time. You really have been watching too many movies. I don't need to listen to this kind of shit now.'

The urgency in Eddie's voice stopped Freddie walking away completely. 'I ain't asking to come and rub suntan lotion on yer back. Once I'm out, we go our separate ways. Listen, we can do this. What I can't do is spend the next few years rotting away behind bars because of my missus. I have the contact but I don't have the readies.'

'How much exactly are we talking?'

'Two hundred grand; maybe a bit more.'

'That sounds okay, but how will you be able to get in the same van as me?'

'I've thought about that. On the morning of you going to see Ray-Ray, there'll need to be a fight on the wing. I need to get hurt. Hurt enough for the medics not to be able to deal with it here, but not hurt enough for them to call an ambulance. You'll have to have someone break my arm. The wing will go into lock down whilst they check me over. Obviously you'll be delayed as well. When they realise it's broken, they'll call the security firm to take me. I can sort it for my contact to make sure there aren't any other vans available that morning. And in this day of lags suing the prison authorities, they ain't going to have me hanging around whilst I'm screaming lawsuits. Then, knowing your van is coming for you, they'll probably put me in with you.'

'Probably?'

'Well there's the possibility they might not, but what I thought was, if you put a squeeze on that muppet of a deputy governor who you've got sucking shit out of your arse, you can make *sure* I'm on the van.'

'And what if I can't? What if I can't swing it for you to be on the van?'

'Then at least we tried, but you'll still have a chance of getting away.'

Freddie watched Eddie watching him. It not only sounded good, it also sounded like there could be a chance of them pulling it off, albeit a small one; but as Eddie had said, what did they have to lose? He could easily sort out his men to haul up the van with shooters if they knew which route they were going, and the money wasn't a problem.

With one flash of his gleaming white teeth, Freddie Thompson grinned. 'Okay Ed, let's do it.'

11

Ray-Ray Thompson was only half listening to the blonde haired nurse talk as she changed his dressings. He liked her. She'd been kind to him, comforting him when he was crying out in pain, staying with him as he screamed out from the nightmares. Now she was telling him about her boyfriend. From what he could gather he was a bit of a player and no more in love with her than he was in love with his teacher, though he wasn't going to say so. Who was he to spoil anyone's dreams? As the nurse chatted away, Ray-Ray thought about Laila. He missed her. Everything about her he missed. Her smile, her laugh, the way her eyes danced when she looked at him.

There was a part of him that wanted to make sure she was safe. But how was he going to find out? He couldn't ask his mother. He didn't want her knowing anything about Laila. Then a thought came to him. He spoke, interrupting the nurse in mid flow, complaining about the lack of text messages her boyfriend had sent.

'Can you do me a favour?'

The nurse looked at Ray-Ray in surprise, slightly put out she hadn't finished her story.

'Yes, of course.'

'I want you to go and see somebody for me . . .'

* * *

Tasha Thompson stretched, forgetting where she was for a moment. Imagining being back in Soho in her absurdly expensive handmade bed with Freddie lying next to her, and Ray-Ray sleeping safely in the next bedroom. But as the summer sun forced its way through the gap in the curtains, reality seized hold of her.

She turned her head and saw she was alone in the bed. Sitting up, she quickly rubbed her eyes. There, in the corner of the room, perched on the edge of the cream embroidered chair was Arnold. In the dimness Tasha couldn't make out his face properly, only the stillness of his body and the stillness of his stare. A chill ran down her.

'Arnold?' There was no answer; merely the murmur of voices outside in the distance. 'Arnold, you're frightening me.'

Arnold's tone was as still and unmoving as his physical presence. 'I've been watching you sleep. So still, so very still.'

He got up, walking slowly towards Tasha. Crouching down in front of her he smiled. 'You're perfect. Just perfect.'

Tasha laughed, her cockney accent cutting through the air. 'Stop being a soft git; you must be bleeding on something. I'm hardly God's gift.'

Arnold tilted his head to one side, catching a beam of sunshine on his cheek. 'Oh but you are to me, you really are.'

She stared at him, always surprised at how beautiful he really was. She could stare at him all day. For a start, he certainly didn't realise how good-looking he was and how many heads he turned when he walked down the street. He was tall, almost six foot five. Wavy blonde and honey-brown hair. Big green eyes with a mesmerising stare. His face was square and chiselled with a wind-tanned complexion. His body was naturally muscular yet he showed no vanity, wearing clothes befitting of a man twenty years his senior. Bleeding hell, her granddad, God bless his soul, wouldn't even have been seen dead in the shirts she'd seen Arnold in. Though perhaps that was what she liked and trusted about him. Quite

81

why he would choose *her*, when he could quite frankly have the pick of any woman, she didn't know. Stroking Arnold's face without saying anything, Tasha got up from the bed, heading towards the bathroom. He was sweet, but compliments made her feel uncomfortable. What she really wanted to do was get showered then go straight to the hospital.

She picked up her phone. It was on silent. There were eighteen missed calls. One from her sister Linda. Seventeen from Freddie.

'Why did you say I'm frightening you?'

Tasha turned round, her thoughts preoccupied with not having answered Freddie's calls. 'Come again?'

'Why did you say a minute ago I'm frightening you? You're not scared of me are you?'

'Scared of you? Christ almighty, I'm more likely to be scared of me own shadow. You're the gentlest man I know Arnie, and I appreciate that.'

'You called me Arnie.'

'Don't you like being called that?'

Arnold smirked. 'You know I do.'

A flash of puzzlement crossed Tasha's face for a second before disappearing into a frown. 'I said it, because when I saw you sitting there, I thought you'd changed your mind about us. You know, perhaps you thought better of getting involved with the likes of me. I don't know what impression I've given you, but I don't do this all the time; in fact, it's the first time I've done anything like this before. I ain't ever cheated on Freddie before.'

'Who's Freddie?'

Tasha shook her head. 'I swear you're worse than me with names, or maybe not listening is just a trait all men have. Freddie's my husband's name. Anyhow, I can't stand here quacking. Let me get a shower, I don't want to miss visiting time at the hospital.'

Arnold stood up, walking over to Tasha. He grabbed her arm gently, stopping her from going into the bathroom.

'Husband?'

'Yes. My husband, Arnie. The man I told you about when I met you.'

'Don't say that. Don't spoil things. Let me hear you say that it's only you and me.'

Again the puzzlement crossed over Tasha's face, but this time the crease in her forehead was much deeper. She held Arnold's intense gaze. She could see he was urging her to say something but she didn't know what. Then it slowly dawned on her what was happening. He wanted her to pretend. To role play. She and Freddie had often done it. Although her husband had cheated on her so often she'd given up counting, they still had a very healthy sex life and role playing was part of it. It was harmless fun.

She smiled sadly at Arnie, slightly despairing at men. How could he think her mind was in the mood to play games when her heart was with Ray-Ray in the hospital? But she supposed she should try. Arnie had been so kind to her, so supportive. She guessed it was the least she should do.

Tasha feigned a smile and took one step towards Arnold. Her face was centimetres from his. Licking her lips she spoke in a husky voice. 'You're right baby; there is no husband. It's just you and me. I just like teasing you. I can show you what a tease I am if you like.'

Gently Arnold held Tasha's shoulders, pushing her away. Sidestepping her, he winked, his face becoming relaxed. For just a moment he'd believed her, but then he should've known she was teasing because that's what she always did. Izzy always teased.

The water pounded down on Tasha's skin. Even though it was July, she had the shower turned onto hot, slightly too hot. The sting of it felt refreshing, making her alert to her thoughts.

She wanted to keep her mind off Freddie; there was nothing to be solved by thinking about him. What had happened to Ray-Ray was because of Freddie. She knew that and didn't need to go there in her mind. It was too painful. She was furious and she could never forgive him for putting their son in so much danger. But even though he was wrong, if he found out what she was doing, it'd be over, both for her and for Arnold. The thought really hit her for the first time. She hadn't thought of it in those terms. She hadn't *really* thought about Arnold's safety.

She was being selfish continuing her affair with Arnold. She knew the risks. He didn't. The problem was, she felt she needed to hold onto something; something safe, to get her through what had happened to Ray-Ray. She couldn't cope alone – or she didn't feel as if she could.

Arnold was everything Freddie wasn't. Kind and warm. He was a gentleman in the old-fashioned sense; shy almost. They'd shared a bed together several times but not actually had sex, in fact nowhere near to having sex. The nearest he'd got was a moment ago when he'd wanted her to role play.

All Arnold had done when they were in bed was hold her close, rocking her gently and very quietly singing a song she couldn't quite make out the words to.

'*He's fucking off his bollocks. What's wrong with him? Don't sound normal if you ask me. Some queer boy no doubt, trying to pretend he's not,*' was what her sister Linda had said when Tasha told her that they hadn't slept together.

'Not everyone wants to get their bleeding leg over Linda.'

'Show me a man that don't, and I'll show you a corpse.'

'Oh God, everything in life ain't about sex you know Lind.'

'Clearly bleeding not. Just be careful Tash, he don't sound all there to me.'

Tasha hadn't said anything to Linda, but not having sex with Arnold had at first felt very strange. She'd worried there was something wrong with her; worried he didn't find her attractive. But after a while it felt quite refreshing. Refreshing that Arnold didn't want her for her body. He was kind in his words, complimented her even though it made her feel uncomfortable, and he didn't want her for sex, he simply wanted her for her.

* * *

'Can't we go even a little faster Arnie? You've got the whole of bleeding Bradford lined up behind you.' They were in the car and Tasha was desperate to see Ray-Ray.

Arnold looked in his rear view mirror and saw over a dozen cars bumper to bumper, following him as he did a steady thirty miles per hour. 'I don't think being pulled over by the police will get you to the hospital quickly. Sorry, but I have a thing about breaking rules.'

He glanced over at her and Tasha shook her head warmly. Arnold was different from anyone she'd ever known. There was nothing complicated about him. He had an innocent simplicity. He didn't mask who he was; the complete opposite of Freddie. For the first time in her life Tasha understood what it was like for a man to treat her with respect. 'You've driven past it.'

Tasha swivelled her body in her car seat as they drove past the hospital.

'I know. I just wanted to show you something. Please.'

'Can't we do this later? I really need to go and see Ray-Ray. Besides anything else, I can't afford to raise any suspicions and have me old man find out you've been staying at the hotel with me. I wouldn't be surprised if he didn't have someone checking up. It wasn't just because the house was damaged by the fire I'm staying there, Freddie's told me I have to in case of any other attacks. And if Freddie tells you to do something, you do it. I just don't think it's safe for you darling. I ain't told you much about Freddie but he's not a man who likes to be crossed. Point is, I'm worried about you; I'm afraid something bad might happen because of me.'

Tasha turned her head to see Arnold's reaction. But he wasn't listening and had the same faraway look in his eyes she'd often seen. There was a part of her that wanted to ask him more questions about himself. About his life. But she knew not to. Not asking questions was part of her life since as far back as she could remember. Whatever he did, it was clear he didn't want to talk about it. He'd tell her if she needed to know. In that way he was no different to Freddie.

'Arnie?'

'Mmm? . . . Sorry, did you say something?'

Turning away, she watched the rain from the sudden cloud burst hit against the passenger seat window. 'No. Don't worry darling; it was nothing important. Okay, half an hour, that's all and then I really have to go and see Ray-Ray.'

'So, you'll let me take you?'

'Looks like I've got no choice.'

The flats were nondescript; a low rise block like thousands of other low rise blocks which had been built in the sixties for working families. The outside was clean, almost sterile with a few trees lining the pathway to the communal front door and Tasha was struggling to conjure up any enthusiasm for the place. 'Is this what you wanted to show me Arnie, a concrete block of flats?'

Aware it was almost midday, she glanced at her emerald-encrusted Rolex, a treat to herself after finding Freddie humping one of the little tarts from Frankie Taylor's club, a good friend of Freddie's and a known face back in Soho.

'No, of course not. You should know me better than that. Today's the day. 28, 7, 98. Remember?'

Tasha frowned. Arnold was forever quoting numbers at her. It was one of his little quirks. She'd given up asking him what they represented a while ago, after one too many long-winded explanations. It was odd to Tasha to see anyone love numbers the way he did, lighting up when he talked about them as if someone had just given him the biggest diamond on Bond Street. She'd always hated maths at school and even now it took a calculator for her to work out the simplest of sums. Yet Arnie seemed to have a passion for numbers, seeing an equation to solve or a pattern of numbers in the most ordinary of things.

Arnie was looking at her with expectation. 'Don't tell me you've forgotten?'

Shit. She'd no idea what he was talking about, but the look in his eyes told her it was something important; something which mattered and something she'd clearly forgotten. Was it his birthday? She wasn't great with all that stuff at the best of times, and with the added anxiety of Ray-Ray it must have gone clean out of her head. Actually, she couldn't even recall the conversation they'd had about it. Still, she didn't want to hurt him and let on she'd forgotten. He'd been so good to her.

'Oh course I remember silly . . . Today's the day.' Tasha smiled weakly, hoping Arnold wouldn't pick up on the fact she wasn't entirely sure what she was supposed to be getting excited about.

'Come on then. I can see you want to get on with it,' Arnold said as he opened the driver's door. He paused and leaned back in. Reaching across to the back seat, he smiled as he grabbed the twisted rope from the back seat.

Inside, the flats were just as spotless as the outside of them, with a smell reminding Tasha of the hospital; the place she should really be getting back to.

Arnold had gone ahead in front of her and from the stairwell, she could hear the sound of him opening his front door. Sighing, she continued to make her way up the stairs, hoping that they could leave soon.

'Jesus, Arnie, what's that smell?' Tasha walked into Arnold's flat covering her nose.

'You can smell it too?'

'Yeah.'

Arnold blinked. 'Really?'

'Too bleeding right I can, open one of them windows darlin'. I reckon you must have a blocked drain. Haven't you reported it?'

'Thought perhaps it was just me, so I didn't want to cause a fuss.'

'Arnie, you're a sweetie but Christ, sometimes you've really got to grow a bleeding pair. You ain't getting nothing done in this life if you can't give it a bit of bollocks when you need to. I'll get them to sort it. Where's the number for the management office?'

'Over there on the table next to the phone. There's a list of numbers.'

Tasha walked across to the table. The place was tiny. She didn't know what she'd been expecting, but certainly not this. Apart from the smell, the place was pristine. Nothing seemed to be out of place. The row of cups she could see in the small kitchenette were lined up with regimental precision and she watched as Arnold straightened the last mug, making sure the handle was turned the same way as the others.

The brown kitchen worktops gleamed nearly as brightly as the stainless steel sink did. And the two tea towels left on top were folded up into what Tasha could only describe as an origami type bird.

Catching Arnold staring at her, she smiled back, feeling slightly annoyed at the length of time it was taking for the phone to be answered.

Walking out of the kitchenette, Arnold watched her from the back. Her blonde hair was tied up in a high ponytail, giving him a glimpse of her neck. Smooth, long and beautiful.

Arnold tightened his grip on the rope. Perhaps he wouldn't need it. Maybe she'd be happy to stay. She seemed so keen. So helpful.

He didn't know why, but he could feel his breath beginning to become shallow. The drips of sweat were prickling at his skin and running down his forehead. His palms were wet, causing the texture of the rope to feel rougher on his hands. Taking one step closer to her, he shut his eyes. He was ready.

The knock on the door was loud. Tasha swung round with her hand on her chest.

'Bleeding hell, that frightened me. Scared me half to death.' They held each other's gaze for a moment before Tasha glanced down to see what Arnold had in his hand.

'What you still holding onto that for? Put it away, it's filthy.' The second knock on the door was louder and more prolonged. 'Hold on, we're coming,' Tasha shouted as she put the phone down, gently pushing past Arnold and going to open the door.

A small man dressed in jeans and a stripy blue jumper followed Tasha back into the living area. 'Sorry to bother you, but I heard you come in. I'm from number twenty-five by the way. It's a bit embarrassing, but there's a really nasty smell and I sort of worked out it was coming from here. I wondered if you had some drainage problems?'

'Oh that's fine babe; I was actually just trying to get through to the caretaker about it now. No answer though. I don't suppose you know anything about drains do you?'

The man smiled, eyeing Tasha's well-proportioned body.

'A little bit.'

'Maybe you want to take a butchers in the bathroom then? See if there's anything to see.'

The tiny width of the flat meant Tasha could reach the bathroom door without needing to move. As she put her hand on the door and began to open it, Arnold who'd been frozen to the spot, leapt across the room, frightening the man and stopping Tasha from opening the door fully. He pulled it shut with force and spoke in a trembling voice. 'No. Not yet, it's not ready for you yet. You can't go in there.'

Tasha glanced at the neighbour who looked slightly shocked and mildly embarrassed. She smiled warmly, then giggled, sounding like a teenager.

'Your face is a picture. It's a surprise; I'm not allowed to see it yet. Been going on about it all day, though really it should be me giving him the surprise; it's his birthday.'

The man beamed at Arnold and a moment later a grinning

Tasha and the neighbour burst into an impromptu rendition of 'Happy Birthday' to a pensive-looking Arnold.

'I'll meet you downstairs in the car.' Arnold spoke monosyllabically as Tasha walked down the stairwell with the neighbour, chattering away.

Everything seemed to be going wrong. It was supposed to be so simple, and now he'd let her down. If he hadn't been so hesitant he'd be giving her what she deserved. His father had always told him he was hesitant. Hesitant and stupid. Stupid and hesitant Arnold.

Putting his head round the bathroom door, Arnold scowled. 'Well, would you look at that.' He walked into the windowless room as he spoke to himself and picked up a towel lying on the floor. As he straightened the towel, putting it back on the rail with meticulous care, he caught a reflection in the mirror. Mess. Mess seemed to be everywhere.

Standing over the bath, Arnold brought out a tissue from his pocket and began to rub the offending tile, which held the tiniest of black marks. Stepping back to admire it, a scowl appeared on his forehead. There was another mark. He'd no idea how they got there. He was grateful Izzy hadn't seen the mess.

After a few minutes of rubbing the ceramic clean until it squeaked, Arnold gave a final check before leaving the bathroom, closing the door and ignoring the headless torso lying in the bath.

'Pull over here.' Tasha felt sick. Her stomach turned in a cramp and her heart began to race faster. There, outside the hospital, she saw the figures of two large men standing by the entrance. They were Freddie's men and they couldn't be more obvious if they tried. Dark glasses with expensive leather jackets. Designer jeans with handmade Italian shoes. They stuck out like the proverbial, especially as this was Bradford, not Soho.

Her stomach lurched as Arnold slowed down the car, bringing

it to a stop in full view of the men. 'Arnold, I'm sorry but I have to go. I'll call you. I'm sorry about spoiling today.'

Arnold looked at her. He'd been quiet the whole journey.

'I'm the one who should be apologising to you. I know this isn't how you expected it to work out but . . .'

Tasha interrupted sharply. 'Not now Arnold. Like I say, I'll call you.'

The car door was slammed as Tasha got out and she was oblivious to Arnold's car driving off. Her mind was on other things. Taking a deep breath, she walked towards the men who she knew by name, trying to ignore her legs wanting to give way underneath her.

They saw her and nodded. No smile. No wave. Only the small acknowledgement telling her they were here for a serious reason. Freddie.

Tasha couldn't see their eyes behind the Ray-Bans but she could tell they were watching everything around them.

'Who was that?' The cockney accent growled out at her.

'Who was what?'

'The car you just got out of. Whose was it?'

Tasha swallowed and looked directly at them. 'A cab. I felt too tired to drive. Problem?'

'Not particularly; not yet anyway. We need a word.' The men stood unmoving, waiting for Tasha to give them their full attention.

'Freddie's coming out.'

A look of astonishment crossed Tasha's face. 'What?'

'He's coming out. We're springing him out on one of his visits to Ray-Ray. We'll have to move fast when we get the nod. So you need to be on standby.'

Tasha's face drained of colour. 'Is he off his fucking head Johno?'

Ignoring her comment, Johno continued to talk. 'He asked me not to give you any details. Oh, and you'll be driving one of the cars.'

Tasha opened her mouth to say something but her shock silenced her.

'You'll only have to take him to where the helicopter will be waiting. He'll worry about the rest but once Ray-Ray is out of hospital you'll both go and join him.'

'Just tell me why? And how he thinks he's going to pull it off?'

'Listen Tash, you ain't got to worry about that. He wants to get out. Get whoever did this to Ray-Ray and once he has, you'll all be shooting abroad.'

Tasha shook her head. 'You don't get it do you? There's been enough shit already. My son's lying inside there and you lot are talking about breaking out and fucking revenge. You make me sick.'

She began to walk away but her arm was grabbed by Johno. 'Don't make this hard for yourself Tash. Just be ready for our phone call. I've always liked you, but Freddie ain't happy with you and however I feel about you won't come into play if he gives me the nod . . . I don't want to have to hurt you.'

Tasha shook off Johno's hand and walked away without saying anything, feeling not only their stare but the chill of their warning.

12

Laila Khan looked at the man who was waving his arms about and shouting, not understanding a word he'd just said.

The hostility in the old man's voice holding the cart was evident but the words didn't make any sense. Tears stung Laila's eyes but she refused to cry again. It seemed as if she'd been crying for the whole of the journey. Her nose was so blocked she could hardly breathe out of it and the combination of the dust and the heat wasn't helping.

'He's telling you to move. To get out of the way before you're killed. Did my brother teach you nothing?' Mahmood stood behind his niece, once more despairing at the lack of teaching his dead brother had given his children.

Moving back, Laila braved herself to look around. Only a few days ago she was struggling over her maths homework, texting her friend Jasvinder and wondering how she was going to persuade her uncle to let her have a Saturday job to afford the jeans she'd seen in Topshop.

Yet here she felt virtually in a dreamlike state; a sense of almost being removed from her own being, looking down on herself standing by the side of the dusty road, in a country which looked as if every house, every road, every village had been scorched by the sun.

Terror ran through Laila in powerless, uncontrollable waves, the fear gripping her mind, instinctively putting her body on heightened alert and sending panic signals to her brain, telling her to run; to escape the danger she was in. But where would she go? Where would she hide, when she knew her uncle would stop at nothing to find her.

Ray-Ray came into her head, but the thought of his kindness, contrasted so much with what was happening around her that she blocked the thought out of her mind.

'Stop daydreaming Laila, we've got a lot to do and you're slowing us down. Tariq take the bags off the cart, I'll get someone to help us. Stay here with your sister.'

Laila watched in horror as Mahmood walked towards the clay buildings. She'd presumed they'd just been taking a break from the unforgiving journey. Her body ached and she was exhausted. They'd taken the plane, a taxi and then a train, squashed in a stifling, squalid carriage with women, children and even a goat.

They'd then got the cart, pulled by an ox and guided by the old man, which had trundled along the dust road, wheels hitting every stone as her bones were jarred whilst the clouds swiftly flew by, hurrying to veil the dazzling sun of its blazing heat.

She didn't know where she was. The signs had disappeared on the outskirts of Islamabad. Though Laila didn't need to know the name of the place to know she didn't want to be here. She couldn't even call it a village; it consisted of five flat-roofed houses, ashen in description, almost as if the colours had been sandblasted away.

Dried mud replaced any paths. An undernourished dog lay panting under the shade of the single mulberry tree, chickens wandered for feed by the crumbling stone wall, and wide-eyed, curious stares watched Laila.

Turning to her brother, her voice was strained and pitiful. 'Tariq, please help me. Please, I'm begging you. We don't have to do this.

94

We'll be okay without uncle; we can manage. I won't go back to school, I can help out; I'll get a job. Anything you need me to do. But please, please, don't leave me here.'

Tariq's eyes flickered; glimpses of hesitation and uncertainty showing in his brown eyes. A moment later it was gone, passing away like the breeze. He had to stay strong. If he didn't he'd be letting her down, no matter how hard it was for her . . . for him. This was the only way. He had to keep believing he was doing the right thing. The only thing to keep Laila safe. If only she could see it was best. If only she'd stop asking him to help her. This *was* him helping her. He couldn't allow himself to feel sorry for her. Better this than the family do what they'd originally wanted to do to her. Besides, he had to remember this was her duty. *His* duty as her brother was to show her what was expected. And surely doing something in the name of duty wouldn't harm her?

Angry at himself for letting doubts come into his mind, Tariq snapped at Laila.

'What do you want from me Laila? What do you want me to do? Just tell me. Tell me how I'm supposed to help you.' Tariq threw down the cigarette he was smoking, kicking a stone out of the way. 'Look, we're here now Laila; get used to it, make the most of it.'

'We're where? Where are we Tariq? You tell me where we are and then tell me this is what Daddy would've wanted.'

He didn't know where they were, although he wasn't going to admit that to Laila. But mostly, he wasn't going to admit his father would never expect him to leave Laila here. But what else could he do? In a way, Tariq felt as trapped as Laila did.

'What difference does it make to you if you don't know where you are? If you wanted to know, maybe you should've paid attention in your Saturday morning lessons; then you would've been able to read the signs.'

Not being able to look at Laila any longer, Tariq stormed off to find out why their uncle was taking so long.

It took Laila to the count of three to start running. She turned left, not wanting to go along the same road they'd come down. She could hear the children who'd been watching her shrieking with surprise and excitement as she darted along the road. She cried out a small cry as her ankle bent over to one side as she ran on the uneven stones in her dolly shoes, making her escape slower than she would've wished for.

Laila looked up and saw nothing but the road ahead looming in front of her. A barren stretch going on and on into the distance. How far was it? One mile? Two miles? It was impossible to tell, but she knew if she stayed on this road she'd be seen.

She couldn't turn back and run past the houses, the children's screams were bound to have caught her uncle's attention by now. Almost without thinking, Laila swerved into the undergrowth. Her burka caught on the tall hard reeds, forcing her to drag and yank at it to make her escape. Within seconds she could feel her feet being covered in water, then her knees, and before long her waist. She began to cry; a loud audible howl. Scared, lonely, hollow cries of terror and pain.

Pulling herself together, Laila slowly and carefully began to wade, waist deep in water and sludge. Her burka was water-logged and she had a sense she was dragging a heavy weight behind her. The reeds towered above her, obscuring her view.

Not having any sight or landmarks, Laila looked up to the sky, making sure to keep the sun in front of her. She paused, tired and shivering in the heat of the day. She didn't want to think or look round because she knew if she did she would panic; panic at the sheer hopelessness of the situation.

She wanted to focus on home, to try to imagine she was in her room, but however hard she tried, she couldn't. The sounds, the smells, the feel of this foreign place she found herself in overwhelmed her senses, making it impossible for her to imagine she was anywhere other than here.

A sudden noise made Laila freeze. Her heart speeded up and her breath became short. Coming towards her through the thick beige reeds was a snake; winding its body with graceful ease towards the ballooned floating cloth of her burka.

Laila's natural instinct was to scream out but as she continued to watch its long dark brown body with light gold sides and dorsal blotches, she was overcome with wanting it all to end. Wanting the snake with its concealed venom to poison her body; putting her out of the misery of her toxic life.

She made a purposeful sudden movement, aware of the fear it would cause the snake; hoping its instinctive reaction would make it turn and bite her. Closing her eyes, Laila waited, embracing the fact it would soon all be over.

Laila's eyes were scrunched up so tightly they were beginning to hurt. Slowly she opened them only to see the snake weave its escape through the soaring reeds. 'No!' Laila shouted as the frightened snake disappeared from sight. Watching it vanish felt like the fleeting glimmer of hope had left with it too.

Not knowing what to do, she put her head in her hands and cried. Cried for herself, for Tariq, for Ray-Ray, for her father and for the life which had been snatched away from her.

She heard voices coming through the rushes.

'Hello?' Laila was startled by the voices. Her heart was racing faster. She couldn't see who was there or even know how many people there were and for a second she wondered if she'd done the right thing by answering. She didn't think it was her uncle or his friends; the tone was warm and kind.

They were speaking in Urdu and Laila thought hard, trying to understand and remember what little she knew. It was unlikely they'd be able to speak English; they were so far away from any large towns or cities.

The same question was repeated and then it came to her. They were asking if she was in trouble, telling her they couldn't see her but wanting to know if she was all right.

'Yes, help . . . I mean . . .' Laila took a deep breath and then slowly and not very confidently, spoke her plea for help in Urdu.

Laila listened as she heard a different voice answer her, louder than the first but again seemingly void of hostility. The sound of something breaking made Laila turn her head. She could see the top of the reeds being pushed and moved to one side, opening up her view.

Standing just a few feet from her, waist-deep in water were two men. They stared at Laila, not unkindly, but puzzled to see her there. Their dark faces held a multitude of questions but they said nothing, only waved their hand for Laila to follow them.

It took a couple of minutes for them to reach the other side of the river and clamber up the muddy banks and immediately she felt exposed. No longer did the reeds give her sanctuary from being seen by her uncle and his friends. Laila knew she needed to move and fast.

She looked at the men who had their eyes firmly on her but talked to one another in quick quiet voices. They looked almost identical in their clothing; both wearing a thin clothed cream shalwar kameez; something her uncle always wore. The usual loose-fitting trousers and long sleeved tunics, now wet, clung to their bodies, showing off their sinewy frames.

Laila wasn't certain what to do now. She looked both ways and the road was as long and barren as the road on the other side. She knew a woman on her own in Pakistan immediately drew attention and that was something she didn't need to do. Clearing her throat, she spoke, more self-assuredly this time, as her Urdu began to come back to her. she asked the way to the nearest town. The men seemed to understand, though Laila could see the hesitancy in their eyes. Instantly she began to feel nervous again, turning her head to the thick reeds as if she was expecting to see her uncle appear out of them at any given moment. The younger and skinnier of the men pulled a face before gesturing and turning to walk. Taking this as a cue, Laila followed them. What other choice did she have?

Her feet were hurting. Sweat was dripping down her back, adding to the discomfort of her wet clothing. She looked at her watch which was still set at English time, causing her to catch her breath once more at the reality of her situation.

They'd been walking for fifteen minutes and with every second, Laila had to fight the fearful thoughts rushing through her mind. They could be taking her anywhere. Even back in Bradford she would never go somewhere with two men she didn't know, yet here she was putting her trust and effectively her life in the hands of these people.

As they walked along the road, the stares from the passing strangers seemed fewer. As long as they didn't notice she was wet, there was nothing unusual about a woman dressed in a burka following a few feet behind two men. It was the only time Laila was thankful she was wearing traditional dress. Wearing western clothes would've certainly brought more trouble.

They stopped and one of the men turned to Laila, pointing.

'Here?'

The man nodded his head as they stood outside a house which was almost a replica of the one she'd been standing outside with Tariq. 'No, I want to go to the nearest town.'

The man pointed again and said the word, *here*. Laila couldn't understand why he was saying the word, *here*. She didn't want to be here, she wanted to get to the nearest town. Though quite what she'd do when she got to it she hadn't worked out.

There was no one to call. Her family, besides from her mother – who'd be too scared to help anyway – were all here in Pakistan. They'd been the ones who'd brought her. Her friends were all family friends and the ones who weren't, for their own safety, wouldn't dare get involved. Laila Khan was quite literally alone in the world.

The men started to walk towards one of the houses, turning back occasionally to see if Laila was going to follow her. She stood, unable to make a decision. Part of her wanted to keep on going, but going where? It could be another few hundred miles to the nearest town for all she knew. The other part of her just wanted to rest. To put her faith – which in the past week had been taken away – back into people. To trust they would be kind and help her.

A minute later she'd made her decision. Though it wasn't her head or heart helping her to make up her mind, it'd been her bladder. She needed to go to the toilet. Taking a deep breath, Laila hurried to catch up to the men.

It wasn't a toilet. Not the sort she was accustomed to anyway. It was a hole. A reeking, foul hole behind the house of the woman she'd been taken to. What made it worse was the old lady standing, watching her. Sensing Laila's hesitation, the woman gestured, then contemptuously flicked her head towards the fly-filled hole.

The humiliation Laila felt as she squatted in front of the old lady brought her head down and caused the tears to return. This couldn't be the life she was going to lead. Somehow she had to get away.

Standing up, and knowing it was pointless to even think about toilet paper, Laila walked back towards the door of the house.

The two men had gone and Laila stood in the dark room, grateful for the coolness and the escape from the relentless heat.

The old lady smiled a toothless grin as she asked Laila to sit down. Too tired to search her brain for the word in Urdu, Laila gently gave her reply in English, her large beautiful eyes lighting up with genuine gratitude as she did so. 'Thank you.'

A bowl of rice topped with what looked like curried lentils was placed in front of her, and Laila accepted it gratefully, ignoring the stained, chipped bowl it came in. She lifted up the upper portion of her burka with her left hand so she could get to her mouth. Expertly using her fingers, she hungrily scooped up the rice.

When her uncle had moved in, he'd insisted on them putting most of the cutlery away, seeing the practice of them using knives and forks as another indication she and her family had been ruined by the western ways.

The curry hit her lips, tingling at first and then burning, her mouth almost calling out distress signals as the heat of the sauce refused to ease off. Laila glanced around, catching the eyes of the old lady, who cackled with laughter as she poured Laila a glass of milk.

The milk was like a balm, cooling down the insides of her mouth and throat. She was still hungry but didn't dare venture to eat any more of the curry. Sighing, and with her stomach still rumbling, Laila turned to the woman. Without needing to say anything the old lady pointed at the large floor pillow in the corner.

It looked so inviting. The white cover might be off-grey and the stained sides might have turned brown, but to Laila it meant she could rest. It looked like a piece of heaven.

She was exhausted and perhaps if she had a few hours' sleep her mind would be clearer. Not being so tired would help her decide what she was going to do next. Laila knew it wasn't unusual for someone in Pakistan to offer hospitality like this. Her uncle had told her countless stories about the kinship and warmth of the people of Pakistan, often unfavourably comparing it to the hostility he found in England, where neighbours didn't speak to neighbours and people walked past each other in the street as if each one were invisible.

In truth, Laila really wanted to get some more distance between herself and her uncle, especially as in a few hours it would be getting dark. But as she looked at the cushion, the heaviness of her eyes, the aching of her body, and the weariness of her feet told her she needed to sleep.

Curling up in a ball on the floor, Laila rested her head, put her hand under her burka to suck her thumb, and within moments was asleep.

13

'I want a mirror.' Ray-Ray Thompson struggled with the words but his look was determined.

'I don't know babe. I don't think it's a good idea at the moment. You need to get yourself better first. Maybe we should wait for the doctor.' Tasha tried to keep her voice light as she spoke, but she could tell it wasn't working. The edge of fear was audible in her voice as her eyes darted round for a nurse to intervene.

It was the second time in less than two days Ray-Ray had asked to look at himself when his bandages were being changed. The last time, one of the junior doctors had come round to discuss pain management, saving her from having to find a way to discourage him from looking in the mirror. Tash had then made a hasty exit, out of the hospital, into the car park where she'd promptly been sick.

She was a coward. She knew that. But how could she let her son see his face or what was left of it? *She* could hardly bear to look. It wasn't disgust. It certainly wasn't shame. It was pain. Pain that Ray-Ray had been put through such torture; such undeserving agony.

He'd been lucky; if you could call it luck. The acid hadn't been thrown all over his entire face, only part of it, but she was scared she couldn't be strong enough for him. It was pathetic, but she didn't know how to stay strong for her son when she couldn't stay strong for herself.

'I said pass me the fucking mirror, Mum.'

Ray-Ray snarled, twisting his mouth at Tasha, partly through anger, partly through pain, but mainly from the damage the acid had caused the top part of his lip. Tasha thought he looked like Freddie when he did that. Full of anger. Full of hate. Full of fear.

'Ray-Ray, it ain't a good . . .'

'Now, please.' The appeal in his voice tore at Tasha's heart, hardening it towards her husband, Freddie. With shaking hands she passed him the mirror and looked across, at the nurse who gave her a sympathetic smile.

'Don't cry Mum.' Ray-Ray's voice was hoarse and quiet. His voice no longer sounded like his own because of the acid attacking his vocal chords, and they could both hear it.

Tasha saw him take a deep breath, mirroring the one she was taking. 'You ready babe?'

'Ready.'

Ray-Ray stared but he didn't recognise who he saw. Who he was seeing in the mirror wasn't him. It couldn't be, because he had blonde hair falling across his forehead. His face was fresh and handsome. Tiny freckles covered the bridge of his nose. His cheeky, dimpled smile pulled more birds than any guy could wish for. Ray-Ray Thompson, son of the handsome Freddie and beautiful Tasha Thompson. Blonde hair. Blue eyes. The best-looking guy in Soho.

That's who he was; yet the mirror was telling a different story. This person, this imposter who stared back at him blankly, was nothing short of a grotesque monster.

Red, inflamed, weeping skin. Raw burns deep into his face, taking away the top part of his lip, displaying his gums. A hole where part of his nose had been. His eyelid deformed; eaten away by the acid. Unlikely to see again out of the once dazzling blue, now dull grey, filmy, fish-like eye.

Ray-Ray swallowed. He wanted to throw the mirror to the other side of the room but he was transfixed by what he saw. Tortured by it. He could feel the tears coming but with it came more pain. His tear ducts had been damaged too.

The shiny skin on the top of his head was taut. His hair had gone. Tufts were all that was left, giving his head a bizarre, tragically comical appearance.

Ray-Ray slowly moved his gaze to look at the other part of his face. The part which hadn't been touched by acid. This was the smooth, handsome Ray-Ray he knew, a glimmer of the young man he once was. And in a way, having a reminder of what he'd looked like was worse than none at all. It was as if the beautiful part was taunting him, reminding him of what had been.

He felt his mother touch his hand. 'Ray-Ray, I'm . . .'

'Ain't nothing to say. I look like a freak. No wonder you didn't want to give me the mirror.'

Tasha's eyes filled with tears again. 'It wasn't that babe. It was just . . . I knew how difficult it would be. I didn't . . .' Tasha gave up mid-sentence. She was exhausted. Ray-Ray was right, nothing she could say was going to make it better; only actions.

'Your dad's going to sort this babe. He ain't going to let whoever did this get away.'

Ray-Ray quickly turned away his head. 'Leave it. I don't want him doing anything. It's nothing to do with him.'

Tasha's voice took on a tone of resentment. 'It's got everything to do with him. The least he can do is try to sort it. I knew. I just bleeding knew this would happen one day.' She stopped, realising her voice was getting too loud and slightly hysterical. Taking a deep breath, she continued in a whisper. 'Listen babe, you ain't got to defend your dad. I know you love him and I ain't trying to put no wedge between the two of you, but Christ, Ray-Ray, look at you.'

The moment Tasha had said it, she knew she shouldn't have. She watched her son turn his face from her, wounded by her tactless comment. 'Ray-Ray, sweetheart, I'm sorry. I didn't mean anything by it. You know me; my mouth's too big sometimes.'

'Forget it Mum, you're just telling the truth.'

Tasha squeezed Ray-Ray's hand. 'Please honey, let your dad sort it out. He's going off his nut. He can't stick it inside, knowing some low-life scum has done this to you. It's killing him not being able to be with you.' Tasha paused, making sure the nurses were out of earshot. 'He's planning to do a break.'

Ray-Ray shot his reply, causing a darting pain to run down the side of his face. 'No, he can't. Is he stupid or something? Mum, you've got to tell him not to do it. Not for me. Please tell him I'm okay. I'll be okay.'

Tasha bit her lip. Perhaps she shouldn't have told Ray-Ray about Freddie's plan but he'd find out soon enough, especially once the Old Bill started to sniff around. Better he have a heads up now.

'Just tell me what happened babe. Can you remember anything about it? Would you recognise their faces? Do you know who did this?'

Ray-Ray looked up at the ceiling. He knew exactly who'd done it. He could see their faces clearer than he could see his mum's. Everything about that night played out in slow motion in his head. He could feel it. He could hear it. He could smell it. The smell of melting flesh. *His* melting flesh. The hot, searing pain. Pain which he didn't think was even possible. Oh yes, he knew exactly who did it. He turned back to face Tasha. 'No, I can't remember nothing. Last thing I remember is you dolling yourself up and going out. After that, nothing.'

Tasha's eyes narrowed. 'Maybe it'll come back to you.'

'I doubt it.'

'You don't know that doll. You hear all sorts of stuff about people's memory coming back to them.'

'I know it won't, let's leave it at that.'

Tasha looked at her son. He was stubborn like Freddie, but the problem was he couldn't afford to be. Not with this. He needed to remember, because Freddie *needed* revenge. She was so angry with her husband, but at the same time she hated the idea of him hurting, and he would be, knowing Ray-Ray was in pain. Revenge would be like a balm for Freddie; soothing and healing his wound.

The nurses came over to re-dress Ray-Ray's face and Tasha moved quietly to one side. Her phone buzzed. She checked the caller ID and frowned. Ignoring the call, she sat down by the side of Ray-Ray's bed deep in thought, waiting for the nurse to finish and the phone to stop ringing.

Gently and expertly, the large West Indian nurse placed the fresh white bandages back on. It was so painful, and just trying to bear the pain and not let anyone see him flinch was exhausting.

To distract himself, Ray-Ray put his headphone into the ear which hadn't been damaged by the acid, listening to the CD Laila had made for him. The music played and his thoughts drifted immediately to her. The reason he couldn't tell his father who'd attacked him.

It wasn't as if he didn't want revenge himself; he did. It was like an unquenchable thirst but the fact was he couldn't have it. Not now, perhaps not ever. And that was okay. It was okay because it would mean Laila would be safe, and that superseded the simmering anger he had within him.

He knew his father, and he knew what he and his cronies were not only capable of doing but *would* do to Laila's family – and potentially even to Laila if they ever found out. Even if they didn't hurt her directly, hurting her family would be hurting her.

By not saying anything he could try to put the wrongs right. He'd always known by the look in her eyes that Laila shouldn't have walked to the bus stop, shouldn't have taken his hand gently, and probably shouldn't have even spoken to him, but she had. She'd done it for him. And this was what he was going to do for her.

After all, it wasn't her fault any of this had happened. Laila was gentle and would never hurt anyone. He wasn't going to cause her any problems by letting his father have his revenge, no matter how much he loved him and wanted it himself. It wasn't about his father anyway. It wasn't *his* revenge to have. It was about him and about Laila.

Ray-Ray didn't want it to go any further. He would put a stop to it by keeping his mouth shut. Her family had settled the score. Warned him off and now they were satisfied, and so was he. It comforted him to know that Laila, with her stunning beauty, her shy demeanour, her dancing warm eyes, would now be safe. Carving out a happy future for herself. Excelling in everything she did before going off to the university she'd spoken about.

Once he found out from the nurse if she was safe, he'd try to contact her again, but he'd leave her to get on with her own life. Besides anything else, he wouldn't want her to see him like this. She could remember him as he once was. And he would be happy to always remember the sweet girl he once knew.

Ray-Ray gritted his teeth as the pain hit him again, but this time, through his agony there was a glimmer of a smile.

14

'Bitch.' The word coming out of his mouth made Arnie slam his hand across his own face, causing a red welt to start to form. He didn't want to talk like that. Especially not about Izzy. But what was he supposed to do when he'd called her and she hadn't answered?

At first he'd thought something had happened, so he'd driven round to the hotel. And within the length of time it took the castaway on *Desert Island Discs* to get to their luxury item, he'd seen her. Smiling, laughing, and looking very much alive.

Arnold couldn't understand it. He wasn't sure what he'd done. The last time they'd seen or spoken to each other was when he'd dropped her off at the hospital. He had a sinking feeling that she was disappointed with him as she had always been when they were children.

He'd promised her a special day and he genuinely thought he'd be able to deliver it. He'd had everything prepared and she'd seemed keen; excited almost, but then it'd all gone wrong. What should've happened, didn't.

Sighing, Arnold wandered to the area of the room with a tarpaulin sheet laid on the ground. A large green bucket sat innocuously on top. Bending down, Arnie murmured a little ditty to raise his spirits as he swirled the red water gently.

'1, 4, 9, 16, 25, Izzy, whizzy, let's get busy.' The ditty made him chuckle at first, then laugh out loud as he repeated it with much more gusto, making him topple over from his crouching position onto the floor; bringing more hysterical laughter.

Uproarious tears ran down Arnold's face as he lay on his side, clutching his tummy as it started to hurt from all the hilarity. He shouted now, screaming the ditty as loud as he could; hoping passers-by would hear his rhyme. The thought of people outside wondering what the noise was took Arnold over into frenzied laughter. Saliva ran down his chin and onto his bare chest as he twisted and rolled around.

Then he froze. Almost as quickly as it began, the laughter stopped, and the tears turned from ones of happiness to ones of sorrow. A deep, sad growl came from Arnie. Izzy was playing games with him.

He looked up to see a pair of blue eyes staring at him through a mass of blonde hair. In his confusion he'd got it wrong again. How many times had he got it wrong now? Five times? Six, if you counted the foul-mouthed girl from Aberdeen, but he didn't like to count her. He'd just been so desperate for Izzy to come back, he'd assumed this person was her. It wasn't. He didn't even know her name.

It wasn't his fault. If Izzy had just answered the phone, came to see him as she'd promised, then he wouldn't have made this terrible mistake. Standing up, Arnie knew there was only one thing to do. The gentlemanly thing to do. He must apologise, as his father had always told him to do. 'I'm so sorry; I do apologise. I mistook you for somebody else.' With one swift movement, Arnie swung the axe.

Arnold wrapped the dismembered body and placed the limbs in the black bin liners. He felt tired; exhausted from all the chopping. But he also felt tired from all the emotional games. Izzy was making him pay for making her wait.

110

He didn't want to get angry but he was starting to get annoyed. She was wasting their precious time together. Well, he wasn't going to put up with it. If she wouldn't come to him, he would go to her. He'd show her he was someone who could be relied upon; that he was as good as his word. If she wanted a special day, he'd make sure she had exactly that. One she'd never forget.

'Bitch.' Freddie Thompson gripped the phone between his hands, squeezing it, but having the restraint not to smash it apart. He'd never known anyone *not* to answer their phone as much as Tasha lately. And it was pissing him off. Big time. If she wanted to mess with his head by playing games with him, then it was working. If she wanted to grab his attention by blanking him, then she was doing a bleeding good job of it.

He didn't know what the fuck he was supposed to have done to her. He'd been a good husband; *was* a good husband. Okay, so he'd dipped his dick in tasty bits of pussy, but that was hardly a crime.

He hadn't done the mushy crap. But she'd seemed okay with that; she'd never complained anyway. More to the point, he was Freddie Thompson, the biggest face around and it wouldn't do his rep any good to be seen to be a soppy cunt. He was married to her, what more did she want?

So she blamed him for Ray-Ray. She was angry. Furious. He got that. But it seemed too little, too late. It didn't really make sense for her to be pissed now. She'd always known the risks and for all the years so far she'd managed to ignore them. Brand new Bentley convertibles and a wardrobe full of designer clothes seemed to have that effect.

Confusion and emotional shit didn't sit well with him. It made him edgy. Paranoid. Dangerous. If it was a game she was playing, then Freddie hoped for her sake she knew what she was doing. No one fucked over Freddie, not even his wife.

He rubbed his chin, thoughtfully. He didn't need this. He was trying to focus on the bigger picture. He needed to have a clear mind, with no distractions, if he and Eddie were going to pull this off.

Looking around his bleak cell, Freddie could almost taste the freedom. There was a sense of wanting to get it over and done with, but he knew he only had one chance. One chance to get it right.

It had to be planned meticulously, otherwise he was fucked. He'd be banged up in a cell tighter than a nun's fanny. There'd be restricted visits, all done through a thick pane of reinforced glass. A twenty-three hour lock-up regime. Isolated yard exercise, and worst still, life would probably mean he'd be locked up until he was pushing up daisies.

Freddie sniffed, trying to ignore the anxiety which lay heavy in his stomach when he allowed himself to focus on what was at stake. Yet however anxious he was, he knew that if he pulled it off, it would be worth it. It'd be sweet.

He clenched his fist, as images of what he'd do and how he'd torture the person who'd turned over Ray-Ray shot through his mind. He had to focus on that. Remember the reason he was doing this. Once it was done, he'd get the hell out of the country. Maybe to Spain, then on to Morocco, before hitting Brazil. Tasha and Ray-Ray would join him as soon as they'd got the all-clear from the doctors and finally, he could be with his son.

He'd heard there were excellent cosmetic surgeons out there. Hopefully they'd be able to do something to help Ray-Ray, but if they couldn't, Freddie was sure his son would feel a whole lot better knowing that the people responsible for his injuries had a long, slow, tortuous death.

'How's tricks?'

Eddie walked into Freddie's cell. He was the only person who could walk in without knocking. Pushing away the thoughts of his family, Freddie grinned. 'Not too bad, you?'

Eddie smiled back. 'Good. In fact, fucking class mate. I've got word from my driver it's a goer; only problem is he's not back at work until beginning of September. Is that going to be a problem?'

'No, in fact, I spoke to the Governor and he was telling me some crap about not being able to have a visit to Ray-Ray until the 27th September, so it works out perfectly.'

'So that's what? Just over two months from now? Shit.'

Freddie tapped his friend on his back, laughing at his friend's sudden glum face. 'Patience, Eddie. Good things come to those who wait. It gives us plenty of time to make sure there'll be no cock-ups. You'll be sorted on your side by then?'

Biting on the apple he had in his pocket left over from lunch, Eddie said, 'Nothing much to sort really. Everything's really tied up, apart from the money of course.'

'I'll arrange with my men to drop off half the money up front, then the other half after the job's done,' Freddie replied. 'Eddie, he does know if he fucks me over, he'll be watching whilst I bury him and his missus alive?'

Eddie gave a half smile. He liked Freddie. He knew what he wanted and got it. His fearsome reputation was justified. Though admittedly, he wasn't too taken by the next part of the conversation.

'And Eddie, I don't know this guy, but I know you. So I'm making you his guarantor. If he screws me Ed, as his guarantor, I'll be coming after you first.' Eddie's half smile vanished.

'When they jump the prison van, my men will be waiting for me in a car. Then they'll take me to another before finally taking me to the last car. The one Tasha will drive.'

'Tasha's going to drive you?' Eddie sounded incredulous which was picked up by Freddie. He cut his eyes at Eddie as his expression darkened.

'What's the tone for Ed?'

'I . . . I'm just surprised that's all.'

'Why?'

Eddie didn't like to be put on the spot, especially when it was by Freddie. 'She's a woman and women can't drive.'

Freddie burst out into laughter, along with Eddie. The tense atmosphere was immediately lightened, bringing Freddie back to being upbeat. 'Don't let Tash hear you say that about her driving, she'll be cutting off your balls.'

'I'm just impressed I guess.'

'Impressed?'

'Yeah, that anyone could put something so big in the hands of their missus. It's like saying you're putting your life in her hands. You must really trust her.'

About to answer his friend, the cell door knocked, but not before a nagging doubt started to creep into Freddie's head first.

'Come.'

Deputy Governor Martin Warner walked into Freddie's cell. He nodded his head to Eddie, who took the pointer and left. Freddie yawned, lying back on the hard spring mattress of the prison bed. 'How's your face?' Freddie grinned, his eyes mocking.

Automatically, Martin Warner touched his face. It didn't hurt now but the humiliation did. The knowledge that the whole of the wing, and no doubt the whole of the prison, knew he was under the thumb of Freddie Thompson didn't sit comfortably with him. It wouldn't be so bad if he were in Freddie's pocket. At least then he'd get something out of it. But he wasn't that lucky, all he got out of it was a headache and the knowledge his family could sleep easy in their beds. Well at least for tonight.

'What is it you want Thompson?' Martin Warner's tone had an air of authority but he knew it held none.

'Less of the lip, Mr Warner. I don't appreciate being spoken to like a cunt in my own cell.'

The deputy dug his fingernails into the palms of his hands to stop himself getting angry. Noticing, Freddie laughed. 'Temper, temper Mr Warner. Why don't you go right on ahead and say what you want to say. Come on, I dare you. Grow some balls.'

The deputy retorted angrily, full of resentment and hostility at being pushed around by Freddie. 'Listen here, Thompson. There's only so much you can push a person before they snap.'

Freddie stood up. The bed creaked behind him. Walking slowly across to Warner, he was amused to see the sudden fear in the deputy governor's face. But he didn't show his amusement; instead he held his mouth in a tight, grim expression.

Inches away from Warner, Freddie could hear the man's fast-paced breathing. He jabbed his index finger hard into Warner's chest. 'Go on then; snap.'

He jabbed again, several times, in quick, aggressive succession. 'I'm pushing you Warner. Snap.'

Martin Warner's humiliation was complete as tears of frustration and anger stung his eyes. His face paled, marked with his cheeks turning red. He had no other place to go besides backing down. 'It's just a turn of phrase. You can imagine how difficult this is.'

'No, Warner I can't. I could never imagine what it's like to be a man like you.'

Freddie laughed out scornfully as he watched Warner quickly wipe away a tear. 'You're pathetic.' He turned away, disgusted at the man's weakness.

Going over to make a drink from his new espresso machine, an item which was prohibited in the prison but an item which Martin Warner was all too well aware he'd been required to bring in on Freddie's insistence.

Freddie winked. 'Fancy a coffee, Mr Warner? Marvellous things these machines. You should get yourself one.'

Martin Warner shook his head stiffly, realising he was being mocked.

'I need you to do something for me Marty. You don't mind if I call you Marty do you? I got word I can go and visit my son on the 27th September.'

'Yes, I heard. What are you telling me about it for? It's ages from now.'

'Let's call it due warning. The thing is Marty, I need you to make sure you're working that day.'

Puzzlement showed on Warner's face. Freddie rolled his eyes at the stupidity of the man. 'I don't understand what you're asking me.'

'I'm not asking. I'm telling. I need you to work on that day and I also need you – and this is *very* important – I need you to make sure Eddie Davidson is in the same van as me.'

'Davidson? He's not due to go anywhere.'

'No, but he will be. Let's just say I'm a bit of a Mystic Meg and I'm predicting he gets a bit of an injury on that day.'

Warner stared in horror at Freddie. 'If you're suggesting what I'm thinking, you can forget it. I'll pretend I didn't hear it.'

Martin Warner turned to walk out of the cell, but with the swiftness and agility of a man half his age, Freddie ran in front of the deputy, blocking his way and slamming the cell door closed.

Nervously, Warner jangled his keys hanging from his worn black leather belt. 'This has gone too far, Thompson. It needs to come to an end. Get out of my way.'

Freddie leaned in, speaking through gritted teeth. 'It only comes to an end when *I say* it comes to an end. Don't let me have to show you that by sending one of my men to come and pay a cosy visit to that wife of yours. Patricia her name is, isn't it?'

Beads of sweat formed of Warner's forehead, and he licked his dry lips. 'I can't, I just can't do what you're suggesting. I could get into serious trouble.'

'Tell me Marty. Which frightens you more? Getting into trouble from the authorities or getting into trouble with yours truly? Point is Marty, if you help me then there's a real possibility no one will ever know. You can get on with your life as if I never existed. If you don't help, then how shall I put it? There'll be no possibility of you, your wife, or your daughter, ever getting on with life.'

'I need to think about it.'

'No you don't. There's nothing *to* think about. Just make sure Eddie gets in the van.'

116

Freddie could see the hesitation still in Warner's face. He walked over to the grey tatty locker and opened the top drawer. Banging it hard to open it where it'd stuck on the runners, he pulled something out. Turning back to Warner he winked.

'I want to show you something.' Freddie smiled as he spoke, the exact opposite to the expression on Warner's face.

'Where . . . where did you get that?'

'One of my men took it. I must say your missus takes a nice photo.'

Martin Warner snatched the photograph held in the air by Freddie. He studied it. There was his house. His garden. His wife and his daughter in the front driveway, oblivious to the fact they were being watched.

Freddie cleared his throat. 'So what do you say now Marty? You going to get Eddie in that van or what?'

Martin Warner screwed up the photo in his hand before throwing it at Freddie who grinned broadly. He swung open the prison cell door and without looking directly at Freddie, he spoke in a hoarse whisper. 'I'll do it. But Thompson, I hope you rot in hell.'

15

The cold water hit her with such sudden sharpness, Laila wasn't sure what it was. She scrambled to her knees, clawing the cushion she'd been asleep on as if she were tumbling down a soaring, crumbling mountain. A dog barked in the distance and the realisation of where she was made her stop moving.

In slow motion she turned her head and body round. Standing above her were the two men from the river and next to them, glowering, his face red with fury, was uncle Mahmood.

Laila's body lurched, in a hopeless attempt to escape, and she felt the top part of her burka being pulled, causing it to fall off. Her thick, long hair tumbled out over her face. She could see only the floor and the bare feet of the three men.

The searing pain on her head made her scream. Laila jumped to her feet, onto her tiptoes, hoping to stop the mass of black hair being torn out of her scalp. Her uncle began to yell in her face. Spit showered her as he bellowed, first in Urdu and then in English.

'Answer me. Why have you done this? Did you think you were going to run away? To go back to England, to that boy in Bradford? Well whatever you thought, it's not going to happen. You will do your duty.'

118

'Please stop uncle, you're hurting me,' Laila's words were staggered as she spoke, between the flashes of pain. The back hand caught Laila's head hard and the force behind it sent her flying across the tiny room. She hit the wall, sliding down it in a mix of blood and tears.

Her uncle came towards her screaming. Raging. Words she couldn't understand. She curled up in the corner, pushing herself into it as she felt the blood trickling down past her ear. Eventually Mahmood squatted down to her level. 'You are coming with me now. I don't even know if there will be a wedding. Who wants a bride who acts like an animal?'

Through her pain and fear, Laila's spirit broke through. Spluttering her words, she defiantly answered back. 'Good, because I hope there isn't a wedding. I don't want to get married and I don't want to be here with you . . . I hate you.' Her last words shrieked out with all the emotion she had.

The shock on Mahmood's face clouded over in seconds into a snarl of disgust. He stood up whispering his chilling warning. 'You will do what I say Laila, otherwise I won't hesitate to kill you. Do you hear me? I would rather go to prison than you bring dishonour on me and my family.'

Mahmood turned to leave but as he did he grabbed Laila's hair once more, pulling her up from the corner. Her legs scuttled quickly to keep up with the lengthy strides of Mahmood as he continued to drag her along by her hair. She screamed out to the two men and the old lady.

'Help me please, help me. I'm begging you.'

Tariq looked at his sister kneeling in the middle of the room. She wore a bright red shalwar kameez with a bejewelled matching dupatta. The dupatta covered her hair and hung down by the side of her face. He watched, conscious of the ten other people in the room inspecting her. She was looking down. No eye contact. No smiling. No emotion. The sign of respect. But Tariq was sure that

119

given the chance she'd try to escape again, and increasingly he felt that he wouldn't blame her.

He continued to think as he watched his sister move her hand and wipe away the tear trickling down her face. Then she was motionless again. Tariq sighed, which sounded much louder in the silent room than he would've wanted. Uncle was getting angrier by the day. Tariq didn't want to see her hurt and he didn't know how to explain to her that she had to stop and accept her fate.

He could see her lip bruised and starting to swell. If only she'd not put up such a fight. He'd spoken to her briefly earlier, when uncle had dragged her back, looking dishevelled and hurt.

'Laila, please, this isn't helping you. People are going to start turning against you. Make life easy on yourself. If you can't do it for yourself, do it for me.'

She'd glanced at him then, but said nothing. A moment later she'd been ordered to change and await the arrival of her future in-laws.

Tariq noticed a heated discussion taking place on the other side of the room. Their voices were low but he could still make out the words of the astoundingly short but obese old lady, the matchmaker of the wedding, speaking angrily to his uncle.

Tariq raised his eyebrows at the old woman's request, at his uncle's insistence over the past year, he'd worked hard at understanding his language. He shot a quick stare at Laila to see if she'd heard or understood what had just been said. If she had, she wasn't giving anything away as she stared at the floor, trance-like. The old lady made a noise in the back of her throat, then limped out of the room, her face sealed with disapproval. The others nodded and silently followed behind.

Mahmood walked across to Laila and bent down. He hissed in her ear, grabbing hold of her arm and squeezing it too sharply.

'See what your behaviour has brought me? Shame. Humiliation. Never did I think my brother's children, who I've shown nothing but kindness to, never did I think they'd bring me so much trouble and pain. Everything I try to do is selfless, yet I'm the one who is disgraced. I've just been told there will be *no* wedding unless a virginity test is performed Laila. They want to make sure you're intact before they allow you to marry their son. Do you know how that makes me feel, hey? Answer me.'

Laila's head turned towards Mahmood but he raised his hand and she quickly lowered it. Her whole body was trembling from fear and from her uncle shaking her violently. She screamed out as a cutting pain hit her back, followed by another sharp pain. She fell forward, her body tense as she waited for the next blow, but it didn't come. She turned her head slightly to see Tariq holding onto their uncle's arm which was holding a thin cane.

'uncle, no. Please don't.'

Tariq spoke in Urdu, appealing to Mahmood. At first he thought his uncle was going to take his anger out on him as he stared with blazing eyes, but instead, he stopped, lowering the cane and dropping Laila's arm.

'She is going to come back in half an hour with two other ladies and your future mother-in-law to check you.'

Laila's voice quivered, it was barely audible. 'Uncle, can I speak?'

Mahmood straightened himself up, rubbing his left leg. It was all getting too much for him. He'd thought it before, but he knew now he was right in thinking he'd been cursed to have been burdened with his irresponsible niece. 'Go on.'

'Uncle, there is no check.' Laila paused, her words catching in her throat. Tariq heard the urgency and fear in her voice as Laila tried to recover her composure.

'I know there isn't a test. It's impossible to tell. Riding a bike or a horse could make a difference. Please uncle, I'm telling the truth, being able to tell is just an old wives' tale.'

Mahmood shouted, angry at the suggestion. 'How dare you. It's only an old wives' tale for those who have something to hide, and when did you *ever* ride a bike or a horse?'

Laila swallowed, her cheeks turning red as her teenage

embarrassment showed. 'Tampons. They would do it. They could break the hymen.'

Mahmood's dark eyes fixed on Laila. The loathing on his face was apparent. He struggled to talk as his revulsion with Laila and her boldness in discussing a subject so foul, so unclean, so offensive, threatened to overwhelm him. 'I hope for your sake Laila you are intact; otherwise I won't be held responsible for my actions.'

Laila stood in the tiny bedroom. It was no larger than the pantry at home. It held a bed, larger than her single one but smaller than the double one her parents had shared, occupied now by her mother and uncle who'd given his mother no choice. A carved wooden chest of drawers sat in the corner, with a large colourful prayer mat resting up beside it. The window had bars but no glass, and was covered by a simple piece of muslin cloth.

The door opening made Laila jump. From behind the door came the matchmaker, flanked by two other women of a similar age to the old lady and a similar body type. The final person to enter the room was a tall, slender woman in her fifties dressed in a peach sari. No one said anything, only stared at Laila, who tried to smile out of politeness. The hostility for her was etched on the three old ladies' faces, who continued chewing on the betel nut which had turned their lips a dark shade of red.

The tall woman stood observing the room, eventually turning her attention to Laila. She was surprised to hear her speak English, albeit laden with a heavy Pakistani accent.

'Laila. Your uncle has explained to you what is going to happen. I'm very sorry but we feel it necessary. A girl who runs off and disobeys her family is a girl who cannot be trusted. Perhaps cannot even be trusted to respect her own body.'

'But . . . I . . .'

The lady held up her hand as Laila tried to speak, and she fell silent.

'For a young girl, for a young woman, you have a lot to say.

Too much. You will have to learn if you want to be a good wife, you must hold your tongue.'

Laila sounded childlike as she spoke, frantically looking from one woman to another. 'I don't though. I don't want to be anybody's wife. I'd like to go to university. I'm good at science and my teacher says if I work hard I'll be able to get into a good place, possibly even somewhere like Cambridge. That's what my father and I always dreamed of. He always wanted so much for me. Maybe you could explain that to my uncle; you could explain to him I'm not a bad person and I don't mean to show him disrespect or seem ungrateful . . . I just want to go home. Please. Please, help me go home.' Laila burst into tears, covering her face with her hands.

The woman walked towards her. Her eyes showing no compassion, she gently took hold of one of Laila's hands, bringing it down from her face. 'That won't be possible. If this test turns out to be fine, tomorrow you will marry my son.'

'Your son, I . . .'

Laila's future mother-in-law held her well-manicured finger over Laila's mouth. 'I told you. You have too much to say. Lie down.'

Laila's eyes were wide open with fear. 'No . . . please, I don't want to.'

'I said, lie down.'

Laila started to shake her head, her hair sticking to her face as it came into contact with her tears and running nose. 'Hold her down,' the tall woman ordered the others, and they immediately grabbed hold of the now-hysterical Laila's arms and dragged her towards the bed. Her resistance came to an abrupt end as a small leather strap whipped across her face. Laila's fear increased as she stared at the face of the woman who tomorrow would become her mother-in-law. Clutching the strap, she glared at Laila, her voice coldly level. 'You don't want to make an enemy of me. If you want me to make sure I tell your uncle you're still a virgin you need to behave. Open your legs and don't move.'

'But I am a virgin. I've never even come close to kissing anyone.'

'I don't think you quite understand, Laila. I will only find you a virgin, if I choose to find you one.'

The threat was unmistakable. Having no choice, Laila lay back and closed her eyes as she opened her legs. She was shaking and momentarily she tried to resist as the old women held on to either knee and started drawing them wider apart.

A sharp pain seared through Laila. It felt like a sharp instrument was being forced inside her. She screamed out, wincing through the intense agony.

'When was your last period?'

Laila could hardly think, let alone speak. The pain was unforgiving. 'I said, when was your last period girl?'

With the end word of the sentence came the end of the sharp pain, only a dull throbbing was left. The woman stood above Laila, her arm outstretched with two of her fingers covered in blood. Laila watched as the matchmaker hurried round the bed with a small white bowl Laila hadn't noticed before.

The woman dipped her hand in, quickly washing it before drying it on the towel.

'Well?'

'It finished about two weeks before I flew out here.'

'Good. Perfect timing. Then there'll be nothing stopping you getting pregnant as soon as possible. Tomorrow, after the wedding is a good time to try.'

The woman turned away and nodded her head to the old ladies as she spoke.

Laila's Urdu didn't need to be fluent to know they'd just been ordered to lock her in. Now there was no escape. She had become their prisoner.

Outside in the dark, below Laila's room, Tariq wiped the tears from his face away. Even though he was on his own he felt foolish crying. He was a grown man, but he'd heard everything that had been said. Heard Laila screaming. Heard her pain.

Throwing his cigarette away, he listened to the crickets and strange noises of the night. He didn't move, although the hard stone he was sitting on was uncomfortable enough to do so. But he wanted to think. He needed to think of a way to help his sister before it was too late.

16

The early morning brought the sound of a cockerel and with it an oppressive heat. It also brought thoughts of Ray-Ray. She imagined his blue eyes. Warm, kind and dancing. His cockney twang which had always made her laugh. His tough demeanour but soft heart, and the fact he could've sat next to any girl but had chosen to sit next to her.

Laila frowned at the thought. She refused to allow herself to think that's where the trouble had started, because she hadn't done anything wrong. Hadn't shown any disrespect. If it hadn't been Ray-Ray, it would've been somebody else, *something* else. A look, a word, playing the wrong music, taking too long to come back from the shops. Anything could've given her uncle the excuse he was looking for. Her sisters, who she never saw or heard from any more, had been married off, but they had seemed to accept their fate quietly and she wasn't like them.

She'd desperately wanted to ask her uncle about Ray-Ray again, but she hadn't dared, thinking it best if she left the subject of him well alone. Bringing him up in conversation would certainly cause more misplaced suspicion from him and she didn't want to ask Tariq either for the same reason.

It might also bring more repercussions for Ray-Ray. This way, if she kept her mouth shut she was sure he'd be safe from any more harm.

Laila wished she could see Ray-Ray again, but she knew that wasn't possible. Not now she was getting married. It wouldn't be safe for him, even more than her. She was terrified he would hate her now. Worried he would think she'd let her family go round. And now no doubt Emma Gibbs from 6C would be trying to get her hooks into him by now. What she wouldn't do to see his face again, to be able to laugh at one of his silly jokes. To feel the same kind of butterflies in her tummy she'd felt when she'd walked along the street with him; dizzy with excitement.

She smiled sadly as she looked out of the window through the bars to the distant mountains. He would be getting on with his life now and she was happy for him. Going back to London after the summer. Forgetting she ever existed. But she knew she would always remember him. Ray-Ray Thompson, the sweetest boy she'd ever known.

Laila continued to lie on the bed. She thought about Tariq and the way he'd stepped in to stop her uncle hurting her. He'd never done anything like that before and she was grateful to him.

She was still in the clothes from the day before. She felt numb; disconnected. She hadn't slept, or she didn't think she had. The night had carried a cold fear and she'd lain on the bed shivering, unable to get warm.

In the early hours she'd given up calling out and asking for someone to come and had banged on the door, until her hands were raw. In the end she'd had to crouch in the corner and do a wee. She could smell it now, the strong stench of urine mixing with the heat and the smells of the cooking coming from the kitchen below.

Even though it was early she could hear the sound of music playing in the distance. The celebrations had already begun.

The door being unlocked made Laila sit bolt upright. She immediately felt dizzy, realising she couldn't remember the last time she ate a proper meal. She watched as her future mother-in-law walked in with a grim expression on her face. As she spoke, she sniffed the air disdainfully. 'Laila, you need to start to get ready.'

'Yes, er . . . I don't know what I should call you.'

'Auntie, will be just fine. Now get up, there's a lot to do. And Laila?'

'Yes Auntie?'

'No tricks. No trouble. No shame.'

Laila looked first at her Auntie's face and then down at the leather strap she was holding tightly in her hand. Not for the first time, Laila Khan wished she was brave enough to take her own life.

Two hours later Laila sat in the chair, two women by her feet, two women by her side, all of whom she hadn't met before. They didn't speak to her, only with each other as they painted her hands and feet in decorative red henna.

'A symbol of blessing and a symbol of fertility. You're a very lucky girl Laila,' Auntie said, nodding her head in approval at the artwork.

Laila said nothing and watched the intricate patterns being drawn. Her father had once told her of another reason why the delicate designs were painted on. It was to ward off evil. And as Laila closed her eyes, empty of tears, listening to the drums being played outside, she hoped above all that what her father had told her would hold true.

'You look beautiful.' Tariq walked into the room and admired his sister. His eyes though, rested on the swollen lip and the bruised right side of her face. The make-up was heavy and although Laila looked more stunning than he'd ever seen her before, she looked older, as if the years had been added on overnight.

Looking into her eyes he could see the sadness and he felt ashamed. He whispered, not wanting anyone else in the tiny room to hear, 'It'll be all right, Laila. You'll see, I promise. I'll do everything I can.'

A hint of puzzlement crossed Laila's face. 'Tariq, thank you.'

'What for?'

'For yesterday. For standing up to uncle.'

Tariq said nothing as his new Auntie frowned at them both, coming closer, wanting to hear anything which was said between them. He drew his eyes from the hostile stare and focused on the heavily embroidered pink shalwar kameez and dupatta his sister was wearing.

A tikka, the traditional gold head chain, lay sparkling in the middle of Laila's forehead, encrusted with diamonds. Gold and emerald earrings hung from her ears. A matching necklace hung heavy on her neck and a large round nose ring, which was connected to a gold and ruby chain, hung from her nose and across her cheek. Both arms and both feet were adorned with delicate silver and gold bangles.

'Ready?' Auntie spoke as she drew down the dupatta to cover Laila's face.

'Tariq!' Laila's voice verged on the hysterical and although Tariq couldn't see his sister's eyes he was certain they were wide open with fear.

'Shhh Laila, it will be okay. Trust me.'

'Of course it will,' the woman snapped. 'How could it not be? She's marrying my son. Now let's get on with this, I don't want to keep anyone waiting.'

From beneath the long pink dupatta, Laila's hand reached out and grabbed hold of Tariq's wrist. Her voice was strained and urgent. 'His name. Oh my God, I don't even know my husband's name.'

The bridal procession marched slightly quicker than Tariq thought was necessary. He could see the old ladies hurrying to keep up with his newly acquired Auntie, who strode as if she was on a bracing country walk rather than a regal marriage parade.

As he followed, the smell of the roast meats hit Tariq's senses. He felt guilty for feeling hungry when he knew he should be thinking about his sister rather than his stomach. Behind him the sound of drums started up.

They walked into the tattered marquee, which was decorated with red and white flowers as well as several large candles. A sea of bearded white-robed men sat chatting to each other on one side of the tent. On the side the women and children sat, dressed in brightly coloured salwar kameez. At the far end of the marquee there was a makeshift platform covered in petals.

Tariq saw his uncle helping Laila onto the platform. She knelt down unsteadily, her face totally covered. He wished she could see him, just to make eye contact, to let her know he was here for her. He sighed and turned to look for somewhere to sit. Out of the corner of his eye he saw the groom entering, dressed in a silk cream Nehru collar jacket and matching trousers, several garlands of flowers hanging around his neck. Tariq wasn't able to get a glimpse of his face either as it was covered by a heavy gold tinsel veil hanging from his pleated red turban. The only thing Tariq could do now was watch and hope for the best, hoping he'd come up with a plan to help his sister.

Laila knelt, unable to see anything apart from the chiffon dupatta covering her face. She felt protected from what was going on around her but the sound of clapping told her the man she was about to marry had entered the marquee.

Her heart was racing from the shallow breaths she was having to take. Her stomach tightened, making her feel as if she needed to rush to the bathroom. A moment later she felt someone brush her arm as they sat down next to her.

The temptation to take her dupatta off to stare at him was overwhelming. She'd forgotten what he looked like. The photograph she'd been shown hadn't been a good one and she'd only looked at it briefly, before pushing the image of his face out of her mind.

The voice of the imam, the man conducting the ceremony, growled out loudly, giving Laila a fright. She jumped. A hand touched her knee. It was him.

The sound of the ceremony began to drown out as Laila became aware only of the person next to her. She could feel him there; almost sense his breathing as he knelt next to her. She closed her eyes which were tired and sore from all her crying. She was about to be married and there was nothing she could do, nothing, apart from hope and pray.

Laila's dupatta was lifted up. She squeezed her eyes shut, then braved herself to quickly open them, expecting to see the man she'd just married. Laila was surprised however to find herself staring into the steely brown eyes of her mother-in-law, her Auntie. 'You need to come with me so you can get changed into your next outfit. Then we can get on with the celebrations.'

Laila strained to look past her Auntie, wanting to catch a glimpse of her husband, but all she could see was the back of him, surrounded by the other male guests who were loudly congratulating him. She saw her uncle turn around. Catching his eye he looked away quickly, but not before he'd given her a look of disdain. The next person in the crowd she recognised was Tariq. He smiled and stepped towards her but a hand belonging to their uncle reached out and held him back. Tariq mouthed a sorry as he was led outside to join the festivities with the other men.

As the marquee emptied, Laila looked down at her hand. The large, almost gaudy, gold wedding ring decorated her finger. Twenty diamonds, eighteen emeralds and five tiny sardonyx stones. Made especially for her; made to let her know she was no longer Laila Khan, and from now on her life would never be her own. Still kneeling on the unsteady platform in the scorching heat, Laila bowed her head as her Auntie stood waiting for her sour-faced, feeling totally alone.

* * *

'Thank fuck that's over with. Can't get this flipping turban off quick enough.'

Laila stared at her new husband in amazement as he threw off his turban. His northern English accent punctuated the air, not quite fitting with his handsome dark features.

'You're . . .'

'English? Were you worried? Did you think you were going to be marrying a foreigner? Afraid I'd be one of them ignorant Pakis?'

She was shocked by the way he spoke. She could see the amusement in his eyes, though she didn't understand how using such a derogatory term was funny in any way. She took in his face as she spoke. 'No, no, I didn't know what to expect. I guess I am slightly relieved though.'

Laila watched as her husband's eyes darkened. He walked towards her taking the ends of her hair in his hands and rubbed it between his fingers. His six foot muscular frame towered over her. His face, no older than thirty, stared down.

'Why are you relieved Laila? Tell me?'

'Maybe it'll be easier. You know, speaking the same language.'

His tone was cold and sinister. 'So you're expecting I'll be wanting to talk to you? And what gave you that idea, beautiful?'

Laila didn't know what to say. She traced his face with her eyes, looking for something which might let her know how to answer. A grin spread across his face.

'Don't look so serious. I'm kidding. This is your wedding day, you should be smiling.'

He placed a kiss on her forehead, then went to walk out of the room. As he did, he pulled Laila to him, put his hands on her face and began squeezing until her face was contorted under the pressure. His eyes stared at her coldly.

'I know all about you Laila. I've heard about you running away. Don't think for a moment you're going to try that with me. You're mine now. My property – and I never did like losing things. Try it and I'll kill you. Apart from that, I'm sure we'll get on just fine.'

He let go of Laila's face, leaving a bright red mark on both her cheeks.

The door was opened and Tariq walked in. He looked at his sister who seemed upset, then at his brother-in-law and froze. He was the man at the house. His uncle's friend; the one he hadn't known. And the man who'd taken delight in throwing the acid at Ray-Ray.

Tariq looked at Laila. He could see she was wondering why he hadn't introduced himself. Gathering himself, he reached out to shake hands with his new brother-in-law, but only a hostile stare was returned. Struggling, Tariq tried to act as natural as possible.

'We . . . we . . . haven't been introduced. I'm Tariq, Laila's brother.'

'Gupta. Baz Gupta.'

Tariq narrowed his eyes. The man sounded like a fool. Hell, he sounded like he was auditioning for a Pakistani version of *James Bond*, but he wasn't *just* a fool, he was a dangerous one. 'You wouldn't mind if I had a word with my sister? In private.'

'She's all yours but make the most of it, because she'll be all mine tonight.' Baz walked out of the room whistling, leaving Laila and Tariq to stare at one another.

Half an hour later, Tariq stood face to face with Baz in the privacy of a dark corridor. 'You better look after my sister. I'm warning you.'

Baz laughed, sneering at Tariq. 'Save the brotherly heroics for someone who cares. I'll treat her the way she deserves and if she gets out of line, I'll put her in her place. I thought you would've known that by now. Funny how you didn't mention we'd already met in front of Laila.'

Tariq slammed Baz against the wall, who grinned at him nastily. 'Tut, tut, Tariq. You can serve time for putting your hands on a serving police officer.'

Tariq looked at Baz in amazement.

'That's right. I'm a copper. West Yorkshire Police. Bradford South, to be correct. You need to keep on the right side of me Tariq. You don't want me to start sending my officers to come and knock on your door, asking questions about what happened to poor Raymond, do you?'

Stunned, Tariq let go of Baz, who brushed down his top.

'Don't look so shocked. What? What's the matter Tariq?'

'But it wasn't me. It was you!'

'I don't know what you're talking about Tariq; surely you can't be suggesting it was a decorated police detective who harmed that young lad?' Baz winked, adding, 'I think it'll be in your best interest to tell your sister to be a good wife, don't you?'

'And if I don't?'

'Then you'd be an idiot.' Baz tapped Tariq on the cheek. 'All you need to do is to make sure she gets rid of any ideas you're going to help her. She needs to know you're on my side Tariq. Then you, her, and I won't have any problems, will we?'

Baz stepped away as he began to open the bedroom door. He paused and looked back at a crestfallen Tariq. 'You can listen if you like. They say virgins scream louder than whores.'

Laila stood in the middle of the room with only a small white pair of knickers on. Although it was a sweltering night, she was shivering. He mother-in-law scattered the last rose petals onto the bed as Baz walked into the room.

'I'll leave you two together. If she's difficult, give her this.' Laila watched as Baz's mother passed him a glass of milk. He nodded, placing it on the side and waiting for his mother to leave the room.

Baz walked across to Laila. It was dark apart from the candle flickering momentarily.

'Put your arms down.' Baz barked out his order as Laila stood covering her breasts. Slowly and timidly she dropped her arms as Baz stood watching her. He licked his lips and could feel the swell of his erection.

She might be trouble but she was certainly beautiful. Smooth, delicate brown skin. Curves in all the right places, and soft pert breasts. He walked towards her and he could see her trembling.

'You afraid of me?' Baz laughed as he said it. He pulled her towards him and pushed his hand roughly down her pants. He started to groan and at the same time he heard Laila whimpering. He felt a hard push in his chest as Laila struck him in panic.

'No, please, get off me. Don't touch me.'

She ran towards the door but she didn't get far before she was being dragged back. Frightened, she clawed out at Baz, feeling her nails scratching his body.

'Oh you like to play games do you? Like it rough? If you want rough, I'll show you rough.'

He grabbed her hair, pulling her down on the floor with him. He pushed his lips hard onto her mouth, biting down on her already bruised lips, and slammed her arms down above her head to stop her trying to fend him off.

Alarm filled Laila's mind. She kicked out, trying to push Baz away, but all she felt was him pressing harder on her body. She kicked out again, but this time it had an effect as Baz fell backwards, banging his head on the wooden chest of drawers. His face turned into a sneer as he rubbed his head. 'Bitch.' Leaping up he grabbed her arm, twisting it behind her back till she cried out. With the other hand, Baz snatched the glass of milk left by his mother from the top of the locker. He yanked on Laila's arm, sitting her up.

'Drink it. Drink it.' Incensed, Baz pushed the glass onto Laila's lips. The milk turned pink from the blood from her lip. 'I said, drink.'

Laila opened her mouth, afraid the glass would break on her face. The milk spilt down the sides of her mouth as she started to choke, then her nose was pinched closed by Baz. She couldn't breathe and she began to bang on the floor, trying to communicate with Baz to stop. 'Swallow, have you swallowed?' Terrified, Laila managed to nod.

Baz let go. The minute he did, Laila fell forward, coughing and struggling to take a breath. She tried to stand, pulling herself up by the bed post. When she got to her feet, she started to feel dizzy. The room began to spin. Holding on to the side of the bed for support, Laila tried to walk, but her knees gave way below her. She dropped to the floor. There was a sense she'd hurt herself, but the sensation in her leg was so strange she wasn't quite sure if she had or not.

Her mind was hazy, but clear enough to know whatever was in the milk had caused this to happen to her. Laila tried to crawl along the floor, but found she couldn't move. She felt Baz's hands start to move up and down her body, creeping over her skin like a thousand spiders. She tried to resist but she couldn't make her limbs work, she couldn't even move her head. She tried to speak but her mouth wouldn't move either. She felt something heavy on top of her, then a burning pain between her legs before she passed out.

Laila stared at herself in the mirror. Her body was bruised and she could see bite marks on her breasts. Between her legs was sore and on her inner thighs she could see dried blood. Her head hurt, throbbing tightly, encased in what felt like a migraine.

It was painful to walk but she wanted to get to the bathroom to try to wash herself before the rest of the household woke up. She looked around the room, the empty glass of milk lay on the floor and her torn pants lay next to it. She pulled on her robe, grimacing at the pain in her arms as she raised them. Trying not to wake a sleeping Baz, Laila tiptoed out of the room. She counted the doors, knowing the third one along was where the washroom was.

It took Laila over an hour to clean herself up. Every part of her hurt. She couldn't even pee properly; it burnt too much. In the end she'd had to sit in the bucket of water to do it, to try to ease the burning sensation from the urine on her swollen and sensitive insides.

She needed to find Tariq. He'd help her. After what he'd said to her yesterday, once she'd told him what had happened he was bound to. Tariq could stand up to their uncle. To Baz and to her mother-in-law. And once he'd done that, he could take her home.

On her way back to her bedroom, Laila stopped to knock on Tariq's door. She tapped quietly, almost inaudibly; scared of waking anyone else. There was no answer, or rather he didn't hear. Laila knocked again, looking round anxiously. This time she whispered, pressing her face into the door.

'Tariq. Tariq, it's Laila.'

A minute later Tariq opened the door. The shock of seeing his sister's swollen face almost had him running to Baz's room. But he stopped. Remembering the conversation he'd had with him. He looked at Laila, whispering harshly, pretending he didn't see what damage was standing before him. 'Laila, what are you doing here? Go back to your room.'

'Shhh, they'll hear us.'

'Then go back to your room before Baz wakes up.'

Laila looked at her brother. He seemed different; almost the same as he'd been at home to her. Cold and distant.

'I can't Tariq. You don't know what he did to me.'

Tariq didn't need to know exactly. He could guess. He spoke awkwardly in hushed tones. 'You'll get used to it. It will just take time. The first time, well it's bound to hurt.' He trailed off and couldn't meet her eyes.

'He gave me something to drink Tariq. He drugged me . . . I've got marks all over my body.'

Tariq rubbed his mouth. He didn't want to hear this. Especially not now he knew there was nothing he could do. He didn't say anything and continued looking down as Laila talked.

'You said everything was going to be okay. Tariq, you promised.'

Tariq's head shot up. Angrily he hissed at his sister. 'Well I lied, okay. I lied. There's nothing I can do for you.'

'What's the matter? What's happened?'

Tariq looked at his sister face on. She was crying and scared. His guilt was killing him, making him feel like shit. 'You're married, that's what's happened, and whether you like it or not that's the way it's going to be from now on. So stop the tears Laila. They're not going to help you and neither am I. Just drop it.'

'Tariq, please.' Laila reached out her hand to touch Tariq. He jumped back as if he'd been electrocuted.

'Just leave me alone, Laila. Just leave me alone.'

Tariq slammed the door in her face, but even through the closed wooden door he knew Laila was still standing there, lost and full of pain, knowing her last chance of any hope had quite literally been slammed in her face. Crouching down on the floor, Tariq put his head in his hands and for the first time he cried for his father.

17

'What are you trying to tell me?' Freddie stared at Martin Warner with the contempt he felt the man needed.

'I'm saying your hospital visit to your son is being moved back Thompson.'

'Mr Thompson, Marty. Don't forget your manners.'

Warner bristled. There'd only been two people he'd ever hated in his life. The proper kind of hatred. The deep-seated, burning kind. The first person went by the name of Terry Jenkins, a boy he'd gone to school with. On a regular basis the boy had taken to ambushing him in the boys' changing room, dragging his trousers off in front of a cheering, baying crowd prior to sticking them down the toilet. There'd never been any reason. Not even an exchange of heated words. Only a desire to humiliate and make Martin's school days tortuous. Jenkins made sure he saved his piece-de-resistance for the last ever day of school; not only putting his trousers down the boys' toilets, but his head as well.

And the second person? He was standing right in front of him. At first he'd had sleepless nights at the thought of what Freddie had asked him to be part of; *forced* him to be part of. But then in the early hours of the morning, when he'd been the only one up in the house, he'd remembered Terry Jenkins.

Whilst the problem had been there, life had been intolerable. Take the problem away and there wasn't anything to worry about. It was the philosophy he knew he needed to take with Freddie Thompson. Being at his beck and call, having the constant threat of harm coming to his family, and being the butt of his jokes most days made life unbearable. Get rid of him, and life could get back to normal.

So as he'd made his coffee in the kitchen whilst his wife and daughter slept peacefully, Warner had come to the conclusion that helping Freddie break out, was the best possible situation. And now far from dreading it like he had been before, Martin Warner was looking forward to getting Freddie Thompson out of his life, as much as he had Terry Jenkins.

'Then you'll have to change it back.'

'Impossible. There's nothing I can do. It was the governor's decision. The prison is going to have an inspection and he wants all prisoners on site.'

Freddie glared at Warner. 'You're taking the piss.'

'If I was taking the piss, I wouldn't be giving you due warning would I?'

Freddie sat down on his bed, clicking off the PlayStation. He had no respect for screws, especially spineless ones like Warner, but it was true what he was saying, he could have quite easily kept it to himself. Then he would've been totally fucked. The next thought which came to Freddie's mind was, *why*? Why let him know then?

'I hope you ain't setting me up Warner.'

'As much as I'd love to see you rot in a cell Thompson, I'd much rather see you gone.'

A small smile started to form on Freddie's face. Then he grinned before bursting into laughter. 'I get it; you want me out from under your skin. Well believe me Marty, I want me gone just as much.'

Martin Warner said nothing but he doubted it. He doubted

Freddie Thompson wanted to be gone as much as he not only wanted, but *needed* the man gone.

'Alright babe. Looking good.' Freddie Thompson sat leaning his chair back on two legs as he watched his wife walk towards him. He wasn't just saying it. Tasha *was* looking good. Too good perhaps for someone whose husband was inside. Her honey-blonde hair tumbled down just past her shoulders and her make-up was immaculately done, classy without being tarty. Her clothes were top gear. Designer. A black, fitted Westwood number. Corseted and down to her knees. Perfect for a woman of her age. Topped off with a pair of Louboutins.

'I try.'

'Looks like you did more than try. Hope it's on my behalf?'

'Who else would it be for, besides meself?'

Freddie cracked his knuckles and sniffed loudly in disdain. 'I dunno, that's why I'm asking. But you wouldn't tell me anyway would you? Leave me to have to find out myself.'

Tasha looked at Freddie from under her false eyelashes. She'd seen him have that look before, on several occasions. More than she cared to remember. Something was bugging him. Eating him up. She could see he was fuming. She knew all the signs; chewing on the side of his mouth whilst trying not to explode and say what he really wanted to. Coming across slightly preoccupied, when she knew his brain was ticking overtime.

It was tricky to know how to treat him when he was in one of his moods. Freddie might be her husband but it was never far from her mind that she was dealing with a very dangerous man. If she ever forgot, she only had to remember Freddie had come into prison looking at serving only a few years and ended up doing life for murder. Another one. Only this time he'd been caught.

Sometimes he'd be happy for her to tease him, coaxing him out of his foul mood. On other occasions, it'd only make things worse, and the calmer approach was the only way to deal with him.

Sitting down opposite Freddie in the visiting hall, Tasha didn't feel like doing either.

She was sick of having to mollycoddle his emotions. What about hers? Yes, he'd given her money, cars, holidays, even houses. All the usual clichés. But he'd never given her himself. So in the absence of having a husband, she'd taken the Bentleys, the Tiffany jewellery, the house in Marbella; because if that was all that was on offer, it was better than nothing. But now it was too late. Tasha didn't want *him* or anything he gave her at all.

She hadn't appreciated being dragged to the prison to come and pay him an emergency visit either. She wanted to be with Ray-Ray, who the doctors had said could come home in a few weeks after almost two and a half months in hospital. Instead, she'd been given no choice but to come. She sighed. She wanted to stop being angry with Freddie, then life would be easier, but she just couldn't bring herself to.

'I always try to look nice Freddie. Got a problem with that? Would you rather me walk round in one of them burkas, covering meself up?'

'I'd rather you didn't give me so much fucking lip.'

Tasha said nothing. She didn't argue with Freddie. No one did. Her way of showing him she was annoyed was by saying nothing, knowing he'd be the first one to talk.

They sat in silence for a few minutes, which always made Freddie feel slightly uncomfortable. Eventually he spoke, gruffly but not as harsh as before. 'I ain't got a clue what's going on with you Tash. You seem different somehow.' He stopped, then shrugged his shoulders, knowing that was as far as his emotional speak went.

'I'm fine.'

Freddie decided it was pointless trying to go on with the conversation. He'd find out soon enough what was going on, once he was out. He looked round cautiously, making sure no screws or lags were close enough to hear.

'The date's been put back but we've got no choice other than to roll with it.'

Tasha felt a slight sense of relief, although she wasn't fool enough to show it. The idea that Freddie would be out of prison unnerved Tasha for lots of reasons; not least because Arnie hadn't stopped calling her. She'd expected a few calls, but then she'd expected him to take the hint when she hadn't returned them.

At first she'd been sorry to see him go, sorry he'd needed to keep calling her. And it'd hurt her. She hadn't been in love with Arnie but she'd been close to it, caring about him deeply. But the minute Johno had told her they were going to spring Freddie out she'd known they'd had to stop seeing each other. It was the only way if she wanted him to be safe from Freddie finding out and hurting him. There was simply no two ways about it.

She'd hoped by now Arnold's calls would diminish. But they'd increased. Five. Ten. Fifteen. Even twenty calls a day. And her sorry had quickly turned to unease, not helped by her sister, Linda.

'Bleeding hell Tash, if you want my opinion you've got a right nut job on your hands. What did I tell you? Any bloke who ain't looking to get his leg over is a bloke who's looking for trouble.'

Tasha had snapped at her sister then. 'And which great philosopher did you get that quote from, hey?'

'All right girl, no need to machine gun the messenger. I ain't trying to wind you up babe. I'm just worried for you.' And she wasn't the only one. Tasha Thompson was worried for herself.

Unlike Linda though, who always liked to walk on the melodramatic side of life, she didn't imagine for a moment Arnie was some looney tune. She knew him better than that. What she was concerned about was something far more real, far more worrying. She had a strong suspicion Arnie's male pride – or whatever it was which was driving him to bombard her with phone calls day and night – would make him do something silly. Something silly, like tell Freddie what'd been going on. And as Tasha sat across from her husband, watching him crack his knuckles, Tasha knew *something silly* would turn into something very nasty indeed.

Wanting to block the thoughts of her problems out, Tasha concentrated on talking about their son. 'Ray-Ray doesn't want you doing it. Well, not for him anyway.'

'You told him?'

'He was going to find out sooner or later wasn't he? Best me tell him rather than some copper.'

'He doesn't know what he's talking about. He can't see he needs me to do this. *I* need to do this. I want to be with him, Tash. I want to be with you.'

'Nothing I can say is going to stop you is it?'

Freddie stared at Tasha. 'You could try talking to me like you want to be here. I'm putting my neck on the line for you and Ray-Ray. I ain't seen you for a while and now I feel like I'm just some surplus cunt. Have you got somewhere else you'd rather be Tash? Or should I say, *someone* else you'd rather be with.'

Tasha blushed. It didn't go unnoticed by Freddie but he didn't react, just listened. Waiting for her to say something to hang herself.

'Don't start, Freddie. If you must know, yes, I *would* rather be somewhere else, with *someone* else. With Raymond. Now go on, tell me you've got a problem with that an' all.'

'Why are you still angry with me Tash?'

'If you have to ask, then you'll never understand.'

'Maybe I don't Tash, but don't worry. I will. I'll make sure I sort out any concerns I have once I'm out . . . Uncomfortable?' he said, looking at her sharply.

He stared at Tasha who was shifting in her seat, making out it was the hard orange plastic prison chair which was making her move awkwardly. But they both knew different. He was giving her a warning.

'So why's Ray-Ray holding back on me doing this for him?'

'I expect he's sick of trouble. Just wants to concentrate on getting better.'

Freddie smiled to himself, shaking his head. 'He's a good boy but he's got a too soft ticker. I'd be jumping at the chance if my old man had bothered half as much with me as I do with Ray-Ray. Not to mention springing out for him.'

Tasha snapped. 'Don't lay that on Ray-Ray. It's your choice to do this, no one's put you up to it. Like it was your choice to beat the flipping brain out of that bloke.'

Freddie spat his words out. 'He was a fucking nonce. What would you have rather me done? Let him walk out of here after only serving half a sentence, only for him to do it again to some poor kid? Whatever you think of me Tash, give me some frigging credit. Yeah, I fucked up. But mainly I fucked myself up, but at least I put a stop to some perv hurting anyone again.'

Tasha couldn't argue with Freddie there. She sighed as the prison officer called time. 'I better go.'

'Johno's going to give you a call to sort out some money for you. So make sure you answer.'

Tasha gave Freddie a tight smile. 'Are you sure you're doing the right thing?'

'Leave me to worry about that, okay? I'll see you on the other side.' He winked at her, then squeezed her bottom. He felt her tensing up and he wondered if Eddie was right. Perhaps he *was* being a fool to trust her.

The rain began in earnest and hadn't stopped by the time Tasha had reached Bradford. She jumped in a cab from the station to her hotel. She was exhausted, and looking forward to soaking in the bath. There was too much to think of to even bother trying tonight. All she wanted to do was have a large glass of red wine and worry about everything tomorrow.

'Sorry love, I can't go any further. Roadworks.'

Tasha groaned, realising she'd have to walk the extra two hundred metres in the pouring rain. Getting out of the cab, she pulled her jacket collar up to stop the rain dripping down her back. It was dark and the shoes she was wearing weren't suitable to be walking in the wet, but she'd rather wear a pair of Louboutin's and stumble and slip in the wet than wear a pair of flats. That was one thing Tasha was quite clear on.

Tottering along carefully, she thought she heard a sound behind her. There it was again. And again. Just as she was telling herself to stop imagining things, she felt a hand on her back and she screamed, turning round in the dark to face a familiar person. 'Jesus Christ Johno. Want me to piss me pants?'

Johno laughed. 'Not really. Sorry babe, didn't mean to frighten you. I saw you getting out of the cab, I shouted but you didn't hear. Come on, let's get out of this rain.'

Watching them, Arnie sat in his car. He smiled sadly, speaking quietly to himself as he stretched out his arm, touching the windscreen, his fingers following them across the glass as they walked into the hotel. 'Hello Izzy, have you missed me? It doesn't look like you have. But I've missed you, and soon I'm going to show you just how much.'

18

Ray-Ray looked at the nurse's face with anticipation. It'd taken forever for her to go and see if Laila was fine, and on the couple of occasions she had before, she'd come back not having found anything out; although Ray-Ray did have his suspicions she hadn't been at all.

'Well, what did you find out?'

'Oh apparently she's well.'

'Did you see her?'

The nurse answered, slightly distracted as she looked at Ray-Ray's hospital chart. 'No.'

'Then how do you know she's all right?'

'I spoke to one of the neighbours; she told me Laila had gone on holiday with her family. That's nice isn't it? I couldn't tell you the last time I went on holiday and I can't imagine my boyfriend asking me . . .'

Interrupting, Ray-Ray snapped at the nurse, not wanting to hear about her love life at the moment. 'On holiday – are you sure?'

'Yeah, totally. Why did you think she wasn't ok? Hasn't she been in contact?'

Ray-Ray ignored the nurse and closed his eyes. Why was he feeling so angry? He should be happy she was on holiday with her family. But he wasn't. For some reason he felt betrayed. It was stupid, but for some reason he'd imagined her worrying about him when he wasn't in school – wanting to know where he was, even trying to find him – but all along she was having the holiday of a lifetime with her family.

Clenching his fist to stop the anger swelling, Ray-Ray kept his eyes shut as he listened to the pretty blonde nurse and her colleague talk beside him, thinking he'd fallen asleep.

'How's he doing?'

'Oh fine.'

'Poor guy.'

'You're telling me. He had his whole life in front of him and now look. Pretty rotten really and from what I can gather his girlfriend hasn't even been in touch with him. I'm not being horrible, but can you blame her? It'd be bit of a shock for anyone wouldn't it to have this happen to your boyfriend?'

'And it's not like it'll be easy for him to find love again, not looking like that anyway, and I reckon if he did it'd probably be because someone felt sorry for him.'

Ray-Ray kept his eyes shut as the nurses walked away. He could hardly breathe. The pain he was experiencing now was worse than any acid burn could ever bring.

* * *

'Pack your stuff. I *said* pack your stuff.' Laila watched Baz from the door as he walked into the bedroom. She hadn't a clue what he was talking about. Fearing she'd done something wrong, Laila huddled up against the bedpost.

Seeing his wife not budging after he'd ordered her to, Baz notched his voice up an octave. 'Move it, Laila. Unless of course you want me to leave you here?'

'I don't understand, where are we going?'

Baz sneered. 'Oh wonderful, not only have I been blessed with a frigid wife, I've been blessed with a stupid one.'

The sting of Baz's words hit Laila as hard as his hand had done the night before. She put her head down, hoping if she showed a sign of respect, Baz's temper wouldn't escalate. She felt him sit down on the bed next to her. 'We're going back to England.'

Laila's head shot up. She studied his face to see if he was mocking her but it gave nothing away. She was afraid to say anything, just in case the tiny glimmer of hope she was feeling inside was ripped away; to find out this was her husband's idea of a joke, making her already dark world seem even darker. 'You're not going to say anything Laila? I thought you'd be jumping all over me to say thank you.'

'Is it true? We're really going back to Bradford. When? Why? Not that I don't want to. I do, but . . .' Baz pulled her down on the bed and she froze like always. Tensing her body as his hands wandered all over her, like she'd done on the first night, on every night since.

Baz rolled on top of her. She felt his hands work their way to the inside of her thighs. She closed her eyes trying to shut out what was about to happen, imagining herself to be somewhere else, somewhere far away.

'It makes you smile. The thought of Bradford. It's the only time I've seen you smile; you should do it more often. It suits you. But don't get any ideas Laila. Don't think you'll be going back to how it was before you were married. You're mine now. My wife. Take it as a warning.'

'I hate him.' Tariq spat out a pomegranate seed as he spoke to his uncle.

'It was a good match Tariq. A good family, not to mention your sister is finally married and now I no longer have the weight of a mountain disguised as an unmarried niece resting on my shoulders. Surely that alone, is a reason to rejoice?' The relief in Mahmood's voice was palpable as he sat under the bay tree brushing off flies. Their bags were packed and now all they had to do was wait for the man from the next village to come and take them to the train which would take them to the plane and home to Bradford.

Tariq looked at his uncle, who'd been more relaxed in the last two months than he'd ever seen him before. He had a sneaking suspicion it was to do with passing the responsibility of Laila on to somebody else. This was the first time he'd had a chance to speak to his uncle alone since they'd arrived in July.

'Why him? Why someone who was born in England, uncle? Not to mention someone in the police force?'

'Why not?'

'It just seems such a strange union.'

'No stranger than the moon and the stars.'

Tariq shook his head. His uncle always did that. Talked in riddles when he didn't quite have the answer or didn't wish to give a straightforward response. 'I don't trust him and I don't think you should.'

'Tariq, he's your brother now and you need to trust him like one.'

Taking another bite of the pomegranate, Tariq watched a tiny ant scuttling about under the dripping juice. 'I've been wanting to tell you this for a while now. On the night of the wedding, Baz mentioned Ray-Ray. Threatened me with it.'

Mahmood turned to Tariq. 'A threat? Tariq I think you must be mistaken, Baz would never threaten you.'

'No, uncle, I'm not mistaken, I know exactly what I heard. He told me in no uncertain terms that if I didn't stay away from Laila, we'd be in trouble for what we did. He'll make us take the blame for Ray-Ray.'

'*We*, Tariq?'

Tariq thought for a moment and a frown appeared on his face. 'Yes, *we*.'

'No, Tariq, *you*. I think if memory serves me right, only *you* were there that night. I was at home, having dinner with Baz.'

Mahmood looked at the shock and hurt on Tariq's face as he stood up, shaking the sand off his trousers. Mahmood waved to the man who'd come to collect them to come nearer with his cart. He turned round to Tariq who hadn't moved. 'Don't look so worried Tariq. All you have to do is listen to his advice and keep a secret, and then there won't be any problem from him . . . or from me.'

The journey was as uncomfortable going back as it had been arriving, but however hot and tiring it was, Laila welcomed every moment of it. Within three hours of Baz telling her, they'd packed everything up and waved goodbye. And with every plant they passed, every pothole in the road they went over, Laila celebrated, because each jolt, each crossroad they came to meant a step nearer to Bradford. The home she'd never thought she'd see again.

She hadn't known anyone could change in just a couple of months the way she had. She remembered coming here and even though she'd been terrified, she'd given a wry smile when she'd seen the sign for McDonald's in Islamabad. But she didn't smile now. She couldn't. Until she landed in Bradford, she couldn't trust anything. For all she knew, they could be taking her somewhere else. The news of Bradford had come so quickly, so unexpectedly, she still couldn't quite believe she was finally going home.

As much as Baz had warned her things wouldn't be any different, at least she would be in England. And that's where she needed to be. Somewhere familiar. Because now she had more than just herself to think about. She now had to think about her baby.

Baz watched Laila, touching her stomach as if she was the first woman ever to become pregnant. Though admittedly she had done well, or rather *he'd* done well, getting her pregnant so soon. He was sure it must've happened on their wedding night, but whenever it had, he was proud of himself.

For the past week and a half his mother had insisted on making

Laila do pregnancy tests. 'What is the point in being married to a woman who can't conceive? I take it you want her to be pregnant before she returns to England? Otherwise you might as well look for another wife, and then you'll just have to return alone.'

And that had been the plan; for Laila to conceive before she returned to Bradford. Everyone had known it. Himself, his mother, Mahmood, even Tariq had known. Everyone apart from Laila.

He knew it wasn't unusual for new wives to be married in Pakistan and kept in the country until they were pregnant. It was a way of making sure the marriage was worth continuing. Sometimes a way of making sure a visa application would be stronger for the husband if there was a British-born baby involved. Not that he had to worry about that. He was a British citizen, born and raised in Bradford. Laila getting pregnant was never about a visa. It was about something much deeper, much more important. It was about honour. His honour.

Even though he'd known that the week after the marriage Laila was at her most fertile and all her body clock's timings were right, he'd still been shocked when his mother had told him the test was positive. Laila was so tense and becoming so skinny. She didn't eat properly and spent most of her time crying. It surprised him she could carry herself, let alone a child.

He was pleased it'd happened so quickly. His leave was up and he was due back at work. He'd been lucky he'd been allowed to take extra unpaid leave but he hadn't fancied the idea of coming back on his own. If Laila hadn't been pregnant, his mother would've insisted on Laila staying in Pakistan with her, and if that had happened, who would've cooked and cleaned for him then?

Laila had been shocked as well when she'd found out but did what he expected her to do; cry. The pregnancy had happened so quickly, the thought of the baby not being his had crossed his mind. He knew how Laila had acted like a cheap whore with the boy in Bradford and for a moment he'd been worried. But that idea had quickly passed; she was so frigid there was no doubt in

152

his mind she had been a virgin when they'd got married. He supposed the pregnancy was just as his mother had said; perfect timing. He had been 'blessed'.

Tariq stood waiting for passport control. Islamabad airport was as hot as Bradford airport had been. No air conditioning, only stifling, oppressive heat. He hadn't spoken to Laila properly since he'd turned her away at his bedroom door the day after her wedding, which seemed an age ago. She'd tried to plead with him with her big eyes as was her habit since they were children, but he'd purposely avoided her gaze.

He hadn't wanted Baz seeing him making any contact with her. And why? To save his own skin, and for that Tariq felt deeply ashamed. Laila needed him, but he'd been warned off by Baz and by their uncle, and instead of fighting it, he'd taken the warning and turned away. He'd wanted to go back home to Bradford before, but his uncle had insisted on him staying.

Moving forward in the queue, Tariq realised he was just as much a prisoner as Laila was.

'Laila! . . . Laila! Bloody hell, look at you. What are you wearing that long thing for? You look so different. Where've you been? Miss Davies absolutely did her nut when you didn't turn up for the end of term exams and when you didn't show up at the start of this term, well you should've seen her. Julie Fowler had to take your place on your science experiment; apparently she totally messed it up. She's such a stupid cow.'

Laila listened to her classmate as she stood in Leeds Bradford airport car park, feeling awkward and conscious of the difference in their appearances. She'd seen Yvonne a moment before Yvonne had seen her, and instead of waving, Laila had tried to put her head down and walk away unseen, but Yvonne had spotted her, racing up to launch into school gossip.

Laila watched Yvonne, with her flowing brown hair and

tight-fitting clothes, happily not taking a breath as she excitedly recalled the events of the end of term. It'd only been two months or so but it seemed so alien to her. School and all it had to offer seemed a world away from her reality now.

Everything seemed not quite real to Laila as she stood ill at ease, her hair tightly plaited under her headscarf and her long plain Shami dress on.

The carefree chattering of her school mate stamped harder on Laila's reality. Her eyes filled with tears and she was grateful Yvonne was too busy talking to notice. 'So anyway, Miss Davies says you're not going to be Head Girl now because you let everyone down. She was so bloody angry. I wet myself laughing. But don't worry, those geeks you like to hang about with are going to have a protest, Emma says she'll lead it. No one knew where you were. It was like you'd just vanished. And you'll like this; everyone thought you'd run off with Ray-Ray, because he wasn't in either. Bloody hell, how cool would that have been eh, to rock up with him?'

Yvonne paused to take a much-needed breath, then almost as if something had struck her, turned to Laila; her face showing a look of genuine concern. 'Oh shit, you wouldn't have heard what happened to Ray-Ray then. Get this; apparently he was at home . . .'

'Laila.' Baz's voice sounded behind her, startling her. She didn't know how long he'd been listening and hoped it hadn't been too long. Her face began to pale when she realised Yvonne, affronted by the interruption, was going to say something to Baz.

'Er, hello? Excuse me. Can't you see we're talking?'

'And who would you be talking to?'

Yvonne rolled her eyes at Laila. 'Thicko, I'm talking to her.'

Baz's eyes cut narrowly at the girl. He took in her overly tight, pink nylon top showing off her youthful midriff, her denim cropped shorts with sequinned pockets, and even though it was a hot September day, the scuffed cowboy boots she was wearing.

She was a silly little tart, but it made for interesting viewing to see what sort of friends Laila had.

'When you say *her*, I take it you mean my wife?'

A look of bewilderment came over Yvonne's face. Laila could see she was trying to process the information in her mind as she opened her mouth, then closed it, only for her to open it again and say precisely nothing. Putting her head down, Laila wondered why she felt so ashamed.

The once-excited voice of Yvonne changed into a small, quiet, caring one. She held Laila's hand and it took all Laila's willpower not to break down completely. It was the first real touch of affection she'd had since Ray-Ray.

'I didn't know. You didn't say anything. Is that why you look so different? Are you okay?'

'She's married, not dead,' Baz interjected.

'I was talking to Laila, not you.' Yvonne's words were quick and harsh and Baz stepped closer, trying to intimidate her. But undeterred, Yvonne carried on. 'But you're coming back to school aren't you? We'll talk then?'

'No, she won't be back at school. Now do yourself a favour, and get lost,' he snapped at her.

'What is it about you, mate? I'm talking to my friend. You don't scare me.' Yvonne got out her mobile phone, turning back to Laila. 'Let me check I've got your number. I'll call you.'

Baz grabbed hold of Yvonne's arm, pulling the mobile phone towards him. 'Get off me! Ouch, you're hurting me.'

Frightened, Laila looked on. This was her friend and even though she knew she'd get into trouble for stepping in, she couldn't stand by and do nothing. 'Baz, leave her alone. Baz!'

Ignoring Laila and the tug on his sleeve, Baz twisted Yvonne's wrist. She yelped and dropped the phone as she pulled away, giving time for Baz to pick up the mobile before Yvonne could.

'Hey, give me that back.'

'I warned you to get lost.'

'Do you know what you are? You're a bully. Just wait till I get me step-dad on to you.'

Baz stuck his face into Yvonne's. He grinned. 'Tell him I'll be waiting and if you want your phone, have him come and pick it up from the police station. Tell him to ask for DS Gupta.'

Baz turned and walked away, followed closely by Laila. She couldn't face looking at her friend to say goodbye. She didn't want to see the expression on Yvonne's face as she stood in amazement in the middle of Leeds Bradford airport car park. But as she got to the car, she heard Yvonne screeching.

'I want my bleeding phone back! You haven't heard the last of this mate.'

19

Laila lay in her room. The same bedroom she'd slept in as a girl when her father had come to tuck her up at night. The same room she always felt safe in, and the same room she'd thought about Ray-Ray in. But those were all distant memories now. Everything had changed. It was no longer her room. It was now her and Baz's room and she was a prisoner in it. Though she supposed she was grateful she hadn't had to stay in Pakistan with Baz's family, who'd all moved back there recently. She couldn't say her uncle was happy about the arrangement; she had a sneaking suspicion he'd wanted her to stay in Pakistan and be rid of her completely. When her family left the house, they locked her in the bedroom. Her mother had spoken to her a couple of times through the door but Laila knew there was nothing she could do to help. Though she wasn't angry with her mother. The last few weeks had made her really see it wasn't just her who feared her uncle, it was her mother as well. From the first time her uncle had entered the house he had been cruel and sadistic. Not caring how any of them thought or felt. Forcing his views and his ways onto them all, as well as forcing himself into her mother's bed, and no-one had been able to do anything about it.

There was no chance of calling anyone because they'd already taken away her mobile, and sticking her head out of the window and shouting for help would only be asking for trouble. Most of the street and the surrounding area were people from her community, and they were either friends of her uncle or friends of friends. One bellow from her and someone would be calling her uncle, brother or husband to inform them of her behaviour.

Laila winced as a sharp pain ran down the middle of her stomach. It'd begun before they'd got the plane home but it was slowly becoming worse. Coming and going in waves.

She'd told Baz who'd ignored her, apart from shrugging his shoulders. It would've been pointless telling her uncle who would've only scorned her, disgusted at the idea she would speak to him about such matters. Her mother had gone to stay with one of Laila's sisters, so that had left only Tariq. She'd tried to speak to him last night but it seemed he was frightened to talk to her.

And now as the pains were becoming worse, Laila was getting more worried. But she didn't have anybody to tell or anyone to go to. What she really wanted to do was go to the hospital, although she knew it was never going to be an option. So all she could do was sit and wait, hoping everything was going to be all right.

A tap on the door, then the rattle of keys made Laila turn sharply around. It was Tariq. He smiled at her. 'Hey. Are you okay? I was worried.'

Laila's eyes filled with tears. She knew he was taking a risk coming to see her. Tariq put his head down as he spoke.

'I brought you these.' He passed her a bag of chocolate buttons – her favourite since she'd been a child. 'I'm sorry Laila. I'm sorry I haven't been the brother you deserve.' Laila began to interrupt but Tariq put his hand up to stop her speaking, wanting to continue with what he was saying. 'I thought I was doing the right thing, I believed what uncle was telling me; or rather, I made myself believe it. But I know now, I was wrong. Can you ever forgive me? I don't know how to make it better for you Laila, but I will. I promise. In the name of our father, I will.' Tariq stopped, breaking down into tears as Laila wrapped her arms around him, crying along with him too.

'I want to talk to Yvonne.'

The woman on the doorstep sniffed, then spat some phlegm into the unkempt hedges by the side of the path. She wore her hair in large pink rollers, and wore a low-cut acrylic top showing off her crinkled chest. Dark circles of sweat sat in the armpits like dark rain clouds. Her legs were skinny and chicken-like under a short mini skirt.

Her face looked disdainfully at the man on her doorstep, standing too close and looking too smug for her liking. She drew on her cigarette, kicking the cat out of the way and almost losing her balance as she moved her foot. She hated Pakis at the best of times. But a Paki copper was pushing it.

'What you want her for? Cos whatever it is you say she's done, she didn't do it. She was with me.'

Baz smiled nastily. He knew her type. Didn't give a shit about her kids until someone else told them what little bastards they were, and then they played the doting, protective mother.

'Is she in?' Without waiting for an answer, Baz pushed past the woman who gave an indignant cry. 'Hey, you need a search warrant to come in. You can't just barge your way in here you know.'

'Really? I thought that's exactly what I'd just done.'

Baz curled up his face. The kitchen was as messy as the front entrance which was as messy as the front garden. The place had a heavy smell of old chip oil and the heat of the day was clearly making it worse.

The wallpaper was stained, as was the ceiling with yellow nicotine. Unwashed pots and pans piled up in every corner. Overflowing ashtrays and newspapers lay around. And sitting in the middle of the kitchen table were a pair of muddy boots, displayed as if they were the centrepiece on a dining room table. 'Nice place you've got here.' Baz smirked.

'Piss off, I know my rights. I want you out of here.'

'No problem, just tell me where Yvonne is.'

'I don't have to answer any of your questions.'

'No, you don't, but rather here than down at the police station.'

'I haven't done anything.'

'Maybe not, but I'm sure I can think of something.'

'You're fucking bastards you lot are. Worse than the fucking criminals.'

Baz could smell shit and he looked down at the cat litter tray which looked like it hadn't been cleaned out for a while. He was tired and he wanted to get out of this dump as soon as he could. 'Just tell me where she is. You don't want me nicking your fella as well do you?'

'Leave him out of it.'

'Or what? He'll sue me? He's got form hasn't he? On parole. You don't want him bringing back in for violating it do you?'

'She's upstairs.'

'Easy when you know how.' Baz winked as he walked out of the kitchen. The woman began to follow him but Baz blocked her way. 'No, I want you to stay down here. All I'm going to do is have a quiet little word with her, then I'll be out of your house.'

Yvonne lay on her bed staring at the posters on her wall. She'd never bothered having pictures of popstars or footballers on her wall before, but it was either that or stare at the damp stains and the holes in the wall, an angry reminder of her stepdad's drunken rants. The sooner she could get out of Bradford, the better.

The job she was working at was paying her well. She was working in a strip club on the other side of the city. She was underage but the owners of the club didn't care if she was seventeen or seven. As long as she got her tits out that's all that mattered.

It was long hours and the men made her skin crawl but if it meant being able to leave the shit hole she was supposed to call home, then she was more than happy to continue. She'd saved up over two thousand pounds. Mainly in tips for extras. But money was money.

Of course, she hadn't told her family about it because she knew within forty-eight hours all her hard work would be pissed up against the wall. Neither had she opened a bank account. Her money was hidden. Hidden in the wall behind the poster.

Yvonne jumped as the door was kicked. She sprung up from the bed, presuming it was her stepdad pissed up to the eyeballs, looking for a fight. Seconds later the door opened, hanging precariously on one hinge.

Yvonne stood on the other side of the bed, shocked to see it wasn't who she'd expected, but even more shocked to see who it was. 'Hey, what the hell do you think you're doing? Does my mam know you're here?'

'Who do you think let me up?'

'I want you to get out of my room.'

Baz smiled. 'What is it with you lot, not very hospitable are you?' He picked up Yvonne's blouse which was lying on the bed before throwing it across to the other side of the room. 'I thought you and I could have a little word.'

'I've got nowt to say to the likes of you.'

'The "likes of" me? Now we're a stupid tart and a little racist.'

'You what? I don't give a shit what colour you are pal. I'm talking about you lot. Coppers. Pigs. The Old Bill. You're all the same. Bullies.'

'Now that isn't very nice Yvonne. I like to think of myself as special.' As he spoke, Baz walked round to where Yvonne was standing. She wore only a tight t-shirt with no bra underneath, showing off her enormous breasts, and a pair of shorts.

For the first time since Baz had smashed down the door, Yvonne's demeanour changed. The air of confidence she had began to diminish, though she kept her voice steady, holding Baz's stare. 'What do you want?'

'Now we're getting somewhere. Easy really. I want you to stay away from Laila. Not only that, I want you to make sure all her friends do too. I don't want some little hooker like you coming to my house and walking round telling everyone my business. So *stay* away.'

'And what if I don't?'

'Then you'll be a silly girl. I want you to pretend you didn't see her.'

Yvonne snarled at Baz, snapping back with self-assurance.

'Yeah, of course you do because you don't want me to tell everybody how unhappy she is. Laila doesn't want to be married to someone like you.'

Baz smirked, prodding her in her chest. 'And how would you know that?'

Childlike, Yvonne answered, shrugging her shoulders.

'Dunno, but I do and not only that, I'm going to tell everybody you came into my house today.'

Baz grabbed hold of Yvonne's hair. 'And who do you think they'll believe, hey? Some little scrubber like you or a police officer like me?' He let go of her hair. 'You've been warned, Yvonne. You'd be very silly to try to take me on.'

After Baz had gone, Yvonne lay on her bed and thought about Laila. In truth, she hadn't thought too much about her since she'd seen her at the airport. She didn't have much time for her. What she did have time for though was gossip, and after no one had known where Laila had disappeared to, seeing her had meant Yvonne would be the first one with the news. She'd only been at the airport to earn some extra money. One of the girls at the strip club had told her it was a good pick-up place for punters. Most of them only required hand jobs which was a good thing, as she was still a virgin and didn't fancy giving it away for twenty quid. Her stepfather had tried hard enough to get it, so after fighting him off for the last five years she wasn't going to give it to some random stranger waiting for a cut-price Thomas Cook holiday.

At the time the only thing that had really pissed Yvonne off

162

about the encounter with Laila's fella was the way he'd spoken to her. The mobile phone being taken had been annoying more than anything. She'd lifted it from one of the punter's pockets at the club the night before, so technically it wasn't even hers.

Within an hour of seeing her at the airport, she'd forgotten all about Laila and her chump of a husband. Until now. The one thing Yvonne Scott hated above all was being told what she could and couldn't do. All her life she'd been pushed around by people, and she certainly wasn't going to add this man to the list. In fact, Yvonne was going to do quite the opposite. It was high time she went round and paid Laila a visit.

20

Whoever was ringing on the doorbell didn't seem to want to go away. Tentatively, Laila tiptoed to the window, hiding behind the red curtain and trying to peek through the nets without being seen from the upstairs front room bedroom.

The bell was still ringing but she couldn't see who it was, as they were standing out of sight, too near the door. A pang fluttered through Laila. What if it was Ray-Ray? What if he'd heard about what had happened and was coming to rescue her? Her heart began to race at the thought. Nervously, Laila craned her head, pushing her forehead onto the cool of the glass pane. She pulled back, dropping the net curtain as if it had stung her. Whoever it was had seen her. She hadn't got a look of their face, only their brown hair, which meant it couldn't be Ray-Ray. A wave of both relief and disappointment hit Laila. Pulling her jumper tightly round her, Laila retreated back to her bed, wondering why she felt so afraid.

Tap. Tap. Tap. Laila wasn't entirely sure what the noise was at first. She lay staring at the ceiling unmoving; thinking it might be a moth trying to get out. The noise got louder and she realised it was coming from outside. Somebody was throwing stones at the window.

'I know you're there Laila, I saw you.' The person's voice was loud and distinctive. And Laila knew straight away who it was. It was Yvonne.

'Come on Laila, I'm not going away until I see you.' Laila wished Yvonne would go. She would only get her into trouble. What was she doing here anyway? She'd never been to see her before, come to think of it, she'd never even bothered with her at school.

'Laila!'

However much she put the pillow over her ears, it was impossible to ignore Yvonne's raucous voice. It was obvious she wasn't going to go away until she got what she came for.

Laila went to the window. She could see Yvonne looking in the gutter for more stones to pick up. She knocked on the glass to draw her attention, frowning as she spoke.

'What do you want?'

Yvonne crinkled her nose. 'Well that's charming. I come to see my mate and that's all the greeting I get. Open the door so I can come in.'

'I can't.'

Puzzled, Yvonne spoke. 'Why not?'

'It's locked.'

Laila could see the exasperation on Yvonne's face.

'Well, open the window.'

'I can't.'

'Why not?'

'I'm not allowed.'

With her hands on her hips, Yvonne raised her voice louder. 'Hey up Laila, what's the gig? We're not going to get very far this way. Just open it.'

Tears came to Laila's eyes. 'Please can you go away?'

'No, not until I see you proper like.' Laila moved from behind the curtain. She opened the window and leaned out, but not before she looked nervously up and down the street.

165

'Here, I brought you McDonald's, you lot can eat it can't you?' Yvonne smiled at her warmly, taking a bite of her burger.

'Now you've seen me, can you go away now? I don't mean to be rude.'

'What's that on your face?'

Laila touched her cheek absent-mindedly. It hurt. A penalty for not cooking the dhal curry the way Baz liked it.

'It's nothing.'

'Has he been knocking you about?'

'Who?'

'Your fella.'

'No.'

'I bet he has. All blokes are the same. My stepdad knocks me about.'

'Does he? What do you do?'

Yvonne shrugged, nonplussed. 'Nowt, besides call him a prick.' Yvonne paused and took another bite out of her Big Mac. 'Sure you don't want some? I'll lob it in through the window. You know your fella came round to see me?'

'No . . . no, I didn't.'

'He thought he was *The Big I Am*. Told me not to come and see you.'

'Then why have you?'

With a wry smile, Yvonne answered. 'Because he told me not to come and see you.'

For the first time in the conversation, Laila smiled. She spoke quietly to Yvonne, still aware any one of the neighbours could be listening. 'Did he frighten you?'

'No. He's just a big bully like me stepdad. He scares you?'

Laila paused then answered, 'Sometimes.'

'So is it really true you're married?'

'Yes.'

'What's it like?'

It was Laila's turn to shrug this time. 'All right I suppose.'

166

'Let's see your ring.'

Laila pushed her hand out of the top window of the low rise terrace bedroom. Yvonne pulled a face when she saw it. 'It's big. Do you like it?'

It was Laila's turn to shrug. 'Not really.'

'Seems funny, you being married. Did you want to?'

Laila answered haughtily, trying to convince herself as well as Yvonne. 'It's my duty.'

'Bugger that, if my mam tried to marry me off to some old fella I'd do me nut.'

'He's not that old. He's only thirty-four.'

Taking another bite of the burger, Yvonne fell silent for a moment then asked, 'You all right? You look a bit pale.'

'I don't feel so good. Got a few pains in my stomach.'

'From what?'

Sheepishly, Laila replied, 'Dunno.'

'Well what does your mum say?'

It was an uncomfortable question for Laila to answer. She put her head down, not wanting Yvonne to see the hurt in her eyes. 'She's not here.'

'So you're stuck at home on your own?'

'Yeah.'

'They locked you in?'

Laila's head shot up, her face a picture of fear. 'Shhh. They'll hear you.'

'Who will hear me?'

'Please Yvonne, the neighbours. They're good friends of my uncle. I'll get in trouble. I've said too much already.'

After a moment, Yvonne asked warmly. 'You want me to come and see you tomorrow?'

Laila didn't say anything. There was no way Yvonne could come back. It would only lead to trouble. But then the idea of having someone to talk to was more than she could ever have hoped for.

'If you like, but not in the morning. Baz will be home, he'll be angry if he sees you. And Tariq won't be back till late.'

'Okay. You want me to bring you something?'

'Some chocolate buttons would be nice.'

'Okay. See you tomorrow.'

Laila waved and closed the window. A moment later a sudden panic passed through her. What was she thinking of, asking her to come back? Baz was sure to find out. She struggled to open the window again, wanting to call and tell Yvonne not to come. But it was too late. She'd gone.

Laila sat back on the bed, wondering why she'd just brought more trouble on herself.

It was late by the time Yvonne got back to her house and she was exhausted. There'd been trouble in the club with one of the girls being found in the toilets with a punter. The owner of the club had thrown them both out, but the man had come back with some of his friends and all hell had kicked off.

It had pissed her off. Yvonne had had to work the high stage because of it, which meant less tips than the middle stage where she usually worked. She'd earned just under eighty quid which was less than she normally would have earned on a Tuesday night and she'd had to work doubly hard for it.

Putting her earnings in the hole in the wall behind her poster, Yvonne thought of Laila. Funny thing was, she'd initially only gone round to Laila's house to wind Baz up; wanting to show him he couldn't push her around. But she'd found herself genuinely liking her. Perhaps it was because she felt sorry for her, but Yvonne felt it was more than that, she couldn't put her finger on quite what it was but strangely, she was looking forward to seeing her again.

Laila had always been the goody-goody at school. She'd always seemed so perfect. Beautiful, kind and clever. And it was because of these traits Yvonne had disliked her. Everything Laila was,

Yvonne felt she wasn't. So she'd done what her family had done to her all through her life. She'd bullied Laila.

So it was a turn-up for the books to discover what a sweet person Laila was. Strangely enough, she was looking forward to seeing her again tomorrow.

The door banged open. It was her stepdad. Yvonne glanced at the clock. Two-thirty a.m. He was early. Usually he wouldn't get in till at least four o'clock, staggering drunkenly up the stairs. Yvonne watched her stepdad stumble into her room with a look of disgust on her face. His trousers had a wet stain at the front from where he'd pissed himself, and his shirt was unbuttoned to his belly, his enormous pasty white flesh on show. He fell on to the bed and landed on something.

'What the fuck is this?' Pulling it out from underneath him, Yvonne went to snatch it back.

'Not so fast, Yvie. Let's see what you're hiding.'

'I'm not hiding nowt. I just don't want a fat lummox like you sitting on them.'

'Oi, less of your cheek.'

Yvonne rolled her eyes. She was used to the nightly visits. Coming in for nothing more than to look for a fight or an argument. The only time she'd been free of them was when he had had been inside for GBH. It'd been the best eighteen months of her life but then when he'd been released, her silly cow of a mother had let him back in, for it to start all over again.

Yvonne watched her stepdad trying to focus his drunken eyes on what he was looking at. 'Chocolate buttons! Hey up, they're my favourite.'

'Well it's a shame they're not for you then. Buy your own you tight git.'

With a smile on his face, he ripped the purple bag of chocolates open, stuffing them into his mouth by the handful. Yvonne's eyes filled with tears.

'You bloody prick. Them aren't yours.' She reached across to get the bag furiously.

'It's my house and anything in this house is mine, you bloody cheeky mare.'

Yvonne shouted, red-faced, at the top of her voice.

'This isn't your house, it's me mam's house and I'm sick of it. I'm pig sick of you. You bloody bugger.'

'Come here.' Her stepdad swiped at her, grasping hold of her sleeve, dragging her down to the bed. 'You're a cocky little cow and you need teaching a lesson.'

Yvonne was scratching wildly, throwing her arms into the air as her stepdad held her down.

'Get off me you fucker.'

'I'll show you who's boss missy and we'll see how cocky you are then.' With a swift movement, he pulled off his belt, wrapping it expertly round his hand. Yvonne heard the whistle in the air before she felt the stinging lash on her back. She screamed out in pain, managing to sit up. 'I hate you. I hate you.' Tears rolled down her cheeks as the buckle of the belt connected with her face, filling her mouth with saliva and blood.

21

Laila thought it was strange. Not the fact that Yvonne hadn't turned up as she said she would, but it was the devastation she felt by her not doing so.

She didn't even know Yvonne well, but she'd sat staring out the window all day yesterday waiting for her to come, and now, a day later, she was doing the same. Watching, waiting, hoping the empty street would be filled with the approaching figure of her new friend, Yvonne.

She'd stood and waited for her so long yesterday that her legs had begun to ache, so today she'd pulled up the wooden chair from the corner of the room, placing it in front of the window.

Laila heard the key in the bedroom door. It was Baz.

'What you doing there?'

'I just like watching everyone go by.'

Laila could sense the panic rising inside her as Baz walked across to the window, pulling the net curtains right across to get a full view of the street. She had thought he was working and the idea Yvonne would appear just as Baz was looking out was beginning to frighten her.

'What's up with you? You look like you're up to something.'

Baz grabbed hold of Laila's hair, pulling her head back. 'You better not be. I've warned you.'

'No, no, I'm not. I just wanted to see out.'

'You're lying.'

'I'm not, I swear. I thought you'd be at work.'

Baz's eyes hardened. 'Oh so because you thought I was at work, you assumed it was okay to make a show of yourself at the window?'

'It wasn't like that Baz.'

Laila hadn't time to explain what it *was* like before she found herself being sent across the room by the back of Baz's hand. He stood above her, then brought his foot down into her side. She moved, quickly scurrying along the floor, trying to protect her stomach with her hands.

'Please, Baz. I wasn't doing anything wrong.'

Baz mimicked Laila as he spoke. '*I wasn't doing anything wrong, I never do anything wrong, because I'm little Miss Perfect.*'

Baz grabbed her top and Laila heard it tear, the material cutting into her armpit as he held her up. 'You're pathetic.'

Baz brought his foot down into her side again. She screamed, terrified not for herself but for her pregnant stomach.

'No Baz, please. The baby.'

'You're not fit to be a mother, you know that?'

Laila scrambled under the bed for refuge. She felt Baz grab hold of her ankles and, desperate to protect herself from him, held onto the bed leg, preventing him pulling her out.

'Oh no you don't.' Baz continued to pull her as her fingers began to slip, betraying her grip. A few seconds later Laila felt Baz let go of her ankles, but it was followed by a cool waft of air as he lifted the bed up.

'What did I warn you Laila? I told you nothing was going to change when we came back to Bradford, but you seem not to want to hear me.'

'I do, I do. I'm trying Baz. I'm trying to make you happy.'

'No you aren't, and if you don't want to hear then, my little beauty, you'll feel.'

Laila was aware of the pain shooting through her, but it was secondary to her survival instinct. She ran for the door, just as Baz hurled the wooden chair at her. It missed. Fractionally, smashing on to the wall and bringing down the framed pictures.

'Laila, stop acting the fool.'

Baz ran out after her onto the landing. It didn't take him long to catch up. He clutched hold of Laila's clothes as she stood at the top of the stairs begging him.

'Baz, please.'

He drew her close to him, staring into her beautiful brown eyes. As he held her, Laila could feel his body beginning to become aroused and his hand starting to explore her body.

'Princess frigid, aren't we?'

Laila yanked away but the force of the movement made her lose her balance and she grappled, desperately searching for Baz to cling on to. Briefly, Laila felt her fingers touching Baz's arm before she tumbled backwards, floating in mid-air for a moment before crashing down and hitting the hard edges of the stairs. Then there was nothing but darkness.

'Laila? Laila? Wake up.' Laila's eyes fluttered open to see Tariq's worried face staring at her. Unsure where she was, Laila turned her head to discover she was somehow back in her bedroom, lying on her bed. Her whole body hurt, and the pain in her stomach which had already been there had become worse.

'Are you okay? Baz told me you fell down the stairs carrying the chair.'

'Where is he?'

'He's gone to work. Do you want me to get you a drink?'

Laila reached for her brother's hand. 'No. Just stay with me.' She smiled weakly at Tariq.

'Laila, I'm so sorry.' Laila shook her head.

'Don't blame yourself Tariq. It's not your fault.' She squeezed his hand harder as she saw the tears come into his eyes. 'Don't, Tariq. Please don't.'

'Did he do it Laila? Did he do this to you? Just tell me.'

Laila shook her head again. She didn't want trouble and she certainly didn't want her brother saying anything to Baz. 'No, Tariq. It's like he said. I fell.'

The pain shot through her again and Laila twisted her body to the side. It was a while before it subsided enough for her to talk.

'Tariq, I think there's something wrong.'

'Just lie still, try not to get upset.' Tariq stroked his sister's hair gently as she closed her eyes.

'What's going on here?' Mahmood Khan stepped into Laila's bedroom and immediately screwed his face up in disdain. Every time he saw his niece he was overwhelmed by a sense of despair. Even though she was now married to Baz, her presence still bothered him. He'd thought it would disappear, but seeing her only reminded him of his brother's weaknesses and the lack of guidance he'd instilled in his children. His late brother and his family were a disgrace to the Khan name and the sense of shame was almost too much to bear.

Tariq jumped up from the bed. He hadn't seen his uncle in a few days. 'Hello uncle. Laila's not well. She had a fall.'

Mahmood didn't bother to enquire how or why it'd happened. 'Tariq, I need you to come with me. I have a few things I need to do.'

'But what about Laila, uncle?'

'Just lock the door as usual.'

Tariq's face blushed red with shame. 'I didn't mean that. She's unwell. Don't you think someone needs to stay with her?'

'What for?'

'She's having pains. The baby, uncle. Perhaps there's something wrong.'

Mahmood waved his hand. He didn't wish to discuss anything like that, especially as he had no doubt that his niece's stupidity, not to mention her wilfulness, most likely caused it. Walking out of the bedroom, Mahmood spoke without taking so much as a glance at Laila.

'Let whatever needs to take its course happen Tariq. Who are we to question what is given or taken away from us?'

Laila heard the sound and immediately knew what it was. She sat up quickly, then threw herself back down as the pain travelled through her. She needed to let it subside but she also knew she needed to get up before it was too late. Pulling herself up again, Laila ignored her dizziness and the pain, slowly making her way across to the window.

A smile crossed her face. It was Yvonne.

'Hold on.' Laila tapped on the window getting her friend's attention. Unlocking the bolt, it took Laila three attempts to lift it. She knew it wasn't heavier than when she'd lifted it yesterday, in fact she knew it wasn't heavy at all, but every movement hurt, as if it was pulling her insides out.

'Hi.' Laila greeted Yvonne shyly. She wanted to tell her what a relief it was to see her. How she'd feared she wouldn't come back and how the thought of that had started to sink her into a dark despair. But how could she? How could she tell Yvonne, a person she hardly knew, that she was her only contact to the outside world.

'I suppose you thought I weren't coming back.'

'I never really thought about it.' It was a lie but Laila was too embarrassed to say anything else. Not quite knowing what she should say, Laila added, 'But I'm glad you're here though.'

'I nearly never came.'

'Why not?'

'Just because.' It was Yvonne's turn to lie now.

'What you been doing?'

'Owt and nowt. Sorry I didn't bring your chocolate buttons.'

'That's okay, I don't really feel like them now.'

'What's up? Your stomach still hurting?'

Laila nodded. 'Yeah, feels worse today.'

'I told you, you need to get it seen to. Could be a bit of Delhi belly.'

'I was in Pakistan, not India.'

'No, soft lass. I mean you might be getting the runs or something. Maybe it's something you ate.'

'I don't think so.'

'How do you know?'

'Cos I'm pregnant.'

Yvonne's mouth hung open. She felt in her pocket and got out a packet of cigarettes. She lit one up before she said anything.

'Bloody hell, Laila. I thought it'd be Mary in Mrs Jacobs's class who got preggers first. She's always putting it about. Everyone thinks she's a right slag; I think she's alright meself.'

'But I'm married.'

Yvonne shrugged her shoulders, crossing her eyes to watch the smoke come out of her mouth. 'I suppose.'

'So why didn't you come yesterday?'

'Had a bit of trouble with me stepdad. He's a bit too handy with his fists if you know what I mean. Anyway, I really came to say goodbye. I've had enough.'

Panic hit Laila. She stammered, trying to get her words out, 'What . . . what, do you mean?'

'I'm sick of it. Me Mam just lets it happen. Most of the time she's too pissed up to care, but even when she's not, she lets him use me as his punchbag. I suppose she sees it better me than her. If I ever had kids, I wouldn't let any fucker touch them. Would you?'

Laila shook her head. 'So what you going to do Yvonne?'

'I'm off. I'm out of this place.'

'But you can't just go.'

'Why not?'

'Where will you go? What will you do for money?'

'I've been saving up. Got meself just over two thousand pounds.'

'How?'

'Stripping.' Yvonne watched as she saw the astonishment on Laila's face. 'Close your mouth girl, you'll let the flies in. You shocked?'

'No. Well a bit.' Laila smiled warmly, not wanting to hurt her friend's feelings.

'I don't like it. All those horrible blokes drooling at you like you're a piece of chicken. There was this one bloke right, who tried to get on the stage. When he was climbing up, he got his foot caught in a pair of knickers left on the floor. He ended up crashing into a table, landed badly and broke his ankle.' Laila giggled at her friend who giggled along with her.

'I wish you weren't going, Yvonne. I'll miss you.'

'Don't be silly. You've got a baby to think of now.'

Tears came to Laila's eyes. 'I'm not being silly, I will miss you. You don't understand.'

Yvonne's voice was warm, taking out some of the harshness of her Northern accent. 'What don't I understand?'

Laila clammed up, afraid she'd spoken out of turn.

'Nothing. It's fine. You're right, I'm just being silly.'

Yvonne glanced at Laila, her face looking serious. 'Why don't you come with me?'

'Where?'

'London. Come with me to London, Laila. Nobody will find us there. I've got enough money for both of us for the time being. We can get a job and you can pay me back. It'll be fun. What do you say?'

Laila saw the eagerness on Yvonne's face, and for one crazy moment it felt like it'd almost be possible. Then the reality dawned on her again. She answered sadly, 'Thank you but I can't.'

'Okay, but the offer's there. I'm leaving on Thursday. I'm getting the midday train. If you change your mind you can come but I won't wait for you. I better go now. You won't breathe a word of this will you?'

'No, I promise. You can trust me.'

Yvonne smiled. She had the feeling she could.

'I know I can Laila. Goodbye, and if I don't see you again, good luck.'

Laila only nodded her head, choking back the tears, unable to say anything. As she watched Yvonne walk up the street, she knew she needed more than luck to get her through.

22

Laila touched the bed sheets she was lying on, then looked at her hand. She saw it was covered in blood. She ran to the bedroom door and started to bang on it.

'Tariq! Tariq! I'm bleeding.' There was nothing but silence. Laila banged again and eventually she heard the sound of footsteps running up the stairs. The door was unlocked.

'Tariq, I'm bleeding.'

'When did it start?'

'I think when I fell down the stairs; I don't know. But it's got so much worse. Please Tariq, you have to do something. Please.'

Tariq looked panic-stricken. 'What do you want me to do?'

'Take me to the hospital, Tariq.'

'Baz will be home soon.'

'I know, and when he does I'll have no chance of getting help. Please Tariq. I'm begging you. Help me.'

Laila dropped to her knees. Desperate and in pain. Tariq bent down to pick her up. He couldn't bear to look in her eyes. 'Please Laila, get up. Don't beg me.' He felt his sister grab his hand. The same sister who used to always play with him. The same one he'd pulled the pigtails of when she was little, and the same sister he'd promised his father he'd look after. It took him only a moment to say it, but Tariq had a feeling he might regret it for longer than that.

'I'll help you Laila, but hurry, we have to try to get back before Baz or uncle.'

The hospital sister smiled sadly at Laila. 'I'm sorry sweetheart, but I'm afraid you've lost the baby. Is there anyone I can call? Your boyfriend . . . your parents?'

Laila's voice was filled with shock. 'No . . . no, but are you sure? Are you sure I've lost it?'

'I'm certain. You'll be able to go home soon but you need to take it easy. You'll be in some discomfort so we'll give some pain-killers, but the pain shouldn't be worse than period pain. If it is you need to come back to the hospital.'

'How did it happen?'

'We can never be entirely sure, but these things sadly do happen, especially at the early stage of pregnancy you were. Sometimes it's just nature's way.'

'Do you think a fall could do it?'

The nurse nodded. 'Is that how you got the bruises?'

Absent-mindedly, Laila touched her face. 'Yes . . . yes. I fell down the stairs.'

'Well it's entirely possible. Like I say, it could be any number of things, but if you had a nasty fall it could easily happen. You can pop your clothes on now or you can wait till after the doctor comes round. I'll send someone in with a cup of tea. Hey, I know it's hard, but you're young. There'll be plenty more chances to try again.'

Laila walked slowly to the hospital toilets. She wasn't quite sure how she was supposed to feel. She needed to go and find Tariq and tell him. She'd left him waiting for her in the casualty depart-ment. That had been nearly two hours ago.

'Well?' Tariq looked at his sister with concern. She shook her head.

'I don't know what to say Laila.' He took hold of his sister's hand as they walked in silence down the corridor towards the exit.

The doors opened, bringing in a cool breeze. Laila wrapped her coat round her, feeling the chill of the evening air. Tariq turned to Laila, dropping her hand.

'Go, Laila.'

Laila studied her brother's face, to see if she was understanding correctly what he was trying to say to her. Tariq stepped forward and kissed her head. 'Go.' Laila turned and as she did he grabbed her hand again, speaking in a whisper. 'I love you.'

A moment later, Laila ran out of the door.

'Gone? She can't have gone. Why the hell did you take her to the hospital without my permission?'

'She was bleeding, what did you expect me to do?'

Baz raised his voice and slammed Tariq against the wall, watched by Mahmood. 'I expected you to do nothing. I warned you, Tariq.'

'Yeah you did. And I'm ashamed to say I listened to you. If you want to report me for what happened to Ray-Ray, fine, but it won't bring her back. She needed help and I wasn't going to leave her like that.'

'Why not?'

'Because she's my sister.'

'No, Tariq – she's *my wife* first and your sister second. How am I going to explain to people she's run off? Don't you understand the shame that brings? Your sister was lucky anyone wanted to marry her. I did her a favour and she repays me like this.'

'It's got nothing to do with other people.'

Baz shouted; tiny drops of saliva splattering out of his mouth. 'It's got everything to do with them! What sort of man will they think I am? A man who can't keep his wife. I'll lose all the respect I've worked for. Do you know how much shit I've had to put up with to get where I am? Paki Gupta. PC Paki. Detective Curry Gupta. Do you know how much they'll laugh at me down the station now? Laugh at me back home? Oh there goes Baz Gupta; thought he was so much better than all of us but he can't even keep a wife. You've humiliated me.'

'I did what was best.'

Baz pushed his face, centimetres from Tariq's. 'If we don't find her, I'm holding *you* responsible.'

'She's gone Baz. You won't find her. Laila doesn't want to be here and I don't blame her.' Tariq stopped as his voice cracked. Pulling himself together, he hardened his tone. 'Uncle forced her to get married. *We* forced her.'

Mahmood went to say something but Baz put his hand up to stop him.

'It was her duty, her culture. She has brought dishonour to me.'

'No Baz, what we put her through had *nothing* to do with duty, culture or honour. I think we both know that. Why don't you leave her alone now? Let her go.'

'Never. But you'd like it if I did, wouldn't you Tariq?'

Tariq stared at Baz. He pushed him away. 'Yeah, I would. Because she deserves so much better than you.'

Baz grabbed hold of Tariq, trying to put him in a head lock, but they were both matched in height and strength so he struggled to get a firm grip. Tariq quickly moved to the side, knocking over the ornaments, then lost his balance slightly, giving Baz the slight advantage for a moment. Tariq grappled with Baz, yanking his top to try to pull him down. He managed to twist Baz round who fell awkwardly, sprawling across the glass table.

'Enough! Stop! Stop!' Mahmood shouted loudly, making Tariq turn to his uncle. Baz saw his opportunity and slammed Tariq with his fist. Mahmood walked across to Tariq, bending down to where he was sitting, holding his face.

'You have brought shame and dishonour to my family Tariq. Both of my brother's children are unworthy to carry the name of Khan. We need to find her and bring her back.'

'You won't be able to find her.'

Baz stood up by Mahmood's side. 'Oh but we will. And Tariq, *when* I find your sister, which I will, I'll kill her.'

Laila huddled up under the tree in the graveyard. The rain was pouring down. She was shivering, sending spasms through her body as she sat drenched through to her skin. The raindrops dripped down her neck and she'd long since stopped trying to wipe her face dry from the rain and tears.

Darkness had come early and the dark grey storm clouds were still visible in the black sky. The shapes of the gravestones seemed eerie, making Laila's imagination run away with her.

She moved slightly, trying to find comfort on the wet ground. What had she thought she was going to do? Where did she think she could go? The questions ran through her mind, shooting at her like poison arrows.

Tightening her arms round her knees she put her head down, tired of her tears, tired of her pain. She was scared and she didn't know what to do to make the fear go away. She didn't know how to bring back the feeling of safety and care she'd once had in the arms of her father.

She had nothing. There was no one to turn to. Tariq had helped but there was nothing more he could do. She shuddered. Even the thought of her brother made her afraid; she was scared for him. Terrified he'd be hurt for helping her and she would be responsible for that, just like she'd been responsible for Ray-Ray. She took a sharp breath as she thought about him and wondered, not for the first time, if he hated her now.

She couldn't even go back home, the repercussions would be unimaginable. They'd make her stay with Baz or worse still, send her to her mother-in-law's back in Pakistan. And she just couldn't. She just couldn't go back.

She'd always thought this happened to other people. She'd known girls in the community who'd been sent to Pakistan and hadn't come back. Girls who'd been forced into unhappy marriages. But it was never spoken about, never discussed. And now she'd become one of those girls. She'd had such hope, such dreams. She'd been ready to take on the world. Her father had told her she could have it all, but most importantly, he'd told her she could have her life. Now though her life wasn't hers and she knew it would never be. And if she didn't have that, what did she have?

Going into her pocket, Laila pulled out the bottle of painkillers the hospital had given her. She thought about her father, her mother, her brother and Ray-Ray. She thought about how it once was and how it should've been.

Undoing the top of the container, Laila poured the tablets into her mouth before curling up under the tree, hoping it'd soon be over.

'No sign of her.' Baz snarled as he got back into the car. Tariq was driving and they'd been searching the streets of Bradford for a few hours. Baz and Mahmood had taken it in turns to get out and speak to all the people they could think of. Uncles, Aunties, friends, religious leaders had all been spoken to, with nobody having seen or heard from Laila.

Baz smashed his fist on the dashboard. He turned angrily to Tariq as he drove past the fire station.

'This is because of you, Tariq. The whole community will now think I can't keep a wife. How will people be able to respect me? Do you know how that feels?'

'The shame is on my hands as well. How will I be able to walk down the street with the weight of dishonour on my shoulders?' Mahmood added dramatically from the back seat.

Tariq carried on driving, praying they didn't see Laila.

'Pull up here.' Baz shouted and pointed at a small terraced house.

'Here?'

'Yes, I want to go and speak to Laila's little friend.'

'It's nearly three a.m. You can't, it's too late.'

'Just watch me.'

Tariq, Mahmood and Baz stood in Yvonne's kitchen with Baz questioning a sleepy-looking Yvonne.

'If I find you aren't telling me the truth . . .'

'I am. I haven't seen her since you told me not to.'

'I'm warning you.'

Yvonne smirked. 'Listen, I can't help it if you can't keep your wife, pal.'

Baz dived across the table to grab Yvonne but she jumped out of the way, used to being on high alert from years of living with her stepfather.

Tariq pulled at Baz, wanting to get out of the place as soon as possible. 'We better go. She hasn't seen her. It's no good.'

Baz looked at Yvonne with disgust. He turned to go but as he did he picked up the kitchen table, flipping it over and sending the piled up mess on to the floor, before storming out.

'Yvonne?' Tariq spoke with quiet urgency as he watched Baz and Mahmood march out along the path. 'If you hear from . . .'

Yvonne snapped angrily. 'I told your mate, I haven't seen her, okay?'

'Please, I'm not trying to cause trouble. I'm her brother. If you hear from her, call me. Just let me know she's all right. I don't even want to know where she is. I just need to know she's safe. Here.' Tariq scribbled down his number on a piece of paper and stuck it in Yvonne's hand, rushing off out to the car as Baz started calling him.

23

'If anyone wants me I'm going to the hospital, but then I'm going to do some shopping so I'll get some lunch whilst I'm out.' Tasha Thompson spoke to the receptionist, making sure she made them part of her alibi if of course she needed one later on. 'Oh, and by the way, I don't want you taking any messages from Arnold either.'

'Certainly, Mrs Thompson. Now, is there anything else I can help you with today?' Tasha shook her head; the reply from the hotel receptionist was almost robotic. Whether she'd actually do what she'd asked her was another matter; she seemed more interested in taking a sneaky peek at the magazine next to her. Without answering, Tasha walked towards the hotel car park. The receptionist was the least of her worries. Today was the day Freddie was coming out.

Johno had given her firm instructions on what she had to do. He'd told her to make sure she kept to the same routine for today, tomorrow and the next few weeks. The police would be sniffing around and she would be one of the first people they came to. It was essential the hospital staff saw her at the same time as they did every morning, as well as the hotel staff, and especially the car park valets.

After seeing Ray-Ray, she would come back to the hotel as she normally did, make sure her presence was known, then head out again on foot to pick up the car they'd organised for her to drive. It was parked in a street on the other side of Bradford. From there she'd go and meet Freddie on the outskirts of Ilkley. Sixteen miles outside the city centre, in the heart of the country.

Tasha didn't actually know the exact whereabouts of where she was going to drive Freddie after she'd picked him up; Johno had told her it was best she knew as little information as possible. The only thing she did know was that he was planning on a helicopter taking him out of the country later tonight.

Thinking about the plans made her feel queasy. If they were caught, it wouldn't just be Freddie serving time; it'd be her as well. She really didn't want to think about it any more, otherwise she might find herself wanting to do a disappearing act. It was still early and she didn't need to go and pick up Freddie until later. Already Tasha Thompson knew it was going to be a very long day indeed.

Freddie was pacing. If he was honest, he was shitting himself. Almost literally. Thankfully they hadn't been on lock up and he'd been able to use the lags' toilets off the recreational room. He was losing it. For him to be nervous was unheard of. But then, he supposed he had a lot riding on it. In fact, he had everything fucking riding on it. He *had* to make this work. He was worried about Eddie's contact; never before had he put his trust in a person he didn't know. He hadn't even let a stranger look after his bleeding rottweilers, let alone himself. Fuck. He had to stop this worrying. It wasn't helping him at all.

He turned and saw Eddie on the other side of the room and he nodded an acknowledgement. A few feet away was Martin Warner, looking as if he was standing in a police line-up after committing the Great Train Robbery. He was a bleeding chump. The look on his face made him look more than shifty. Even from across the room with less than perfect eyesight, Freddie could see him standing in his cheap blue suit, tiny droplets of sweat on his forehead. Now what the fuck was Warner doing? Oh God, he was waving and calling him over. For fuck's sake, he'd told him not to do anything out of character, and calling him over was just that. Freddie couldn't just ignore him because no doubt the man would only bring more attention to him if he did.

Talking through his teeth so no one could lip read what he was saying, Freddie angrily spoke to Martin Warner. 'What's the matter with you? Do you want to get us nicked before we even get out of here? I told you not to speak to me.'

'It was just, I . . .' Warner stopped to dab his damp forehead.

'Pull your fucking self together, Marty. You look like you've thrown a bucket of water all over yourself.'

Warner was clearly in a panic. What Freddie really wanted to do was ram his fist down his whiny little throat. The man was a pussy. It wouldn't surprise him if he burst into tears. Warner spoke to Freddie, far too loudly for his liking.

'I've been thinking. I'm not sure if I can do this. What happens if we get caught? What will happen to my family then? Listen Thompson, let's call this off and then say nothing about it.'

Freddie was holding it in, but he felt he wanted to burst. This man was already messing things up. Still speaking through gritted teeth, Freddie narrowed his eyes.

'I swear to God Marty, if you don't want me to order my men to fuck you and your whole family up, then you need to get a fucking grip. The only way you're going to back out on this is in a body bag. All you have to do is stay there and say nothing. Once it starts, you know exactly what you have to do.'

The sweat now started to pour off Warner's forehead. 'Just repeat the plans for me; I'm not sure I can remember everything.'

Jesus, it was like he was dealing with a child, and people were starting to notice that he, Freddie Thompson, was talking to a screw. 'No, Marty. I ain't standing here any more. If you value your family in any way, I'm sure even *you* will remember. Okay?'

'Motherfucker!' a lag shouted at the top of his voice on the other side of the room, followed closely by a loud bang. It was starting to kick off. Freddie looked over to see one of the prisoners in a headlock over near the pool table. The lag screamed as a prison-made weapon was used on his face and a razor blade attached to a comb slashed the man's cheek. Blood spurted everywhere, covering the green felt of the pool table.

Freddie knew it was a signal for the other prisoners to join in. A cracking of wood was heard as the cue stick was broken across a knee, leaving a lethal jagged edge. Fists and feet were flailing. Ten, twenty, fifty men started to jump in; battering one another with pent-up anger and excitement. The prison alarms were going off and Freddie heard the running of feet before he saw the back-up officers charging along the corridor.

It was chaos and Freddie could hardly see through the throng of men. He was searching for Eddie. Then he saw him, down on the floor, his face covered in blood as a lag booted him in the face. He saw the lag grab Eddie's arm, twisting it round at the shoulder until it popped out of the socket.

'Fucking hell! Me arm! Fucking hell!' Eddie rolled around on the floor in excruciating pain, unable to stand as the shock hit his body.

Freddie stood back in the entrance of his cell, watching the prison officers haul the men off each other. Cell doors slammed and security gates shut. Some men continued to shout as they were dragged back into their cells or towards the isolation block. A few minutes later, the only people who were left in the recreational room were the prison officers and Eddie, who was still shouting in agony. As Freddie's cell door was slammed, he smiled to himself. Eddie had done well.

'It's broken.'

'Well give the man a medal, of course it bleedin' is.' Eddie grimaced through the pain of his dislocated shoulder and his broken arm as he spoke to the medics. Freddie had sorted out the attacks with one of the other lags, but Eddie hadn't known who it was going to be until he actually got pounced on.

'The element of surprise is what's needed, kid.' Freddie had said to him. And it certainly had been a surprise when the biggest, hardest, craziest lag had nailed him to the floor, kicking the shit out of him, before clean snapping his arm.

It was typical Freddie to choose the terminator – the nickname everyone called him on the wing – to batter him senseless. The geezer was serving life for a triple murder. Asked why he'd killed the three strangers during a bank job, his only defence had been, 'because I felt like it.' No doubt using the terminator, when there were so many other lags to choose from, would've appealed to Freddie's sense of humour. And Eddie would bet any money Freddie would rib him about it later.

They'd given him painkillers, but the pain was still shooting through Eddie's body.

'You really need an injection Davidson, until you're taken to hospital. A couple of paracetamol won't do the trick.'

Eddie shook his head. He had to be straight-thinking, not hazed-up with shit. Yes, he was in agony, but if it meant getting out of this crap hole, then he would've happily had his other arm broken.

'Fuck me, watch what you're doing Governor.' Eddie recoiled back, trying to protect his arm as Deputy Governor, Martin Warner stumbled into the medical room, bringing a couple of prison screws with him and banging Eddie's arm in the process.

Eddie looked at Warner. Jesus what was wrong with the man? All he had to do was keep a low profile and act natural. Yet here he was with his face pallid, waxy and wet with sweat. He looked like he was going to pass out. Fuck. He was the one with the broken arm, yet Warner looked like he was the one who'd been injured.

Eddie watched as Warner went to the tap, splashing his face with water, as the medics looked on, concerned.

'Are you alright Sir?'

'I'm fine; I think I ate something dodgy for supper last night.'

'I can give you . . .'

'I said I'm fine!' Warner shouted loudly at the medic – who was taken aback by the sudden outburst – before apologising profusely. 'Sorry . . . sorry. I'm sorry.'

Eddie's heart was racing. The man was clearly losing it. Catching Warner's eye, Eddie gave him a warning stare. All eyes were on the governor as he dabbed his face with a handkerchief. Eddie saw one of the medics smirk to his colleague as they watched Warner's hands visibly shaking.

'Thought I'd let you know Davidson, I've spoken to the depot and there are no vans free to take you to the hospital at the moment. But clearly you need to go. So what I suggest is, you wait for the van which will be taking Freddie Thompson on a compassionate visit, then I'll have you dropped off. By the time you're finished, there'll be a van available to bring you back. Any problems in the meantime, let your wing officer know. You can take him back to his cell.'

Eddie stared at the deputy. If he were any more wooden, the man would've turned into a tree.

Freddie couldn't see anything through the van windows so he didn't know where they were, but by his reckoning the van should be sprung within the next half-hour. The driver would be taking the long route, where there were no cars, no cameras and where his men were waiting in ambush. Exhaling hard to calm himself, Freddie put his head in his hands. All he could do now was wait.

The van came to a screeching halt, sending both Freddie and Eddie forward. Freddie heard his friend scream out in pain. A second later the sides of the van were being banged. The screws sitting with Freddie struggled to get up, then yelled to the driver. 'Radio in, radio in, there's a raid.' A shot was heard. Then another. Then there was the cranking open of steel as the back door of the van was forced open. Five men in balaclavas appeared, holding sawn-off shot guns and bellowing at the top of their voices. 'Get down, get down. Put your hands on your head.' Without hesitation, the prison officers went down on the floor of the van. The youngest officer knelt as he pleaded for his life. 'Please, I've got a wife and kids mate.'

'Yeah, so have fucking I, now do I look like I give a shit? Keep your mouth shut or I'll blow your fucking head off.' The man took the butt of his gun, smashing it into the face of the officer who fell unconscious with the sound of crunching bone and cartilage. The other officers said nothing, but the steel butt was smashed on the tops of their heads, sending the last screw forward to smash his chin on the steel edge of the partition. He dropped down with a sickening bang, biting off the tip of his tongue as he went.

'Round the corner, drive the fucking van off the road.' Freddie barked his orders at the driver, who immediately sped to the lay-by.

Once down the isolated lay-by, Freddie was frantic to escape the van. 'Quick, get me fucking out of here.' Quicker than searching and struggling with keys, one of Freddie's men brought out his silencer from his back pocket. As Freddie held his hands up, he shot the middle of his handcuffs, then did the same for Eddie, whose ankles were chained instead due to his arm.

Rushing out of the van, Eddie spoke. 'I'm getting out of here now. Thanks Freddie, and good luck mate. Hope I'll see you again.'

Freddie was surprised to find he was suddenly emotional and heard his voice betraying his feelings. 'You're going to be all right Ed? You know to get in touch with Johno if you need anything. Money. Shelter. Anything.' He paused. 'And Eddie, cheers. I couldn't have done it without your help. Oh, and hey, watch that arm.' Grinning, Freddie tapped Eddie hard on his dislocated shoulder, laughing as he cried out in pain.

Freddie ran round to the driver. 'Get out.'

Not arguing, the man got out of the van, nervously staring at

Freddie as he spoke. 'Eddie told you what was going to happen now. You know I'll have to get one of my men to knock you about before we go.'

The driver nodded. Freddie tapped him on his back in thanks then watched him close his eyes as Johno began to batter him senseless. It was good to be out.

24

Freddie was pumped. The adrenalin rushed through his body as he hid on the back seat of the second getaway car. He couldn't believe it. He was free. There was still a long way to go before he could properly relax, but it'd been surprisingly easy. As easy as getting a shag from a whore.

It'd been a couple of hours now. A good distance had been put between him and the break out, and it would take some time before the prison realised what had happened. The van had a tracking device but Johno, whose many skills included safe-breaking, had disarmed it without any problems.

The screws and the driver had all been left stripped down, unconscious and handcuffed to each other, as well as being chained to the van. So there was no chance of them calling for help.

The only person who might have raised the alarm would've been Martin Warner, after the realisation of what he'd done had sunk in. But if he had been going to do that, Freddie doubted he would now. Not after the little visit paid to him late last night. A lit petrol bottle, to do a small amount of damage through his letterbox, was probably all the reminder he'd needed not to do anything silly today. Freddie smiled to himself, undoubtedly that's what had made Warner look so anxious this morning.

'How long till we get there?' Freddie spoke to Bobby. He was the cousin of Johno and another man who'd been in his firm for a long time. He'd done a lot of driving for him and had never fucked up once. It was good to have people around him who he could trust.

'About another two hours. We're making good time, boss.'

So far nothing had been reported on the radio, so hopefully it was a good sign. Even when the prison did realise, it'd still take them some time before they actually located the van. It was parked down in a country lay-by and according to the reccy his men had done, no one went there.

It was a touch. Great they were making good time. It was important for his men to get back to their usual routines and places. Johno would probably be back in Soho by now, and once Bobby had dropped him off he could easily get back to the Midlands before he was missed. Then the last leg was down to Tasha, and apart from her morning routine when she went to see Ray-Ray, she had no structure to her day as such. It was all going nicely to plan. Lying back on the floor of the car, Freddie allowed himself to breathe a small sigh of relief.

Tasha looked at her watch. She still had plenty of time until she had to meet Freddie, but she was feeling anxious. She didn't want to go and pick up the car too early. If she did, she knew she'd wind herself up to the point of panic. What she needed to do was distract herself. She couldn't wait in the hotel, in case the van had already been found. After what had happened to Ray-Ray the police knew where she was staying; she'd had to tell them in case they'd needed to contact her in connection to the attack. So it wouldn't be long until they came to talk. Perhaps they were even there now, watching the hotel, wanting her to lead them to Freddie. Putting not only him in the frame, but Tasha as well.

She was pleased she was well away from the hotel. In an hour or so she'd make her way to the car, and from there drive to Ilkley. It was only sixteen miles out from Bradford but the vastness of the moors made it feel a world away. It was an ideal place to meet Freddie.

She and Ray-Ray had gone up there when they'd first come to Bradford, deciding to try to embrace the move from London, to learn to love the differences, not hate them. But they'd failed miserably. And even now when she thought about it, it made her chuckle.

One look at Rombald's Moor was all it took. The ruggedness, the expanse, the sheer enormity of it had them looking at each other, immediately turning back to do some late-night shopping in Bradford. They were from Soho. Born and bred in London. There were a lot of things the Thompson family did and were known for, but the countryside just wasn't one of them.

Tasha looked at her Rolex. She'd had enough of sitting in the cafe. There was no shade and the Indian summer sun was beating down on her. The last thing she needed right now was a headache. Paying her bill and leaving a generous tip, she walked slowly through the back streets of Bradford, thinking how surreal the peace was. In a matter of a couple of hours, life would never be the same again for any of them.

As much as she was pissed with Freddie, she didn't want any harm to come to him. With every cell in her body she hoped nothing would go wrong, but then, why would it? Freddie might not be the best husband, but he certainly was one of the best faces. If anyone could get away with this, he could.

Stopping dead, Tasha suddenly realised where she was standing outside. A thought came to her. This may be the only chance she got. Then the only thing she had to worry about was her family. It didn't need to take more than five minutes, but it certainly would give her peace of mind. Bracing herself, with a determined look on her face, Tasha marched towards the block of flats. Once and for all she was going to tell him it was over. Perhaps then, Arnold would get the message.

*   *   *

The stairwell smelt the same. Arnold had told her most days, sometimes twice a day, he'd clean the stairs. She'd found that odd but had said nothing. And Tasha supposed the smell of cheap bleach was better than the smell of piss. The place was so sterile and drained of any personality, almost depressingly so, it was hard to imagine why anyone would want to live here. But she could see why Arnold would like it. Clean, simple and unassuming.

She sighed as she came to Arnold's landing. She guessed the reason she hadn't returned his calls was because there was a part of her hoping she wouldn't have to be the bad guy, that Arnie would've either quickly disappeared or phoned to tell her he'd met someone else. And she would've been pleased for him. At least one of them could've been happy.

But neither had happened; Arnie hadn't gone anywhere, nor had he met anyone else. So the only fair thing to do was tell him to his face it was over. Give him the watered-down version of why it couldn't continue. Christ, even the idea of telling him made her feel rotten. She still cared and didn't want to hurt him, but it was essential for both their sakes, especially now Freddie was out.

'Hello there. Izzy isn't it?'

Tasha stopped knocking for a moment to look at the man who'd sidled up next to her. 'Excuse me?'

'Your name. It's Izzy, isn't it?'

'No.'

'Are you sure?'

'I'm certain.'

'But . . .'

'Bleeding hell, don't you think I'd know my own name?'

'I'm sorry, I know I sound ridiculous. It's just I could've sworn Arnold said your name was Izzy. In fact I'd put my life on it.'

Tasha gave him a tight smile. His face looked familiar but she couldn't place it. Seeing the puzzlement on her face, the man, slightly disappointed that he hadn't been remembered, gave Tasha the prompt she needed. 'I sang 'Happy Birthday' with you? I'm his next-door neighbour.'

Tasha gazed at the man. She remembered him now, and he looked as lecherous and as oily as he had done the last time.

'Oh God, of course babes. Sorry darling; got a lot of things on me mind.'

'No answer?'

He was really trying her patience. What she wanted to say was, *'Would I be standing out here in the corridor knocking if there was?'* Instead she smiled and politely said, 'No.'

'Do you want me to give him a message?'

'No, it's okay.' Tasha looked at her watch again, checking she was still okay for time, and hoping the man would stop staring at her chest.

'In a hurry?'

The geezer was getting on her nerves now. But it wasn't really in her nature to be rude, unlike her sister, Linda, who would've already told him to do one.

'Yes, sort of. I have to go and . . . er . . . meet a friend. So if Arnie doesn't come back in fifteen minutes I'll miss him, which will be a shame. My own fault. Should have called.'

The neighbour looked both ways before speaking quietly to Tasha.

'I shouldn't do this, but I'm sure he won't mind. Whenever I see him, you're the only thing he talks about. But as I say, I swear he said your name was Izzy.'

Tasha rolled her eyes; she'd no intention of starting the same discussion all over again. 'It's *Tasha*.' As she said her name, she watched Arnold's next-door neighbour take out a bundle of keys from his pocket.

'I've got the master key; I can let you in if you like. Oh don't worry, I haven't stolen them. It's just while the caretaker's away for the week. His mother's had a stroke or something, but I'm the resident committee chairman, so I do the emergency cover. We have a master key to spare anyone having their doors broken down if they lose their keys or leave the stove on. Those kinds of things.' He grinned in an expectant manner.

'No, it's all right. I hardly think it's an emergency. I don't think Arnie would appreciate coming home to find me sitting there.'

'Why not? If I walked in to find you waiting for me, I wouldn't be complaining.' The man licked his lips as he finished off the sentence. Tasha shuddered, and turned away.

'He wouldn't forgive me if I let you just walk out of here. He really has missed you.'

'I don't know, it doesn't feel right.'

'What are you going to do? Snoop about in his drawers?'

'Of course not.'

'Well then, there's no real problem is there?'

Without waiting for a reply, the neighbour started to unlock Arnie's door.

'If he doesn't come back in time, then you could always leave him a note. I'll lock up again when you've gone. Give me a knock or I'll be down in the car park trying to get the graffiti off the wall. Little bastards.' The man left Tasha, waving as he went down the stairwell.

Tasha's hand rested on the handle of Arnie's front door. She hesitated, not feeling entirely comfortable with invading his private space like this. But then she was only going to wait and like she'd said, she certainly had no intention of snooping. Pushing open the door, she stepped into the flat.

25

'Hey, you all right?' The voice sounded distant. 'Hey lady.' There it was again. 'Lady, should I call an ambulance?'

A hazy vision was in front of Laila as she began to open her eyes. It lifted, and a man came into focus. He was staring at her with concern as deep and ingrained as the dirt on his face. Laila looked round to see where she was. Then it all came back to her as she saw the empty container of pills lying next to her. It hadn't worked. She couldn't even do that properly. Her mouth was dry and her head was throbbing. She tried to stand up, but her legs gave way.

'Here, hold on to my arm love. I don't suppose you've got any spare change have you?'

Laila shook her head and looked at the tramp. Was that how she was going to end up? Was she seeing her future standing in front of her? An existence, rather than a life?

She looked around again. How long had she been unconscious for? 'What time is it?'

The man grinned. 'You need to stay off them pills, love. It's Thursday morning.'

'Are you sure?'

'I'm certain.'

She looked up at the church clock. It was already eleven-fifteen. Laila froze, realising what that meant. Thursday, eleven-fifteen. It meant Yvonne was leaving for London in forty-five minutes. She'd forgotten all about that until now. Laila watched the minute hand move round to the top, and then she started to run.

Laila's clothes were still wet through from the night before. As she ran, she fought off the dizziness as she began to notice the stabbing pains in her stomach. She had to try and ignore it. She needed to get to the station before midday. Fifty yards ahead of her, she could see a bus pulling up, one which would take her to the train station.

'I haven't got any money but I need to get into town.'

The bus driver stared at Laila. His shirt was off-white and Laila could see the patterns of his string vest through it. 'If you haven't got any money, why am I going to let you get on my bus?'

'I'm meeting my friend. I don't want to miss her. Please.'

'Go on; scram. Off.'

'You don't understand, it's really important.'

'Listen ducky. You lot come over here and then want everything for nothing. My granddad fought in the war so we could keep England English. Fat lot of good that did. Sometimes I think I've taken the wrong turn and instead of ending up on the high street I've ended up along the streets of New Delhi.'

'That's in India, my family are from Pakistan.'

'Don't get smart with me young lady; it's all the same anyway. You might be able to get a free ride with the taxpayer's money, but you're not getting a free ride on my bus. Now do one.'

Laila watched the bus fade into the distance. She wasn't sure if she was going to make it now. She began to run along the pavement, looking behind her occasionally to see if there was another bus coming.

She needed to be faster but Laila found she had to keep stopping to ease the pain. 'Stop, please stop.' Laila waved her arms in the air, flagging down the oncoming car. It went past her, then slowed down.

Laila ran to it, not wanting the car to drive off again. She opened the door. 'Please help me. Can you get me to the station? I need to be there as soon as possible.'

The driver looked shocked to see the tear-stained young woman begging for a lift. 'Yes, yes of course. Jump in.'

Laila looked at the car clock. It was twenty minutes to midday. She might just make it. The warmth of the car and the relief she wasn't going to miss Yvonne made her relax slightly. 'Thank you. Thank you for the lift.'

The driver smiled reassuringly. 'Don't mention it. My name's Arnold by the way, but my friends call me Arnie.'

A short time later, Arnold pulled up outside his flat in the car. He looked down at his hands, seeing the scratches on them, wondering how they'd got there. 8, 10, 14. Fourteen scratches and he simply couldn't remember how he'd got them. And where had the blood come from? He shook his head, aware it wasn't the first time he'd no memory of what had happened in the hours before. Though he did remember a girl. Oh yes, he remembered her very well.

'Arnie! Arnie!' Scrubbing brush in hand, Arnold's next-door neighbour waved as he saw Arnold. By the time he got up to the car, he was out of breath.

'So glad I caught you. I got a little surprise for you. I hope you don't mind, but you know that lady friend of yours? I let her into your flat. I just didn't think you'd want Tasha having to wait outside.'

Arnold's face darkened. 'Tasha? I don't know a Tasha.'

'The lady who was there the time I came round. I let her in.'

Arnold turned the engine off, stepping out of his car. 'I think you mean Izzy.'

'Izzy, yes. That's what I said. I said to her, your name's Izzy but she insisted it was Tasha. How very strange.'

It wasn't strange. That was Izzy, always wanting to play games, and now she'd come back to him. Arnold smiled.

'I hope I haven't done the wrong thing Arnold, letting her in without you being there? I was so sure you wouldn't mind.'

Arnold started to whistle, then turned and headed towards the block of flats. 'I don't. I don't mind at all.'

26

'We're early. I better wait till Tasha arrives.' Bobby turned to look at Freddie, who was tucked down on the back seat of the car.

'Is it clear?'

'Yeah.'

'Thank fuck for that. My back's giving me right jip.' Freddie sat up as he spoke, kneading his fingers into the base of his back. Even though the car had blacked-out windows, he'd felt exposed sitting up, so he'd spent the whole journey lying on the floor of the back seat.

Gazing out of the window, Freddie could see nothing but space. Wide open space. No bars. No steel door. No continual noise; only silence and freedom. A huge grin crossed Freddie's face, showing off his immaculate white teeth.

'Get fucking in. Look at that, Bobby. We did it; can you believe we actually fucking did it?' Freddie yelped with joy, slapping his old-time acquaintance on his back.

'Listen, you get off Bobby,' he told him. 'You've done me a favour actually getting here early. I need to get me head round all of this. One minute I'm looking at spending a lot of me natural inside, the next, I'm fucking here, on the moors.'

'I dunno boss. Why don't I just wait here with you for Tasha to arrive? Makes more sense.'

'Appreciate it, but like I say, I need this bit of space to get me head round it all.' Bobby heard the steel in Freddie's voice and decided not to push it any more. He knew his boss and he knew when to open his mouth, and when not to.

Freddie talked whilst staring at the moor, sucking up the freedom as if he was a thirsty man in a bar.

'I'm supposed to be meeting her on the other side of those woods, so instead I'll just wait in them for her to come. Best thing for you to do is get back to the Midlands. Take the missus out or something. Be visible, and if there are any problems, contact Johno. He knows how to contact me.'

Freddie watched Bobby drive off. He could hear the engine well after the car had disappeared into the distance. Normally he'd hate having anything to do with the countryside; all this birds and nature stuff really wasn't his scene. But standing with his feet on a cushion of heather and looking at a whole heap of nothing meant he was free. And that made it the most beautiful fucking sight he'd ever seen.

Heading towards the small thicket of trees, Freddie even allowed himself to whistle; something he hadn't done since he'd lain in bed with Tasha, the day before he was nicked.

Thinking of his wife made him smile. There was a whole load of shit to get to the bottom of. And he hoped she hadn't done anything stupid whilst he'd been away. He hoped it was nothing more than a woman having a moody. If it was, everything could go back to normal. But if it wasn't, if she'd done something stupid, whether he loved her or not, he wouldn't even let Tasha live to regret it.

Tasha sat down on the tiny sofa bed at the bottom of the room, getting no comfort from it; the springs almost certainly had gone.

She could still smell the drains or whatever it was and with the window shut it made her feel quite nauseous. After a moment she moved to the other end but found it no better, wondering if it was just her unease at being in Arnie's flat which made her uncomfortable.

From where she was sitting now, she could see the front door, and for the past couple of minutes Tasha had found herself staring at it intensely, as if looking hard at it would make Arnold walk in. She hadn't been looking forward to telling him, but now she was here, she just wanted to get it over and done with.

She looked at the clock on the wall. It was really time to go. Well, she'd just have to leave him a note. Quickly explain she was sorry, but wouldn't be able to see him again. If that didn't give him the message, then she didn't know what would.

Looking in her bag, Tasha saw she had a pen but no paper. Damn. She walked towards the phone, hoping there'd be a pad next to it. Nothing. She glanced around and couldn't see any. The worktops were free of anything apart from the tea towels, folded up in origami shapes, as they'd been last time.

Tasha stared at the locker. She didn't want to start opening drawers, but she didn't want to leave without at least writing a note. And she certainly didn't want to give any message to the creep next door. Therefore there was only one thing to do. Open the drawer.

Bills. Menus. Leaflets, but no paper. She closed it, then opened the second drawer; praying it wouldn't be at this point Arnie chose to walk in, to what could only be described as her rooting through his things, albeit innocently.

Moving some leaflets to one side, Tasha froze. Catching her breath. She stared at the photograph. It was her. She looked at another. And another. More photos than she could count. All taken without her knowing. All taken by someone who'd been watching her. All taken by Arnold.

206

She quickly studied the black and white photos. This one was taken when she was coming out of the hotel. This one when she was coming out of the hospital from visiting Ray-Ray. And this one. Oh my God. This one was taken when she was sleeping.

Hurriedly she put them back. Shit. Her finger had scratched on something sharp. It was bleeding. Tasha looked down and saw she'd cut it on a jagged edge knife lying on the bottom of the drawer.

She sucked it but her finger continued to bleed. She needed to wrap it, then get the hell out of there. Some toilet paper would do it for now. Rushing into the bathroom, Tasha froze.

She pressed her body against the tiles as the door shut behind her. Her feet wouldn't move but her brain was screaming for her to run, all the while her eyes were fixed with horror at the bathtub. Her stomach turned over and vomit rose to the back of her throat. She swallowed it back down, pushing her hand across her mouth, not wanting to be sick. She had to get out.

Tasha turned her head slightly, trying to coax her body to turn with it, unable to take her eyes off what was left of the dismembered body. Edging backwards, Tasha felt the handle of the door behind her. As she made her way into the tiny hall, she heard a noise. A key in the lock. It was him.

Arnie was home.

'Izzy? Izzy? I know you're in here. Coming, ready or not.' Arnold stood in the doorway of his flat and sniffed the air. She was here. He could smell her. The perfume Izzy had in her hotel room. Floral oriental fragrance hung in the air. Izzy had come back to him.

Tasha crouched in the bathroom in the corner. Her whole body was shaking as she desperately rummaged in her bag, covering it with the blood from her finger as she frantically searched for her mobile.

'Emergency services – which service do you require?'

'Police.'

'I'm sorry caller I can't hear you, can you speak up?'

'Police.'

'Can you put the phone to your mouth caller, I can't . . .'

Tasha cut off the phone. It seemed the person on the other end of the phone was speaking louder than she was, filling the bathroom with a shrill voice. She didn't dare speak any louder. Her mind was racing. She could hear Arnie in the flat calling somebody else, but he was bound to come in. She had to try to stay focused. Perhaps it was all a mistake. Perhaps there was an explanation and he didn't know anything about it. Someone else could have placed the person in the bath and Arnie hadn't even seen her . . . him . . . *it*, was even in there. Bullshit.

Tasha's eyes filled with tears as she caught the horror of what was in the tub again. It was Arnold. There was no pretending. The man only a few feet away from her had done this. And once he found Tasha in there, she would be next.

Arnie smiled to himself. He loved it when she played games with him. Especially hide and seek. 'Izzy, come out.' He made a point of opening the cupboards and drawers, slamming them closed loudly so she could hear; letting her know he was going along with her game. But he knew she wasn't in here. He knew exactly where she was. Arnie squeezed his mouth together and gulped to stop the chuckle coming out. He didn't want her to think he was spoiling her game. That just wouldn't be fair.

Arnie stood by the bathroom door. 'I can't find Izzy; perhaps I should look in the bathroom.' He bent forward, stifling laughter, pressing his ear against the door to see if he could hear any sound from her. Nothing. She was obviously taking it very seriously. Straightening his face, he opened the door.

Tasha watched Arnie walk slowly in. She was holding her breath, desperately trying to stop crying out with fear. He hadn't turned round to see where she was crouching yet, but he would. Any moment. And when he did, she knew he would see her. She knew she was almost dead.

'Izzy? Izzy?' Arnold's voice bellowed in the bathroom. It echoed eerily. He felt so happy and the least he could do was let her have fun. Arnie walked to the sink and studied himself in the mirror which was hanging above it. He stood staring, wide-eyed for a few seconds and although he didn't turn round, a huge grin spread across his face.

'Oh, there you are.' Arnold watched her in the mirror, crouched in the corner. Curled up, hugging her knees, to stop him finding her. She was so clever but he was more clever. He had found her.

As he stared at her in the mirror, Arnold was surprised to see she wasn't smiling. He could see she had something on her face. It was blood. He turned round quickly, his face full of concern.

'Oh my God Izzy, have you hurt yourself? Let me have a look at you.' Arnie rushed to Tasha, sliding himself along the floor. She pulled away, terrified, unable to speak. She looked at him. He was so handsome, so tall, so softly spoken – yet he was the stuff of nightmares.

'Let me see to your finger, Izzy.'

Tasha, still frozen, didn't want to contradict him. Didn't want to tell him it was her. Tasha. Not this person he and his next-door neighbour referred to as Izzy. She didn't know what to do. If she screamed, she was sure it would make whatever horrors were going to happen worse. Much worse. Maybe if there was a way for her to manage to keep calm. Play along with him, then he wouldn't hurt her, or at least not straightaway. If she could gain his trust. After all, they'd spent plenty of time together and he hadn't hurt her then. But then he hadn't ever called her Izzy, and she'd never seen that look in his eyes before.

Tasha heard a whimper and realised it was coming from her.

Calm. Keep calm. Think of Ray-Ray. Think of Linda. Think of a way to get out of here.

'Does it hurt?' The concern in Arnie's voice sounded so genuine. Tasha blinked, unable to respond with the simplest of replies. 'You're crying, Izzy. Don't cry. I'll make it better, I promise.' Holding Tasha's gaze, Arnold put her finger in his mouth, sucking away the blood. She shivered in horror, then her whole body began to judder. 'You're cold. Let me sort this out for you then, I'll get you warm. Okay?'

She watched him run the bath tap, putting his hand under it to test the temperature, his fingers centimetres away from the dismembered corpse. 'Here you are.' Arnold stretched out his hand for Tasha to take. Frantically she shook her head, opening her mouth to breath, gasping for air. 'I can't, I can't.'

Arnie frowned in puzzlement. 'Whatever is the matter? Don't you want your finger to get better? You can't leave it to bleed. Now stop being silly and come here.' His arm stayed outstretched and very slowly, Tasha reached for it, remembering she needed to make her think she trusted him.

'There you are. That wasn't difficult was it?' He pulled her towards him and held her hand firmly, pushing it under the water. The angle of Arnie's hold made it impossible for Tasha to stand up and she found herself having to kneel. Her body was pushed up against the bathtub, her face inches away from the remains of the person in the bath. She turned her head, letting out a small cry. It was almost as if it was invisible to Arnie and he couldn't see the bloody mass lying there.

Tasha couldn't stand it any more. Her stomach erupted and this time there was no holding back. She vomited over the tiled floor, heaving loudly as her body twisted in shock.

Tasha felt Arnie's hand on her back. On all fours she scrambled away from his touch, her hand sliding in the mucusy vomit as she escaped back into the corner. She couldn't stay calm. She couldn't do it. He was going to kill her anyway. She screamed at him, 'Just stay away from me Arnie. People know I'm here. So just let me go.'

Arnold sat back down on the edge of the bathtub, his face quizzically tilted to one side. 'But Izzy, you've only just got here. Why would I want you to leave when the fun hasn't even begun?'

Sit and way the time and how the pit winds had been. He must

27

Sit and wait. That's all Freddie could do. Until of course it'd got dark and then he'd had to find cover from the cold summer rain. And the sitting and waiting had turned into a whole fucking night.

As Freddie sat on the moss-covered stone, looking out into the distance, it was hard for him to think of anything besides he'd been fucked over. His wife, his Tasha, had well and truly fucked him over.

Brooding wasn't doing anything to help. He had to try to be practical, to keep focused on getting himself out of the mess, but his mind kept drifting. He couldn't actually believe what had happened. It'd all been going to plan. To actually break out was almost unheard of and he, Freddie Thompson, had been the one to do it.

Had he really believed it was possible? He wasn't sure. But what he *had* believed in was his wife. Marty, the driver, even Eddie or Johno at a push. But Tash? Turning him over? He would've put his life on it she wouldn't have. But then he had, hadn't he? He *had* put his life on it.

All the warning signs had been there and he, like an absolute muppet, had ignored them. Why the hell had he trusted her? He should've known by the way she was behaving. Sneaking around, not answering his calls. Not coming to visit. And tarting herself up like one of the Toms from Soho.

He'd been made a mug of. Eddie had even warned him and he'd been right. So right it was a joke. He should never have trusted a woman. Freddie was not only learning the hard way, he was paying one heavy fucking price for it.

He stood up, stretching and feeling last night's dampness still in his clothes. Where was he? In the middle of fucking nowhere. The road they'd driven along yesterday was the only road leading on and off the moor. Besides a car driven by some old geezer sucking up the scenery as if it was something to admire, Freddie hadn't seen anyone else.

He decided this was a good thing and a bad thing. Good, because it meant the likelihood of anyone seeing him was very slim. Bad, because he was now stranded. To make matters worse, he still had no signal on his phone to contact Johno. He'd turned his phone off in the night to save his battery, hoping that when he turned it back on there'd be a message, but he'd been wrong.

Stressing, Freddie wiped his lips. They were dry and he didn't have any saliva to wet them with. A combination of nerves and thirst. Looking back at his mobile, Freddie smiled ruefully to himself. There was half a bar. Not enough to call anyone, apart from, ironically, the emergency services.

He reckoned if he could get out of the immediate area, away from the highest peak, there was a chance he could get a signal. Carefully glancing round, Freddie began to jog across the moor.

'For fuck's sake.' The pain from banging his toe on what seemed to be the fiftieth stone sent Freddie rolling down the side of the slope. The place seemed to be made up of nothing but rough potted land, overgrown with heather, bracken and dry grasses, with large hidden stones hidden every twenty yards or so.

Even though it was early morning the day was beginning to get hot. The sun was already beating down, drying out the moor from last night's rain, but Freddie had still managed to step into a waterlogged peat bog. One leg of his trousers was now covered in stinking black mud and his white trainers squelched as he walked, pushing out stale water. Moor. Hill. Mountain. To him it was all the fucking same, and his anger at being in this situation began to supersede his anxiety and paranoia at being seen.

The tiny path leading across the moors seemed well walked and Freddie hoped he didn't bump into any ramblers. Although he was out of his prison gear he was conspicuous in his blue jeans and white Abercrombie and Fitch top.

His feet were hurting him and he didn't want to look at his watch to see how long he'd been walking. His wet trainers rubbed on the back of his heel, causing a blister. Shit. Freddie stopped, realising he could be walking round in circles. He was sure he'd just walked this way. The landscape looked the same as it did fifteen minutes ago. But then, everywhere looked identical. Fucking countryside. Getting out his phone again, Freddie saw instead of getting a full bar, the flashing black line had disappeared to nothing.

'Christ.' His voice sounded loud against the quiet. He didn't want to start to panic; it wasn't his style anyway. He didn't do panic. He did a lot of things. Anger, revenge, even murder, but panic; no.

Wiping his face with the sleeve of his top, Freddie decided he didn't even want to start to analyse it. All he knew was that when he'd got to safety, Ray-Ray's attackers would have to wait. Lucky for them they were no longer at the top of his list.

Beginning to walk again, he touched his Cartier wedding ring. The person whose name was at the top of the list, flashing in neon writing, was so much closer to home. Without a doubt, Freddie would see to it that Tasha got what was coming to her.

The sound of pop music made Freddie crouch down. He turned his head, looking around, but couldn't see anyone. It sounded like it was coming from the other side of the large boulders and slowly he started to move, crawling along the ground at first, then on to his knees before running to the boulder, pressing his body up against it.

Freddie listened without moving. He could now hear the sound of voices. A woman. A man; yes he could definitely hear a man.

Freddie put his hand behind his back, lifting up his top to place his hands on the gun.

'Hello.'

The voice behind him made him jump. Instinct had Freddie pulling out his weapon but common sense stopped him. He turned round to face a woman who wore a large smile and the most hideous floral dress. She kept eye contact with him as she poured out a flask onto the ground, turning the purple heather brown. 'We're camping, well, we were. Funny how time seems to stand still when you're out here. We've got to head back now, but I'm trying to steal a few more minutes. Glorious isn't it?'

Freddie nodded his head. He could feel the cold of the gun against his skin. The woman continued to stare and it didn't escape Freddie's attention she was getting a full on clock of his face. It made him more than uneasy. The question now for Freddie was what to do. He didn't have a problem with shutting up people forever, but even to him it seemed slightly extreme at this present moment. However, if he had to, he would; he wouldn't even hesitate.

Answering the woman's question, Freddie smiled, moving round slightly to see if he could get a glimpse of who she was with.

'Yeah, beautiful. Love it up here darling. Me and the missus always come when we get a chance.'

'You're not from round here though are you? That's a London accent you've got isn't it?'

Freddie gritted his teeth. The woman had only just met him and she was already sticking her beak into his business. 'Yeah, you're right, but when I have the chance to come, I do.'

'Wife's not with you? On your own? Did you park round here?' The woman fired questions, glancing in all directions.

215

'Sometimes it's nice to take a bit of time out, you know how it is.' It was obvious by the woman's face she didn't know how it was. 'My car broke down and now I seem to have got meself a bit lost.' Freddie pointed to his trousers, hoping the muddied leg would add some credence to his story.

'Oh that's a shame. My husband knows a bit about cars. Perhaps we could drive round to where you've parked it and take a look for you?'

Freddie was sidestepped for a moment, but he pulled himself together quickly. 'Oh no, ta babes. Really kind of you and all that but I'd rather cadge a lift if that's okay. Think it's the electrics so it'll be pointless looking at it. Needs to go to a garage. So perhaps . . .' Freddie trailed off purposefully. He didn't want to push this woman and make her nervous, but there was no question about him not getting a lift. It was just a matter of how. Hopefully she'd do it the easy way. Offer him a lift and then he wouldn't have to resort to anything he didn't need to.

'Where are you heading?'

'Anywhere it'll be easy for you to drop me off sweetheart.'

'Let me just check with Andy, I can't see there'd be any problem, but you hear all sorts.' She trilled out a laugh irritatingly, making her way down to the man who was struggling with getting the picnic mat back in the hamper.

Freddie watched them talking. He saw her point at him, so he waved, holding a smile and trying not to feel paranoid. He walked down the heather-covered slope towards the couple, his feigned grin fixed on.

Standing, hovering by the open car door, Freddie could hear the radio turn from music into the local news. It was the usual. Politics. International war. Who's shagging who in the world of entertainment, and then he heard what he was hoping not to hear. '*Finally, police are still searching for the escaped prisoner, Freddie Thompson, who escaped early yesterday morning after the prison van he was being transported in was held up by five armed men.*

216

Thompson is known to be the head of one of Britain's most powerful and dangerous criminal organisations. He's described to be six foot tall, blonde streaked hair, blue eyes and well-built. He also has a very distinctive London accent. Police believe he may be heading for the north of England. They are warning the public not to approach him. They are also looking for another man, Eddie Davidson, who was sentenced last year to life imprisonment for killing his wife. He's believed not to be travelling with Thompson.'

Freddie swivelled round slowly to face 'Andy' and the woman. Their faces were drained of colour, and the frightened glaze in their eyes told Freddie all he needed to know. They stared at one another. Nobody moved.

Freddie saw the woman's eyes starting to dart about. Unable to stand the tension any longer, she blurted out, 'Egg roll anyone?' Hysteria cutting into her tone.

Her hand trembled as she held out an egg mayonnaise sandwich wrapped in cellophane. Freddie raised his eyebrows, shook his head in bemusement.

'I ain't here to mess about. So as they say, I can either do this the easy way or the hard way. But understand this, either way is fine by me.'

Andy spoke up and it amused Freddie to see him plumping out his chest. 'Listen here you. Just tell me what you want from us.'

Freddie walked towards Andy, who straightaway looked like he knew he'd been foolish to try to show any bravado.

'For a start Andy, I think you'd be wise to get rid of your attitude mate. It really won't do you or your missus here any good to play daydream hero with me.'

Andy put his head down, humiliated.

'Okay, so what I need to do is get out of this area, and you guys need to take me.'

'What about your car?'

'He *hasn't* got a car Brenda; he was just saying that.' Andy snapped at his wife who blushed, though still looked slightly puzzled.

'But his electrics have gone.'

Ignoring her, Andy spoke to Freddie, this time making sure the deference was heard in his voice.

'Why don't you just take our car and leave us here?'

'So you can call the police within a moment of me going? I ain't born yesterday.'

'We wouldn't do that.'

'Then you really are more stupid than you look Andy. Listen, I want to get to the viewpoint on the north side of the moor, but I've no idea where I am now, so you have to drive me.'

The woman turned to Andy. 'We should drive round fell way.'

'I've never been keen on that route, Brenda. It takes you too far round. I prefer the Ilkley Quarry way. Past the cow and calf rocks, I . . .'

Freddie shouted, interrupting the couple who both jumped in fright. 'Jesus Christ, I've been landed with John fucking Craven. This ain't an episode of *Countryfile*; I don't care how we do it. Just fucking take me there.'

'How long will it take?' Freddie listened to Johno on his mobile as he sat in the back seat, his gun out on his lap. If he was going to get caught and sent back to prison, then he was as sure as hell going to blaze a hole in anybody who tried to put him there. Though there was probably no need to play hard ball with these two. They didn't seem the type of couple who'd start with the heroics. Not now anyway.

Freddie glanced at the side of Andy's head. His temple showed an angry red mark. Freddie had given him a little slap about before they'd got in the car; 'a taste of things to come' as he'd put it. A warning to Andy not to do anything stupid as he drove.

Freddie finished off his call to Johno. The helicopter could be at the viewpoint in forty minutes. Thirty, at a push. Although Johno had asked what had happened, he hadn't explained anything to him about Tasha, not with Bill and Ben sitting in the front. He had heard the relief in Johno's voice when he'd spoken to him. The guy had been worried and oddly enough, it had made Freddie feel good. At least there was one person he could trust.

'Can't this tin box go any faster?' Freddie turned and watched the smoke billowing out of the back of the Ford Fiesta as he shouted at Andy over the noise of the engine.

'Don't like to push her. She's fifteen, but still manages these hills pretty well. She's been all over with us.'

Freddie rubbed his head. He was talking about a car like it was his own child. Of all the people he could run into, it was these two. Then what did he expect? He was never going to meet anyone near normal on a moor. Rambling. Bird watching. Picnicking. Camping. All kinds of crazy shit. There was only one type of person on the moor. And he'd certainly been landed with them.

'Just put your foot down on the pedal and move it.' Freddie could see Andy's worried expression as he shifted up into fifth, scraping the gears with a screeching sound. From the back seat he could see the speed dial as it changed from forty to sixty, then eighty. The road dipped and curved. The Fiesta took the tight bends as they hurtled along. Freddie watched Brenda holding on tightly to her seat as Andy pressed his body into the steering wheel. The car began to push out more strange noises and more smoke, almost obscuring the view of the road.

'You'll kill us all Andy. Slow down.'

'I'll tell him when to slow down, keep going.'

'Brenda's right, the car won't make it.'

Freddie pointed the gun at Andy. 'You better make sure it makes it.'

Brenda's piercing scream rang in Freddie's ears. The minute Andy saw the gun at the side of his head he began to shout in panic, swerving all over the road dangerously.

'Oh my God. Oh my God. Oh my God.'

'Calm down for fuck's sake.' The combination of the screams,

219

the shouts and the noisy engine made it impossible for anyone to hear Freddie. He took a deep breath and followed it by a loud bellow. 'Stop.' The car screeched to a halt.

Hitting his head on the back of the seat, Freddie glared at Andy waving his gun in his face. 'What the fuck are you doing?'

'You said stop.'

'Stop shouting, not stop the fucking car. Move it.'

'The engine's stalled.'

'Oh Jesus, get out. Get the fuck out. I'll drive.' Freddie pushed open the passenger door, running round to the driver's seat; almost dragging Andy out. Getting into the front seat, Freddie looked up and saw they were in front of a tiny three-way junction.

'Which way Andy?'

'I don't know. I've got a map in the boot though.'

A few seconds of rummaging in the back had Andy jumping back in the car, frantically poring over the map. Sweat from his forehead dripped down, spotting it with dark smudges.

'For goodness' sake, you've got it the wrong way up.' Brenda turned the map round without any warning, and promptly caught Andy's eye with the corner of it.

With one hand held over his watery eye, Andy snapped in annoyance. 'No, you're wrong. It's the other way.' He turned it back round, attempting to straighten out the folds.

'I think you'll find it's not.' Brenda haughtily snatched the map again, spinning it round. It was all too much for Freddie.

'Are you two trying to take the piss?' They stared at him, bewildered. 'Never mind. Never fucking mind.' Freddie glanced at his watch. They needed to hurry. He turned the engine on putting the car into gear. While he was deciding which way to go, he heard a distinctive loud noise, the sound of a helicopter flying overhead. With no hesitation, Freddie wheel skidded the Fiesta straight across the junction and down the hill, following the distinctive grey helicopter.

The car bounced over the cattle grids, slamming down the

suspension. Freddie could still see the helicopter ahead as he glanced up to the sky. He needed to get to the viewpoint as soon as possible. An unauthorised helicopter would certainly bring attention.

Racing down the road, Freddie's heart dropped. From the corner of his eye he saw a white vehicle, then a blue flashing light. Instinct kicked in. He reached over to the dashboard, leaning for his gun, cocking the hammer of the M92 in readiness.

He needed more speed. His foot was right down on the pedal, pressed into the floor, yet he still wasn't able to push the Fiesta past ninety. He could almost feel the police car on his tail. Shit. He had to think, but the noise from the back was beginning to distract him. He quickly glanced round to scream at Andy and Brenda who were in the throes of hysteria,

'Shut up! Unless you want a bullet in your head.' Almost immediately, they fell silent.

With a sudden movement, Freddie veered off the road, onto the bracken-covered moor. In his rear-view mirror he saw the police car furiously reversing back after shooting past. Then a sight he was hoping he wouldn't see. Over the horizon, coming the other way, drenched in sunlight, were three more police vehicles, speeding up the road.

The Fiesta wasn't going to outrun the police cars. The only thing Freddie could do was make a run for it. The viewpoint was just over the other side of the fell.

'Take my phone. Last number. Call it.' Freddie barked the order at Andy.

'Voicemail. It's just gone straight to voicemail.'

'Fuck. Ok, find the name, *Eddie*. Call it.'

Andy's fingers fumbled with the phone. 'It's ringing.'

'Put it to my ear.' Freddie anxiously looked in the driver's mirror. He could feel the wheels of the car getting stuck in the ground and he pulled the Fiesta up, grabbing the phone from Andy. Freddie opened the door and jumped out, taking a quick glance round, trying to judge the distance between him and the police. Then he began to leg it.

Running with the gun in one hand and the phone in the other, Freddie stumbled over the heather. He had to talk to someone; this might be his last chance. He could see the helicopter four hundred meters in front but the police were gaining.

Freddie could feel the tightness in his lungs as he ran. He was panting hard and it felt like he could hardly breathe. He heard the click of the phone. 'Ed! It's Freddie, listen to me. Don't say anything. Tash never turned up. I need you to sort it . . . Whatever happens, sort it.'

Without cutting off the phone, Freddie shoved the phone in his pocket as he tried to speed up. He ran, turning and shooting blindly behind him. Two hundred meters. He wasn't going to make it. One hundred meters. He could see the helicopter just in front, hovering a couple of feet above the ground.

Glancing round, Freddie could see the police had fallen back after the shots were fired. Only another fifty meters. He pushed forward but as he did, he felt himself start to lose his balance. His foot landed in a hole, sending him sidewards, tumbling on to his side. He hit the ground, losing the grip on the gun, but pulled himself up quickly, running faster than he'd ever run before. The two policemen almost now catching back up with him.

The pain in Freddie's chest was almost unbearable as he struggled for breath. The spinning helicopter blades muffled out all sounds.

'Take my hand boss!' one of Freddie's men yelled, reaching out his hand as the helicopter began to rise into the air. Freddie grabbed on. For a moment, he thought he was going to be pulled in two as his men held onto his arms and two police officers held on to his legs. He heard shots being fired and a moment later the grip on his legs were released.

Freddie was pulled into the helicopter on his stomach as it soared above the moors. He sat up, watching as the figures below got smaller and smaller until they became small dots. He leant back, his eyes closed but there was no relief. Tasha had betrayed him and the only thing Freddie Thompson felt was hate. Pure, revengeful, hatred.

Eddie clicked off the phone.

'Who was that Ed?'

He gazed at the woman and sighed. He looked at her tits, her curvaceous body, her red puckered lips and his wasted erection. Getting off the bed without saying anything, he started to get dressed. Heading for the door, Eddie decided Freddie owed him big time.

28

Eddie Davidson couldn't have been more pissed-off if he tried. He was frustrated for a few reasons. One, he hadn't had the shag he'd so carefully lined up. Two, he hadn't been able to track Tasha down, and three, unless he was being paranoid, it seemed every television channel had his face on it.

The problem was, to find Tasha he had to start speaking to people. And speaking to people meant the likelihood of being caught was ever more present.

He had a lot of time for Freddie. Owed him a lot and his loyalty to him never came into dispute. But it didn't stop Eddie wanting to wring his neck at this moment. By rights he should be tucked up in bed getting his balls sucked by a Tom, whilst another sat on his face. Instead, he was being Freddie's foot-soldier, something he'd never signed up for. Then again, who did sign up with Freddie? Freddie was the type of man who *told* you what to do and there was never any question of not doing it, unless of course you wanted to end up bobbing in the Thames.

He'd been looking forward to getting back to London. The north had never been his bag. Come to think of it, he couldn't actually think of a place where he'd ever felt at home, apart from the streets of Soho.

He had a mate in Portugal who ran a bar. The idea of going over there had briefly passed through his mind, but the idea of spending the rest of his days in the sun and not waking each day to the grimy smells, sounds and sights of London was more than he could bear the thought of. And even if it meant having to look over his shoulder for the rest of his life, he was more than willing to take the chance if it meant being able to have a cup of Rosie Lee in Lola's Cafe on Berwick Street.

However, he was now stuck with his nose to the ground, still up north looking for Tash, who no doubt was blanketed up with some geezer. Eddie sighed and rubbed his balls. They were aching. He had to try to stop thinking about getting laid. It really wasn't helping.

Freddie had told him to sort it. And Eddie knew exactly what that meant. It was a shame really; Tasha was one of the good ones. It was still hard to believe that she'd betrayed Freddie. He would never have thought it of her, other than the fact Tash was a woman. No matter how well you thought you knew them, eventually they'd screw you over.

When he'd been working for Freddie full time, Tash had always looked out for him. She'd opened her house and made him feel welcome. And although it'd been her personal chef who'd cooked the meals and the maid who'd made up the bed for him when he'd needed to crash out, it'd been Tash who'd made him feel he was part of something special.

Eddie never had a family himself and it hadn't really bothered him. He didn't know who his mum and dad were, and he was more than happy for it to stay like that. How he saw it was they didn't owe him anything and he didn't owe them. Like everything in his life, he'd just got on with it.

He'd been dumped in a children's home when he'd been six

months old and left when he was sixteen. The closest he'd got to family besides Tasha and Freddie had been his missus, until he'd caught her with the next-door neighbour's cock in her mouth. And he'd dealt with it the only way he knew how. An axe in her head.

The psychiatrist who did a probation report told the court he had all the classic signs of betrayal bond and abandonment syndrome. Both diagnoses Eddie had found to be utter bullshit. He didn't know one man who wouldn't have done the same if they'd found their other half with a face full of hairy balls.

Crouching down behind the car park wall, Eddie kept his eyes on the receptionist of the hotel Tash had been staying at. She was the person he needed to talk to, though from what he could see of her she looked like she had her finger tightly up her arse. Getting information out of her might prove tricky. There was only one thing for it. The Eddie Davidson charm.

The receptionist rummaged in her bag to find some change.

'Here you go, get yourself a cup of tea.' Eddie looked at her in bewilderment as she tried to give him a handful of coppers. The cheeky cow thought he was a tramp. How on earth she could mistake him for one, Eddie didn't know. Okay, maybe he hadn't slept as much as he'd liked to have done, and the copious amount of cocaine he'd taken to keep him awake hadn't done his skin any favours. But a tramp? She was having a giggle.

He was wearing some pukka designer gear which he'd got off the doc who'd sorted his arm out so it couldn't be the clothes. Perhaps it was the glasses he was wearing; making him look like a numpty. But better a numpty than being caught. It was amazing how something so simple could disguise who he was and take away his handsome looks.

Eddie decided perhaps a little bit more was needed, aside from charm alone. 'I ain't no tramp darling, but I appreciate the gesture. Nice to see a woman with a heart for once.' Eddie smiled his best smile, breathing his stale breath all over the woman.

'You know you shouldn't be here. This is private property.'

'I know but I'm trying to find somebody. An old friend.'

'Then what are you doing in a car park? I doubt you'd find him here.'

'Her. She's a her.'

'Well whatever, but as I say, you need to leave, otherwise I'll have no choice but to phone security.'

He'd been right. She was a haughty cow.

'She's been staying in your hotel. I haven't seen her and I'm a bit worried.'

'I can't possibly divulge guest information sir.'

'No?' Eddie went into his pocket and pulled out a wad of fifty-pound notes. He saw the receptionist licking her lips as if about to taste something nice.

'This might change your mind.'

Looking left to right, the receptionist's face took on a softer appearance. 'Not here. There's a pub two streets away called The Oceania; I'll meet you there in fifteen minutes.'

Money talked. It always had, and as far as Eddie could see, it always would.

'So what happened to not divulging guest information?'

The receptionist looked flustered as she took a sip of her house white wine.

'I'm only trying to help. If you think it's about the money; it's not. I just don't like the idea of someone not being able to find their friend.'

'Well if that's the case, you won't want paying.'

Eddie thought the woman was going to choke. She spluttered her mouthful of wine on her chin and on the table as her cheeks turned red.

'I didn't say that . . . I . . .'

Seeing Eddie laughing at her, the receptionist stood up, affronted.

'Listen, I don't have to take this from you and I don't have to help.'

'Sit down darling, we both know what you want, so less of the performance.'

'I won't be made fun of.'

'I'm sorry, okay? How does that suit you?'

'I suppose.'

Eddie rolled his eyes. The one good thing about being inside was it had meant he hadn't had to deal with the female of the species.

'Tasha Thompson. She's a guest of yours.'

'Yes, I know her. The police came wanting to talk to her. You're not the police are you?'

Eddie scrunched up his face. He preferred to be called a tramp than the Old Bill. 'Don't insult me darling.'

'Why do you want her?'

'I'm asking the questions. When was the last time you saw her?'

'The other day.'

'Don't you find that peculiar?'

'No. She's a long-term guest which means she's paid three months in advance, so what she does or doesn't do is no concern of ours. She's free to come and go as she pleases. It's a hotel, not a prison.'

The mention of the word prison had Eddie squirming in his seat. 'Okay, but have you any idea where she was going the last time you saw her?'

'No.'

'You're not being very helpful for someone who wants to earn a few bob.'

'All I know is the last time I saw her she said she was going to the hospital and then cancelled her lunch and then something about a man called Arnold.'

Eddie sat up. This was the sort of information he wanted to hear, though he didn't expect Freddie did. 'Arnold?'

'Yes.'

This was becoming hard work now. 'Who's Arnold?'

'Her boyfriend I think, or he *was*. I used to see him about a lot. Tall, very good looking, but quiet. Anyhow, he stayed over a few times. It's really against hotel policy but as she was a long-term guest the hotel chose to turn a blind eye. I can't remember when it was but he started calling several times a day. Could have been as many as twenty times.'

'He was psycho dialling?'

'Well I wouldn't put it like that, but it was lots of times. She wouldn't take his calls and then she asked me not to take any messages. She even wanted me to tell him she'd checked out.'

'How did he feel about that?'

'I don't know because he hasn't phoned back. I'm glad really. I'm not really good at lying.'

'No, I'm sure you're not darling.'

The receptionist cut a look at Eddie, wondering if he was being sarcastic or not, but he held his face steady, not giving away any clues. Still unsure, the woman carried on.

'Anyhow that's all I know.'

'What was this Arnold's last name?'

'I don't know, like I say sir it's a . . .'

'Hotel not a prison. I know, I know. There must be something else.'

'No. If you like I can call Pete.'

'Who the hell's Pete?'

'The hotel car park manager. He keeps records for a month of

229

all the car registration plates. He should have Arnold's. I know Mrs Thompson asked for a permit a couple of times for him to be able to park.'

Eddie's face lit up. Bingo. 'You, my darling, have earned every penny.'

29

Tasha Thompson stared in dread. She'd watched as Arnie had sat in the corner rocking, muttering numbers under his breath. He'd been sitting there for what seemed like an eternity but according to the clock on the wall it'd only been just over an hour. She'd also watched as he'd switched between crying and rage. Head buried in his hands one minute, shouting and waving his hands around the next. And now, to Tasha's horror, he was starting to sing. A song about her. Or who he thought she was. A song about Izzy.

'Izzy sweet, Izzy mild, Izzy sweet my little . . .'

'Stop! Stop . . . I'm Tasha. Arnie, it's me.'

Arnold looked at Tasha, his eyes red and puffy from crying. He crawled across to her on his hands and knees, gazing up into her face curiously.

'Don't you like it? Don't you like my song?' He reached out and touched her leg. Immediately Tasha recoiled, slamming her back into the wall, pressing herself as far away from him as she could.

'Please, Arnie. You've got the wrong person. I don't know who this Izzy is. I swear. Just let me go . . . please.'

The thunderous bellow made Tasha freeze.

'Why do you keep saying that to me Izzy? Why are you teasing me? Stop playing games with me.' Arnie's eyes flashed in anger, his pupils hugely dilated. He put his hands over his face and sat motionless on the floor.

His fingers started to spread open, stretching across his face and exposing his eyes through the gaps. 'Peek-a-boo. I can see you!' High-pitched laughter exploded from Arnie. A second later, Tasha burst into tears.

Arnie reached up, grabbing hold of Tasha who was violently trembling.

'I'm sorry Izzy. I'm so sorry. I didn't mean to frighten you. I didn't mean to shout. Say you'll forgive me.' He smiled at her and carefully placed the restraint over her mouth again.

He stared at her for a minute, transfixed, then leapt up from the floor, sitting next to Tasha on the tiny sofa bed. He began to stroke her hair. Whispering quietly, he nuzzled his head into her neck as she sat shivering naked.

'It just makes it so hard for me; for us, when you play the pretend game Izzy. It spoils what we need to do, especially as today is our special day.' Tasha's body didn't move, only her eyes, looking down at the knife Arnie held in his hand.

The intensity was broken by Arnie bounding up from the bed. He ran across to his CD player and pressed play. Tasha watched in horror. This was worse than him screaming at her. He was acting as if nothing was wrong.

'I think this is the best version of the song, don't you?' He smiled warmly, shuffling his feet to the sound of 'Feels Like I'm in Love' by Kelly Marie.

'Oh this is the part; this part's my favourite.' Arnie giggled as he sang out the chorus in a low droning voice. He was about to launch into the next verse when he looked across at Tasha. He stopped as he noticed for the first time the tears running down her face.

'Whatever's the matter baby?'

He went over to her, bending down to Tasha's eye level, with the music still on full blast. He saw she was still shaking.

'Sorry, my darling, you're cold. I always presume everyone's as warm as I am. Maybe if you danced, it would warm you up. Come on, dance.'

Arnold pulled Tasha up, dragging her off the bed as he swayed vigorously in time with the music, moving from one foot to another as the CD player looped Kelly Marie to play again.

As he pulled her, holding her tightly against his body, Arnie could feel she was tugging at her ropes on her hand. Holding her at arm's length, he could see the restraint was keeping her quiet but she was still crying and he could see the mucus coming down her nose, leaving bubbles on the front of the home-made leather gag.

He really had no idea what the matter could be, but then Izzy had always been prone to tantrums. Silly little Izzy; forever wanting her own way, but he didn't love her any less.

'Are you trying to dance Isobel? That's it, move side to side to the beat.'

Arnold watched proudly as Tasha's body shook. She wasn't quite in time with the music but enough for him to see she was really trying; not everyone had rhythm like he did he supposed, although he knew better than to say anything; he didn't want her any more upset than she was already was.

The only thing which would probably cheer her up was what they'd both been waiting for. He smiled as he hugged her hard, making sure he didn't cut his fingers on the knife.

Freddie sat on the top deck of the private yacht, watching as the light bounced and reflected off the sea, shimmering like precious stones. He hadn't moved since this morning. He was too afraid to, certain that if he did take his eyes from the rippling sea he might never recover.

He needed to wait for this feeling to pass. For the rage, unlike any anger he'd ever experienced before, to leave him. Though he didn't know how long the wait would be; it could be a day, a week or even a year of sitting, staring at the sea.

But he would wait as long as it took. After all, time was what he had plenty of.

Moment by moment, minute by minute. Anything to get him through. The only way he knew he'd stop staring at the sea was when he got the news from Eddie. The call to tell him that Tasha, his dear beloved betraying bitch of a wife, was face down in a shallow grave.

30

Eddie put down the phone and laughed. It was easier than taking a piss. Whoever this guy was that Tasha had been shagging, he certainly didn't seem to mind who knew about it. Pete the car park attendant had come up trumps.

When he'd passed on the car plate number to one of his contacts to find out who it belonged to, he'd half-expected it to be registered to somebody's pet fish. Instead, he'd just been informed of the address and date of birth of one Arnold Wainwright. Eddie smiled, thinking that he'd probably get that shag with the tom sooner than he expected.

Sitting outside the flats in his car, Eddie shook his head again. It was almost as if Tasha wanted Freddie to find out what she was up to. He knew it couldn't be the case though; she, more than anyone else, knew what her husband was capable of and what he would do if he even suspected her of cheating. Putting on his black leather gloves, Eddie took a deep breath before getting out of the car. It really was a shame. He'd liked Tasha a lot.

The stairwell smelt of bleach, reminding Eddie of the children's home in Mile End where he'd spent three miserable years. Taking in the doors, he saw they all had spy holes. For all he knew, the neighbours could be spying on him now. He wasn't sure how he was going to play this. Knocking would bring unwanted attention, as would booting the door in. Shit. He was worrying too much. As long as he got out and back to London without being caught, that was really all that mattered. He didn't know why Johno wasn't doing all this, but he knew it wouldn't do to ask questions.

Eddie made sure the corridor was clear before he stepped on to Arnold's landing. He walked along, listening at the different doors for people talking, until he came to the right one. He was going to make this as painless as possible. Well, for Tasha anyway.

He'd sort out the geezer first then get Tasha out of there, before taking her away to sort her out too. He hoped he wouldn't crash in to find Tasha naked with the guy. He wasn't sure if he could take that.

'Hello? Are you lost?'

Eddie had his foot raised in mid-air, about to kick down the front door. He froze and turned to see a slippery looking man standing next to him.

'Can I help you?'

'Yes mate, you can do one. Get lost.'

'I suggest you leave before I call the police.'

Usually Eddie would've baited the man some more, not giving a shit if the boys in blue turned up or not. Things were different now however, and he certainly didn't have an ego so big it wouldn't allow him to back down.

Trying a new tactic, Eddie grinned, lowering his leg as he did so.

'Sorry mate. I didn't mean to be rude; I'm just a bit tense. I'm looking for the missus. Found out she's cheating on me. Broke my heart it has. I'm not looking for trouble.'

Eddie saw the man's face turn into a veil of curiosity.

'I'm sorry to hear that. May I ask who you're looking for? Perhaps I could help.'

It took Eddie all his willpower not to sneer at the man. He was like a woman, hungry for gossip, with his eyes lighting up for information.

'No, it's fine. I'd rather sort it myself.'

'I see you've hurt your arm. Is it broken?'

Eddie looked down at the cast on his forearm. He'd been lucky it hadn't been his shoulder which had been broken, only dislocated. Though it'd been excruciatingly painful when they'd popped it back in. One of his contacts who'd been a doctor in his time had done the handy work for him. It still hurt like fuck but at least now it had a chance of healing.

'Yes, I did it playing rugby.'

The man nodded, then looked at Eddie's hands. 'Aren't they hot in the gloves?'

'I have psoriasis. I prefer to keep them covered.'

Again the man nodded, taking in and seemingly analysing the information. 'Was it Arnold you were looking for? I'm his next-door neighbour. He doesn't seem the type to mess around with other people's wives. Nice man.'

'Sorry to break the news to you but your nice man is the very same one who's shagging me wife.'

It was almost like a light had gone off in the man's head. He spoke in a rush, full of excitement.

'It all makes sense now. Why Arnold was calling her Izzy. I fell for it completely. Called her Izzy myself, but it was only when she let slip her name was Tasha I thought something was strange. When I asked him, he swore it was Izzy. Covering up you see; didn't want anyone to find out. Well I never. Arnold, the old devil.'

'Now you know, I hope you can just let me get on with it.'

'Oh no. I can't possibly let you kick down the door. I'm on the housing committee you see. I cover for the caretaker when he's away.'

'Well, I won't tell if you won't.' Eddie leered at the man, who backed off feeling slightly threatened.

'I really think you should knock don't you?'

'And I really think . . .' Eddie stopped himself and remembered the magic word. Money. He went into his pocket and pulled out the wad of fifty-pound notes which were rapidly disappearing. He started peeling them off, seeing the greed in the man's eyes.

'So, how about you didn't ever see me? You didn't see and you won't hear anything in the next ten minutes. Do you think you can do that?'

The man didn't say anything. He didn't need to. Eddie watched him hurrying back into his flat, holding tightly on to the money.

Eddie waited for a couple of minutes. The neighbour had given him pause for thought. He couldn't now go the whole way with this Arnold geezer.

It was one thing for the next-door neighbour to keep his mouth clamped about a few slaps to Arnold's face, but a different one to keep his mouth shut for murder. A change of plan was needed. He'd give the guy a few kicks to give him a warning, then he and Tasha would get out of there. He'd deal with her in private. He didn't think Freddie would have a problem with the new plan. After all, he knew it was Tasha he wanted sorted; anything else was only a bonus.

Eddie raised his foot once more in readiness. He savoured the moment. It was the best part. The quiet, before the fucking storm.

'See Izzy, you don't need these on if you're going to behave, it was only ever for your own good you know.' Arnie smiled as he untied Tasha's wrists after taking off her gag. 'That's better, now we can have fun. I know you've been looking forward to it as much as I have.' He smiled in contentment, heading towards the bathroom.

The crash of the front door caving in had Tasha screaming for a moment until she saw who it was, making her blood run cold. Arnie jumped in fright, his face drained with shock.

Eddie stormed in, shouting and kicking at the side of the wall. He grabbed hold of Arnie, shaking him viciously, before head-butting him, his nose exploding into a fountain of blood.

'You're lucky mate; you're not really the one Freddie's pissed off with, otherwise you'd be pushing up daisies. So do yourself a favour and keep it closed.' Eddie slapped Arnie hard, using the knuckledusters he was wearing over his gloves to do most of the damage. The metal sank into Arnie's cheek and he stumbled towards the side, knocking the lamp over.

'Get your fucking clothes on Tash, we're going.'

Tasha stood up, she blinked but didn't move.

'I said put your fucking clothes on.'

Eddie could see Tasha was in shock to see him. He looked round and saw her clothes meticulously folded up in the corner of the room. He grabbed them, throwing them at her.

'Hurry the fuck up, Tash.' As he waited he saw Arnold moving to get up but he pushed him back down with his foot.

'Don't bother mate, not if you want to ever wake up again.' Eddie turned angrily to Tasha, when he saw she still wasn't moving or bothering to get dressed, but was just staring at Arnold who had curled up into a ball, whimpering. He grabbed her arm at the same time as throwing her shirt over her. 'I said, put them on. It's no good eyeballing loverboy over there. It don't look to me like he's going to be doing you any good.'

'Izzy, please don't leave me.'

Eddie jumped on Arnie's fingers, hearing the crack. 'I said, shut the fuck up.'

Seeing Tash had at least got her trousers on, he dragged her out by the arm, ignoring Arnie's cries.

'What do you expect me to do Tash? Go on, tell me. Just tell me what I'm supposed to do.' Eddie stared at Tasha a few hours later as they stood in the countryside above Bradford. He was finding this harder than he imagined, especially as she was trying to tell him some story about the fella. But then from his own experience he knew women would tell you anything to get out of shit.

'I expect you to listen Ed.'

'I ain't got time to listen darling. Freddie didn't ask me to hear some *Jackanory*. You knew the score babe.'

Tasha's voice was pleading. 'Ed, I ain't saying what I did was right. But what you saw just now, well it wasn't what you thought it was.'

'You don't even want to know the last time I heard some woman tell me that Tash.'

Tasha shook her head, trying to keep her composure, but she could hear the hint of hysteria coming into her voice. 'I ain't Nora, Ed. Please Ed. I ain't your wife babe. I know how she treated you, we all did.'

'But none of you thought to tell me?'

'Look . . . I dunno, maybe we should've done it differently, and I'm sorry, but it's hard to tell someone their missus is bringing half a dozen men home to shag each week.'

'So what's the difference between you and her?'

Tasha's eyes implored him, needing him to believe her. 'You've got to believe this is the first time I've ever done anything like this to Freddie, and unlike Nora, I didn't do it to hurt him. I never even slept with him darling. Ask Linda if you don't believe me.'

'Linda? You're having a bubble ain't you Tash? Your sister would swear the day was twenty-five hours long if it meant sticking up for you.'

Tasha fought back the tears. 'I'm telling the truth.'

'I don't think it matters to Freddie one way or another if you slept with him or not, do you? All that matters to him is you never turned up because you were shacked up with another fella.'

'I was all ready to come to him. I'd gone to tell Arnie it was over because he wouldn't leave it. You know me Ed, I ain't ever turned anyone over in me life. As much as I'm pissed with Freddie, I'd never wish bad for him.'

Eddie stared at Tasha. She seemed so sincere. Unlike his wife, no one ever had anything bad to say about her. Hell, it didn't matter what he thought or didn't. Freddie wanted it sorted, and that's what he was here to do.

'He was going to kill me.'

'Now you're talking fucking shit. I can believe it when you say you didn't have any intention of hurting Freddie; I can even believe it you never actually got boned by that geezer. But him wanting to kill you? I ain't buying it Tash. Didn't you see the way he was blubbering in the corner? He makes a postage stamp look hard.'

Tasha began to cry. 'You saved my life Ed.'

'Yeah, and now I'm about to take it away.'

Eddie walked up to Tasha, ignoring the fear in her eyes. He pulled out the gun from his pocket.

'On your knees Tash.' He pushed her down. It surprised him she wasn't begging for her life like he'd seen a lot of men do. He was surprisingly touched by her dignity. Her voice was a whisper.

'Tell Ray-Ray . . . tell him I love him, and tell Freddie, well, just tell him I never wanted to hurt him.'

Eddie pushed the gun into the back of her head. His finger trembled as he began to pull back on the trigger. Pull it. He just needed to pull it.

'Fuck!' He let out a shout as he fired the gun into the air. 'I can't do it. Shit Tasha, I can't fucking do it.'

Eddie stood with the gun pointing into the air. He reached down and gently touched the top of Tasha's head with his other hand. Tasha turned slowly round. She was shaking and tears of pure relief ran down her face. It was a few minutes before she said anything.

'Thank you Eddie.'

Eddie gave a wry smile. 'You won't be thanking me when Johno catches up with us both.'

Tasha looked at him, confused. 'Why didn't you do it Ed?'

Eddie stared at her then quietly said, 'Because you're family. As near to family as I'll ever get and I never knew it meant anything

241

until now. I love you, you dozy cow. I love all of you.' Eddie turned away rubbing his head, the gun still in his hand.

He felt Tasha's hand touch his shoulder gently. She leaned up and kissed him on his cheek. 'If it matters any, the feeling's mutual Ed. I love you too you donkey.'

Eddie walked towards the car. He didn't want Tasha to see him choked up. It was the first time in his life anybody had said they loved him.

Back in the car, Tasha and Eddie sat in silence, both looking out on to the rolling barren landscape, contemplating their next move. Opening the window to smoke a cigarette, Eddie talked, sounding slightly absentminded. 'Thing is now Tash, we've got to work out what we're going to tell Freddie.'

'You worried?'

'I ain't going to lie to you honey. I'm shitting fucking boulders.'

'You mean bricks?'

'No babes. When it comes to Freddie, you know as well as I do that shitting bricks just ain't enough.' They both laughed before falling into silence again.

'I need to use your phone Ed.'

'What for?'

'To call the police.'

Eddie sprang backwards as if he'd just been burnt. 'You are clowning me?'

'No. I need to make a call about Arnie.'

Eddie sighed. 'Listen babe. We sort things out ourselves. You know that.'

'I know, but not this. This is different. *Please*. When I get me head round it, I'll tell you about it.' Tasha swivelled round to face Eddie, her face drawn with anguish.

Eddie studied Tasha's face. The whole thing was beyond him. 'No, Tash. I don't know what's going on babe. It's bad enough I'm going to have to make some story up to feed to Freddie. So please

242

Tash, leave me out of anything else. I don't want to know. Don't tell me nothing. If you care for me at all, at least do that for me.'

Eddie blew smoke out of the window before shaking his head and passing the phone to Tasha. She stepped out of the car to make the call.

31

'Women's problems?' Johno stared at Eddie as he spoke.

'Yeah, women's problems.'

'What the fuck are women's problems?'

'How the fuck do I know?'

'So why didn't you ask her?'

'What the hell difference does it make what's wrong with her fanny? It's women's problems.'

'So you're trying to tell me her fanny stopped her being able to meet Freddie?'

'Yeah, exactly.'

'I ain't buying it Ed.'

'It don't matter if you do or not, you ain't a gynaecologist are you?'

'So you saw it?'

'Of course I didn't see her fanny, what do you take me for?'

'I meant her doctor. Did you see him?'

'Yeah, I saw her in hospital and spoke to him.'

'But I only spoke to her the other night. She seemed perfectly fine to me.'

Eddie opened his arms in a huge gesture. 'What can I say? That's women's problems for you. Just happens when you least expect it.'

'Are you taking the piss Ed?'

'No. I'm just uncomfortable talking about Freddie's wife like this. Call me old-fashioned.'

Eddie sat, holding Johno's gaze, feeling the sweat dripping down his back. Johno had always been suspicious, especially when it came to him.

When he and Tasha had been brainstorming what they were going to tell Freddie and Johno, it'd been Tash who'd come up with the idea. He hadn't questioned her about it. It'd sounded convincing at the time. But as he sat there opposite Johno and some of Freddie's other heavies, he wished he'd asked Tasha slightly more about it.

'Here Johno, I managed to get her report from the hospital. Odd or not, Tash is telling the truth.'

Eddie passed the report over and watched whilst Johno studied it. What the hell he was studying it for, Eddie didn't have a clue.

'Seems in order.' Eddie had to bite down on his lip to stop laughing. At times Johno was the biggest bullshitter he knew.

Eddie had got his doctor mate to write a report, which had cost him a monkey, but he guessed it was worth it. He stood up and walked towards the door, picking up his jacket. He turned to Johno as he spoke.

'Eddie, Freddie appreciates your loyalty. He understands you put your freedom on the line to sort it out for him.'

'So is that it?'

'Yeah.'

'So can I tell Tasha that she'll be okay?'

'I'll have to run it by Freddie, but as far as I'm concerned she will be.'

'Well?' Tasha grabbed hold of Eddie's sleeve the moment he got back in the car. He gazed at her and smiled.

'Well it looks like you're in the clear.' Eddie laughed as Tasha hugged him in excitement. It was such a relief. It meant she could live her life without always looking over her shoulder. It meant Linda would be safe and it meant for the time being at least she was going to see another day.

Eddie gently pulled her off him.

'Listen Tash. I need you to promise me you ain't ever going to talk about what really happened. Not even to Linda. Christ, especially not to Linda. I put my neck on the block for you babe. Don't let me down and I don't want us to ever discuss it again. Is that clear?'

'Crystal babe. I promise, on me life.'

Eddie turned to look at Tash, cocking his head to one side.

'Now I need you to do one other thing for me. You need to tell me something.'

'Anything darling.'

'Please explain to me what the fuck women's problems are.'

'Women's problems?' Freddie stared at Roger as he sat on the deck of the yacht anchored a couple of miles from the coast of Marbella. 'What the fuck are women's problems?'

'Beats me boss. It's just the message Johno asked me to pass on to you. He's seen the hospital reports; seems it's all pukka.'

Freddie shook his head. 'I can't get me head around it. I don't understand.'

'Said it's got something to do with her fanny.'

Freddie pushed his glass across the table and glared at Roger. 'That's not what I meant. Talk about my missus like that again, and I'll cut your tongue out.'

Freddie got up and stomped below deck to the master bedroom. Sitting down hard on his bed, he thought about Tasha. This hadn't been the news he'd been expecting. He'd been tense all week, expecting to hear Eddie had dealt with her the way he'd wanted him to. But this? This had well and truly thrown him.

All this time he'd thought she'd been sneaking around behind

246

his back shagging some toerag, but all this time she'd been ill with women's problems, whatever they were. He felt ashamed. He didn't even want to think about what would've happened if Eddie had actually pulled the trigger. Fuck. It was too awful to think about.

That had always been his problem. He'd get a bone between his teeth and wouldn't let it go. Act first, think afterwards. And only thanks to Eddie did he still have his wife. He owed him big time. He'd make sure he was well sorted. But he also owed Tasha big time. What must she think of him? Christ, he hoped she hadn't said anything to Ray-Ray. He knew his son loved him but he also knew if Ray-Ray thought for a minute he'd put a target on his mother, he would never speak to him again.

Freddie rubbed his head. It really was hard to get his bonce round it. It was stupid for him to start to become arsey, pointing out the fact Tash should've told him about her illness. He knew he wasn't the easiest person to talk to and for all he knew she tried to tell him. Freddie would be the first one to admit he didn't do women's talk.

He hoped there was a way Tash could find it in her heart to forgive him. He'd been a mug. Freddie decided that when he actually looked back on it all, he had never really doubted her in the first place. He knew his Tash would never screw him over; it was everyone else who thought she would.

'You all right boss?' Roger knocked, then walked in carrying a glass of bourbon on the rocks for him.

'I'm fine. I want to go back.'

'Back?'

'Yeah, back.'

'But boss, it's too early. It's too dangerous, you'll get caught. The police will be . . .'

Freddie stood up angrily, stopping Roger from saying any more. 'Just sort me out a house for when I'm there. Move Tash and Ray-Ray in, but keep it low-key. I don't want to risk going home,

247

the Old Bill will certainly be watching, but to tell you the truth Roger, the way I'm feeling I wouldn't give a shit if I was caught. Perhaps I deserve that. I'm going to go back to Soho because it's the least I can do. I want to see my son and I need to tell my wife I'm sorry.'

32

Baz Gupta knocked on the door. He narrowed his eyes at the man who was busy peering out of his front door.

'Is everything all right? I'm Arnie's neighbour. If there's some kind of problem maybe I could help.' The gleam of curiosity lit up the man's face, but Baz and the other officers ignored him, much to the man's disappointment.

'Police! Hello? Mr Wainwright?' Baz thumped on the door with the side of his fist. 'Mr Wainwright, open the door, it's the police.'

A minute or so later, Baz heard the door being unbolted. He was taken aback for a moment when a tall, blonde, good-looking man covered with bruises opened the door.

'Arnold Wainwright?'

'Yes, but my friends call me Arnie.'

Baz gave a small frown, then flashed his badge. 'Detective Sergeant Gupta. We've had an anonymous call and I was wondering if I could have a few words?'

Baz glanced to the side, to see that the next-door neighbour had stepped into the corridor to listen.

'Can we come in?'

Arnie's face paled. 'I'd . . . I'd rather you didn't.'

Baz's voice took on a nasty tone. 'And why would that be, *Arnie*?' Before Arnie could reply, Baz, not worried about formal procedure or a search warrant, pushed past, knocking Arnold towards the wall. He strode into the tiny front room, with the other officers following close behind.

Arnold ran forward, dropping to his knees in the front room, desperately trying to pick up the photos which were scattered all over the floor. Baz stepped on his fingers, crunching them to a stop. 'Not so fast Mr Wainwright. What's with the photos?'

Sweat began to drip from Arnie's forehead. His eyes were full of panic as Baz bent down to pick one up. Baz looked at the photo, then at Arnie. 'What happened to your face? Where did you get the bruises from?'

'He got them from Izzy's husband. Bit of a dark horse our Arnold.' The voice came from behind them as Arnie's next-door neighbour walked in through the open door. Delighted all eyes were on him, he continued full of exuberance. 'Bit of a rough sort if you ask me. When I saw him he was all ready to kick down the door. Gave it a good kicking as well. If I hadn't been forceful with him I'm sure he would. There she is. There's Izzy.' Without waiting, the man grabbed hold of the photo in Baz's hand.

Baz, annoyed with the interruption, snatched it back. 'I don't think anyone was talking to you. Now if you don't mind.'

'Oh no I don't mind, all I'm saying is Arnold's the victim here. Broken-hearted, though I don't blame him, she's a bit of a sort.' A lecherous grin appeared on the man's face as he bent down to pick up all the photos of Tasha off the floor.

'Is this true sir?'

'Of course it's . . .'

'I was speaking to Mr Wainwright.' Baz glared at the neighbour who saw the look on his face and decided it was better to say nothing.

'Izzy, perfect Izzy. She said she wouldn't leave me.'

Baz curled his lip as he looked at Arnold distressed on the floor, staring at the photographs. He had no time for pining men. It was nothing short of pathetic.

'Do you mind if we look around? Is this the bathroom?'

Baz walked to the door. Reaching his hand to open it he was shocked to see Arnold spring up, his face contorted with alarm as he threw himself in front of him, knocking Baz's hand off the door. 'No! No . . . you can't go in there.'

Baz stood almost nose to nose with Arnie. 'I think, sir, that it'd be in your best interest to step away from the door.'

Arnie shook his head. 'No, really.'

Anger appeared on Baz's face. 'Move.' He used his forearm to push Arnie out of the way before throwing open the door. He walked in, then froze. Oh Christ. He turned to Arnold, his eyes wide open. 'What the hell?'

'I'm sorry . . .'

'Sorry?'

Arnie put his head down.

'I've got paint all over my shoes and you're sorry? And what the hell are you doing putting paint on your floor?'

'I did try to tell you. I thought the tiles needed a bit of a facelift. The man in the shop said it would dry in twelve hours but it seems he gave me the wrong information.' Arnold smiled sheepishly as Baz scowled and walked back out of the tiny bathroom.

'I've seen enough.'

'You said you'd had a call?'

The tone in Baz's voice was hostile. 'I did. And I've seen everything I need to see.' As an afterthought, Baz added, 'The worst thing the force ever did was to agree to have the anonymous tip-off line. You wouldn't believe the time wasted on following up calls from people who think it's a joke to make up things like this. Some sick individuals out there. Problem is there's no way of finding out who they are.'

Marching towards the door, Baz nodded his head to the other officers, signalling for them to leave.

'20, 18, 5.'

'Excuse me?' Baz spoke with his hand on the front door handle.

'20, 18, 5.'

'What are you talking about?'

'20, 18, 5. Your ring. Twenty diamonds, eighteen emeralds and five rubies. It represents the original Mayan calendar doesn't it? They used base eighteen. Each month contained twenty days and each year contained eighteen months, leaving five days at the end. The belief was these five days held bad luck and were filled with fear.' Arnie smiled holding Baz's glare.

'I'm supposed to be impressed Mr Wainwright? Is that your party trick?'

'Oh no, there are no tricks in numbers detective. They're merely a series of symbols of unique meaning in a fixed order that can be derived by counting. Actually, as unusual as your design is, I've seen a ring just like that one before.'

Baz narrowed his eyes, feeling irritated. 'I don't think so.'

'Oh I have.'

'Like I say, I don't think so.'

'I have.'

'Look, Mr Wainwright, clearly this is an issue for you, so why don't we draw a line under it? Let me explain why I *know* you haven't seen one like this before. It was specially made, so as much as you say you've seen one like this, you haven't.'

Arnold shrugged at Baz as he began to walk out of the flat. 'Perhaps you're right, it wasn't quite the same. The ring this young lady was wearing had five sardonyx stones in the centre, instead of the rubies.'

Arnie paused, seeing Baz freeze, then turn to him.

'"Young lady"?'

'Yes, brown eyes, black hair. Nothing like Izzy at all.'

'Are you sure? How long ago are we talking about?'

Arnold looked at the clock on the wall. 'Twelve days, three hours and twenty-six minutes, give or take a minute or so for my unreliable car clock. She was on her way to London with her friend. Her friend seemed quite excited to see her at the station.'

Arnie smiled again at Baz, who leaned forward, inches away from Arnie's face. With a nasty sneer, he said, 'Tell me, what else did this *young lady* say?'

Arnie sat on the tiny bed in his flat, cradling a photograph carefully in his hand. His fingers moved across the picture of Tasha, tracing her hair, and along her face until finally he circled her lips. She was beautiful. And she was his.

He'd let her down, letting the bad man drag her away from his flat. She still wanted him to be close to her. He could feel it. He was sorry and he needed to tell her he was. Growing up, his father had always told him to apologise; even the times when it wasn't his fault. *'Say you're sorry Arnold. Say it, say it. Bad things happen to boys who don't say sorry.'* But this time he really meant it. He had to go and tell her – and he knew exactly where she might be.

Smiling, Arnie stood up. He opened the bottom drawer of the locker, carefully taking out the jagged-edged Gerber knife, and placing it in his suitcase before heading out the door.

33

'That's it baby, just lie there. Just lie there for Daddy. Feels good huh?'

With a start, Laila woke up, feeling the rough hand of a stranger beginning to explore her body. She sat up with a cry, scrambling to the safety of Yvonne who was asleep on the other side of the bare-floored room.

Bleary-eyed, Yvonne rolled over on the stained mattress.

'What's going on?'

The man stood up unsteadily, his unshaven chin jutting out, elongated in anger. His eyes rolled drunkenly as he began to unzip his trousers which were tight from his bulging erection.

Seeing what was happening, Yvonne's eyes flashed in anger. She got up quickly, facing the man straight on.

'Do one, you little prick.'

The man reached to grab hold of Yvonne, but his actions were awkward and slowed by his intoxicated state. He tumbled forward, stumbling into Laila who squealed, jumping aside.

'Flipping whore. You bitches are all the same.'

In disgust, Yvonne looked down at the man who was attempting to pull himself up. With a smile she glanced at Laila. 'Come on, let's get out of here.'

*   *   *

Outside the squat, Yvonne leant on the wall and lit a cigarette, drawing deeply on it. Going into her bag she pulled out a bottle of vodka. Unscrewing the red top she handed it to Laila. 'Here, get this down you. It'll take some of that tension out of you.'

'No thanks.'

Yvonne shrugged. 'Okay. Suit yourself.'

After a couple of swigs, Yvonne tucked the bottle in her bag again. She looked at Laila who was swinging her legs as she sat on the other end of the wall. 'Hey up, my top looks grand on you Laila.' She paused, then added. 'We'll be all right kid. From today there'll be no more dossing in squats. My contact's put me in touch with someone. I've still got most of the two grand so I can pay the first two weeks' rent. Things are going to start looking up.'

Laila began to shake her head as her eyes filled up with tears. 'I don't think I can do this. You're different to me.'

Yvonne's expression hardened. 'How am I different to you Laila?'

'You know, you can do stuff. Stuff with men. It's easy for you. You're used to it.'

'Used to it? Is that what you think?'

Laila shrugged.

'You think I've got used to waking up to find me mum's boyfriend in the same bed as me? Having to fight him off night after night and me mum doing fuck all about it?'

'No, no I didn't . . .'

On a roll, Yvonne interrupted Laila angrily. 'And I suppose because I'm not all prim and proper like you, you think I've got *used* to giving hand jobs in car parks to men old enough to be me granddad, just so I can get enough money to get the hell out of the place I call home?'

Laila looked down, upset at the anger directed towards her but mainly upset for her friend.

'And I tell you something else Laila; I never *want* to get used to it. I never *want* to get used to me skin crawling at the touch of a stranger. 'Cos if I do, if I get used to *that*, it's over. I know there's no chance of getting out.'

'But you had a choice?'

Yvonne threw her cigarette down in exasperation, grinding the sole of her shoe on to the butt. 'That's a matter of opinion. But I know I have a choice in how I see life, and I choose to count myself lucky. You should try it.'

'Lucky? You call being here with you lucky?'

A flash of hurt darted through Yvonne's eyes.

'I didn't mean it like that Yvie, I'm sorry . . .'

Yvonne picked up her bag and stormed down the path, she turned to Laila. 'All I've heard from you since we've arrived in London is you complaining. It's not great I know, but it could be worse. You could be back in Bradford with Baz, or worse still Laila . . . he could've killed you.'

'I just keep thinking maybe it'd be easier back home. Perhaps if I tried harder with him . . .'

Yvonne shook her head. 'Listen to yourself Laila. Nobody can help you if you don't start to help yourself. If you want to go back, go, but you're on your own. I'm through.'

Yvonne marched along the street wanting to get away from Laila, to stop her seeing the tears in her eyes. It took Laila only a few minutes before she began to run after her friend.

'Yvonne . . . wait! Yvonne, I'm sorry!' Yvonne carried on walking and it took Laila an energetic run to catch up with her. 'Please, stop!'

Yvonne came to an abrupt halt. Choosing her words carefully, Laila spoke. 'I'm sorry. I didn't mean to say anything to hurt you. I don't want to go home, I'm just scared. I don't know where I'd be if it wasn't for you. You've done so much . . . you saved my life. Please don't leave me. I've nowhere else to go. I need you to be my friend.'

Yvonne's cheeks pinked. Nobody had ever said they needed her before. Her tone was soft as she spoke to Laila. 'I know it isn't easy for you, and I promise I'll do everything I can to look after you, but I need you to help me too Laila. I need you to *try*. Just try. Do you think you can do that?'

Laila nodded her head and a moment later the two friends embraced in the middle of Lewisham High Street, giving each other a much-needed hug. Feeling slightly daft and pulling away, Yvonne grinned at Laila. 'Right then, we better get a move on.'

'Where we going?'

'Going to meet a fella in Soho. His name's Johno Porter; my contact says he'll sort us out.'

Johno Porter went into his pocket to get out a packet of cigarettes. He passed one to Yvonne as he talked. 'Rent by the end of the week. Rule one is, I don't want trouble. Rule two, no working the streets. There'll be other girls sharing the main rooms with you, but you'll have your own bedroom. You'll also share the maid, who'll be my eyes and ears. Sometimes I'll need you to do some work for me.'

Yvonne's eyes narrowed as she looked at Johno. Her contact had told her that as pimps went, he was one of the better ones. Working for Johno meant they could rent rooms from him both to work and live in. They were clean, secure and most importantly they were safe. 'What kind of work?'

'Parties, special clients. Problem with that?'

'No. But it'll only be me who does that. She doesn't.' Yvonne nodded to Laila who was standing on the pavement outside the walk-up in Greek Street.

'What? Is her pussy made out of gold? Does she think she's too good to be a whore? Because if it looks like one, smells like one and moves like one, then in my experience, it is one.'

'Leave her be.'

Johno snarled, taken aback by the front of this Northern girl. 'I'd watch your mouth if I was you.'

Yvonne wanted to tell Johno where to stick it. Instead, she just lit up, blowing the smoke out and into the path of a passing stranger. Johno eyeballed Yvonne, who matched his stare and held it as long as he did. It was Johno who gave in first, begrudgingly respecting the feistiness of Yvonne.

'Fine. What's her name anyway?'

Yvonne's mind went blank, before saying the first name which came into her mind. 'Janie. Her name's Janie.'

34

Ray-Ray Thompson stood in his mum's bedroom looking into the mirror. He never knew why he looked; the despair he felt never waned when he saw his reflection. It was as if a tiny part of him hoped that when he looked, his face wouldn't be so scarred, so disfigured. But of course it always was, and each time his circle of misery began all over again. As he stood staring, Laila came into his thoughts, but he pushed her away. Not wanting to see her beautiful face in his mind. Not wanting to remember how she made him feel. Not wanting to remember what the nurse had said.

He'd become a person of the night, rarely adventuring out during the day. The stares, the looks, the comments from passing strangers had made him feel ashamed of who he was. If he'd wanted to, he could do as his father had always done and resort to violence at every comment and sly gaze he got, but where did it stop? He'd end up having to spend his days fighting and already he was tired. Sometimes, even too tired to get up in the morning. So instead of going out during the day he found it easier to sit with the toms, the boozers and the lost souls of the night in one of his father's clubs. Seen, but left alone.

'All right babe? We're going out. Let me have a look at you.' Tasha came into the room followed by her sister, Linda. Tash walked up to him and stroked his face. Ray-Ray never knew if she touched his face to help her come to terms with the way he looked, or if it was to help *him* come to terms with it, showing him there was at least one person who was still willing to touch him. Either way it made him feel uncomfortable and the pity in her eyes when she looked at him always made him pull away.

Ray-Ray held Tasha's wrists gently, pulling her hands away from his face. 'Don't Mum. Please.'

'Babe, I want to.'

'And I don't *want* you to.'

'What you need is a good woman, she'll sort you out.'

Ray-Ray's smile faded, and seeing it disappear, Tasha knew straight away she'd made a mistake saying such a stupid comment to her son. She reached out to him, but he turned away from her. 'Ray-Ray.'

His tone was hard when he answered. 'Don't apologise. It only makes it worse.'

'Stop making out you're some sort of monster, darling.'

Ray-Ray raised his voice. 'Look at me. Just look at me. Would you want to be with someone who looked like me? Well, would you?'

'Ray-Ray, please.'

'No, don't fucking Ray-Ray me. Answer the question.'

'Darling, you're an incredible person. A girl would be lucky to have someone like you, ain't that right Linda?'

Ray-Ray banged his fist on the side table. 'You still ain't answered me.'

Tasha shook her head, wiping away the tears which were already pouring down her face. 'Don't do this to yourself babe.'

Ray-Ray walked back across to his mother. He pulled her to him, putting his face close to hers. 'Look at it, look at it properly and then tell me it's the face someone would want to wake up and see each morning. Tell her Auntie Linda, *tell* her. I want to hear her tell me the truth. I'm sick of hearing her crap. Tell me what you see when you look at me? What would you see if I was a stranger to you?'

Linda walked between the two of them, looking hesitantly at Tasha then back at Ray-Ray. The tension he was holding in his shoulders was let go and his whole body stooped in weariness as he listened to his auntie talk.

'I'm not going to lie to you darling; you ain't no oil painting, but that don't matter. I believe there's a special somebody for everyone and that special somebody will be able to see beyond the scars on your face.'

'What the bleeding hell is going on? I could hear raised voices from outside. I felt right at home.'

Freddie Thompson stood in the door grinning. Tasha blanched whilst Ray-Ray ran up to his dad to give him a hug.

'Dad, it's good to see you. I didn't know you were coming.'

'That was the plan, can't have the Old Bill knowing I'm here. Alright Lind?' Freddie smiled at Linda then winked at his son but avoided looking directly into his face, unwilling to look at the damage. He bent round to look at Tasha. 'Ain't I even going to get a hello?'

'Hello Freddie.'

'You could try looking pleased to see me.'

Linda looked at Ray-Ray, knowing it was their cue to leave. A moment later, Freddie stood alone opposite Tasha. She looked good, but then she always did.

'It's good to be back Tash; you're looking well.'

Tasha said nothing and Freddie could sense the tension. Hating his wife's silence, he tried to push the conversation further.

'You okay?'

'You're taking a risk coming back here, but yeah, I'm as good as can be expected.'

Freddie worked hard to keep the defensiveness out of his voice. 'What do you mean by that?'

Tasha turned to face Freddie. 'You should've warned me you

were coming home. I'm just supposed to smile and put up with it?'

'I need to warn my own wife her husband's coming home?'

'I was getting used to being on me own.'

Freddie was surprised how hurt he felt by Tasha's words but he still kept control over his emotions, talking quietly, but aware he was gripping the door handle.

'Then babe, you'll have to get un-used to being on your own, cos I'm here to stay.'

'Not in here you're not.'

'Excuse me?'

'You heard Freddie. I'm not sharing a bed with you. I'll share the house, but for the time being, that's all.'

It was too much for him. Freddie lost it and exploded, standing up in pent-up frustration.

'There's someone else ain't there? This is what it's all about.'

Tasha ran across the room in anger and threw a pillow at Freddie which missed but landed on the vase of roses, knocking them everywhere.

'You see that's it. *This* is the problem, right here. The reason I can't just pick up from where we left off. You ain't changed Freddie; but I have darling, and shouting at me as if you've got a nasty case of constipation certainly won't work.'

'Okay, I'm sorry. I'm a jealous man but I've got reason to be; look at you, you're beautiful.'

'Oh turn it in Freddie. I ain't the schoolgirl you met in the club. It's not about your jealousy anyway.'

Freddie looked at Tasha, full of sincerity. 'Is it women's problems?'

Tasha didn't know whether to laugh or cry. She raised her eyebrows as well as her voice. 'Women's problems?'

'Yeah, I thought you might have them.'

'No it's fucking not. My problem, Freddie, is with you.'

'I've only just walked through the door, what have I done?'

'You can honestly stand there and look me in the face wondering what you've done?'

Freddie pulled a baffled face. 'Yeah.'

'You asked somebody to *kill me* Freddie. To take me up to the moors and put a bullet in my head.'

'Oh, that.'

Tasha brought her hand back and slapped Freddie across the face. The first time she'd ever done it. He looked at her, not quite knowing how to react.

'Yes, *that* Freddie. Did it just slip your mind darling? Did it slip your mind you got someone to make me kneel down as they put a gun to the back of me head?'

'I didn't know he was going to do that.'

'Well what did you think he was going to do? How else would you have wanted him to kill me? Did you think about Ray-Ray in all this? And what he would've done without me? No, you didn't, because you're a selfish bastard Freddie Thompson. I don't even know if I love you any more. And another thing, hell would have to freeze over before I shared a bed with a man who wanted me dead.'

'All right son? How you doing mate?' Freddie sat down next to Ray-Ray, picking up the other controller of the PlayStation. He clicked to join the game and began to start shooting, staring at the screen, almost on autopilot. 'You won't beat me. I was D-wing's reigning champion.'

'I think I've put enough hours in myself as it happens.'

There was a pause before Freddie said anything else.

'Your mum told me you never go out, or only at night.'

'I'm surprised she talked to you long enough to tell you that.' Freddie grinned as he blew up one of the enemy soldiers.

'Yeah well, she did. That and throw a pillow at me, telling me what a useless husband I've been.'

Ray-Ray spoke seriously but there was no maliciousness to his voice. 'Well you have, haven't you?'

Freddie smiled. 'I expect my son to back me up, not stick another bleeding knife in.'

'Just telling you the truth Dad. She's hurt; she hasn't told me why, but I know Mum.'

Freddie glanced at Ray-Ray, regretting it immediately as he was shot down and lost another life on the game. He had to respect Tasha for not saying anything. She would've known as much as he did how much it would've irrevocably damaged his and Ray-Ray's relationship if his son ever found out he'd put a hit on her. A lot of women he knew would've been chomping at the bit to tell all, so it was really fair play to Tasha. 'She told me she didn't love me.'

'Have you ever told her you do?'

'She knows I love her.'

'How?'

'Because she wants for bleeding nothing.'

'For women it ain't enough. They want to hear it.'

'You something of an expert?'

'What do you think Dad?'

Freddie put his controller down. 'I'm sorry. It was a stupid thing for me to say. If only you could try to remember who did this to you. One of them hypnotherapists or shit might work.'

'Dad, I don't want to go through this again. I don't remember. Just leave it. I have.'

'But I can't leave it. I don't want to. It eats me up inside to think the person who did this to you is still whistling down the wind. Christ, Ray-Ray, don't you want revenge?'

'No, I don't.'

'Why not?' Freddie said disbelievingly. 'Look at you!'

Ray-Ray got up from his chair. His tone levelled with the icy glare his father was giving him. 'Yeah, look at me. *Me*, Dad, not you. My face, my problem, my revenge.'

'Why are you so flipping stubborn? I sprung out for you.'

'No, you did it for you. You just went ahead and did what felt right for you. I didn't want you to.'

'You aren't thinking straight. You don't know what you want.'

Ray-Ray's voice was loud and he could feel the pain in his eye from where his blocked tear ducts were trying to cry.

'Why can't you respect me enough to listen to me? Don't you think I haven't agonised over it? Don't you think when I look in the mirror I don't want to do the same to them as they did to me?'

'Them, you said *them*.' Ray-Ray turned away but Freddie grabbed him. 'You know who it is, don't you? Look at me son.'

'Leave it Dad, just fucking leave it.'

'Tell me. Tell me who it is. Why won't you tell me? Did they threaten you? Is that it? Did they say they'd do something to me? Are you trying to protect me? Whoever it is, I ain't scared of no one.'

'Will you listen to yourself? Why does it have to be about you? Maybe it's about me, maybe it's about somebody else.'

'Tell me then. Please tell me.'

Freddie's eyes filled up with the tears Ray-Ray couldn't shed. Ray-Ray went towards his father, putting his arms round his dad. 'You've got to let it go Dad. For me, let it go.'

Freddie choked back the tears. 'I don't know how to son. It eats me up and I know your mother blames me.'

'It ain't your fault Dad.'

'Maybe I could've protected you. If I hadn't sent you up to Bradford; if I hadn't done the deal with the Keenan brothers from South London, or even the deal I did with the Turks.'

'Stop, Dad, stop. I want you to listen to me, you're not to blame.'

'How do you know? How do you know it wasn't someone wanting to hurt me by hurting you? I just can't live with myself son, it's doing me nut in.'

'I promise you it's not your fault – because I know exactly whose it is.'

An hour later, Freddie sat in his front room with Johno. What Ray-Ray had said was still playing on his mind; in truth it was gnawing at him, but for the time being he wanted to try to focus on other things. Things which he was sure would make Ray-Ray feel better.

'I want to give him his confidence back. I reckon he needs some fun.'

'Who?'

'Ray-Ray. I want you to organise a party. Booze and birds. White, black, S&M, threesomes, twins. The whole lot. I want to give him a party he'll never forget.'

35

His elation made his cappuccino taste even sweeter, though it could also have been the excessive amount of chocolate he'd got the waitress to sprinkle on top of it.

Arnie stood on the doorstep of the large white London house and rang the bell. He looked round and smiled. He had come to London especially to be with her. Bradford was nothing without her. He was so close he could almost smell her. The door opened and a woman answered. 'Yes?'

'I'm here to see Izzy.'

'You've got the wrong house mate. There's no Izzy here.'

Arnie frowned as Linda gave the once over to the incredibly handsome man standing on the doorstep.

'I'm certain this is the one.'

'Afraid not, never heard of her. Now if you don't mind, I'm busy.' The door slammed shut, leaving Arnie perplexed. He was sure this was the right house. Perhaps the woman was wrong; she hadn't been very helpful, in fact she'd been verging on rude.

Another frown appeared on Arnie's face as another thought came into his head. Perhaps the woman had been lying and Izzy *was* in there after all but just didn't want to see him after he'd let her down? Contemplating this, Arnold slowly walked away, putting his hand in his pocket and feeling the sharpness of the jagged-edged knife.

Eddie Davidson pushed his body against the wall as he was about to turn the corner. It couldn't be, could it? A minute later he craned his neck round to make sure his eyes weren't deceiving him. The sunglasses he had to wear indoors or outdoors to stop him being recognised weren't helping, but he was certain. What the hell was Tasha's ex-boyfriend doing not only in London but outside her house? More importantly, what the hell was he going to do about it?

Eddie felt like a muppet. Though it wasn't a new feeling. He'd felt like that ever since he'd been on the run and had to walk around in shades and a hat looking like something from a bad seventies' detective movie. He'd dyed his hair but it still looked like him, only with a different colour barnet, so he had no option but to wear a stupid disguise. And standing outside the block of flats – where he'd followed Tasha's ex to, trying to look discreet – was turning out to be harder than he thought. He had no idea the man had moved down to London, but then why would he? It wasn't as if Tasha would tell him. This was her dirty little secret.

The concierge had come out twice already and now this third time he was actually speaking to him. 'Can I help you sir, you look a bit lost.'

'I ain't lost; I'm waiting for someone. I couldn't come in and wait could I?'

'I'm sorry. Residents or guests with residents only.'

'Do you want me to say the magic word?'

The concierge looked haughtily at Eddie. 'I really *don't* think saying please will make a difference sir.'

Eddie went into his pocket, pulling out some fifties, and pushed a dozen or so into the concierge's hand, whose eyes lit up. 'But I guess it depends on what *sort* of please it is.' Eddie gave a wry smile. The magic word worked every time.

* * *

Inside the flats, Eddie whistled to himself. They'd only just been built and the spec was higher than the one Freddie had put him up in, and that was saying something. Black marble covered the floor and the walls. Red roses sat on mirrored tables. Chandeliers hung from the ceilings and a sweet smell of orange blossom hung in the air. The man must have a bit of dough tucked away unless of course Tasha was footing the bill for him.

The corridor was clear. Eddie put his head on the door to see if he could hear anyone. Nothing. Without hesitation, he used the electronic door pick he'd acquired from Bobby, Johno's cousin, to undo the lock and enter the flat.

The moment he entered, Eddie could hear the shower running. He took the opportunity to have a quick look around. As he did, he began to think and the more he thought about it, the clearer it became to him. Tasha and this fella hadn't ever really finished in the first place. He wasn't so much of her ex as her current. She obviously hadn't been able to live without him and had brought him down to London to be near her.

How Tasha thought she could get away with it he didn't know, especially as Johno had given him the nod to tell him Freddie was back in the country and hoping to start again with Tash.

Oddly, Tasha's betrayal, even though it wasn't directed towards him, hurt Eddie. More so than Nora's betrayal had. Perhaps it was the lies, or maybe even the fact he'd put his neck on the block for Tasha, going against Freddie's orders. Whatever the reason, it cut deeply. Thankfully he wasn't a fool to it any longer, and Tasha Thompson would regret trying to dupe him.

Opening the drawers, Eddie found nothing of interest. The closet was the same. Though for a runt like Arnie, he was surprised to see the stash of knives he kept. It was a shame the bloke hadn't tried to use them in Bradford, instead of rocking in the corner like some kind of basket case. It might even have made Eddie have something resembling respect for him.

'Well, well, well.' Eddie spoke out loud to himself, belatedly clocking the fact he sounded too much like a policeman for his liking. He studied the contents of the large beige envelope, his eyes opening wider with each document he looked at. Photos. Paperwork and a few letters. There was certainly more to this fella than he thought. Folding up the envelope and stuffing it in his inside jacket pocket, Eddie sat at the table and waited.

'Hello son, remember me?' Eddie grinned his best smile; part sneer, part menace and amusement, as Arnold walked out of the bathroom, wrapped only in his towel. Arnie froze and turned to run back through the door, but the sound of the trigger made him freeze. 'Oh I don't think it would be wise to run, mate. I never did like shooting anyone in the back.'

Eddie laughed as Arnie turned round in what seemed like slow motion. He was as he remembered him to be; a fucking coward. Eddie could see the colour drain from the man's face.

'I don't know if you're a fool, or just like being damaged mate, but I know you ain't brave. I wonder if Tasha knows what a pussy she got together with?'

For the first time, Arnie spoke, although it was barely audible. 'Who's Tasha?'

'Now I know *you're* a fool but worse still, you think *I* am too.'

Eddie got up from the leather chair. He backslapped Arnie with the butt of the gun, wiping off the blood which splattered from Arnie's mouth onto his face. Eddie yelled, towering over Arnold, who lay stunned on the floor. 'I told you didn't I? I warned you mate. Stay away. Clearly I never did a good enough job of it, cos you're here.'

Eddie booted Arnie in the ribs, bringing his foot down again and again. 'I don't want to damage you too much because then how are you going to walk away? So count yourself fucking lucky geeze, cos I'm giving you a day to disappear. If you haven't gone by then, I'm going to do the job for you. I'll make you disappear permanently.'

Giving Arnold one last kick in the head, Eddie left, feeling like it was a job well done.

Arnie hugged his knees, his head tucked down into them as he laid tightly curled up on the floor. He heard the passing traffic outside, the shouts of children, the noise of a plane flying above and the people in the corridor outside coming and going.

After a long time, finally he sat up slowly, wincing at the pain of his injuries. The man had come back. The bad man from before; but this time it was going to be different. This time Arnold wouldn't let him take Izzy – because this time he was going to make sure she was safe.

36

'Get up; I've got a job for you.' Johno shouted at the top of his voice, amused at Yvonne's groaning under the cover. 'I said, get up.'

'Do you have to shout Johno? My head's thumping.'

'Who's shouting darling?'

'You are. Now please shut the fuck up.'

Johno scowled. He barely knew this girl and she was already crossing the line when it came to the way she spoke to him. He walked into the tiny galley kitchen, coming back with a glass of water.

'Hey! What the hell did you do that for?' Yvonne leapt out of bed, her hair dripping wet. She stared at Johno who was grinning, an empty glass in his hand.

'I was just about to get up.'

'And you babe, are a mouthy cow. Keep it zipped and maybe you won't need a glass of water poured over you to keep yourself cool.'

Yvonne got up and went to pour herself a drink. It wasn't even midday, but she needed the hair of the dog to help her get through it. A large whiskey was poured to the top of the glass, some posh stuff she'd never heard of that belonged to one of the other girls. She drank it and immediately poured herself another one. Too smooth for her liking. She liked to feel like she was drinking something. What was the point in alcohol if you couldn't taste it?

'What's the urgency anyway?'

'I've got a job for you. A nice little earner for you and Janie.'

'Look I told you, *I'm* fine about it but not Janie. That was the deal.'

Johno leaned forward. 'You don't get to make the deals.'

Yvonne decided that backing down might be the better option this time. She softened her voice, trying a different tact.

'I'm not trying to Johno. She's just not ready. Give her time.'

Johno sniffed. 'Fine, but make sure you're here tonight. I'll tell you all you need to know when I come and pick you up. Here, I want you to wear this.'

Yvonne held up the dress. It was a beautiful cream Stella McCartney dress cut on the bias, with a waterfall neckline giving it the feel of a vintage twenties dress.

'Crikey, this is a bit of all right.' She put it down on the bed, turning to Johno with a slight look of apprehension on her face. 'It ain't nothing weird is it? I'm not into any weird stuff.'

'No, don't worry it ain't. Not in the way you're thinking anyway.'

Yvonne's face brightened. 'Nice one. Cheers Johno. What time will you pick me up then?'

'Eleven – and make sure you're ready, Yvonne. I don't want any fuck ups.'

'And you can do one too.' Yvonne screamed as loud as she could as she stumbled backwards out of the Archer Street bar in Soho. Her feet were hurting her and her head was spinning. She bent down and took off her shoes, walking along the filthy pavements in her bare feet. She was tired, and she was supposed to be doing this special job for Johno. She hadn't meant to drink so much, but then she *never* meant to drink so much. She really needed to go home and make sure Laila was all right. She also needed to

273

get ready, but all she really wanted to do was to go to bed. Perhaps if she had another pick-me-up drink then she'd feel more up to it. Deciding it was a good idea, Yvonne stumbled along Shaftesbury Avenue.

Walking into Layman's Pub on Brewer Street, Yvonne headed straight to the bar. There were two men in the far corner. They looked like they had a bit of money. Well, enough money to buy her a drink. She moved towards them. The taller one spoke to her immediately.

'All right beautiful?' He spoke with an accent she couldn't place.

Yvonne's face crinkled up and she didn't bother trying to disguise it. 'I know you're not talking to me.'

'There's no one else here who's making my heart skip a beat.'

Yvonne snorted with laughter at the tall sinewy stranger who'd stood up from the bar stool to stand beside her.

'You seriously use that line? Take it from me chuck, it won't get the girls running to share the sheets with you.'

'What will?'

Yvonne licked her lips. Perhaps she could get this one in the bag. 'Money.'

'How about I get you a drink and we can discuss it further? What's your poison?'

'Double brandy please.'

Taking the drink off the man, Yvonne knocked it back in one. The man laughed. 'Looks like you're thirsty. Another?'

'Don't mind if I do.'

The man grinned, waving the barman to pour another, and turned to Yvonne who was rocking gently back and forth, a glazed expression on her face.

'So why don't we talk about what we were saying earlier?'

'You'll have to remind me, that brandy's gone straight to me head.'

'I was asking how much?'

'For what?'

'How much do you charge?'

Yvonne smirked, remembering the conversation again. He wasn't bad looking and it'd mean money towards the rent. 'A ton for full sex. Twenty-five for a hand job. Oh and I don't do bareback.'

'Sounds wonderful babe. Or it would do if you weren't nicked. I'm arresting you on suspicion of soliciting. You do not have to say anything but it may harm your defence if you do not . . .'

Yvonne rolled her eyes. 'Just do me a favour pal and put the handcuffs on.'

'Where the fuck is she?' Johno stared at Laila, his eyes dark and full of hostility. He looked round the bedroom, pulling sheets off the bed, as if she'd magically appear from beneath them.

'I don't know.'

'What do you mean you don't know?'

'I don't. She said she was popping out to do something.'

'Do what?'

'I don't know.'

'Fuck me, why do I bother with whores? You lot are more trouble than they're worth. Try calling her.'

'I did. Her phone's off.'

'Well try again then. Fuck me, don't bother. Don't bother. Give it me here.'

Johno snatched the mobile and pressed last number redial. It went straight to voicemail but it didn't deter Johno from leaving a message.

'I hope you get this fucking message because it's the last fucking message you'll ever hear if you don't get your arse back here, now.'

Johno threw the phone down. As he did he got a glimpse of the Stella McCartney dress he'd given Yvonne earlier. 'She's not even pissing changed. You'll just have to do it.'

'Pardon?'

'I said you'll have to do it.'

Fear ran up and down Laila's body. 'What . . . what do you want me to do?'

'Stop flipping asking me questions for a start.'

'But . . .'

'Oh listen, don't think I'm happy about this either. Just put the dress on and I'll tell you the rest in the car.'

'So you understand what you have to do? There'll be other girls there as well. And when you go in I want you to go and look like you're having fun.' Johno sat in his Mercedes, rubbing his head. This girl seemed to be as much use as a nun on a stag night.

Freddie had asked for the party to be full of girls, which had been easy to arrange – they had enough working for them – but he'd also asked for a fresh, drug-free girl which was harder said than done. Most of the girls who worked for them were up to their eyeballs, so Yvonne had been perfect; but thanks to her disappearing act he had no other choice but to take this girl.

'I'll go across and talk to him first, then afterwards I want you to go and talk to him like we discussed. Make it as natural as you can Janie. Make out you like him.'

'What if I don't like him?' Laila's eyes were wide with terror.

'Give me bleeding strength. The magic word is *pretend*. Janie, just *pretend*. And it don't matter if you do or not. *You understand me?*' Johno's words sounded menacing at the end.

'Yes, but . . .'

Johno put his fingers on her mouth. 'Janie, will you do me a favour?'

'Yes.'

'Shut the fuck up.'

Johno locked the car and started to walk across the car park with Laila, noticing how beautiful she looked. Only on occasion did he ever sample the goods. It wasn't his style to mix business with pleasure. But looking at her in the cream dress, the way it fitted

276

over her curves, tonight might well be the occasion he did a bit of sampling.

Once at the back door of The Tash club in Hanover Square – the club owned by Freddie and named after his wife – Johno looked at his phone to see if Yvonne had called. She hadn't. He pursed his lips. When he saw her, he was going to show her what happened when she let him down.

'You ready?'

Laila could feel herself shaking, though she wasn't sure if it was the late September night or the fear of what she was about to face which was making her do so. She was petrified. Without Yvonne she felt lost. She was also worried about her.

When Yvonne hadn't answered the phone, the thought had passed through Laila's mind that Yvonne had left her, and it'd taken every ounce of strength not to fall apart and run. But once the initial panic had gone, Laila remembered her friend's words. *'I need you to help me too, Laila. I need you to try. Just try.'* And that's what she was doing, but it didn't stop her being terrified.

'Johno, I won't have to sleep with him, will I?'

'You'll do whatever it takes and whatever he wants.'

'I can't.'

Johno held her shoulders, not too tightly, but tight enough to let her know he wasn't messing about.

'That shit don't work with me sweetheart. Whether you want to fuck someone or not, it's irrelevant now. Thanks to Yvonne, you're going to be thrown in at the deep end babes. She well and truly stitched me up and I don't take kindly to anyone doing that to me; especially not a bleeding tom. If you want to make sure your friend stays alive to see the light of day, you'll do whatever it takes.'

Montague's private club was full to capacity. The music was pumping and the deep bass vibrated through the guests. Multi-coloured lights flashed and the atmosphere was filled with people having a good time. The four red velvet decorated rooms held London's top faces, pimps, hookers and the Thompsons' close and trusted friends. When there wasn't a private party it was a popular hangout for the rich who didn't want to mix with the famous; a discreet, members only club charging a one-off fee of twenty thousand pounds a year.

Champagne only came by the Cristal bottle and whiskey only came by the single malt. All in all it was more than a nice little earner for Freddie. There was never any trouble, they all seemed too busy losing thousands at the casino table or paying the toms to share their Bolivian cocaine to care.

It was midnight and Ray-Ray sat reluctantly at the party his father was throwing for him. He hadn't wanted the party at all but his father had insisted, and Ray-Ray had seen how important it was to Freddie. So he'd eventually agreed, not wanting to disappoint his dad by refusing to come.

Freddie had decided not to make an appearance himself, thinking it safer, not wanting the whole of Soho to know he was back in the UK, after all he was still a wanted man.

As he sat in the corner, Ray-Ray thought about the conversation he'd had the day before with Freddie. It'd been a bit of a shock to the system seeing his father so upset. His mum, yes, he was used to that, but his father, never. He hadn't realised he blamed himself for the attack on Ray's face. He'd always assumed it was the Freddie Thompson ego going into overdrive that made him seek revenge for his wronged son. But what he'd seen yesterday hadn't been ego; it was just a father loving a son.

'Alright Ray-Ray. How's things?' Ray-Ray looked up to see Johno standing by the side of him.

'Good, thanks.'

'Enjoying yourself? Your Dad wanted you to have a good time.'

Ray-Ray nodded, not wanting to tell Johno he'd rather be anywhere but here.

'That's my boy; I'll get a drink sent over.' He tapped him on his shoulder as he walked off across to the bar, giving a wink as a signal.

'Hi, do you mind if I sit here?' Ray-Ray didn't turn his head to the question. He wasn't taking much notice. He was too busy watching Alfie Jennings, one of the biggest Soho gangsters, trying it on with a woman half his age. 'Yeah, sure.'

'My name's Janie.'

Ray-Ray looked at the woman. In the strobe lighting, he saw the recoil of horror in her eyes as he turned and she saw his scarred face. He froze for a split second as he stared into her face, then sprang back from his chair, instinctively covering his face with one hand.

He pushed back into the wall, knocking the small table over as he tried to disappear into the darkness of the club. The glasses smashed to the floor. The people in the room turned to stare at him as he ran, making his way through the small crowd, knocking blindly into the customers as he sought sanctuary in the toilets.

'No! No! No!' Ray-Ray's voice shouted out in distress in the quiet of the bathroom as he leant against the sink. He looked up to see his reflection in the mirror. With a swing of his hand he smashed his fist into the glass, hitting it so hard shards of glass stuck in his fingers. He turned to the second mirror, smashing it with the same vigour, leaving smears of blood on the cracked glass. He turned to the last mirror, a tall mirror hanging on the end wall and ran into it, smashing into pieces what he saw staring back. Exhausted, he slid down the wall and let out a deep low painful cry.

'You all right Ray-Ray?' Johno's voice was filled with shock as he was greeted by the scene in the gents. Ray-Ray was crouched on the floor, blood oozing from his head and hand, glass spread all around the tiled room. Johno walked over to him, hearing the crunching glass under his feet.

'You need to get that seen to; it looks like you'll need stitches.'

279

'Get out! Get out!'

'Ray-Ray, mate, listen.'

'I said get out! Now!' Ray-Ray shrieked at him.

'Okay, okay. I'm going.'

Ray-Ray didn't move as Johno walked out. He stared at the ceiling, remembering the way she'd looked at him. Remembering the way Laila Khan had just stared at him, the disgust and terror on her face clear to see.

'What did you say? What did you fucking say to him?' Johno shook Laila in the now-emptied club. Her fear was apparent. 'I . . . I didn't.'

'You must have said something.'

'I didn't, I swear, I just told him my name. That's all I said.'

Johno raised his voice up a notch. 'I don't fucking believe you.'

'Please Johno, you're hurting me.'

'This is nothing compared to what will happen when I find out what you said. Now get in the fucking car.'

Johno stomped off, leaving Laila standing in the middle of the room, unaware she was being watched by Ray-Ray.

37

Yvonne sat in the tiny police cell, drinking a tepid cup of coffee. Her head was clearing, leaving her with a nasty headache, though she knew it was the least of her worries after letting Johno down. She'd been a stupid cow and gone against all the basic rules. Written and unwritten. It was the first lesson of anyone who worked the street. Don't talk specifics. Don't talk about money. Yvonne took another gulp of the coffee and knew she'd made a huge mistake.

The door opened and the man who'd arrested her, along with the other man she'd seen in the pub, walked in. The arresting officer sat down, pulling up his chair and throwing a brown file on the table, along with an envelope of money. Yvonne's eyes widened. She'd forgotten she'd had that in her bag. Shit.

The officer leaned over to put his gum in the bin.

'Feeling better?'

'Piss off.'

'Now you tell me how being rude is going to help anyone.'

Yvonne closed her eyes for a moment. She couldn't believe what an absolute idiot she'd been. 'Have you got a cigarette?'

'You need one?'

'Yeah.'

'That's a shame, because the answer's no.'

Yvonne curled her lip. 'You're one flipping muppet.'

'Let's talk about this.' The officer pushed the clear bag forward containing the white envelope. 'There's a lot of money there. Nearly two thousand pounds. Where did you get it from?'

'I saved it. It's mine.'

'And perhaps you'd like to tell us where exactly you saved it *from*?'

Yvonne said nothing, chewing the inside of her mouth.

'You know what I think? I think you stole it.'

'I didn't!'

'So it's money you've earned soliciting? Money for your pimp?'

'No.'

'We're not getting very far are we? I tell you what I'm going to do for you. I'm going to let you off with a caution, but until you can come up with a proper reason and proof this money's yours, I'm afraid we're going to confiscate it.'

It was a couple of hours later before Yvonne Scott was cautioned and released from the police station in Savile Row. The sun was high in the sky and Yvonne was beyond the stage of being tired. She walked slowly back towards Soho, angry at herself for messing up. Her mind was racing. How was she supposed to pay Johno his rent now? He wouldn't think twice of throwing them out on the street and then where would they be? The idea of sleeping rough was bad enough, but the idea of telling Laila, who she'd promised to look after, was ten times worse.

Up in the walkway, Yvonne walked straight into the back room where she knew Laila would be. She froze as she saw her friend. 'Oh my God Laila, what happened?'

She ran over to her, touching Laila's swollen lip.

282

'Who did this to you?'

Laila shook her head as Yvonne held her, rocking her gently. 'Tell me? I'll deal with them, or maybe we can get Johno to.'

With big wide eyes, Laila spoke. 'It *was* Johno.'

'Why? Why did he do it?'

'The job you were supposed to do, I had to do it instead.'

'Oh God, I'm so sorry Laila.'

Laila shook her head, determined to be strong for her friend. 'No, it's not your fault. I went to the club with Johno, everything seemed fine and then it all went wrong.'

'How?'

'I don't know. I didn't say anything, only my name.'

'You didn't say your *real* name, did you?'

Laila smiled warmly at Yvonne, touched by how worried she was. She knew she couldn't afford to be traced, and it was for this reason they could only work for cash, fearing that all it would take was a search of a police computer by Baz to find them. And the idea of him coming to look for her was not only terrifying but never far away from Laila's thoughts.

'Of course I didn't say my name; even I'm not that naive.'

'Who was he?'

'I don't know. It was strange though Yvie . . .'

Before she could finish her sentence, Johno stormed in. 'Where the fuck were you?' he shouted, pushing Laila out of the way. 'I had to take *her* along instead. A fucking disaster.'

'Please, not now Johno.'

Johno Porter turned red with rage. He pulled Yvonne up by her hair, shaking her at the same time.

'Don't "not now" me! I was looking for you. You were supposed to do this job and little Miss No Sex over there became little Miss Big Mouth and put a bomb under the whole evening. Fucked everything up. I want to know what *you* were doing.'

'Leave her alone,' Laila shouted as she ran up to Johno, trying to pull his hands off Yvonne's hair. A quick backhand had her sprawling across the floor. Yvonne bit down on Johno's hand to distract him from going after Laila. He let go with a yell.

'You cunt.'

Johno held his hand as Yvonne grabbed Laila, shoving her out of the door, out of harm's way.

Yvonne closed the door and turned to Johno who had recovered and was steaming towards her, fist clenched.

'I wasn't doing anything. You want the truth; I got mugged. Ended up in A&E with a slight concussion.'

Johno's fist froze in the air. He pushed his nose to Yvonne's. 'If you're lying to me . . .'

'I'm not, I swear on me nan's grave. God rest her soul. I'm really sorry for letting you down.'

Johno let Yvonne go, moving back to sit down on the arm of the couch.

'Don't think I'm just letting this go; Janie messed up big time.'

Yvonne raised her eyebrows, amazed. 'Who is this guy?'

'Remind me, when did whores turn into Jeremy Paxman? Stop asking questions. Anyway, I need my rent.'

'Can you wait Johno?'

'No, I want it now.'

'I haven't got it. When I was mugged they took my purse.'

Johno raised his voice again, flinging all the things on top of the table on to the floor. 'You've lost my fucking rent money? You're taking the piss now Yvonne. I want my money and I want it now. You've got till tomorrow night.'

'What a flipping disaster.' Tasha glared at her sister as they stood outside Ray-Ray's locked bedroom door.

'And you saying that is helping how, Linda?'

'I'm just saying.'

Tasha gritted her teeth; she was furious with herself for letting Freddie go ahead with the party. She'd known it was a bad idea. 'Then don't. Flipping don't.'

Tasha knocked on the door again, pressing her head, hoping she'd hear something, even a stir coming from inside. 'Baby, answer the door. Honey, tell me what happened.' There was nothing. No reply. No sound at all.

Freddie walked along the long marbled corridor towards the two women. 'Johno told me what happened. I'm sorry.'

'Sorry?'

'Yes, Tash, sorry. I thought it would be good for him. I was only trying to make him happy. I messed up and I'm gutted.'

Tasha looked at her husband. This wasn't the Freddie she knew. There was a softness to him; a softness she hadn't seen for a long time, maybe even since before they were married. Her defence went down slightly. 'I don't know what to do. Maybe I should've gone along to the party.'

'He's a big boy and he'll come round. Our son's a fighter, he always was, takes after his mum I reckon.' Freddie winked at Tasha and Linda smiled to herself, watching the exchange between them.

'Do you want me to try Tash? See if he'll talk to me?'

'Would you?'

'Of course.' Freddie reached into his pocket and pulled out a rolled-up bundle of fifty-pound notes. He placed it in Tasha's hand.

'Why don't you and Lind go and treat yourself, buy yourself something nice? Do what women do.'

'I don't know, maybe I should stay here.'

Linda interjected. 'Er, hello? You may not know, but I bleeding do. I'm never one to turn me nose up at splashing the cash. Come on girl, they'll be fine. Leave them to it.' Tash smiled as Linda scurried off. She went to follow her but was pulled back by Freddie.

'Tash . . .' Freddie faltered, unable to say what he felt. Instead he smiled, bent down his six foot three frame and kissed Tasha on the top of her head.

*   *   *

285

'Ray-Ray, open the door mate. Your mum's gone.' There was still no sound. Freddie knocked again blowing his cheeks out in exasperation. He took a quick glance down the corridor making sure Tasha had left. Pulling out a gun from his jacket pocket, he aimed at the lock, fired and blew the door open. Worked every time.

'Only me, son.' Freddie walked into the bedroom, smirking, feeling pretty pleased with himself. Ray-Ray got off his bed.

'Why the hell did you have to shoot the damn door off?'

'You weren't going to open it were you?'

'Get out Dad.'

Freddie pleaded with him. 'Please son.'

Angrily, Ray-Ray shouted at his dad. 'Is that what you think of me? Do you think the only way for me to get a woman is to pay them?'

'It wasn't like that son.'

'Well, what was it like? Tell me what it was like.'

The curtains were closed in the room but Freddie could still see the blood coming through the jumper Ray-Ray had used to bandage his hand. Freddie's tone was light as he spoke.

'Do you know how many people I've put in the ground for talking to me like that?'

'It's all a joke to you.'

'I ain't laughing son.'

'Just go.'

'You'll have to make me – and don't forget who's the one with the gun in his hand.'

Freddie thought he saw a small smile from Ray-Ray. He sat on the end of the bed, slipping slightly on the silk sheets.

'Tell me what happened son. You frightened everyone. Smashing the place up like that. He won't admit it, but I reckon you frightened Johno as well.' Freddie put his hand on Ray-Ray's back and was surprised he didn't move away.

'I missed you Dad.'

Freddie's voice caught in his throat as he struggled with his emotions. 'I'm here now son. I'm back now.'

'She was a whore wasn't she?'

'Yeah, they all were, you know that. She was one of our new girls. What did she say Ray-Ray? What did she say to upset you? I'm going to send Johno round later to deal with her.'

'No! Don't.' Ray-Ray stared at his father. 'Promise me you won't let anyone lay their hands on her.'

'Easy son.'

'Promise me, Dad.'

'Okay, I swear.'

They both fell silent again. Freddie, uncomfortable with any emotional situation, broke the quiet. 'You still haven't told me what she said.'

'It wasn't what she said. It was how she looked at me . . . it was what she *was*.'

'She was a hooker, so what?'

'I don't mean that.'

'You've lost me now son.'

'Have you ever held onto something, only to discover it ain't what you thought it was? And your life is built on nothing more than a dream and you realise you ain't got nothing at all.'

Freddie looked down, pondering the question his son had just asked him. He looked up to the ceiling. He looked across to the door. Then he went back to staring at the floor, before finally looking at Ray-Ray and answering, 'No.'

Frustrated, Ray-Ray kicked out at his clothes lying on the floor. 'Haven't you ever loved someone and they turned out to be someone different to who you thought they were?'

'I married your mother, didn't I?' Freddie, seeing the tension come back to his son's tone took the joking tone out of his voice. 'What has this got to do with that whore?'

'Don't call her that.'

287

'What do you me want me to call her; a tom? A hooker? A ho? Jesus, Ray-Ray, what do you want me to say?'

'She's got a name.'

Puzzled, Freddie shook his head. 'Okay, okay, so let's call her by her name. What is it?'

'Lai . . . Janie, she said her name was Janie.'

'Okay, so it's Janie. I don't get why Janie's got under your skin so much.'

'She hasn't.'

'Could have fooled me. I don't know why you don't just let Johno sort her out. Hell I'll do it, it'd be my pleasure. I think even your mother would after seeing how upset you are over it.'

'No, I told you.'

'Suit yourself, but the offer's there.'

'What do you know about her?'

'Know about her? You being serious? You think I'd know anything about *her*? Why the fuck would I want to know about a hooker? I don't need to. Men want to fuck them Ray-Ray, they don't want their life story.'

Freddie stood up from the bed. Seeing as you won't go to the hospital, I'm calling Doc to come and sort your hand out. I've got some things to do, so I'm shooting off. I'm meeting my new number man. Going to show him the ropes.'

As Freddie got to the door, he smiled at the sight of the blown-off lock. 'Better send someone round to sort out this door before your mother gets home. I'm trying to get into her good books.'

'I want to see her again.'

'Who?'

'I want to see Janie again.'

Freddie stared at his son. He blinked several times whilst he processed the information. He didn't understand. 'But I thought she'd upset you.'

'Let me worry about that Dad.'

288

Freddie knew not to argue. He was just pleased his son wanted to spread his oats. 'Okay . . . okay, great. I'll let Johno know.'

'But I don't want her knowing anything about me. Not my real name, nothing.'

'Yeah of course, that goes without saying. So you don't have to worry on that score. When do you want to see her again?'

'Tomorrow night.'

38

The next day Yvonne still hadn't found the courage to tell Laila she'd lost the money for the rent or that Johno had given her until today to find it. Sighing, she sat on her bed. Going into her bag for her bottle of vodka, Yvonne stopped as she looked at the piece of paper. She'd forgotten all about it.

She got up to close the door, wanting to make sure no one could hear her. Taking a deep breath, she dialled the number. What other choice did she have?

'Hello?'

'Tariq, it's Yvonne. Tariq?'

Baz Gupta didn't say anything, just clicked off the phone and gritted his teeth. Then he smiled, a cold, dead smile which didn't touch his eyes. The phone immediately rang again but this time Baz didn't answer it. He watched Tariq walk into the room to get his mobile.

'Hello?'

'Tariq, it's Yvonne. I need your help.'

'Hold on, hold on a minute.'

Tariq looked at Baz who stared coldly at him, watching as he walked back out of the room. He brought his voice down to a whisper as he talked. 'Yvonne! Are you all right? Is Laila okay? Thank you for calling.'

Taking a deep breath, Yvonne spoke. 'I need your help.'

'Anything, anything.' Tariq answered with urgency.

'I need some money.'

'Okay, how much are we talking about? Fifty, hundred, two hundred?'

'Two thousand.'

The line went silent for a moment.

'Tariq?'

'Yes, I'm here.'

Yvonne bit her nail nervously. 'If you can't.'

'No, no, I can. Where are you?'

'London.'

'Okay, I can get down to London by early next week.'

Yvonne's panic was clear in her voice. 'Johno's not going to wait for his money till then!'

'Who's Johno?'

'The guy I really don't want to have to tell I haven't got his money.'

Tariq fought the temptation to react to what Yvonne had said about owing a man money. The tension in his voice was clear. '*Fine*. Fine. When do you want me to come down?'

'Tonight.'

Baz stood on the station platform. It was raining but it didn't worry him. He didn't even bother to put his hood up. He wanted to feel it. Wanted to feel every moment.

It was all fitting into place nicely. When Arnold Wainwright had told him he thought Laila had gone to London, it was a lead but not a start. But instead of rushing out to do something, he'd waited. Prayed. And, as good men are, he was rewarded by his belief, and his prayers had been answered. It was only a shame

291

that Mahmood had left for Pakistan last week. Still, Baz was more than capable of dealing with this on his own. In fact, he was looking forward to it.

Baz looked down at his ring. He rubbed it before stepping on to the train, three carriages down from an unaware Tariq. The bitch was in London and his brother-in-law would lead him straight to her.

Pulling up in New Bond Street, Freddie parked Tasha's Bentley on the double yellow lines. He was happy to pay the one hundred and fifty pound parking fine to Westminster council if it meant being able to park directly outside Bvlgari jewellers, plus the car was registered to one of his associates. Even though he was wearing a hat and glasses he still needed to be careful, there were cameras everywhere. Like Eddie, he looked a muppet, but apart from having something more permanent done to his face there was little he could do to disguise the real him apart from go around looking like a plank in a hat and dark glasses.

It was only just ten o'clock so Freddie was pleased to see it was open. He was ready to spend some serious money.

After the busy sounds of the West End outside, the Bvlgari shop held an almost-religious hush.

'May I help you sir?'

'Yeah, I want something for me missus. Something which says, *you're all right*.'

'All right?'

'Yeah, you know.' Freddie stared at the well-manicured shop assistant from behind his glasses. Even with the dark shades on he could see the man's face was more or less orange in colour. Dragging his eyes away from the man's face, Freddie went to the cabinet.

'Do you mean you want the piece of jewellery to say, *I love you*?'

'That's what I've just said haven't I?'

'Of course you did, sir. Maybe sir would like the parentesi pendant with chain in 18-Carat gold with pave diamonds.' The man pulled out a tray of beautiful necklaces from the cabinet.

'I don't want her thinking I'm a cheapskate mate. Show me something proper.'

'Certainly sir. How about the parentesi lock chain necklace? This time it's in white gold with full pave diamonds. It's based on one of our most renowned designs, originally inspired by the joints of Roman pavements.'

'How much?'

'Twenty-eight thousand.'

'Twenty-eight thousand for a design of a pavement. Fuck me,' Freddie whistled.

'Sir?'

'I'll take it. Wrap it up.'

'And will sir be paying by Amex, credit or debit card?'

'Cash. I'll be paying in cash.'

'For me?' Tasha's grin was a mixture of surprise and delight.

'You like it?'

'Of course I bleeding do. It's beautiful.'

'Listen, I know you were upset but I've got some good news. Ray-Ray asked to see that tom again.'

Tasha's face lit up. 'You're ribbing me?'

'No. I was as shocked as you are, but he came right out with it. Johno said she was a bit of all right.'

'Is this what the present's for?'

'Yeah, that and other things. Anyhow, I'll see you later. Maybe you and me can do something nice this evening.'

'You and me?'

'Don't look so shocked, I'm not a complete dinosaur.'

Freddie kissed Tasha lightly on her cheek, and for the first time in a long time she didn't flinch. She smiled as he walked out of the kitchen, surprised how she was looking forward to tonight.

Her phone rang. It was Eddie and his tone was cold.

'It's me.'

'I know.'

'We need to talk, but not on the phone. Meet me.'

Tasha was puzzled by the conversation; usually Eddie was warm and friendly. Perhaps he was just having a bad day. 'When?'

'Tonight.'

'Eddie, I can't . . .'

The hostility in Eddie's voice hit Tasha down the phone. 'Tash, tonight.'

The phone went dead. Tasha scowled, surprised Eddie had put the phone down on her. Still, she had more important things to worry about, like what she was going to wear tonight when she went out with Freddie. It'd been so long since she'd wanted to do anything with him, but his suggestion of doing something nice this evening had excited her. Perhaps things were going to turn out all right after all.

Johno watched Laila from the door. From where he was standing he had a nice sight of her arse. Round and pert. Giving that Pippa Middleton more than a run for her money. What she was doing he wasn't quite sure, and why she was on her knees on a dirty old mat he didn't know the answer to. However, if it meant her cocking her backside in the air, he was happy with whatever it was she was doing.

'Janie?'

Laila turned round, startled. She looked nervous. The last time she'd seen him, he'd been so angry with her.

'All right babe? Where's Yvonne?'

'I'm not sure, but she did ask me to tell you it's all sorted. She said you'd know what it meant.'

Johno frowned. He wasn't into cryptic clues, but he hoped it meant Yvonne had the money for him. Funny how a little pressure went a long way with whores.

'So, after the disaster of what happened, for some strange reason he wants to see you again.'

'Who?'

'The flipping prime minister. Who do you think? The guy I took you to; he wants to see you again. Looks like you've had a squeeze.'

'When does he want to see me again?'

'Tonight.'

39

Ray-Ray smiled at his mother. He could see her face all lit up and girly-looking, and even though he was brimming over with anger and anxiety he was pleased for her. She was happier than he'd seen her in a long time. 'I see me dad's started the charm offensive.'

Tasha sniffed the large bunch of red and white roses.

'Hey, leave him alone. It's been a while since he's sent me flowers.'

'What does the card say?'

'Oh I never saw that.' Tasha pulled out the card from the flowers and opened the tiny envelope. She smiled, her eyes twinkling. Ray-Ray leaned in to see. 'Come on, spill the beans.'

'Keep your beak out.' Tasha laughed as she twizzled away, stopping her son from reading the card. With lightning speed, Ray-Ray reached over his mum's shoulder and snatched it out of her hand. Tasha squealed as he stretched his arm high up in the air so she couldn't reach it. 'Give me that.'

'Not unless you let me see what it says.' Tasha tried to jump up, pulling on Ray-Ray to bring his arm down but she was laughing so much her attempts were fruitless.

'Tell me I'm the best son in the world and I might give it you back.'

'You're the best son in the whole entire world. Now hand it here.'

'Tell me I'm just the greatest.'

Tasha stopped laughing. A soft warmth washed over her face as she held Ray-Ray's gaze. 'Yes babe, you are the greatest. I just wish you could see that yourself.' Ray-Ray turned his head away, embarrassed by the intensity of the moment. He gave his mum back the card, not wanting her to get heavy on him. He listened as Tasha read the card.

'*Forgive me.*'

'Is that it? Dad's a man of few words ain't he?'

'Hold on.' Tasha turned the card over; it had an address on the back. 'Looks like he wants me to go on a date.' She giggled shyly.

'Well are you?'

'Going on the date tonight? Of course.'

'No, I meant are you going to forgive him?'

'It's not as simple as that.'

'It never is with you guys. I'd like you to. It's been a long time coming. What do they always say? *His heart's in the right place.*'

'I'll try, Ray-Ray.'

'I'd like you to; after all, you ain't always been the doting wife.'

Tasha squirmed slightly. This was the first time Ray-Ray had ever referred to the situation with Arnie directly. 'Okay, I promise. Happy now?'

'Happy.'

Wanting to ease the moment, Tasha pulled out the Bvlgari necklace from under the neck of her top. 'Did you see this? Your Dad gave it to me this morning; bleeding gorgeous. Your Auntie Linda was salivating over it when she saw it.'

Ray-Ray laughed, making Tasha smile. 'It's good to see you happy son.' Tentatively she added, 'I hear you're going to see the tom again. I'm pleased for you mate.'

Tasha could see Ray-Ray shutting down the minute she said it. The relaxed light-hearted exterior disappeared, and in its place, she could see the tension seep back into her son's body. The next moment, he was gone. She heard the front door slam and once again, Tasha felt she'd lost him.

'He'll see you now, and remember; you fuck up this time darling, and it ain't you who'll get it, it's your mouthy friend, Yvonne. Think about it. How would you live with yourself, knowing you could have stopped her getting cut up? So don't think about trying to keep your legs crossed babe. Do what you're paid to do.' Johno spoke gruffly, pushing Laila through to the lounge section of the hotel suite she'd been brought to.

The dress Johno had given her to wear was exquisite. Long and gold, with sequins, cut beautifully to her body. Laila could feel the silk lines of the dress moving to the sway of her walk.

From the already dim bedroom, Laila walked into near darkness. The curtains were drawn and the only light was the one coming from underneath the door in the corner.

She turned her head as Johno walked out, closing the double doors behind her, before the further distant sound of the hotel room door banging shut.

Standing, trying to adjust her eyes to the dark, Laila sensed someone else was in the room. 'Hello?' Her voice sounded timid and no reply came. She moved slightly forward, but immediately her foot hit something sharp. 'Hello? Is anyone there?' She could almost feel her heart beginning to race faster. She suddenly started to feel afraid, the darkness feeling as if it was closing in on her. She had to tell herself she was being silly.

'Hello? Please, if you're there, talk to me.' Her voice sounded higher this time. Again, there was no answer. It was frightening her now. She didn't want to be there and she turned to leave, running back towards the double doors. As she put her hands on the large brass handles, she jumped to hear the room fill with music. It was a song she knew well. A song she used to play. *Never Tear Us Apart.*

Memories came flooding back, overwhelming her, and as she stood there listening to the chorus of the song, Laila couldn't move. All she could see were rolling images in her head which wouldn't stop.

The music turned off and the lamp in the corner came on. Laila quickly spun around. The person was sat behind the lamp, making it impossible for her to see his face. His voice sounded calm.

'Did you like the music?'

Laila's body trembled, as did her voice. 'Yes, yes it was fine.'

'You sound upset. Should I have played something else?'

'No, it's just I used to listen to that song. It brings back memories.'

'Happy ones I hope?'

Laila didn't say anything even though she could sense the man's voice wanting her to answer. The room fell quiet, until through the dark, Laila spoke. 'What . . . what would you like me to do?'

'What would I like? For a whore you ask stupid questions.'

Laila flinched. His voice was harsh and cruel and from nowhere Laila's eyes began to fill up with tears. She wiped them away quickly.

'Tell me about yourself Janie.'

'There's nothing to tell.'

'Ain't there always a sob story behind you lot? Daddy didn't love you enough, Mummy ran away?'

'I . . . I . . . don't know.'

'Don't know or don't want to tell? Where are you from, Janie?'

'Why are you asking me all these questions?'

'Would you rather not talk? Would you rather just fuck? Is that it? Come on then, let's fuck.'

'Please . . . I can't even see you.'

'Oh you want to see me do you?' Ray-Ray stood up, walking round from the brightness of the light towards Laila. His tall frame towered over her. 'There. How do I look? Beautiful ain't it?'

Laila pulled back, not from his face but from his hostility. She stared at him, taking in his scars on half of his face, tracing them down with her eyes to his neck and to his chest which showed beneath the black open shirt he wore. The other half of his face was hidden by a half mask.

'Do I disgust you *Janie*?'

'No, of course not.'

'Really?'

'No, you don't.'

'Prove it.'

Laila blinked, baffled by this man.

'Touch my face Janie.'

'Sorry?'

Ray-Ray raised his voice, startling Laila. 'I said, touch my face!'

Laila stepped back even more. She didn't know what he wanted from her and why he was doing this.

He grabbed her hands, pulling them towards his face.

'Touch it. Touch it.'

He brought her hands up to his face. She closed her eyes, stopping her tears. Her fingertips could feel the roughness of the heavy lines of the scars; the rise of the scar tissue like mountain ranges, in contrast to the taut smoothness of the other parts of his face.

She could feel him stop moving her hands but she could hear his breathing, she could feel it. She opened her eyes wide, to see him staring intently at her.

He dropped her hands and walked away. With his back to her, Ray-Ray spoke quietly. 'Take your clothes off.' Laila didn't move to undress, her body tensed up.

'I said, take them off.'

It was a moment before Laila moved. Keeping her eyes on the floor, she pulled at her dress. Her voice was small and quiet. 'I can't get it off.'

Ray-Ray walked over to Laila. Standing behind her, he saw his hands shaking as he moved her hair out of the way. His fingers brushed at her skin as he began to undo her zip. He hesitated, bending his head towards the back of hers. He closed his eyes, smelling her perfume, smelling the fresh scent of newly washed hair, the scent of everything pure. Flicking his head back he jolted himself out of the moment, remembering why he was here and what she was. He pulled himself up straight, pulling the zip down with force.

The dress fell to the floor, folding away from Laila's skin with ease. Ray-Ray glanced at her, but found himself unable to look at her for any longer. He walked over to the double doors, opening them wide, and went into the bedroom.

'Come here.'

Laila stood in the doorway of the bedroom. Her mind was racing as she watched Ray-Ray begin to unbutton his shirt, exposing his strong, well-built chest. The scars were on one side of his body, disappearing completely at his rib cage. He walked towards her slowly, never taking his eyes off her.

'Put your arms down.' *Put your arms down.* Echoes from her past hit Laila as she watched the drops of her tears splash to the ground. Almost inaudibly, she whispered, 'I can't. Please.'

Ray-Ray bent down to her ear and whispered back, just as quietly. 'Put your arms down.' *Put your arms down.* Laila squeezed her eyes shut, dropping her arms at the same time. A few moments passed until she found the strength to open her eyes. He wasn't in front of her as she thought he was. He was sitting on the end of the bed, his head bent down low.

'Get on the bed Janie.'

She wanted to run, but remembered the words of Johno, threatening to hurt Yvonne. She had to *try*. What other choice did she have? Slowly she walked across to him, lowering herself on to the bed. Her body was filled with so much tension it made it almost impossible for her to lower herself down to sit next to him. She could feel his body next to hers, just as tense. Just as rigid as hers.

'Lie down.'

'I . . ?'

'Don't say anything; just do it.' He spat out his words.

Laila fell back on the bed, feeling the softness of the mattress catch her body. She lay staring at the ceiling, blinking at nothing, closing her mind off to what was happening to her.

Ray-Ray threw himself down next to her, but the instant his body hit the bed, Laila jumped up, running towards her clothes which lay abandoned on the floor.

'I'm sorry, I'm sorry, I can't do this. I thought I could.' She pulled on her dress, struggling to do the zip up. Giving up, she picked up her shoes, wiping her running eyes and nose on the silk sleeve of her dress. 'I'm sorry I have to go.' Ray-Ray stood, blocking her way.

'Please, let me go.'

He sneered at her. 'What's the matter *Janie*?'

'I don't do this.'

'You don't do what?'

'This . . . I don't do this.'

'What? Not enough money for you? Is that it? You want more money?' Ray-Ray stormed over to his jacket pocket, pulling out wads of fifty-pound notes. 'Here. Is this enough money for you? Is this what you want?' He started to throw it at her, screwing up the notes, firing them at her face.

'No, no I don't want your money.'

His voice was strained, holding back the anger. 'Isn't my money good enough for you . . . or is it me? You can't bear to sleep with someone like me.'

'No, stop, please it hasn't anything to do with you.'

'You're a whore aren't you? Am I so bad even a whore wouldn't touch me?'

'No, no, please.'

'Then why? Why not me?'

Laila's tears were heavy and her voice tried to reach out to him. 'You don't understand. This isn't what I do . . . I've never done it.'

He bit down on his lip and watched her walk towards the door. She was going. Leaving. But he couldn't tell her. He needed her to see. Desperate, he rushed over to the music controls, switching the song on again.

Laila stopped. He watched her breathe. *Turn around. Please turn around.* He wanted to reach out and touch her. Her voice was warm when she spoke. Her back still facing him.

'I need you to know, this isn't anything to do with what you look like.'

'But you're still going?'

'What do you want from me?'

'Look at me. Turn round and look at me.'

Laila slowly turned, clutching on to her shoes. Ray-Ray saw her stare at him blankly. 'Look at me.' Confusion crossed her face and Ray-Ray could feel the panic rise inside him.

'What do you see?'

'I . . . I don't know.'

'Look *harder*. Can't you see?'

Urgency filled her voice as she spoke over the music. 'I don't know what you want me to see.'

Ray-Ray shouted, and tears he didn't think could fall trickled down his face. 'Look; just *look*.'

He could tell she didn't understand. In frustration he swung at the lamp, knocking it and everything else off the table. He grabbed his shirt, pulling it on as he walked out of the door.

For a few seconds Laila stood without moving, trying to comprehend what had just happened. It was the second time he'd run off and she was at a loss to know what to do.

Pulling herself together and trying not to worry about what Johno would say, Laila gathered the things off the floor. She froze. Her eyes transfixed on what lay next to the magazine. Tentatively she crouched down, picking up the CD case. Her breathing

303

shortened, and her heart began to hammer in her chest. She stared at it. It couldn't be. But there in the corner were the smiley face stickers with her initials on. She moved her fingers to lightly brush over them. She looked at the door, and, as the realisation hit her, she covered her mouth, a tiny cry coming out.

Throwing the case down, Laila ran into the empty corridor. Picking up the bottom of her dress, she pushed past the room service trolley and a startled looking bellboy.

She hurried round the corner and there, at the bottom of the corridor, she could see him. She called out but he didn't turn as he stepped into the lift. She could see the doors closing as she neared them, and lunging forward, she hit the call button, but it was too late. They closed, leaving her standing in the corridor. She put her head on the cool metal of the closed doors and under her breath whispered, 'It's you. Ray-Ray, it's you.'

40

'You look the bleeding dog's bollocks.' Linda grinned at Tasha as she came into the kitchen, wearing a low-cut deep blue satin dress, topped off with the Bvlgari necklace Freddie had bought her. 'I take it your old man's on a promise?'

'I'm going to be wined and dined Linda, not taken to a farmer's field for a quick roll in the hay.'

'Are you going to get one of Freddie's boys to drive you?'

Tasha crinkled up her nose. Even though her and Freddie were trying to get on and trust each other again, it didn't stretch to the people who worked for him. She wanted them as far away from her as possible. They'd also been happy to see her six foot under and that was something she wouldn't forget in a hurry.

'You've got to be joking Lind, I'd rather walk.'

'Well it's lucky for you then you've got your own motor parked outside ain't it? Go and have fun babe, you deserve it.'

Tasha found driving her convertible Bentley Continental in her Christian Louboutin shoes more difficult than she first imagined. It wasn't helping either that she hadn't figured out quite how to use the GPS mapping system, nor that it was getting dark and she didn't know the part of London she was in. Half an hour ago she'd driven past Myddeltons deli on the corner of Amwell Street and Lloyd Baker Street which served the best crispy bacon focaccia in town, but now the familiar landmarks had disappeared.

She was certain she'd already passed Battersea Bridge three times and was going back in the same direction as she started from, though she wouldn't let herself concede it probably would've been easier to have got Johno or even Eddie to drive her. Shit, Eddie; she'd forgotten about him. She'd been so swept along by Freddie's romantic gestures that she'd forgotten about Eddie wanting to meet her tonight. Never mind, she was sure Linda would be pleased to see him. How her sister had a secret fancy for Eddie was beyond Tasha, but there it was. Even though they'd all known each other for years, Linda had only let slip this piece of information the other day. She couldn't see it herself, but then Linda had never had the best taste in men. Though who was she to talk?

Sighing, Tasha pushed the bluetooth on the steering wheel to see if she could get through to Eddie, but it went straight to voicemail. She wouldn't leave a message; it was pointless. She didn't even know if it was his number any more. He changed it as often as he probably did his underwear, although she didn't blame him. She knew there was no way Eddie could deal with going back inside again.

The GPS told her to turn left, but instinct told her it didn't know what the hell it was talking about. The potholed road looked more like a drive-up to a builder's yard than a road she thought, until she saw the tealight candles along the path.

Driving slowly, Tasha took in how beautiful it looked. The whole drive was lit up on both sides with flickering candle flames. She smiled, genuinely touched by the trouble Freddie had gone to. It didn't even matter that she knew he would've recruited his men to do it rather than *him* do it himself, but it was the thought that mattered. For all her married life she'd only ever wanted him to think about her and her feelings, and finally he had started to do so.

Stepping out of the car, Tasha couldn't help giggling; she felt like she had done on the day of their wedding. The tiny path leading up to the warehouse had more candles lit along the edge of it and was strewn with rose petals. There was a part of Tasha which wished Linda was there to see it, wanting to share something so beautiful with her.

Tasha touched her necklace, feeling the butterflies in her tummy, and walked along the path, drinking in every intoxicating moment of the starlit night.

Inside the warehouse, Tasha was overwhelmed by how beautiful it was. She didn't even feel foolish as the tears pricked at her eyes. In the middle of the empty warehouse space, a long table sat with hundreds of candles twinkling and flickering, creating a sense of magic.

She walked to the table, picking up the single rose, smelling the gentle aroma of the blossoming flower. Then she heard footsteps behind her. Smiling, Tasha turned round.

'You look beautiful. Thank you for coming. *You look perfect Izzy, just perfect.*'

Ray-Ray was pacing. He couldn't sit down, let alone sit still. He walked over to the window in his bedroom looking at nothing in particular, and seeing nothing but Laila's face in his mind.

What the hell had he just done? He was a fool playing games with her, wearing the half mask on the good side of his face to prevent her recognising him. For what? To punish her? He'd been so angry with her, so betrayed by her – or he thought he had. But when he'd seen her, all he'd really wanted to do was take her in his arms. Wanted to tell her it had been the idea of her which had kept him going through hospital. The possibility of seeing her face and hearing her voice one more time, had given him light in an otherwise dark tunnel. There were so many things he wanted to

307

ask her. So many questions needed answering. What the hell was she doing in London? How had she ended up working for Johno? But instead of asking any, he'd been a prat. Fuck it. Grabbing his coat, Ray-Ray knew exactly what he was going to do.

'What you doing here? Shouldn't you be laying on all the mushy stuff with Mum? Oh don't tell me, you were your usual tactful self and now dinner's off.'

Freddie looked at Ray-Ray as he walked into the kitchen, just as Linda walked in with Eddie. 'It's nice to see you've got so much confidence in me son, or it would be, if I knew what the fuck you were talking about.'

'Oh turn it in Dad, you don't have to be shy in front of us. We won't tell anyone the mighty Freddie Thompson has a heart, will we?' Ray-Ray gave a half smile at the others, as Freddie continued to look puzzled.

Linda piped up. 'And that necklace was something else doll, bleeding hell Freddie, have you thought about giving your sister-in-law one as well?'

'I gave her a necklace but I don't know anything about any dinner. I said we might go out and maybe do something nice but with one thing and another, I've been too busy. Forgot all about it.'

Linda glanced at Ray-Ray as she saw Freddie was being deadly serious. 'What about the flowers?'

'What fucking flowers? Will somebody tell me what the hell is going on?'

Ray-Ray and Linda shrugged their shoulders and Freddie clocked Eddie, looking sheepish. He barked at him. 'You got something to tell me Ed? Have you been sending me missus flowers? Cos if you have, fuck me Ed, whether I owe you or not, I'm coming for you.'

Eddie put his hands up in the air. 'Freddie, it's me you're talking to.'

'Leave it out Dad, Eddie's done nothing. Are you sure you ain't sent them?'

Freddie, overcome with paranoia, snapped and shouted at his son. 'What? Now you're going to accuse me of having dementia as well as being a crap husband? I know if I've sent flowers to your mother or not.'

'Okay, okay calm down. I'm sure there's some simple explanation.'

'Such as? Cos I can't bleedin' think of one.'

Ray-Ray stared at his father, feeling a pressure point start pulsating in his head. He hoped to God there was a simple explanation; like the flower shop had got it wrong and they'd just been delivered to the wrong address, or his father had genuinely forgotten. But how likely was that? Wasn't it more likely his mother had begun to do again what she'd been doing in Bradford? Pretending to him she wasn't seeing anybody behind his father's back, when they both knew she was. Shit. He didn't want to think about it now. He *couldn't* think about it now. 'Listen Dad, I'm out of here, I've got things to do.'

Ray-Ray slammed out of the kitchen, not wanting to be see his father turn from being his dad into the formidable, fearsome Freddie Thompson. The Freddie Thompson that men were terrified of. The Freddie Thompson he'd seen hundreds of times throughout his life. And the Freddie Thompson he didn't want a part of.

Back in the kitchen, Linda was trying to calm Freddie down. 'Think Freddie, think. I ain't saying you're losing your marbles, but I don't get it. She got done up to the nines. I told her she looked the dog's bollocks.'

Eddie raised his eyebrows, wondering if he could slip out without being noticed, while Linda carried on talking. 'She was chuffed to bits you'd asked her to go on a date. I ain't seen her look like that for a long time. She was happy.'

'Happy for someone else to shag the daylights out of her.'

It was Linda's turn to raise her voice. 'Stop it Freddie. It was *you* she said she was going to see. She wouldn't lie to me. She never has done before.'

'Yeah, that's what she wants you to think.'

'No, I know she wouldn't. The last time . . .' Linda began to bite her lip, pulling her mouth back from spewing anything else out. She didn't need to look up to know that Freddie's blue eyes were staring at her.

Freddie lifted her chin up and as he did so, even though he didn't hurt her, Linda could feel the strength in his fingers alone.

'The last time what Linda?'

'Nothing Freddie, I didn't mean anything by it. You know me.'

'I do and that's why I know you're lying.'

Eddie took a deep breath, and slowly moved Freddie's fingers away from Linda's chin, keeping eye contact with Freddie at all times, praying he'd see tomorrow.

'Freddie, I think there's something I need to tell you.'

'You know what I always enjoy in the car? A sing-along.' Arnie quickly glanced back over his shoulder to talk, not wanting to take his eyes off the road. 'Don't look so scared, I think you'll be safe now. The bad man's gone.' There was no response, only a small cry from Tasha who was curled up tightly on the back seat, her hands tied.

Arnie was worried. 'Are you all right? You look awful. Let me do up the window.' He took his hands off the steering wheel and the car zig-zagged across the road, making a passing car steer up on to the grassy bank to avoid a collision.

Having taken control of Tasha's Bentley again, Arnie slowed right down, stopping on the gravelled side in front of an entrance to a farm. He turned off the engine and moved round so he could see her properly, then reached out and stroked her hair, wiping away her tears. He pulled off her gag.

'You're sad.'

'Take me home Arnie. Please. Just take me home,' she wept.

Arnold's face turned to a smile. 'Really? You want to go home? You're not just saying that to make me happy?'

Tasha only stared ahead as Arnie replaced her gag.

'Lovely, then off we go. How about that sing-along?'

41

Ray-Ray. He was the only thing she could think of. Ray-Ray. The words she hadn't dared to imagine she'd be able to say again. The tears streamed down Laila's face as she ran down Greek Street still in her long dress, minus her shoes, and ignoring all the stares she was getting. All she could think was, *Ray-Ray.*

His face. What had happened to his face? She shivered, terrified of the next thought, terrified that she was to blame.

What must he think of her? She'd held on to him in her mind like a person held onto a candle in the darkness. He'd been her everything. On the hardest days the idea of him had kept her going. But she'd messed everything up, and she was not only frightened she wouldn't she see him again but she was also scared he might hate her. That thought, she didn't think she could live with.

Wiping away her tears, she hoped Yvonne would be back soon. She needed to talk; everything seemed to be falling apart. She'd tried to call her but it'd gone straight to voicemail. Probably her battery had died. Heading up the walk-up stairs, Laila hoped Johno wasn't waiting for her, wanting to know why she hadn't called him to pick her up from the hotel.

'Where've you been?' Anita, one of the other girls in the walk-up scowled as Laila came in. 'I've been run off me bleeding feet. If it ain't a blow job, it's a shag. They've been queuing up like they're after tickets for the FA Cup final. God knows how I'll bleeding walk tomorrow. Me fanny feels like a pneumatic drill's been up it.'

Laila smiled weakly, changing into a t-shirt and a pair of jeans. 'Sorry, I don't know where Yvonne is, she's supposed to be here.'

"Supposed' isn't '*here*' though is it? I'm going home. You can finish off.' Anita screwed up her face.

Laila shuddered. She'd only done one massage before and it'd made her physically sick. Yvonne had told her to think of it as if she was a masseuse in a posh health spa rather than a girl working in a walk-up in the middle of Soho.

She stood above the man who was lying face down on the massage table naked to the waist, wishing with all her heart that Anita hadn't been so desperate to go without finishing off this client.

Wanting to get on with it, Laila poured some oil in her hands. She rubbed them together to warm it up, knowing she was putting off the inevitable. Her hands paused above his back, not wanting to touch him.

Gritting her teeth, Laila slid one hand towards his shoulder, the other towards his hip, cringing at every touch she made. She could feel the goosebumps on her skin, adding to her sense of repulsion. Her stomach cramped, and she wanted to retch as she moved both hands to massage his shoulders, kneading away the tension in them but adding to her own. Every fibre of her being screamed out as her fingers slid to the top of his arm, grasping his flesh and turning her hands in circular motions down his arms.

She moved down to his hand, turning it over to massage the palm and down to his fingers, then went round to the other side to do the same to the other arm, seeing the tension in him.

As she got to his wrist, Laila began to slow down, suddenly

313

becoming more uncomfortable than she already was. She could feel her heart pounding in her chest. Slowly, Laila moved her hands down towards the man's clenched fist, her eyes darting across his body and towards the door.

Cautiously, she took one hand away, stepping quietly back as tears stung her eyes. As she moved away some more, the man's hand shot out, grabbing her wrist. Laila pulled away but his grasp was too tight. She screamed as he pulled her towards him.

'Hello Laila, you didn't think I'd let you get away so easily do you?' Baz Gupta sneered as he looked at his wife.

'What the bloody hell . . .' Yvonne walked into the room. At the sight of Baz she froze, glancing over at a terrified Laila.

'Oh look, it's the other tart. How cosy. I've come to collect my wife.' Baz held Laila in an arm lock around her neck as he stared at Yvonne. Her first thought was to wade in and help, but she knew there was a good chance of her being overpowered.

Backing out of the room, Yvonne turned and ran, almost throwing herself down the stairs. She crossed over Greek Street, not hesitating as she dodged the cars and weaved through the late-night partygoers hiding from the summer downpour. Cutting through the side street to get to Charing Cross Road, she hoped it wasn't too late.

'Come on, come on.' The traffic was building up, making it impossible for Yvonne to cross. She didn't have time to wait. Bolting up the same side towards Centrepoint, smashing into anyone who got in her way, she saw the number 38 bus on the other side of the road. 'Tariq! Tariq!' She could see him going to sit down, taking his seat on the bottom deck, but then another bus blocked her vision. She tried to cross but was forced back by the oncoming black cabs. 'Tariq!' She waved her arms but he didn't look out of the window. Running down the road, she kept her eyes on the bus, trying to keep up as it gained speed. The lights at Cambridge Circus were about to change from red to green. If he didn't see her now he'd be gone. Looking right, she saw a car hurtling towards her and closing her eyes, she ran across the road.

She heard the screech of tyres, a horn and people screaming. The car crashed into the back of the black taxi on the other side of the road to avoid hitting Yvonne.

'What the hell are you doing lady?' The car driver jumped out, his face red and his fist waving, ready to have a pop at Yvonne. The whole of the traffic had come to a standstill, including the bus Tariq was on. Tariq along with the other passengers, looked at Yvonne in astonishment. She ignored the driver, running nearer the bus and banging on the window.

'Tariq, quick it's Laila.' She didn't need to say anything else for Tariq to run off the bus.

Tariq panted as he followed Yvonne. 'What's happened?'

There wasn't time for an explanation but she knew the name would say it all. 'It's Baz.' Without a moment's hesitation, both Yvonne and Tariq ran, escaping the shouts and demands of the angry drivers.

In Greek Street, Yvonne signalled Tariq to the walk-up.

'I'll go and find Johno. I can't call him because my phone's dead. It's the first room on the left. Will you be all right whilst I go and get help?'

'I'll be fine.' The words sounded more confident than Tariq actually felt.

Taking the stairs two at a time, Tariq banged into the room. The look on Baz's face was as startled as the look on Laila's upon seeing her brother. She managed to mutter the words 'Tariq,' before Baz ran in front of her, pushing her backwards on to the floor.

'Oh here comes the hero of the hour.'

'Leave her alone Baz.'

Baz laughed menacingly. 'Who? My wife? You want me to leave *my wife* alone? We were just having a nice cosy chat. A little catch up to find out what she's been up to. I was just trying to persuade her to come home with me without a fuss, but it seems like she's got other ideas.' Baz smirked nastily. Tariq's face darkened as he spoke.

'Just walk away.'

'This is about honour.'

'This has *nothing* to do with honour Baz; it never has had.'

Baz leant down, grabbing Laila by her arm. He dragged her up to her feet. 'Move out of my way Tariq.'

Tariq looked at his sister. He could see the fear in her eyes.

'*Move.*'

'No.'

Neither of the men moved. From the corner of his eye Baz saw the metal pole of a broom handle and, seizing the opportunity, he grabbed it, taking a swing at Tariq who was caught off-guard. It knocked him sideways as the pole caught him on the side of his head. He staggered into the massage table, sending the bottles of oils flying.

Baz rushed him again, this time using the side of his body to push him against the wall. He grabbed Tariq's hair, pulling his head back then, smashing it against the corner frame of the cupboard. Blood squirted out of Tariq's nose as Laila screamed. He slid down to his knees, receiving a final kick from Baz in the back.

'Stop, it! Stop it!' Laila rushed over to Tariq who lay slumped on the floor. She cradled Tariq's head in her arms.

The door swung open.

'Laila, I should've said this before, but I'm saying it now. I ain't one for words but I need to get this out, I lo . . .' Ray-Ray walked through the door beginning to deliver the monologue to Laila that he'd been practising on the way over. He stopped dead, taking in the scene that greeted him in the tiny room.

'Ray-Ray!'

Baz slowly turned his head as it dawned on him who this man was. He stepped forward slowly, back kicking Laila to move out of the way. His face was curled with hatred. 'My wife *is* popular. First we have the hero and now the freak show's arrived.'

Laila looked at Baz anxiously; she could see the venom in his eyes and she knew what he was capable of. 'Ray-Ray, just go.'

'I ain't going anywhere.'

'How romantic, beauty and the beast.' Ray-Ray went to move forward but froze as he saw Baz bend down and pick up a green can from the bag he had with him. He watched in horror as Baz hurriedly shook out the contents all over Laila, soaking her in the strong-smelling colourless liquid. It was petrol.

Freddie Thompson couldn't move. It was the same feeling he'd had when he was sitting on the deck of the boat, thinking Tasha had betrayed him; the same cold steel feeling lay in his heart as it did now. And as he had done then, he now decided it was best to do nothing apart from stare at the blank wall in front of him, knowing if he did move he wouldn't be responsible for his actions.

'I'm sorry Freddie, I ain't never lied to you before. But what was I supposed to do? It was Tash you were asking me to deal with. Tash. I couldn't do it.' Eddie paused, knowing it wasn't looking good for him. Freddie hadn't spoken for the last ten minutes, but had just been standing by the marble sink, staring at the wall. And as Eddie went into more detail, explaining as gently as possible what had really happened with Arnie, he wasn't sure if he was going to get out of this alive. And it wasn't helping that Linda was sticking her two penn'orth in either. Her words spilled out in panic.

'Freddie, listen to me. Tash, she wasn't thinking straight. You know how difficult it was, what with you going inside and all.'

For the first time, Freddie spoke. 'Oh so it's my fault now is it Lind?'

Looking at Freddie's demeanour, Linda thought it was best not to say anything else.

'How long was she banging him for?' Freddie shouted, and neither of them said anything, 'I said, how long?'

It was Linda who spoke. 'She wasn't, not really. She never slept with him.'

'You expect me to believe that?'

317

'That's what I said to her.' Linda stopped, realising what she was saying wasn't really helping. She changed tack.

'She knew she'd done wrong Freddie. She loves you, she was just lonely.'

'She made a right fucking mug of me. I bet she was pissing herself laughing. *That's* why she wasn't happy to see me. Spoilt her dirty plans.'

'No Freddie, it wasn't like that. She was scared of him.'

Freddie laughed loudly and Linda heard the edge of bitterness in it. 'Do me a favour. So scared they've run off together?'

'She ain't, I swear.' Linda stopped short of saying she would bet her life on it, not wanting to give Freddie any ideas.

'There's more.' Eddie got the envelope which he'd picked up from Arnie's flat out of his jacket. He threw it on the table. 'The man's minted. There's all kind of documents there.'

Freddie pushed it away. 'That ain't of interest to me. All I'm interested in is payback time and once I've had that, then I'll deal with you two.'

Linda and Eddie looked at each other and in a desperate attempt to placate Freddie she said, 'Freddie, I know you're pissed and in a way you've got every right to be, but if the flowers were from him, I think she's in trouble.'

Freddie's hard exterior didn't falter as he stared at his sister-in-law. 'And that's my problem, how?'

'I know you love her and I know you're hurt but please Freddie, let's just look for them.'

Eddie butted in. 'I don't buy it. I reckon they've just gone.'

'Ask yourself, why the farce then? Why would Tash pretend she's going on a date with Freddie if she didn't believe it herself?' Linda protested.

Freddie raised his voice, throwing the wine glass from the sink to the other side of the room. 'I don't know Linda. I don't know anything any more. But I tell you what I do know, there's no way

I'm running after her. Even if what you're saying is right, she deserves all she gets.'

'Eddie, tell him, please.'

The hammering on the front door stopped all three of them. It was late, and all of them knew no one ever knocked on Freddie Thompson's door like that unless they didn't value their own life, not unless they were the police.

Linda pulled open the door. It was Johno.

'Where's Freddie?'

'In the kitchen.'

Johno ran past her, pushing her to one side. 'Freddie, there's trouble at one of the walk-ups and Ray-Ray's bang in the middle of it.'

'You want me to do what?' Eddie looked at Linda in amazement. He didn't need this. He was already worried about Ray-Ray but when he'd tried to go with Freddie and Johno, they'd refused point blank. Now Linda was adding to his anxiety by stressing about Tash.

'Please, Eddie; help me.'

'We're in enough trouble already.'

Linda snapped at Eddie. 'Then doing this won't make the slightest bit of difference will it?'

'Look, she'll be fine.'

'How do you know?' Linda grabbed hold of Eddie's arm as he turned away, not wanting to be drawn into it any more than he already was.

'Even if I was going to help you, what makes you so sure Tasha hasn't just run off? It seems a bit excessive darling. You lot are all the same.'

Linda looked at Eddie, shaking her head. 'She ain't Nora, Ed. I know my sister, and I know she'd tell me if she was seeing some other fella. She was piss scared of this geezer. Wouldn't even talk about him. She couldn't tell Freddie like she normally would if someone was bothering her, because she knew what he would do to her. So she was on her own.'

Eddie shrugged his shoulders. 'I dunno.'

Linda's eyes pleaded with Eddie as she spoke. 'Well I do. Please. I know you care about her.'

'Where would we even start to look? Did she tell you where she was going tonight?'

Linda shook her head. 'No, she just went off all excited.'

'Then we're stuck. It's been hours. She could be anywhere. We can go by the place he was staying at, but he's probably long gone, so unless you can think of something, it's pointless. I'm sorry.'

Linda sat on the edge of the couch feeling deflated and chewing her fingernails. She rubbed her eyes, not sure what she was supposed to do next. She had to think. Problem was, Tasha had talked so little about Arnie, she didn't have a clue. Then it came to her. Something Tash had said. Linda looked up at Eddie.

'It ain't nothing much but she did say he talked about some place of his father's a lot. He was always asking her to go there with him, but you know Tash, she ain't exactly a wellington boot and mud kind of gal. It was somewhere up north.'

Eddie's face changed from an intense frown into a relieved smile.

'Baby, you'd be surprised how sometimes an *ain't nothing much* can turn into something important.' Eddie picked up the envelope Freddie had thrown on the table. He pulled out documents and letters, discarding most of them until he came to a tatty piece of paper. He scanned it with his eyes. 'Here it is. I knew I saw it. Sole benefactor to his old man's estate.'

Linda snatched it, reading it over. 'Let's go.'

'Go where?'

Linda waved the piece of paper at him. 'Here. To this place in the country.'

'What? You want to go all the way there on a long shot?'

'No, I want *us* to go on a long shot. Eddie, what else have we got?'

He looked at Linda and saw the worry in her eyes. How the hell he'd ever got involved in the first place he didn't know. Women. They'd always been his downfall. With a roll of his eyes, Eddie grabbed his coat. As he got to the door, he saw Freddie's car keys to his brand new Porsche lying on the side. Shrugging his shoulders he grabbed them too. He already had a lot of explaining to do, so he might as well do it driving a hot set of wheels.

Freddie ran along the street, not caring that he didn't have his shades on. All he wanted to do was get to Ray-Ray. He didn't know what kind of trouble Ray-Ray was in or who this woman was, but all that mattered was that his son needed his help. And he was the one who was going to sort it.

Freddie and Johno pulled out their guns and crept up the stairs, leaving Yvonne who was already waiting for them at the entrance. The wooden steps creaked underfoot and Freddie cursed under his breath. At the top of the stairs he could hear voices inside. Pushing his head against the door he listened, wanting to hear how many people there were.

Ray-Ray was frozen with fear, his eyes fixed on the flame of the Zippo lighter which Baz was holding in one hand. His other arm was tightly around Laila's neck. Baz laughed cruelly. He could see the terror in Ray-Ray's eyes and it served only to spur him on.

'Now tell me something. How was my wife when you fucked her? I always found her to be a frigid little bitch. I'm curious to know, was she worth losing your face for? Very quiet, aren't we?'

Freddie burst into the room aiming his gun at Baz who didn't move, just said coolly, 'Hero, monster and now here comes the cavalry. London really is the entertainment capital of the world.'

Freddie stared dangerously, his tone of voice reflected in his eyes. 'Let her go.'

Baz shook his head. 'I don't think so. I think *you're* the one who's going to move away. I'm taking Laila with me. Come any closer . . . and whoosh!'

Freddie stared at Laila properly for the first time, who was shivering in fear. Then he realised what was happening. She was drenched in petrol. The smell was overpowering. He glanced at the flame which was held a few inches away from her; any closer and she would catch fire.

'Listen pal. It's gone past that mate. The minute you get my son involved, you get me involved.'

'How touching. It's a shame you weren't there to protect him before.'

Freddie looked at Ray-Ray, then at Baz, then back to Ray-Ray as it started to dawn on him.

'You? It was you . . .' Freddie felt the pain rise up in him. His hand shook as he pulled back the safety catch on the gun, not caring if the tears were falling. His voice quivered as he tried to keep his emotions under control. 'You ruined my son's life and now I'm going to kill you.'

'Put the gun down or she goes up in flames.' Baz held Freddie's stare, hate cemented on to his face.

Ray-Ray glanced at his Dad, knowing full well what he was capable of. 'Dad, put down the gun.'

Freddie snapped at Ray-Ray, keeping his eyes on Baz the whole time. 'Listen to your son. He's got more sense than you. Now move it.'

Baz began to edge along the wall, keeping his eyes firmly on the people in the room. Laila began to whimper. 'Ray-Ray, help me.'

Baz pulled on her neck. 'Shut up. Loverboy isn't going to help you. I warned you I'd kill you if you ever left me.'

Laila's big brown frightened eyes fixed on Ray-Ray, silently pleading with him. Baz dragged her along as her knees gave way in terror.

'Dad, do something!' shouted Ray-Ray.

Freddie stepped back as Baz shuffled past him. He shook his head, feeling totally powerless, something he'd never felt in his life. 'There ain't nothing I can do son.'

Baz backed down the walk-up stairs, pulling a crying Laila with him as Freddie, Johno, and Ray-Ray stood at the top of them, their facial expressions mirroring each other as they followed down the stairs.

Yvonne, at the entrance to the walk-up, screamed as she saw her friend in a neck lock, the lit flame inches from her. She could smell the petrol as Baz kicked out at her. 'Stay back, Yvonne.'

'Laila!'

Laila was too terrified to speak; her breathing shallow as her airway was constricted by Baz's strong hold. The night air hit her and she saw the passersby bolt in amazement, but she was only half-aware of them as Baz began to shout loudly. She could see a crowd forming around her.

The neck hold was suddenly released. Laila fell towards the ground but was held up by Baz's strong grip on her hair. She screamed in agony, watching the startled faces as they looked on. In the distance she could hear the sounds of the police sirens.

Baz began to shriek, beside himself in anger as she was forced to kneel in the middle of Greek Street. She watched the flame, seeing Baz's hand shaking as he held the lighter.

'I want everyone to see you for what you are. See! See! This is what I was given. A whore for a wife. A whore who has brought shame and dishonour to my family.'

Baz saw some people moving forward towards him. 'Stay back! Stay back!'

Laila was shaking violently, the petrol covering her body, burning her skin, deep into her pores. She looked up through her soaking wet hair. 'Help me! Please somebody help me!' The circle of people stood still. No one moved.

Freddie felt Ray-Ray lurch forward but he held him back, fearing for the girl. All eyes were on Baz and the lighter in his hand. All eyes on the flame. The whole of the crowd had horrified looks on their faces; drawn with fear and curiosity. A child began to shout, but was quickly silenced by his mother putting her hand over his mouth. No one dared to move, realising something terrible was about to happen. The sense of terror and helplessness for Laila was palpable, time seeming to pass in slow motion.

Baz stopped shouting for a moment to look down at Laila, his face contorted with rage. He whispered something under his breath, causing Laila to scrunch her eyes tightly shut. He looked up at the crowd, staring at them in angry disdain. He looked up to the sky then yelled. 'God is great! God is great!'

The next moment, a scream was heard as Laila Khan was engulfed in flames.

Ray-Ray ran forward at the same time as Freddie and Johno. He could see them jumping on Baz, and he stripped off his jacket, trying to smother the flames. He could hear Laila screaming underneath the heat of the fire.

'Roll, Laila, roll! Someone bring some water quick!' The flames began to subside but they were still too hot for him to be able to get close. A second later he felt some water being thrown and looked up to see one of the restaurant owners holding an empty bucket.

'Laila? Laila, talk to me.' Laila didn't move. Ray-Ray rested his head forward, talking quietly to her. 'Laila, please. You're safe now. Please say something.'

Ray-Ray watched the ambulance drive away. He'd wanted to go with her but Yvonne had been so upset he'd let her go with Laila and Tariq to the hospital instead. He sighed, turning to face his dad who was turning away from the chaos, worried the Old Bill would recognise him.

'I'll kill him. Don't worry Ray-Ray, I'll get some of me contacts to turn him over in prison. He won't see daylight.'

Ray-Ray looked at his dad in horror. 'Haven't you learnt anything?

Look at me, look at Laila. How much more do you want, Dad? Enough. It's enough.' Ray-Ray's voice was loaded with anger.

Freddie snarled, not appreciating being spoken to in such a way, and feeling very edgy that he was standing in the middle of Greek Street so exposed. He pulled his son into the walk-up stairway. 'Your problem is you're too soft.'

'No, Dad, I just don't want any more violence, and for some reason you just don't bleeding get that do you? That concept is alien to you.'

Before Freddie could answer, Johno interrupted. 'It's Linda. She needs to speak to you.' Freddie shook his head. He didn't need this shit. Tasha had made her choice. He looked at the mobile phone Johno was holding, and it was all he could do to stop himself throwing it at the wall.

He snatched it from Johno and barked down the phone. 'Yes, yes, what the fuck is it Linda? What the hell are you going to tell me now?'

Freddie listened to the voice on the other end and Johno and Ray-Ray watched his face turn from anger to fear, then from amazement to shock.

'You're where? Put Eddie on the phone.'

'What the hell do you think you're doing?' Freddie listened some more, then slammed the phone at Johno.

'What's happened?' Ray-Ray spoke to his father.

'Not now.'

Ray-Ray raised his voice, refusing to be pushed aside.

'Yes, *now* Dad. If it's about Mum, I want to know.'

Freddie bristled. He didn't like Ray-Ray speaking to him in front of other people like this. He gave him a warning look. 'Turn it in son.'

Ray-Ray shook his head and walked over to his father, standing in front of him. His voice was urgent. 'Tell me what's happened.'

'Okay fine. Linda thinks your mum's in trouble. Satisfied?'

'You're kidding right?'

'No, son.'

'And you're standing here, doing nothing? You have to do something Dad.'

Freddie slammed his hand against the wall. He was raging.

'How exactly do you want me to help her, eh?'

'I don't know Dad, but all my life all I've ever heard is the mighty Freddie Thompson this, the mighty fucking Freddie Thompson that. But truth is, all I've seen is Freddie Thompson wreaking havoc; Freddie Thompson spoiling lives and doing just what he likes. But where is he now when we really need him eh? There ain't much between you and Laila's husband.'

Ray-Ray saw the hurt in his dad's eyes and immediately felt guilty, but he was determined not to stop. 'You just don't get it do you? You never did. Me and Mum, we never *wanted* the great Freddie Thompson, all we wanted was *you*. We love you. *She* loves you. I wanted my Dad, and Mum, well she just wanted the man who she'd fallen in love with all them years ago.'

Freddie looked at his son, then turned and began to walk away. Ray-Ray sighed, but then Freddie stopped. He turned to Johno.

'Johno, how long will it take to get some of our contacts over to Northumberland?

Johno stood staring at Freddie, not quite certain where this was heading. Impatiently, Freddie growled at him. 'Well?'

'Er, a good few hours I reckon. Depends where . . .'

'Enough.' Rubbing his head, Freddie looked at Johno and Ray-Ray. 'I can't believe I'm doing this. Johno, I need you to go and speak to the Old Bill over there.'

'What?'

'Don't fucking question me. Just listen. I need you to go and tell them Tasha's in trouble and we need their help.'

42

'You see, bad things happen to bad girls, Izzy. You know what will happen to you if you tell lies don't you?' Tasha sat, staring ahead, saying nothing.

'I'll ask you again; do you love me?'

With tears in her eyes, Tasha answered in a monotone voice. 'Yes Arnie.'

'Are you sure that's the truth Izzy?'

'Yes Arnie.'

Arnold stared at her, playing with the large knife in his hands. Tasha watched in horror as his fingers bled; he was seemingly unaware of the multiple cuts to them. 'Good, that's settled then. Maybe later we can play a game. You like games, don't you Izzy?'

Tasha said nothing. If she was to have any hope of getting out alive, she knew she had to play along with him. Pretend she was Izzy. She forced a smile.

'There, that's better. Smiling always makes you feel better.'

A moment later Arnie got up, pulling a key out of his pocket. He locked the back door, double-checked it, then walked out of the room. Tasha found herself getting up from the chair and quietly stepping along the highly polished wooden floor to see exactly what Arnie was doing. Through the crack in the door, she could see him standing on a stool, stretching up to the top of the tall side cabinet filled with glass ornaments. The key. It was there he kept the key.

Tasha's hands were still tied in front of her as she sat on the chair in the darkened parlour. She was sure it was almost early morning, as she could see a shaft of sunlight coming through the wooden shutters, shedding light into the room. The whole house was unsettling, feeling as if it had been frozen in time. Tasha shuddered, not only cold from being clad only in the thin blue satin dress, but also chilled from the idea that any child had been brought up in such a massive, eerie house.

Arnie had told her not to move. Just to sit in the room and wait. *'You know what happens to girls that move?'* Tasha didn't, but she didn't ask either. She didn't know how long Arnie would be upstairs for. A minute? Ten? An hour? But maybe it would be her only chance. Terrified, Tash stood up from her chair and tiptoed into the next room.

She pulled up the stool and stood on it, but even standing on her tiptoes she couldn't manage to reach the top of the cabinet. Her hands being tied made it even more difficult. She needed something to help.

The broom stood in the corner of the room and Tasha glimpsed round nervously before grabbing it. The minute she pulled it she sent a dozen cleaning products scattering loudly all over the tiled floor, the clatter of the metal tins resonating in the echoey kitchen. She ran with the broom at the same time as Arnie began to run from the attic.

Tasha used the broom to swipe the key off the top but the angle of it made it impossible to get. She noticed that the cabinet wasn't secured on the wall. Maybe if she tipped it a bit, the key might fall towards her.

Her finger tips managed to grasp the lip of the cabinet, she pulled it and the key fell on to the floor. Jumping off the chair

328

she heard Arnie come down the stairs. Quickly, she shoved the key in the inside of her bra.

'Izzy, where are you?' In the parlour, Tasha was too afraid to answer. How would she explain herself? How would she explain that she'd moved from where he told her to stay, and the things all over the floor?

Tasha could hear Arnie coming along the corridor. She was too terrified to turn around and look at him, but the words blurted out. 'You caught me.'

'I did Izzy, and now you need to tell me exactly what I caught you doing?'

'It's your turn now, Arnie.'

'For what?'

'I was playing hide and seek. I heard you come in and I thought it might be fun, but you caught me.'

The room was silent whilst Arnold contemplated what Tasha had said. His gut was telling him she was telling lies, playing games with his mind as she always did. Something in her words and her breathing was letting him know she wasn't really playing hide and seek, but when she turned round her eyes were big and pleading. Urging him to believe her. Urging him to keep her safe, the way she'd done when Pappy used to come and take her from her room in the middle of the night.

'Sing me a song Arnie. The one I like.' Arnold bristled. He turned away, picking up the things on the floor. 'Not now. Perhaps later.'

Arnold walked to the stool and moved it back to its original place, glancing suspiciously over at Tasha who was standing perfectly still. Part of her wanted to leap at him now and take her chances by attacking him with the broom, but she knew she had to bide her time. It wouldn't take much for Arnie to physically overpower her, then all would be lost. She had to make him trust her. She needed to make him think she was Izzy.

'I don't like mess Izzy, you know that.'

'Yes Arnie, I'm sorry.' Arnold snorted to himself, not feeling as cheery as he had done.

Tasha's fear had made its way into her mouth and she could taste the dry stickiness of her lips. She was holding her breath and she wasn't sure if she could let it go or not.

'I'd like to go for a walk, Arnie. Can we go for a walk? Take me up to the river.'

'Can't this thing go any faster, Ed?' Linda dug Eddie in his side.

'What? You mean can't I go faster than a hundred and forty miles per hour in a top of the range Porsche on a country road?'

Linda smiled. Even though her stomach was twisting over and all her thoughts were on Tash, she was comforted slightly by the fact she was with Eddie.

'Have you got a signal yet?'

'No. Anyway, Freddie didn't sound keen to help. Looks like we're on our own.'

'The turning should be coming up in a minute.' As Eddie spoke, he saw three police helicopters in the sky. 'Shit.'

Linda put her hand on his knee. 'They're not looking for you Ed.'

'Not yet anyway.'

'Probably looking for some poor bastard who thought going for a walk was a good idea before getting lost.'

Eddie tried to smile. Police at the best of times made him uncomfortable; police in helicopters flying overhead made him downright nervous.

Arnie walked slightly behind Tasha. He looked down at his hands, wondering how the dried blood had got on to his hands and arms. 'Can we play hide and seek, Arnie?'

'What, out here?'

'Yes it'll be fun. You count first and I'll hide.'

Arnie looked unsure. 'I don't know, Izzy.'

'Please Arnie. Don't you want to make me happy?'

'You know I do, but how do I know you won't run away and leave me?'

Tasha stepped towards him. 'Because I love you, Arnold.'

They held each other's stare, both feeling the wind getting up and the shower of the summer rains.

'18, 19, 20. Coming, ready or not.'

With Arnie looking the other way from behind the tree, Tasha pulled the key out of her bra. Her hands tied in front of her made it hard for her to manoeuvre properly. She was shaking as she watched Arnie coming towards her hiding place.

'I can smell you Izzy. I know I'm hot.'

Tasha covered her mouth to stop the cry coming out. Her breathing coming in short gasps. She could see the manic look on Arnie's face, his eyes wild and dancing.

'Izzy, I know you're there!'

Crawling on her hands and knees on the moss, Tasha began to make her way up the hill. Her knee snapped a branch underneath her and immediately she heard Arnie shouting.

'Ah ha! You're over there. I knew I was hot. I knew it.'

Tasha began to scramble up faster but found her feet were slipping. She could hear Arnie rushing towards her. Any moment now he would see her. Standing upright, she began to run, but taking a backwards glance over her shoulder she saw Arnie laughing, only a few feet away.

'Give me a kiss Izzy; tell me that you love me Izzy. Tell me Izzy, tell me.'

A large tree stood in front of Tasha. Picking up speed, she ran to it. She felt the bark scratch her skin as she leant against the trunk, then her blood ran cold as she felt a hand on her shoulder. She screamed and ran round the large tree, but to her horror Arnie's face craned round the trunk, laughing hysterically. Taking a deep breath, Tasha pushed herself against the bark and braced herself. As Arnold came parallel to the tree, she jumped out, thrusting the key into Arnie's eye with her bound hands. He staggered back, screaming, holding his face as blood spurted everywhere.

'Izzy!'

Tasha ran as fast as she could up the winding path and along to the top of the hill to where the river ran. She could hear helicopters flying overhead. She tried to get their attention, jumping up and down, but was unsure whether they could see her or not. The wind was blowing much harder up here and she could see the torrents of water hitting the side of the verge.

The rain began to get harder, soaking her blue dress and making it cling to her skin. Trying to hurry was impossible; the mud kept making her slip and her tied hands made it hard for her to keep her balance. She couldn't hear the helicopters any more; the raging sound of the water rushing past was so loud it prevented her from hearing anything else.

She was exhausted. Tasha turned round for the first time to see how far along she'd gone and immediately slipped in terror when she saw, not three feet away, Arnold, covered in blood. He grinned manically, waving as he shouted above the noise of the water. 'Hello Isabel, you're being very silly. Give me your hand and this can all be over with.'

Tasha scrambled faster along the water's edge, slipping and sliding in the mud as she went. She wanted to look behind her but was too afraid. Something touched her leg and she shrieked and turned automatically; it was only a stick but it gave her the opportunity to see that Arnold was still there, still smiling, close behind her.

Up ahead she saw a wall blocking her way; the only way round it would be if she climbed down the verge and along, then up to the stone pathway. It looked almost impossible but rather that than face the prospect of Arnie catching her.

The rain was still streaming into Tasha's face. She glanced round and saw a different expression on Arnold's face. A look of horror, maybe even panic. He was mouthing to her but she couldn't hear what he was saying from the pounding of the water.

Arnie watched in terror. From where he was he could see the bad man at the top of the hill. He'd found them. He needed to warn Izzy, but she was pushing ahead. He could see the man waving. He had to stop him hurting Izzy. Arnie called out to her but she still wasn't stopping.

When Izzy was at the wall, he was certain she'd stop, but he watched her clambering down and his head started to whirl as she tried to cling on to the side. In her attempt to try to get away from the bad man, she was going to fall.

'Stop there Izzy. Please don't go any further,' he pleaded, but she wasn't listening and continued to climb down, precariously close to the surging river. Arnold stood up as best he could, trying to hold his balance. 'Isobel! Stop!' It was no use.

Edging forward, Arnold saw Tasha was stuck on the bottom ledge, attempting to move along with her hands tied and her foot slipping. He stretched out his hand for her to take it.

He couldn't understand why she wasn't taking it. She could hold on to him and be safe. 'Take my hand Izzy. I'll save you.'

Tasha looked directly into Arnie's eyes, then at his hand. She looked at the raging river below. A second later, she jumped.

'NO!' Without a moment's hesitation, Arnie jumped into the water after her.

'Oh Christ. Jump in!' Linda yelled at Eddie as she watched the drama unfold in front of her.

'Me?' Eddie looked at the fast-flowing river, not rating his chances. Out of the corner of his eye he saw at least half a dozen police officers running up the hill. Rather the water than the coppers. He looked at Linda and gave her a resigned look. 'On second thoughts, I'm going in.'

The water smashed over the top of Tasha's head. Gasping, she tried to pull herself up above the water, but the undercurrent was dragging her down. She tried to get her breath, but the water overwhelmed her and caused her to swallow great quantities of it. She went under again, rolling over in the surge of water and attempted to twist her hands out of the rope, but it was too tight. Panic was beginning to take over as Tasha felt herself weakening. Her body was exhausted and she could feel the fight draining from her as she was sucked deeper and deeper into the billowing waters.

Suddenly she felt something around her neck. It was an arm. Arnie's. He was pulling her up, screaming words above the noise of the water. 'I've got you, Izzy,' he was spluttering as he spoke, trying to keep them both up as the flood carried them along. She screamed and struggled, trying to break away. Rather the water than Arnie. Kicking out, Tasha's head went back under the water and this time she tried to open her eyes as it began to fill her lungs. The tightness in her chest felt as if it were going to explode and the crushing weight of her airless body made her want to scream out in pain. Her head began to feel heavy as she started to black out, sinking down to the bottom of the river.

As she sank down, through her haze, Tasha felt Arnie release his tight grip. She knew this was her chance. It gave her a surge of energy, allowing her to find the last bit of strength to kick up to the surface of the water. As she fought to get her breath, she saw Eddie pushing Arnie's head below the raging river. She watched, terrified, as they struggled, thrashing arms everywhere, dipping in and out of sight as the water rushed over their heads. Then both Arnold and Eddie disappeared beneath the bubbling river.

334

43

Tasha sat shivering, wrapped in a blanket next to a shaking Eddie, and a relieved-looking Linda who was holding Eddie's hand. Tasha managed to smile to herself as the police tried to take Eddie's name. 'It's Brown. John Brown. From Scotland.'

'You don't sound Scottish, sir.'

'No? First person who's ever said that to me mate. Maybe you ain't got the ear for accents.'

Tasha leaned over to Eddie and gave him a kiss on the cheek. 'Hey, John Brown, that's the second time you've saved me life.'

Another police officer came in and spoke to Tasha.

'I thought you'd like to know we're going to call off the search, or at least a search and rescue. The divers have informed us they're doing a search and find; looking for a dead body. We're so near the river mouth, in all likelihood he'll probably have been swept out to sea. The river's been torrential because of the floods.'

Tasha looked thoughtful as the door of Arnie's front parlour was opened. Freddie came in, hat down, sunglasses on, looking sheepish and holding a huge bunch of flowers in front of his face, followed by Ray-Ray who looked relieved to see his mum. Freddie nodded his head at Eddie and Linda. The police officer in the room spoke to him.

'And you are?'

Freddie looked around quickly, then pointed at Eddie.

'I'm his brother.'

Eddie piped up. 'He's from Scotland as well. Bob. Bob Brown. From Scotland.'

Freddie frowned at Eddie as the police officer gazed at the two men, dressed almost identically in sunglasses and baseball hats.

Freddie felt very uneasy in the presence of so many coppers and the sooner he was out of there the better, but he'd needed to come and see Tasha. He waited for the police officer to walk out of the room before he spoke.

'Tash. I dunno what to say darling.'

'How about you do what most people do and just say what you're thinking – or ain't that manly enough for Freddie Thompson? Haven't we all come too far now?'

Freddie stared at his wife. Why had he even bothered? He didn't have to come chasing after her. She should be grateful he was even speaking to her, after all he was Fred . . . He stopped his thoughts, shook his head, and smiled to himself. Jesus, Ray-Ray was right. He could be an arsehole.

He looked at Tasha, his eyes full of love.

'You're right. How about if I told you I love you more than I thought it was ever possible to love someone? The idea of being without you frightens me babe. You are, and have always been, the better part of me. I've been a prick for a long time now and I know it'll take more than just a sorry, but I am. Truly I am. I'm asking you to give me a chance to become a better man.'

Freddie looked around the room, and saw Linda filling up with tears, Eddie and Ray-Ray smiling with relief, and Tasha looking at him lovingly. He smiled, giving them the Freddie Thompson wink, adding, 'And if you lot ever repeat what I've just said, I'll blow your bleeding brains out.'

FOUR MONTHS LATER

The flat Ray-Ray showed them was sumptuous. 'My Dad's fine about you guys staying here. As long as you like or until you decide what you want to do.'

Yvonne, Laila and Tariq stood with their mouths open at the luxury of the penthouse flat in Soho Square. It was exquisite.

'Bagsy the biggest room.' Yvonne pushed Laila out of the way as they ran through to see the bedrooms, leaving Tariq with Ray-Ray. This was the first time they'd been alone.

'Thank you for everything you've done, Ray-Ray. This flat, the way you helped Laila . . . They said if it wasn't for your quick thinking, well, things could have been a lot worse. She probably would've been scarred for life.' Tariq realised what he'd just said. 'I'm sorry, I didn't mean . . .'

Tariq looked at Ray-Ray, but couldn't bring himself to look directly into his face. The shame he felt for being part of anything to do with what had happened to Ray-Ray's face haunted him.

Life didn't seem fair. The man was scarred for life, and still he showed no bitterness even though Mahmood had got away with it, hidden somewhere in Pakistan. But at least he couldn't come back to England; the authorities were aware of him, which meant Laila and his mother would be safe. As for Baz, well that was another matter entirely. Smiling gently, Tariq put out his hand to Ray-Ray who took it cautiously.

'I'm sorry. I'm so sorry I didn't do more to stop it that night. I . . .'

Ray-Ray put his hand up. 'Tariq, I know it wasn't you. I don't blame you no more than I blame Laila. She thinks the world of you.' Tariq smiled, touched by Ray-Ray's forgiveness and understanding.

'My Dad says he can sort out a job for you. Don't worry, it's all above board.'

'Why are you doing this?'

Ray-Ray looked slightly embarrassed. 'I don't want to lose her again. It's that simple. You stay, she stays.'

Laila walked into the front room. 'Everything all right?'

Ray-Ray smiled. 'Everything's just fine. I was just telling him about a job which was going down here.'

Laila's face lit up. 'Really? You'll stay Tariq?'

'Yes, great isn't it?' Tariq laughed, overwhelmed by his sister's love as she jumped up, grabbing her brother's neck, laughing with delight. Ray-Ray watched them, before walking out without saying goodbye.

'Ray-Ray. Where are you going?' Laila ran down the corridor. He stopped and smiled. 'I thought I'd leave you to it. Family and all.'

'Don't be silly, we haven't even had time to talk. I want to know everything; everything that's happened to you.'

'There'll be time for that. Go and have fun with your brother and Yvonne, you deserve it.' He turned away but Laila grabbed his hand, her eyes twinkling as she spoke softly.

'Ray-Ray, I love you. Don't you understand that? I always have.'

Ray-Ray turned away, choking back the emotion as he spoke. 'Don't say that Laila, don't say that if you're just trying to be kind.'

'I'm not, I do.'

'Look at you, you're beautiful. You've got your whole life ahead of you. You don't have to feel sorry for me Laila.' The pain in Ray-Ray's voice was audible to them both.

Laila put her finger over his mouth. 'Shhh, don't Ray-Ray.' She touched his face, moving her fingers over his scars, tiptoeing up to kiss him on his face, his nose, his eyes and finally, on his lips. She spoke in a whisper.

'I've always believed there's a special someone for everybody, and you Raymond Thompson have always been, and always will be, my special someone . . . It's always been you.'

'Ladies and gentleman of the jury, have you reached a verdict?'

'We have.'

'And how do you find the defendant on the charge of attempted murder? Guilty or not guilty?

'Guilty.'

Watching from the gallery, Johno smiled as the verdict was read out. He watched the colour drain from Baz's face. The fear and the realisation that he was going away for a very long time etched on his face. The moment Baz began to cry, it was Johno's cue to leave. He didn't need to stay and wait for the sentence. He would get what was coming to him. Besides, Freddie was going to arrange a very special treat for Baz Gupta. A welcome to prison treat; Freddie Thompson style. And that was one kind of treat Johno was happy to do without.

Freddie and Tasha sat hand in hand on the deck of the private yacht with Eddie and Linda, all of them giggling like schoolchildren as they leaned over the side, looking at the crystal-blue water. Tasha had agreed to try again, wanting, like Freddie, to put the past behind them. He'd been ready to lavish her with gifts and cars and anything money could buy, but she hadn't wanted expensive presents, expensive jewellery, expensive anything. She'd only wanted him.

And sitting in the sweltering Mediterranean sun with Tasha, Freddie Thompson was the happiest he'd ever been. He had everything he could ever wish for. He had his son and he had his wife, and by his reckoning that made him the luckiest man alive.

He watched as Tasha got up from her seat and walked across to the other side of the boat. He followed her, worried she was unhappy about something.

'Is everything all right babe?' Freddie asked, a concerned look on his face. It mattered to him how she was feeling.

'Yeah, I'm okay darling. Just sometimes I can't stop thinking about what happened. About Arn . . . about him.'

Freddie's face darkened. He didn't like to think about Arnie either, though some of his reasons were more selfish than Tasha's. Rightly or wrongly, it was a constant struggle to get the picture of Arnie and Tasha out of his mind. After everything that'd happened he knew it was petty, but all the same, it wasn't easy for a man like him. Though he wasn't ever going to let on to Tasha how he felt or let it get between them. She needed him now more than ever and this time he was going to step up to the mark.

Putting his arms around her, he pulled her in softly, his words making her feel safe and assured. 'Babe, he's gone now. You know what the police said. There was no way he would've ever survived. It's over. Nothing is ever going to hurt you again, I promise. I'm here now, everything is going to be fine.'

The sun was high in the cloudless sky and the slower pace of life relaxed the milling tourists, intoxicating them into tranquillity. A donkey clattered along the cobbled street pulling its loaded cart down the road. Mopeds buzzed by and good-natured cyclists hurried along. The trees on the hill surrounded the castle walls and the warm breeze made it pleasant to sit outside in this small rural town, just outside the city of Rouen in Normandy.

'*Excusez-moi, que vous parlez anglais?*'

'Yes, I'm English.'

'Oh what a relief, my French really isn't up to much.' The man smiled warmly, then added, 'My name's Arnold, but my friends call me Arnie.'

THE END

"A false witness shall not be unpunished, and he that speaketh lies shall perish".

Proverbs 19:9 (King James Bible)

LONDON

1990

'Come on out. It's not funny now Bronwin. Mum said we had to be back by seven. She'll skin us a-bleedin'-live if we're late.' The tall, skinny girl shouted loudly in no particular direction before looking down at her bitten nails, scraping off the last of the pink nail varnish as she waited for her sister to come out of her hiding place.

Exasperated, the girl looked up again. It was getting dark and even though she'd known it was cold when she'd come out, she'd only put on a thin t-shirt. Better cold than looking frumpy in the brown coat her mum had bought her last week. The thought of bumping into any of the boys from the Stonebridge Estate looking like something left over from a jumble sale made her shudder more than the evening chill of the October air.

Peering intensely into the darkness, she could just make out the dark silhouette of her sister scuttling about in the thicket of trees, thinking she couldn't be seen. The girl sighed as she watched. What her sister found so exciting about playing in a stupid park was beyond her. Parks and swings and trees were for babies. And she certainly wasn't that.

There were only four years between them, yet her only sibling seemed so immature next to her. Ever since she was little she'd

342

felt older than her years. And even though she'd only just started secondary school, she knew she wasn't a silly little girl any more. Not now anyway. Not now she'd lost her virginity with the boy across the landing. Although it'd only lasted less than the time it took the kettle to boil, and he'd only just managed to get his penis inside her before he'd exploded; groaning and coming everywhere as well as staining her already dirty skirt. It still counted. Counted enough to make her special. For the first time in her life she had something to brag about. Something to tell the other girls in her class about.

She knew she wasn't pretty like her sister, nor was she clever, and she certainly wasn't popular. Everything was always a struggle. Everything she felt ashamed of. Even down to the way she dressed. Hand-me-downs from anywhere and anyone. Musty clothes, ingrained with the stains and smells of poverty, which brought nothing but ridicule.

But that was all going to change now. The sense of being a born loser had gone. She was proud she was the first one in her year to *do it*. Proud that word had got around the class. Now the girls wanted to speak to her and the boys didn't avoid her any longer. Take tonight, she was supposed to be going round to the house of one of the most popular boys in the year after *he* had come up to her; asking her in front of his mates if she would. She knew what he wanted. She wasn't stupid, but neither did she mind. Because it was *her* he wanted it from and nobody apart from her sister had ever wanted anything from her in her life.

Looking back towards the trees, she realised she couldn't see her sister now. The dark silhouette had disappeared, merging into the blackness of the autumn night. She wasn't worried. This was how it always went. Her younger sister's idea of a joke. Hiding and making her search her out. Letting her be on the verge of panic before she'd appear with a dimpled grin and an infectious laugh.

As she stood waiting, chewing on her nails and spitting out tiny bits of skin, the girl thought about her mother. Instinctively, she screwed up her face, convinced the metallic taste at the back of her mouth was that of the bitterness she felt towards her.

Her mother was only fourteen years older than her and had decided a long time ago that even though she'd given birth to two girls, she didn't want the responsibility of caring for them, nor did she want the trouble of loving them; preferring instead to spend her time with any man who'd buy her a drink down the local. With a jolt, the girl quickly broke her thoughts, not wanting to have the bitter taste at the back of her mouth any more.

She walked slowly towards the trees, resigned to the fact she was going to spend the next ten minutes searching for her sister in the woods which were full of horrible creepy-crawlies. Though at least looking and calling for her sister was a distraction from thinking about her home-life which always made her feel sad and empty. And she didn't want to feel sad or empty today. She wanted to think about later on tonight when she'd sneak out of the cramped, run-down bedroom she shared with her sister, to go and see the boy.

'Bron!' She was getting pissed off now. She'd been looking for over ten minutes. Her arms had already been scratched by the bushes and she was certain something nasty had crawled down her top. She was cross, but she wouldn't let her sister know she was. They both had enough of their mother being cross at them without her adding to it. She didn't want to see the hurt in her sister's eyes if she scolded her for hiding and having fun.

Just ahead the girl heard a branch snap. Her head shot up towards the sound. In the shadow of the night, she saw a dark silhouette a few feet ahead.

'Bron! Please, stop messing babe. I want to go now.' There was no reply. Just a strained silence laying heavy in the air. She edged forward, feeling the ground as she stepped carefully through the bracken. A breaking of another branch. Only this time it was coming from the side of her rather than in front of her.

The girl listened, waiting to hear the stifled giggles of her sister.

344

In the darkness she could hear breathing. But not the lightness of breath of a child. From the side came a deep staggered breath. A hungry, urgent, sweet-smelling breath. Warm against her neck. She turned in panic. Almost immediately she tasted blood in her mouth as something hard hit against her lips.

She screamed as she felt her top being torn. Rough hands pushing her down into the damp, cold earth; tugging painfully at her pants under her skirt.

As she felt the hands tighten around her neck, her breath becoming short as the life seeped out of her, it was of some small comfort to the girl that the last words she managed to cry were, 'Run Bronwin! Run!'

Bronwin sat in the corner of the tiny room, watching the uniformed police officers milling about as they came in and out of the bare room. Sat by her was a plain-looking social worker with a cup of soup in hand, oblivious to the large drop of over-stewed tomato soup sitting on her cream blouse, looking like a deep red blood stain.

'Bronwin, you really need to tell us what you can remember.'

'I don't think she's ready to answer any questions.' The social worker intervened as the large detective leaned in to question Bronwin. Annoyed with the interruption, the detective snapped back. 'I think that's a matter for Bronwin, don't you?'

'Officer, she's far too young to know what's best. She's had a traumatic experience and I don't think the questions will help, do you?'

The officer in charge rubbed his empty stomach as he heard it growl. 'Listen, no-one's saying she hasn't had a traumatic experience, but if we want to make sure the perpetrators can't get out of this we need to make sure she tells us everything she can remember. She's an important witness. Where's the mother anyway?'

The social worker, putting down her cup of soup, opened her file, flicking through the notes. 'We don't know exactly where she is at the moment, we've tried leaving her a message but we've had no reply. She told us she'd meet us here but maybe it's all too much for her.'

'She's got responsibilities. This kid for one, and another one lying cold.'

The social worker bristled, furrowing her brow angrily as she took a sidewards glance at Bronwin.

'That's enough detective. Not everything is so clear-cut. The family are well known to us and there are problems. The mother's very young and as I'm sure you'll appreciate, things can get difficult for her.'

The officer's demeanour softened slightly as he looked at a shivering Bronwin in the corner. It passed through his mind how nicely she'd fit the image of Dickensian London. She was elf-like and looked as if she could do with a good hot meal. Her blonde, matted hair he'd bet hadn't seen a brush for days but she was startlingly pretty, unlike her sister who lay on a mortuary slab on the other side of the building. Dead or not, the child had been no looker.

The detective sighed. It was tragic. A shocking waste of life. And what was to happen to this kid? Another care home child for society to pay for until they washed their hands of her when she was old enough to be kicked out on the street, to end up a junkie, a tom or dead.

The future, the officer decided, was more than bleak. Still, it wasn't his problem. All he needed to do was sort out who was responsible and he'd leave the other problems for others to deal with.

'Fine, no more questions, but we need to take her to see the line-up. It's important; we can only hold the men for so long.' The officer turned his head and winked at Bronwin who stared ahead, her eyes vacant and the childlike life drained out of them.

The line-up room was dark and six-year-old Bronwin wasn't sure what she was supposed to do. The woman who kept insisting on holding her hand smelt funny. A bit like the cupboard in the kitchen at her nanny's house. She didn't like the smell and she didn't like the woman. She wanted to go home. Where was her mum anyway? She hoped she'd come and get her soon.

'All we want you to do is tell us if you remember any of the men's faces. We want you to have a good look and if you remember any of them, tell us.'

'Can I have a word, Detective?' A man stepped out of the shadows, making Bronwin retreat behind the social worker. She didn't like her, but she liked the man with the booming voice even less. She listened to him, not understanding what he was saying; only understanding he was cross, like everybody seemed to be.

'Detective, my clients feel it's unfair they're not only being forced to be in the line-up, but also the pick-out is going to be on the word of a child. We all know what children are like Detective. They choose things on a whim. Something as simple as the colour of a person's jumper. I want a stop to this.'

The officer in charge rubbed his top teeth with his tongue before answering. His mouth was dry and the thought of a strong cup of coffee was becoming distracting. He'd been here since yesterday night and he wasn't even sure how he was managing to stand up, let alone have a coherent conversation.

'You and I both know it's going to go ahead. And you know the saying; if they've nothing to hide, they've got nothing to fear.'

The man grinned nastily at the detective, his eyes reflecting the coldness in his smile. Bronwin took a sharp intake of breath. She didn't like this at all. Why wasn't anybody taking her home to bed? She was tired and wanted to snuggle up with Mr Hinkles, the teddy bear her sister had got her. Where was her sister anyway? She'd heard people talking about her and they'd asked her a lot of questions, but she hadn't seen her; well, she didn't think she had.

The last time she saw her was in the woods. But she didn't want to think about the woods, thinking about them gave her a funny feeling in her tummy. But she did want to see her sister.

Big tears began to spill down Bronwin's cheeks. Her eyes had adjusted to the darkness and she watched them fall on to the floor, right next to the foot of the man with the booming voice. Cautiously, Bronwin looked at him from underneath her shaggy fringe. He was smart. Smart and clean. He also smelled nice. The only other person who Bronwin knew smelled nice like that was a man who had come to visit her mum before her mum had got angry and shouted at him. After that he hadn't come back and even though Bronwin couldn't remember his face clearly she could remember the clean, fresh smell.

Quickly, Bronwin dropped her gaze as she saw the man looking at her. Her eyes wandered to his shoes. They were black shoes. Shiny black shoes apart from the bottom part of them which were dirty with mud. She looked up again, edging back as the man bent down to meet her stare.

'Would you like a hanky?'

Bronwin shook her head but the man insisted.

'Here, take it.' Pushing the crisp white handkerchief into Bronwin's hand she noticed some letters embroidered on to it, but she wasn't good with letters, especially fancy ones which swirled and curled like those did.

She could feel her knees trembling. And the funny feeling in her tummy was beginning to come back. Taking hold of the smelly lady's hand, Bronwin buried her face in the woman's skirt, squeezing her eyes tightly shut and hoping that when she opened them again she would be back in her flat with her mum and sister.

'Now is everybody ready? We need to get on with this.' The detective's voice had a tone of weariness. He was tired and didn't expect much from this line-up, although in his gut he felt he had the right men, but he knew only too well with slick, high-powered lawyers like the one standing opposite him, even if the suspects had been caught with the blood-stained knife in their pocket and the word *guilty* written on their forehead, there was still a possibility of them walking free. Sometimes the law stank. Strong and rancid like the crimes themselves.

'Are you ready Bronwin?' The social worker pulled Bronwin away from her skirt as the lights on the other side of the mirrored line-up room went on.

Bronwin nodded, not because she wanted to, but she understood that if she did she'd be able to get out of there and hopefully then she'd see her sister.

'All you have to do is pick out the men who you think you saw in the woods. Do you think you can do that Bronwin?'

Again Bronwin nodded, not wanting to think about the dark horrible woods. She stood on a chair and in front of her a procession of men began to walk in through the door on the other side of the glass.

As Bronwin stood watching, the social worker whispered in Bronwin's ear which made it tickle. 'Don't worry Bronwin, they can't see you or hear you.'

The men stood with their backs against the wall, staring ahead, holding up the boards they were given. The detective adjusted the microphone as he spoke in it.

'Can you step forward number one and then turn to the left and to the right slowly.' The tall man with dark hair stepped forward nervously, turning as instructed in both directions before stepping back to the wall.

'Number two, can you step forward and then turn to the left and to the right slowly.' Without taking his eyes off Bronwin's reaction to the men, the detective stood up slightly as he realised he was too near the mike.

'Number three, can . . .'

Bronwin's mind wandered off. Her legs were getting tired having to stand up and she thought it was funny the way all the men were staring ahead. The smelly lady had said they couldn't see her, but she didn't know how that was possible if she could see them. Bronwin bet she was telling lies. She knew grown-ups told lies as well as children, sometimes more. Even her mum told lies, saying she'd come home and then she wouldn't and it would be left down to her sister to put her to bed.

'Bronwin? Bronwin?' The detective was talking to her. She didn't know how long he had been but she could tell he was cross; his cheeks were red like her mum's cheeks went red when she was angry with her.

'Do you recognise any of them? Were any of them there in the woods?' The detective's voice was urgent as he stared at Bronwin who was busy chewing on her top lip.

'Detective, let me handle it.' The social worker cut her eye at the detective. 'Bronwin, do you recognise any of them? Were any of them there in the woods?'

Bronwin looked first at the detective and then at the smelly lady. She didn't know why they were asking her the same question and arguing about it.

The social worker sighed, looking at her cheap Timex brown leather strapped watch. 'Bronwin, this is very important. If you can remember *anything*, you need to tell us. Can you remember who it was?'

Bronwin nodded her head.

'Show us then. Can you point them out?'

Bronwin nodded again, she raised her hand and pointed, speaking in a small voice. 'It was him.'

The officer sprang into action. 'Number eight.'

'Yes. And him.' She pointed again at the line-up.

'Number two.'

'Yes.'

The detective's face didn't give anything away. In a matter-of-fact manner, he spoke. 'Well done Bronwin. You've done really well.'

Bronwin looked at him, her elf-like face turned to the side. She swivelled around, turning her back on the line-up and staring towards the door where the man with the booming voice stood. 'And him. I saw him in the woods as well.'

'Bronwin do you understand what happens to children who keep telling lies?'

'I ain't lying. It *was* him, it *was* that bloke. Why won't you believe me?'

The psychiatrist tapped his pen on his leg absentmindedly. 'We've gone over this before and we both know why I won't believe you, don't we?' The psychiatrist paused dramatically, then said, 'Because it's simply not true. How do you think a person feels to be accused of bad things, Bronwin? Heinous things. How would you feel if I accused you of doing something bad?'

'But you are. You're saying I'm lying.'

'That's *not* the same Bronwin because you *are*.'

Bronwin's eyes were wide with fear as she cuddled Mr Hinkles, her teddy bear. 'Please let me go home. I think I should go home now; me mum will be missing me.'

Not being put-off but seemingly more determined by Bronwin's tired plea, the psychiatrist continued angrily.

'Bronwin, children who tell lies, *especially* dangerous ones which cause other people harm, sometimes can't go home. How would you like to never go home?'

Bronwin didn't say anything but curled up tighter in her sadness as she listened to the doctor continue to talk. 'And you know what's happened now don't you?'

Bronwin shook her head.

'Now everybody thinks you're a liar. The police, the courts, even your mum does.'

Hearing the psychiatrist mention her mother, Bronwin sat up, her tiny face scrunched up in a mixture of hurt and anger.

'No she don't! She never said that!'

'Bronwin, I don't tell lies because I know it's wrong.'

Rubbing away a tear with the back of her sleeve, Bronwin yelled, 'You're a big fat liar.'

Taking his glasses off to wipe them with the corner of his starched white doctor's coat, the psychiatrist didn't bother to look at Bronwin as he spoke. 'That's why she hasn't been to see you Bronwin, because she doesn't like liars. No one is ever going to believe a word you say. No one trusts you Bronwin which means no one's ever going to believe you when you tell them what happened in the woods.'

At the word *woods,* Bronwin covered her ears.

'It's no good doing that Bronwin. The only way to change this is by telling the truth and stop these silly lies.'

'But I keep telling you, it ain't a lie. I want to go home. I want to see me mum and me sister.'

The psychiatrist nodded to the white-gowned nurse in the corner of the room who stepped forward.

'Bronwin, I've told you this before. Your sister is dead and because you told lies the people who really *were* responsible for her murder are free to go and hurt somebody else.'

Two blinks was all it took for Bronwin to begin to scream. Her wail was fearful and high-pitched; an adult's cry within a child's body. The scream resonated through her and began to take possession of her body as she began to shake, convulsing into a fit.

The nurse who was already next to Bronwin quickly and expertly administered the powerful drug. Almost immediately, Bronwin's eyes began to roll back. Her shoulders began to slump and her mouth gently opened to one side as she lay on the bed in the tiny white-washed room.

After a couple of minutes, Bronwin's eyes slowly regained focus, she sat staring ahead at nothing but the blank wall. Today was her seventh birthday.

In the next room, Bronwin's mother sat nervously pulling down the grey nylon skirt she'd bought from Roman Road market the

352

day before. She'd wanted to look presentable and it was only now she was deciding it might be too short. Perhaps she should've got the other one, the longer one, but it'd been a fiver more and she'd needed the fiver for the electricity key. Taking off her jacket, she placed it over her knees.

She was nervous. Her hands were sweating and she could feel a prickly heat rash beginning to develop on her chest. She knew what these people were like. Knew how they judged. Christ, she'd been dealing with them since she was a kid herself and now they had their hands on her daughter.

Week after week she'd called up to see Bronwin but they'd told her she couldn't. Not even a phone call. She'd even turned up a few times hoping someone would show a bit of compassion, but she'd been turned away, not even being allowed to set foot in the children's facility. Today was the first time she was able to see the doctor in charge, and as her Nan used to say, *she was shitting bricks.*

Gazing around the room made her feel even more nervous. There were paintings of men in gilded frames on the wall looking superior and almost mocking in their pride. It surprised her to see the doctor's office void of any medical books but instead filled with trinkets and thank you cards. Biting her thumb nail down to the quick and then having to suck it to stop it from bleeding, she jumped as the glass door opened.

'Hello, I'm Dr Berry. Thank you for coming.'

Not taking the outstretched hand, Bronwin's mum thought the doctor looked like he should've retired years ago. His white hair and stooped shoulders made her feel as if she was paying a visit to her granddad rather than a child shrink.

She spoke. Her hostility, caused by her nervousness, cut through her words. 'I've been trying to come for a while now but then you'd already know that don't you? What I want to know is when can I take Bronwin home?'

'Well there might be a problem.'

'I don't want to hear about bleedin' problems mate. I just want to take her home where she belongs. She's my daughter, not yours.'

Dr Berry went round to the other side of his desk. He pulled out his chair slowly, staring moodily over his rimless glasses. 'How do you feel about your daughter's death?'

'I ain't here to talk about me other daughter. In fact, I ain't here to answer any questions at all. Just give me Bronwin so we can get out of here.'

As was his habit and his arrogance, the doctor ignored the interjection and continued to talk. 'Do you feel responsible for your daughter's death?'

Filled with painful, angry tears, Bronwin's mother stared ahead. She was pleased to hear her voice was steady as she made a concerted effort to stay calm. Her words punctuated the air. 'I am not responsible for her death. It wasn't me who killed her. It was them animals, whoever they are.'

'But you were the one who let your daughters out. Surely you must hold some sort of guilt.'

Bronwin's mother blinked away the tears as she felt them burning. She bent forward, holding her stomach, and whispered almost inaudibly as her gaze found the window. 'Of course I do. Of course I do.'

'Then let us help you. You do want some help don't you?'

Bronwin's mum nodded, trance-like.

'You know Bronwin is still very confused about what happened and who *was* there. She's a very troubled little girl. She insists on telling these lies.'

'Bronwin ain't a liar. That's one thing she's never done is lie. If she's telling you something then it must be true.'

'That's as maybe, but she's a child and all children lie.'

'She don't.'

Dr Berry sighed. 'Do you want us to help her and at the same time help you?'

'Of course. Anything.'

'I've spoken to the social workers and they're in agreement with me it's probably best Bronwin stayed here with us.'

Bronwin's mother stood up. She wiped away the tears, feeling angry resentment. 'Oh no you don't. You ain't going to mess my little girl up.'

'We won't be doing that, what we'll be doing is untangling the mess which has already been put there in her short life.'

'That ain't going to happen. You ain't going to take my daughter.'

'Of course not. That's why I'm asking you to sign these papers.'

'I'm not signing nothing. I want my daughter and I want her *now*.'

'I'm sorry, but that won't be possible. We've had an extension of the interim care which means you can't take her.'

The shock and hurt on Bronwin's mum's face was so deep it almost penetrated Dr Berry's supercilious gaze. He turned away quickly. Standing up and walking across to the window as Bronwin's mother began to shout.

'You bastards. You fucking bastards.'

'We're not doing this to upset you, we're doing this for Bronwin's benefit and of course yours. You'll be able to get on with your life knowing Bronwin is getting the help she needs. She'll thank you in the end. I just know she will. You can give her what you didn't have yourself. You can give her a chance. A start in life.'

'But I'm her mother. She should be with me.'

'Yes, but only if it's right for her and at the moment it isn't right.'

Bronwin's mother headed for the door, catching Dr Berry raising his eyebrows at her skirt. She pulled it down quickly.

'Well I'm sorry, but no way. I would never hand my child over to the likes of you. I might not be what you think a good mother should be and I'm not saying I haven't got my faults, but I love Bronwin. I loved both my kids.'

'Fight us and you'll lose and then you'll never see Bronwin again. Do it this way and you'll be able to see her. It's your choice. I know which way I'd choose.'

'You . . . you can't do that.'

'We can and we will. Do you really think the courts will agree to you keeping her after both myself and the social workers give evidence of you being unstable and incapable of giving Bronwin what's needed?'

'I love her. Ain't that enough?'

'In an ideal world it is but then we're not in an ideal world are we? Can you excuse me one moment?'

Not waiting for any sort of reply, Dr Berry picked up the phone on his desk. He spoke quietly into it. 'Would you mind coming in now?'

A moment later the glass door opened. The man who walked in didn't bother to introduce himself. He stood with a frozen frown on his face as Bronwin's mum stared at him. 'Who's he?'

Once more, Dr Berry chose to ignore a question he saw as irrelevant. He walked over to Bronwin's mum, picking up the papers as he passed his desk, then reached out with the pen which was always kept in his breast coat pocket.

'Sign them. It's for the best. If you say you love her which I believe you do, you'll listen to me. No one's the enemy here; don't make us into them.'

Bronwin's mother took in the doctor's face. Deep, entrenched lines circled his eyes and cold, small green eyes stared back at her. 'You'll let me see Bronwin?'

Dr Berry pushed the pen and papers forward. 'She'll be in good hands. There's nothing to worry about. I promise.'

Taking the papers, Bronwin's mother grabbed at the pen and hurriedly scrawled her name on the papers. Dr Berry passed the papers to the other man, talking as he did so. 'We need another signature you see, so that's why this gentleman's here. You'll get a copy of this for yourself.'

The other man took out his own pen. Bronwin's mother watched, loathing etched on her face as her eyes traced the flamboyantly written signature.

Dr Berry smiled, his tone over-jovial for the sentiment of the occasion and his clichéd remark inappropriate.

'Right then, that's all done and dusted.'

'Now take me to see my daughter.'

'You've done the right thing.'

'So why doesn't it feel like it?'

Staring through the glass pane of the door, Bronwin's mother wiped away her tears before opening it. Quietly, she walked into the room, feeling the air of hush as she entered. She stared at her daughter. So tiny. So elf-like. So beautiful.

'Bron. Bron, it's me.'

Bronwin's eyes stayed closed.

Dr Berry crept up silently behind. 'It's all right; she's had some medicine to calm her down. She's just in a heavy sleep.'

'Can I wake her up?'

'It's best to leave her. She needs all the rest she can get.'

Leaning forward, Bronwin's mother swept her daughter's mass of blonde hair away from her forehead. She kissed her head before speaking to her sleeping child. 'Bron, mummy's got to go now. But always remember I love you and I'll see you soon. And Bron? I'm sorry.'

Turning to the doctor, Bronwin's mum stood up and went into the pocket of her torn jacket. 'Can you give her this? It's her birthday card.'

'Yes of course. The nurse will see you out. The social workers will be in touch in the morning to sort the other details out.'

Once Bronwin's mother had left, Dr Berry took a quick glance at the card before throwing it into the bin in the corner. In deep thought, he stood observing Bronwin as she began to stir.

The door opened, jarring him from his thoughts. He smiled at the entering visitor and reached out his hand with a welcoming greeting. 'Thanks for signing those papers by the way. I thought for a moment the mother was going to be difficult. I'll just wake her up.'

Walking across to Bronwin, Dr Berry gently nudged her. He spoke quietly. 'Bronwin? Bronwin? Hey birthday girl, you've got a visitor. Someone's here to see you.'

Bronwin slowly opened her eyes before rubbing them gently. She sat up then screamed. It was the man from the woods with the black shiny shoes.

'She's all yours.' Dr Berry smiled, tapping the man on his back as he left the room, leaving him sitting on Bronwin's bed as he began to unbutton his shirt.

The bed was hard and the chair was too. Sparse and unwelcoming. And Bronwin didn't know why she couldn't go home instead of having to stay in a house where she didn't know anybody and didn't want to be. It was the same recurring thought she had each time they sent her somewhere new.

The only place she'd ever wanted to be was with her mum. But they'd never let her. Telling her it was for the best. Only allowing her to speak to her at birthdays and Christmas.

The people who'd met her and her social worker at the door had smiled and had seemed pleasant enough, but she knew; knew they didn't like her. Didn't really want her there, but that was fine with her because she didn't want to be there either.

She'd been in more care and foster homes than she could possibly remember and over time she'd developed a sixth sense. Knowing when people *really* wanted her or when all they *really* wanted was the few hundred quid caring allowance they got for taking in the likes of her.

People wanted cute. Sweet. And once upon a time she'd been just that. The cute child with the button nose and the chocolate box freckles. Blue eyes staring out from under a mass of blonde hair. The tiny frightened child. But then the tiny frightened child had grown up, yet Bronwin knew she'd lost her childhood a long time before that ever happened.

How long had it been now? Eight years, nine even. Nine years of going from one home to another. Settling in, only to have to move again a few weeks, a few days, even a few hours later because someone hadn't filled in the forms, courts hadn't signed the appropriate documents or her file had got lost. But mainly, Bronwin knew she was unwanted because she was no longer a child. No longer someone's toy, someone's plaything to do what they liked with. She was sixteen now and had a mind and an opinion of her own. But most of all she had a voice. A voice that had begun to say, 'No.'

She no longer wanted to be or feel like the unwanted teenager. A problem child. Hard to place. Hard to love. She didn't want to become bitter; hardened to life before she'd reached eighteen. But she could feel it. Feel herself slowly being cemented into the drudgery and pitiful existence of her life.

But she was determined to change it. To take control. And as Bronwin stared out of the window at the rainy night she made a decision. The time was right. She was old enough not to have to listen to a bunch of jumped up social workers telling her what to do. All they really did anyway was find a roof over her head; the rest of it was left to her.

Bronwin stuffed her things back in her bag, pausing at the sight of the bedraggled Mr Hinkles, her teddy bear she'd kept for all these years. She held it tight. Closing her eyes for a moment before opening them wide. Quickly she pushed the bear down to the bottom of her bag, not wanting to deal with the memories it brought up. Of her sister. Of her mother. Of the day in the woods.

Bronwin opened the window. She felt the chill of the evening air and the spray of the rain on her face blown in by the wind. Making sure no one could hear her, Bronwin shuffled on to the ledge. It wasn't so far down. Seven feet perhaps, maybe eight. Eight feet to freedom.

After a count of three in her head and then another one of five, Bronwin jumped, hitting the ground harder than she thought she would. She rolled on the grass and felt a sharp pain in her ankle; shooting pains up the outside of her leg. But she didn't care. All that mattered to her was that she was out. Out of the care system which had never cared for her, and out of the system which had taken away the one person she'd cared about and who, in her own way, had cared about her.

Getting up from the wet ground, Bronwin ignored the pain. She picked up her bag, quickly making sure no one in the house had seen her. It was clear.

Hobbling along the tiny pathway, Bronwin smiled. The rain hit down hard on her but instead of it feeling cold, it felt warm; invigorating. She was free. She was finally free. Today was her sixteenth birthday.